20

20

THE BEST OF THE
DRUE HEINZ LITERATURE
PRIZE   edited by

John Edgar Wideman

UNIVERSITY OF PITTSBURGH PRESS

Published by the University of Pittsburgh Press, Pittsburgh, Pa., 15260

Copyright © 2001, University of Pittsburgh Press
Manufactured in the United States of America

Printed on acid-free paper

10 9 8 7 6 5 4 3 2 1

Contents

Introduction

John Edgar Wideman

In 1992 I enjoyed the honor of awarding the annual Drue Heinz Literature Prize to a book of short fiction by Jane McCafferty. Now, in my capacity as editor of this anthology of stories commemorating the twentieth anniversary of the Prize, I must choose only one of Ms. McCafferty's fictions to include in this volume composed of a story from each winner. I'm pleased to report my task isn't easy. Even with Ms. McCafferty's assistance—she and most of the writers suggested two of their stories for the editor's close consideration—I find myself stymied, second-guessing myself as I attempt to conjure compelling reasons for admitting one excellent piece and omitting another. There are highly charged, memorable moments in most fictions selected by the authors. The dilemma presented by Ms. McCafferty's pair of very different narratives, each with its distinct virtues, both abundantly attractive, is the rule, not an exception. As my criteria for admission blur and morph, it helps to know readers will be well served whether I go with the long or the short one, the apple or the orange.

For the longest time I didn't exactly approve of short stories. The form felt gimmicky to me. Stories seemed to depend too much on special effects—a quirky character's voice or a bizarre situation or pumped-up language or surprise endings—effects laid on to counteract (compensate for) a story's necessarily brief attention span. Stories, I thought, are quick hitters. They engage us for half an hour, forty-five minutes then move on. And so what? As reader I resented being teased, seduced, then biff-bam, thank you, ma'am, the encounter's over. Stories, I suspected, were just too small, too premeditated, too falsely complicated and will-of-the-wisp to deliver authentic punch. As a writer I could see through to the bones of most stories, catching on pretty rapidly to the particular gimmick, the game being played beneath the surface reality of a story. The only reason for remaining on board—aside from borrowing or stealing bits that worked—would be a sort of crossword puzzle–solving doggedness and curiosity—let's keep plugging away to see how this author wrings the changes from the inevitable archetype of beginning-middle-end.

An O. Henryish "surprise," such as Frank Stockton's famous lady-or-tiger ending, or the equally titillating convenient indeterminacy of a sumptuous Joycean epiphany, weren't these predictable, limited options built into the story-constructing kit all writers employed? And even if not, wasn't the market for stories so small and narrow that it exercised a subversive monopoly, determining not only who gets paid but also what kinds of stories are published, what version of reality (political, metaphysical) they contain? Are short stories, I wondered, the ultimate page turners, designed to distract, to occupy fragmentary, fleeting moments of leisure, offering a change of pace as you thumb through colorful, sexy ads, smart cartoons, profiles and photos of the momentarily, fashionably famous?

Maybe my attitude toward stories partly was sour grapes. For years I found it easier to publish novels than short fiction. When my stories eventually appeared, they were collected in volumes, most of them previously unpublished, a few printed in tiny magazines.

Since I'm an American of African descent, in some ways my case is always complicated. Yes and no. Could editors' lack of interest in my short fiction have been caused by my inadequate writing or was my difficulty finding outlets for my stories part of a more general pattern? Browse the major collections of short fiction from, say, 1980 through today and you'll discover how they reflect the apartheid prejudices of the society at large during that period. About twenty years ago, the *New Yorker* returned a story to my agent with a written comment that went something like this. . . . *Nice try, Mr. Wideman, blah, blah, blah . . . but we don't publish vernacular fiction.* Of course the editor who refused my piece could have replied, *We have a long and glorious history of outing vernaculars, but because of the race and class of our traditional readership and the exquisitely insulated, upper-middle class lifestyle our advertisers espouse and pay us to represent, we aren't interested in your particular vernacular.* How race matters varies case by case, but it always does matter, and in this discussion of publishing habits an examination of race is instructive since race can stand generally as a sign of difference.

Difference appeals to the publishing industry when difference is commodifiable, when difference can be reformulated to smooth out risks that difference, by definition, entails. In other words, difference is acceptable only when it can be packaged to function as seamlessly as brand names function in the consumer economy. Gender difference, for instance, once somebody remembered (with Oprah's help) that women constitute the majority of fiction buyers, transformed publishers' lists so that female writers and women's stories now dominate. But what definitions of gender do the best-selling stories generate?

Of course it's never exactly simple. Women writers of extraordinary talent also have helped reconfigure the picture of what's published, sold, and read. Even if I'm willing, for the sake of argument, to entertain for a minute the possibility that for decades my stories and those of other African American writers just weren't good enough to break through into the few mass circulation magazines still offering fiction or into yearly anthologies of "best" stories, the meaning of "best" or "good" remains problematic.

Publishing practices produce more heat than light when it comes to maintaining standards for short fiction. The customary routes and reasons for books of stories coming out are not necessarily investments in either the health, variety, or quality of the form. Commercial houses launch modestly budgeted small printings of short story books as fishing expeditions to test the attractiveness of new writers, and occasionally books of collected fiction are organized to cash in on the reputations (or stroke the vanity) of well-known, veteran authors.

So who consistently presents stories to the public because stories are "good," that is, not chosen primarily by considerations of fashion, politics, brand name popularity, prejudice, or bottom-line financial concerns?

The answer, given the mixed motives and arbitrariness of any definition of quality, is nobody. Another answer is that some folks, a precious few, keep trying. Keep on attempting to present a wide range of stories whose value resides in their ability to teach, to give pleasure, to challenge our certainties about what stories should be—about who we should or could be. Such an effort is what's crucial about the Drue Heinz Literature Prize. Whether or not the volumes of short fiction in the series measure up to some universally acknowledged standard of quality, the Drue Heinz Prize competition is organized to facilitate and honor the goal of publishing a wide variety of fiction that elaborates, interrogates, and extends the definition of quality. Of course the University of Pittsburgh Press would love to sell oodles of the prizewinning book each year and valiantly endeavors to achieve a wide audience. However, because of the generosity of the Heinz gift, the competition is neither driven by nor dependent upon commercial success.

Though only one African-descended writer has garnered the Drue Heinz Prize, the rules and spirit of the contest clearly promote equality of opportunity. As a hedge against the possibility that a single, monolithic standard of aesthetics or politics might narrow the evolving definition of quality, each year a different senior judge is empowered to select a manuscript of stories—from a group of anonymous entries—for publication and a cash award. The University of Pittsburgh Press occupies an enviable position—free at last, free at last—privileged to search out, then share with the reading public, stories that don't claim to be the best, but a volume chosen by someone visibly committed to writing good stories, someone whose contributions to the genre are on record, a fellow sufferer of the new prizewinner, a coworker in the communal, collective effort.

Each judge is granted the responsibility of picking and choosing a favorite, but then must substantiate his or her abstract preferences with concrete, specific examples of what good stories should be: Here are stories I like. Read on. See if you like them, too.

The idea is intoxicating. It's like the idea of public spaces open to all artists where art can meet the people and discover its audience, shape its audience without the self-serving mediation of vested interests accountable to no one. *Ideal* may be a more accurate word than *idea*, but as I said, the Drue Heinz Prize keeps trying, has tried for twenty years, and this volume of twenty memorable tales is confirmation and celebration of that effort, that dream and ideal of endowed, protected public space and public access.

One last comment. I've changed my mind about the possibilities of the short story form. Powerful works of short fiction like the ones in this book lured me into re-engaging, re-imagining the form as reader and writer. I no longer conceive of short fiction as finger exercises for the deeper plunge of long work. The older I grow, more I write, the more I'm confronted by curious readers with the question, *Is that story fiction or nonfiction, sir?* — the clearer it becomes to me that genre is a chimera. Every new story, like every new life, contains the exciting, desirable potential to expand the definition of life or story. Good writing is good writing, a tough, exhausting hustle, ultimately, always seeking to achieve the impossible. As Alberto Giacometti famously lamented, *you always fail.* In this context genre is irrelevant. From the writer's point of view the division of literature into classes and kinds only multiplies pitfalls, resistances, and incompatibilities between language and vision. Genre is seen best as a work-in-progress, a label tentatively attached until somebody smart enough, resourceful enough undermines its authority. At least as pernicious as beneficial for writers, the idea of genre exists primarily for the convenience of marketing, reviewing, for those who insist on hierarchies of artistic kinds, those who divvy up academic or scholarly turf. Writing of any sort consists of setting down one word after another, making something that doesn't exist until it's expressed with the medium of written language. The effort of making is at some level play, like patting clay, beating a drum, or tapping your toes, singing, or spreading paint with your fingertips — play that's a gift to the artist the artist passes on, from the one to the many to the one. Serious play that reminds us we're all in this together, this life, and what we make goes into the collective project to brighten and lighten, to glorify and transform the unavoidable pain and burden of being alive.

Writing is creative play, is sharing the pleasure of making, is respecting and lavishing care on the thing made. The serious side of that play can consume a writer's life yet, simultaneously, doggedly preserve the vitality of language. Whether on the small scale of story or in the roomier expanse of a novel, if a writer demonstrates the power of language to create something out of nothing or rather out of itself (strangely also and not also the writer's self), out of words, their history and tensions and texture and indefinably new/old, oral/written cycling presence, then the writer has achieved mightily. Language stays alive. A present, beckoning, personal resource is bequeathed to the reader. In addition to their practical functions of exchanging information and conducting business, words are preserved as a medium for imagining and entering the silent emptiness surrounding each of us, between us. This emptiness a good writer seeds with words that become real in the reader's mind, this space where the writer desires to express and represent what's real to him or her through the artifice of language is identical in many ways to the featureless, intimidating interior, the private expanse where we construct the narratives of ourselves and of difference, where we figure out the *I* and *we* and *other*.

So here's a gift of twenty narratives from twenty writers, each author a Drue Heinz winner, each story part of a prizewinning collection. They provide confirmation in print that one tentative definition of being human might be: the storytelling animal. Though most authors suggested a pair of stories to choose from, the final selections are mine. I submit them as evidence that the communal process of short story writing continues to expand the notion of just what kind of creatures we might be. If you read attentively, you'll probably find yourself here, but also there's the more intriguing possibility of losing yourself, entertained for a while by the play, the discipline, the weight and freedom of being other.

20

THE DEATH OF DESCARTES

David Bosworth

I

A house on the northern coast of Maine. One story high, its rectangular sections extend in three directions, fitting through the abrupt rise and fall of the promontory rock: prosthetic limbs, mechanical fingers, angle-jointed, clinging there against the wind like the roots of a scrub pine. Easy to frame, and in fact frames itself with an encircling metallic railing, a futuristic boardwalk which flirts with the cliff's uneven edge and overlooks the cove. Two materials dominate—steel and glass. One color—orange. Five hundred feet below, the North Atlantic, a white-capped winter ocean, its dull green brine squeezing like a spittle-tipped tongue into this gouge in the highlands, and interrupted only by jutting thumbs of tide-sculpted rock. Clouds, gray-bellied, blur the gulls. No other life. A few pine trunks, polished of their bark, tucked at gravity-defying angles into the cliffside notches, wait for the next nor'easter to be washed away.

Fact: it is January.

A transparency over the frame: the Detective's first impression. Dissonance. A place out of place. Eliminate the setting, brush out the neighboring houses, the acid-cold pinch of the air, the perpetually overcast sky, keeping just the house framed by its orange railing, and he's not in New England but Southern California, a town with a two-word name, the second of which is always "Beach"; the home of a neon sign artist, a binary theorist, a utopian behaviorist, some Brave New World advocate, riding on the tide of tomorrow's ideas or today's vulgar and inconsequential fads—who can tell, trapped in the present tense? Not the Detective; not anymore. Possible subtitle: "The Motive." Neighbors would not like this house, or the man who built it. Difference is conflict always, if sometimes beneath the surface, and it's conflict that moves us from one frame to another.

A transparency over the frame: the eyewitness account. The time of day is dusk; the angle of vision, from within the cove; the distance, about a thousand yards. Behind the wheel of his boat, returning from a rather fruitless day of fishing, the eyewitness sees this: a figure, its limbs flailing the air midway between cliff top and water—a falling body. Shock freeze-frames the image for him; then, in a series of frozen frames approximating motion, the body jerks downward toward the inevitable ocean. A pause, then the angle changes, the eyewitness drawing a straight line of vision from where the body enters the water to the promontory top. And there, leaning against the orange railing, he sees someone; too far away to identify, or even to distinguish sex or size, but a person nevertheless, and staring, he thinks, down to where the body fell. Another pause and the figure disappears as the eyewitness recovers from the initial shock and steers his boat carefully toward the walls of the cove—as close as he can come without risking the rocks. The search is futile, though, and the witness, a realist; after a half hour, he heads for home.

Fact: one does not survive a thirty-minute immersion in the January North Atlantic.

A transparency over the frame: the corrected image. Every view of a crime, the Detective has learned, is through tinted glass. The first rule: always doubt the witness; check his view before accepting the image. Note that dusk affords the poorest visibility of the day and the most deceptive. Note that dramatic and unexpected events cause selective amnesia, time distortion, astigmatic errors. And the witness himself—sober, respectable enough, no known connection to the house's occupants, but a local man, a stubborn downeaster; for him, all of reality is a frozen frame. The provincial mind, it has no doubt. "I saw what I saw," he says over and over again.

Fact: no one else has reported the "accident."

When the phone rang, the Detective was sitting in his study's easy chair, eyes closed, reading glasses at the tip of his nose, a book folded on his barreled belly. His feet were resting on a cracked leather ottoman, a concession to old age and poor circulation which failed to match the otherwise flawlessly crafted decor of the room. He made the transition from sleep to consciousness without moving his body or opening his eyes; remained that way, a disembodied mind, free of pain. Perhaps this is what death will be like, he thought, as through the study's walls, he heard his daughter's voice, an intentionally soft murmuring on the phone meant not to disturb his sleep. Strange, the Detective thought, how without understanding a word we can recognize someone's voice; how to this day he could still hear his father's cough, as distinctive as a fingerprint; how he could replay in his mind each subtle modulation in Sadie's breathing, although Sadie hadn't drawn a breath in nearly two years now. A concept occurred to the Detective then, a phrase appearing in its entirety as if by magic (he was new to this sort of thinking, this stretching the mind horizontally instead of focusing it into a bright, fine, penetrating beam)—"Identity is more than just content"—but it slipped away from him like an early morning dream whose connection to reality was not obvious. And he didn't follow it. Too sleepy from his postlunch nap, diverted by his indigestion, he forgot it, and instead, thought about forgetfulness itself. Perhaps that was the true cause of senility—a loss of will, of energy, a growing inability to force the connections. Mental tenacity, he had lectured his classes in criminology, was the primary qualification of a good detective.

The Detective heard his daughter's voice rising in the next room, sensing in it excitement, trouble, incipient hysteria (for her, they were all the same), and he suddenly felt a wash of pity for her. Perhaps one of her special projects was foundering, her save-the-beach, save-the-sea-gull, save-the-old-lighthouse campaigns. The locals hated her, Charlie Wriggins had confided in him, this rich alien bitch who had lived here just five years and thought herself a native, self-crowned as Earth Mother and Defender of the Land. Sea Gull Sally, they called her. Poor famous-detective's daughter; people had always made fun of her, even when she had been a girl. She made people nervous. She had no . . . patience—that was it. And no faith. Anyone or anything she loved that wasn't within her sight was dying; she was absolutely sure of it. Her husband lying in the gutter, a mugger's knife in his back; her daughter, Nan, crushed and bleeding under the wheels of a car; her father, dead of a coronary in this very study—better check on them all to make certain they were still breathing. And now, at the onset of middle age, she had adopted the state of Maine, just as she had adopted her widowed father, certain that unless she kept a steady eye on its coastline, the shore would, in a moment's time, be swimming in oil spills and pesticide-poisoned egg shells; appeared on the beaches, just as she appeared unexpectedly in her father's study, afraid that her emotional universe would collapse without her omnipresent vigilance.

Perhaps it was his own fault. What kind of father had he been to her, involved in case after case, often away from home, and then, even when he returned, his mind preoccupied, the crime scene frame-frozen in his inner eye, the list of crisp facts clicking in his head as he searched for the solution? Preoccupied not because it was his duty, not because he was the best detective they could call on, the best they could ever call on, but because he loved it. It *was* a sin to love too much, the Detective was beginning to learn. A man was a finite vessel; emotions, energy, attention were finite gifts to be dispensed with care like the resources of his daughter's environmental plans. Love your work too much and something, someone, was bound to suffer, the vessel empty when his turn came. In the past, when he had thought about it, which wasn't often, he had believed himself to be a good husband, a good father. Now he wondered. Now he did think about it often, too often. Now the inspections were self-inspections; the framed scenes not bars and motels, but the rooms of his own home; the violations subtle, unannounced, shades of the distant past. Now there were no bleeding corpses, just memories—his wife and daughter. He had thought himself a good husband, a good father, but then he had found the letters.

The Detective opened his eyes, superimposed the visual surface of reality over his unwanted thoughts. It was as if he were glancing at a vellum scrapbook or the indexed contents of a museum exhibit, his career laid out there before him on the study's paneled walls: the medals for service, the honorary degrees and newspaper clippings, the Sherlock Holmes cap resting on the fireplace . . . all so "arranged," so dustless and dead, the room embalmed with furniture wax. And he always felt, when he first awoke here from his daily nap—eyes blinking open, body still inert—like some wax figurine, a carved prop for this historical scene: "The Famous Detective's Study," doll-house perfect. Strange, the Detective thought, how Sally hadn't changed. As a child she had played "house" with a kind of grim self-seriousness, and now, some thirty years later, the game still continued, her performance unimproved. Time was on her side, of course. Her adulthood, his old age were inevitable, the doll house a real house now, the doll a flesh-and-blood girl. But Sally wasn't satisfied with simple equality, or with just one daughter; she was intent, instead, on adopting her father, a second child to play mother to: the way she treated him since Sadie's death, the coddling, the solicitude. He had tried to resist it, but because he lacked his old tenacity, because time *was* on her side, he often gave in. Like this study, its decorations; *her* idea, done at *her* insistence: "every growing boy needs his own private room, a place to forge his identity." She always knocked now before entering the study as if afraid she would catch him masturbating.

Perhaps it's revenge, the Detective thought, some sort of emotional revenge, reversing the rage of helplessness she'd felt as a child, still felt, and inflicting it back on her father. "Revenge"—the Detective shook his head at his choice of words. All of this psychology, this self-inspection was new to him, but the words he chose remained the same. He was still the Detective; that was the tint to his glass: his frame of reference, crime; his point of view, the criminal's.

"I will not," he heard his daughter say into the phone. A pause. She dropped to a strained whisper, but latched onto her voice, he understood her now. "He's sleeping."

The Detective straightened up, lifted his left leg by the thigh and lowered it to the floor slowly—a rush of blood, pain, life. "Sally!" he called out; closing the book on his lap, he threw it onto the roll-top desk beside him. "Sally—I'm coming!"

Sally's hurried footsteps approached the study; then (he heard them in his mind just before they began), three evenly spaced knocks on his door, exclamation points for his anger, and in a moment, she was standing above him.

"Dad, you're supposed to be sleeping."

"Never you mind that. Who's on the phone for me?"

"You're supposed to take an afternoon nap every day. I didn't make that up, you know. I'm not the Bangor heart specialist who told you to start taking it easy."

"Sally . . ."

"You have to take care of yourself, Dad. You have to . . ."

"Sally," he said with emphasis. She stopped, waited, the unwilling but still obedient daughter. "It's Charlie Wriggins, isn't it?"

She pursed her lips. The Detective smiled; he lived now for these small triumphs, these feats of detection, minor victories over her insulating secrecy.

"We have to talk, Dad. You can't keep ignoring the fact that you're over seventy and have a heart condition. You have to adjust. You have to come to grips with reality."

That last phrase brought a sneer onto the Detective's face. He had heard it again and again, that almost hysterical voice pleading with her father, with her husband and daughter, with her fellow kitchen environmentalists, to come to grips with reality.

"Yes," he said, rising unsteadily, "but I suppose reality can wait till I get off the phone."

"I . . ." Sally began, then faltered; he turned around. "I hung up."

He stared at her, wordless, shocked beyond anger, waiting though for anger to come. This was new, this insulting presumption of authority, and he waited for the righteous rage of his helplessness to flood him, giving him the strength to fight her back. But his rage never came; instead, he had that old sensation, a dispossession, a time suspension (if only he knew what brought on these moments, if only he could have transferred the gift to his students—the real difference between a great detective and a merely competent one): those moments when the confusion clarified, when the answer suddenly materialized, whole and inviolable. Not logic, but something like instinct which solved the mystery and yet was a mystery in itself.

"He has a case for me," the Detective said softly, half to himself.

Sally sighed; she wasn't surprised. After forty years, she was accustomed to her father's abilities, although perhaps envious of them: she had to burst through locked doors to keep informed; he merely peered through the walls.

"Look, Dad, I'm sorry, but I didn't think that you should . . ." Her apology unraveled, but he brushed it out, just as he had always brushed her and Sadie out when a case had preoccupied his mind—the absent father, the empty vessel. No, he wasn't angry with her; he was beyond emotion, disengaged and moving on another plane as Sally's voice changed, grew soft with resignation.

"He isn't home, but he did leave a number for you to call. I wrote it down on the pad by the phone." Then, one last protest, not out of hope for success, but duty-inspired. "You shouldn't, you know. You're not strong enough."

He limped quickly toward the phone. Her voice followed him there, accusatory and frightened. "He says it's murder."

The Detective dialed the number, steadying his right hand with his left by grabbing it around the wrist. He was magnanimous; he was sympathetic; he was in a forgiving mood. It had been the mentioning of murder that had frightened Sally into hanging up. Not her fault—she couldn't help seeing that knife in her husband's back, that car striking her daughter's body, that oil slick drifting inexorably toward her favorite beach. She was a worrier by nature, so he would forgive her, forgive anyone: he had a case, the first since Sadie's death.

Someone identifying himself as Officer Truax answered the phone, resisting the Detective's questions with officious inflexibility until there was an interruption from an extension.

"Hey, Sherlock, that you?"

It was Charlie Wriggins's voice, and the Detective visualized him in his mind's eye: a seventy-five-year-old, ornery and energetic ex-newspaper man who loved his profession's image and cultivated all its clichés, full of piss and vinegar and newsroom profanity. He was one of the few transplanted residents who got along with the locals (Charlie's term) because, although he was as irascible as they were, he was a reporter and not a reformer by nature; he didn't try to change their lives. The Detective waited until Officer Truax hung up.

"Where are you, Charlie?"

"The Klein place on the shore highway."

"Which one's that?"

"You've been up here two years and you don't know the Klein place? Frankly, Sherlock, you amaze me. You know, the orange erector set overlooking the cove. The one they tried to revoke the building permit on; lost in court."

"Oh yeah, the Klein place," the Detective said, but he didn't know it. A city man all his life, he had barely stepped outside since moving in with Sally, as lost in the New England countryside as a Kansas runaway in New York City. For him, Maine was a jumbled montage of sea gulls and rock and agitated ocean, a place you sent postcards from, returning home before they arrived. But now the Detective wouldn't return. Maine was his home; he would remain there until he died.

"Well, what's this all about? What happened?"

"It seems that someone—maybe Mr. Klein himself—took a walk last night." Charlie paused and the Detective sensed him savoring the drama, the headline potential of the story. "A very strange kind of walk: three feet toward Nova Scotia, and five hundred feet down into the Atlantic Ocean."

"What do you mean, 'someone'?"

"Well, the Coast Guard hasn't found the body yet. We do have a witness, but he was too far away to see who it was. And too far away to see who pushed him."

"He saw someone being pushed?"

"Not exactly. Couldn't print that, though I'd bet my next three social security checks on it."

The Detective sees desks, rows of desks, gleaming under the fluorescence of institutional lighting; he sees faces, young and attentive, propped by pencils, above open notebooks; and then, before him, a hand, his hand, chalk-smeared and gesturing, clipped with authority; his voice emerging as if from a distance, words in amber, preserved in time, to be summoned and repeated for the appropriate crimes . . .

"What's that you said?" Charlie asked him.

"I said: 'No corpse, no crime.'"

"Don't be so sure about that. Listen, Klein's missing. The only one up here is his wife and the police chief is having a hell of a time making any sense out of her. He's been here all morning and doesn't know much more than when he started. Klein was some sort of VIP scientist, and I mean the real thing—physics, the atomic bomb, a Nobel prize about ten years ago; he's practically a national asset, so we're talking about federal authorities and national press if this thing doesn't get cleared up real soon. The Chief doesn't want that, and frankly neither do I—I want this story all to myself. Now Mrs. Klein is some kind of egghead, too, so I talked the Chief into letting me call you in. He's a reasonable sort for a local; knows that these intellectuals speak a language of their own. I told him you might be able to break her down, get through to her."

The Detective cleared his throat, suddenly aware of his daughter's eavesdropping presence behind him. "Can you pick me up?"

"I'll be there in fifteen minutes."

The Detective hung up, avoiding Sally as he walked back to the study. She followed him there, though, as he knew she would, and that enraged him—the predictability, the knee-jerk reflexiveness of her smothering, mothering instinct. What's the matter, he wanted to say to her sarcastically, you didn't knock this time. But he remained silent.

"You're getting involved?"

The Detective searched his desk for his pocket notebook. "I'm going to take a look around, that's all."

"You're getting involved."

The Detective turned to his daughter; searched her face for an excuse to strike out at her, for a hint of the resentment he was sure she still felt toward him. But instead, he found only a sad resignation, her eyes reflecting truths that he didn't want to see:

Fact, they said: you are seventy-two, with a heart that's older.

Fact, they said: your wife is dead and you're lost without her.

Sally shook her head and then left the room, closing the door behind her. The Detective stared after her, ashamed of himself, ashamed that her pity was so well founded. He never should have moved to Maine in the first place. After Sadie's funeral, his first few weeks of absolute solitude had frightened him into accepting Sally's invitation, but now he understood that it had been a mistake. Better to have risked the loneliness, better to have risked a sudden breakdown or better yet, the blocked or burst vessel that would eventually be his end, better anything real or dramatic or painful than this slow rotting in place, this forced self-inspection, this philosophizing.

As his eyes scanned the desk, the Detective suddenly remembered the letters and he felt as if he were going to faint, heart fluttering, mouth gasping, sweat dampening his freckled forehead. He dropped into his easy chair and loosened his collar, closing his eyes. *The letters.* They were always there in the background of his mind like some vulgar jingle, popping into consciousness at the first vacant moment. And he couldn't brush them out, not the idea of them, not even their image—the white, feminine-fancy stationery, the elastic band surrounding them, the slanted curls of Sadie's script. And not the shock he had felt when, the week after the funeral, he had cleaned out her desk and found them; the suspicion. It hadn't been the sort of suspicion the Detective was accustomed to, not the professional curiosity, the teasing shadows of solutions, the pleasant, piquing mental play that directed his detection in case after case; but something more dominating and physical—nausea, paralysis, fear. And a fear that knew its object, for he had read the first two lines of the top-most letter and they had stopped him, sent him reeling. No, it hadn't been the sort of suspicion that the Detective was used to, but rather a suspicion that begged not to be confirmed: he had packed away the letters without reading another word.

———

A bedroom: middle class, modest in all respects, but carefully decorated, color-coordinated, its curtains and bedspread a matching dark blue, its wallpaper print a floral cerulean. It is late, night, and only a small desk lamp lights the room, its corners, the edges of vision, blurred in shadows. At a writing table across from the bed, under the funneled glow of the lamp, spotlit, stage center, the woman sits, with paper and pen, a hand covering what she has written. In profile hers is a striking face, hard-planed and weathered, a middle-aged beauty, the grace of endurance, of suffering done well; but blushing now, too, as she looks to the door where the man stands, hat in his hand, shoes tracking water on the rug. Fact: it is raining outside. The room, the scene, their sudden meeting, is framed in words, her words; her eyes saying, "You should have knocked"; her refusal to avert his eyes, "I've earned my privacy." "I'm keeping a diary," she says aloud.

The man nods, accepts; he's entitling the frame, tagging it for his memory, something like—"We All Need Our Private Times." But now the Detective wanders, peering into, peering from the blurred and darkened corners, of the room, his mind; superimposing new transparencies, the tinted glass of changing realities, trying to assimilate the late-found evidence; but all grows tentative, vaporous, murky—a scene out of focus. A new subtitle floats, flirts like suspicion through the translucency of time's cataract eye: "The Lie?" But who can tell now, trapped in the present tense?

There were three sharp knocks on the study door, and they drew the Detective's attention away from the desk drawer where the letters were hidden. His heart had nearly recovered from its arrhythmic attack, but he was pale and exhausted, and the room seemed to have grown suddenly cold. He fumbled with his handkerchief, dabbing his forehead and rubbing his cheeks, futile gestures to hide the attack, and when Sally entered the room with his sweater, coat, and scarf, she froze, momentarily shocked by his gray-tinged complexion. Then, recovering, she waited for the lie she knew would come.

"I'm all right," the Detective said.

Sally said nothing, slumping her shoulders, watching with a pose of passive resistance she had learned from her mother: kill yourself if you must, but I'm not going to pretend that it isn't happening.

"*I am,*" the Detective said again, but uncomfortable with the lie, he tried to escape it by hurrying on, speeding up time. He stood up quickly, reaching for his sweater; but old age demanded slow transitions, from sleep into consciousness, from sitting into standing, was a slow transition itself from life into death. His left leg, gravity-pumped, swelled with blood, ached until he thought he would cry out from it, then buckled at the knee and he began to fall. He threw out his hand to catch the desk and brace himself, but Sally's arms, younger, quicker, were there first, gathering him around the chest and pulling him toward her. He hung there, dead weight, a drowned body, his heart racing helplessly again, waiting for the slow transition out of pain.

For a moment, the Detective gave in to it; more than physically he surrendered his resistance and clung to his daughter. It occurred to him then to ask her. It occurred to him then that she might know, and that even if she didn't, just to share the burden, to transfer it, letting her ask the questions he couldn't ask, letting her read the lines he couldn't read—letting her be the detective—would be a relief. But what was he to ask her, how was he to phrase it? "Did your mother, did your mother always love me? Was she always, did she ever . . . ?" Words faded; pain faded, pumped away by a steadier heart, replaced by anger, self-disgust. That he should have to ask Sally in order to know; that she should know and not he; that she should have been closer to Sadie than he . . . The Detective placed his hand on the desk and pushed himself away from her.

"Let go of me," he said.

Sally dropped her arms, slowly at first, ready to support him again if he weren't strong enough to stand on his own. She refused to look at his face—for his sake, his pride, the shame she knew he felt at his dependence on her; and, too, for her own sake, to avoid the hate she knew she'd find in his eyes. And the Detective hated her even more for that further kindness—her refusal to rub it in. Fact: their roles *had* reversed. That she believed that and still tried at times like these to pretend she didn't only emphasized its truth all the more to him. He was close to Sally now, closer than he had ever been before, but he had never loved her less. Inequality bred dependence, bred closeness, bred hate and resentment. That she should know and not he . . . no, he wouldn't, he couldn't ask. The Detective reached for his sweater and, turning his back to his daughter, buttoned it slowly, taking refuge in the independence of a simple task.

A car horn honked from the driveway. The Detective hurriedly threw on his coat and scarf, and then, avoiding Sally's eyes by looking toward the floor, he left the room, hoping to avert another confrontation. But by the time he reached the front door, he was acutely conscious of an obligation to reassure her, aware that she would worry as soon as he left her sight. He paused there in the doorway and turned to face her; there were tears in her eyes, tears he had caused.

"Don't go, Dad," she said. "You know you're not up to it."

Sally reached out tentatively, touching his plaid scarf, a gesture so pathetic that the Detective wanted to slap her hand away and to slap away with it all the closeness and dependence and guilt he felt. But his revulsion passed quickly, and instead, he felt sorry for her, bound to her all the more. Sea Gull Sally, the habitual worrier—what had he done to her that she had so little faith? and what had happened to him that he was becoming so like her? The Detective kissed his daughter on the cheek, squeezed her hand reassuringly.

"I'll be all right," he said.

But as he walked down the steps toward Charlie Wriggins's car, he knew that he wasn't all right. All the hope that Charlie's phone call had aroused in him was suddenly gone, Sally's oppressive despair in its place: . . . those strange thoughts which afflicted him now, those concepts that stretched beyond comprehension, so unlike the measured facts of detection—what was he to do with them? what did they mean? Despair was the province of a philosopher, not a detective. To a man without hope, the world appeared hopeless; a man with hope, foolish—but was it actually so? The first rule: always doubt the witness. The Detective no longer trusted his own judgments; everything had become tentative, vaporous, murky. Come to grips with reality, his daughter had told him, but which reality, whose reality? Sally's? Charlie's? His own?

And even as he drove to the Klein house, captive audience to Charlie Wriggins's manic enthusiasm, despair wouldn't leave the Detective. He turned in the seat, pretending to listen, his attention though directed inward; and staring through the windshield into the formless slate of the sky, he thought: "Even murder can't excite me anymore." It was as if he were dead or anesthetized. But then another realization—unsolicited, unwanted—followed: it was as if he were on another case, preoccupied and withdrawn, seeking the solution, and nothing, not even murder, could divert his attention from it. Yes, he was on another case, although he fought it, forcing it from consciousness whenever he could, although he wished more than anything else that the case would disappear. And as they drove toward the ocean, toward the Klein house, toward the scene of the crime, the Detective projected onto that blank and depthless sky, as though it were the blackboard of his old classroom or a clean page in his pocket notebook, the skeletal clues of the other crime, the one that would not leave him. And he saw written there the words of his own mind; recorded, preserved in time, as objective and relentless as the aching in his thighs. Fact, he saw there, fact: I've never found her diary.

2

The Detective sat in what he assumed to be the Kleins' living room, although it was like no living room he had ever seen: tubular, stainless steel chairs twisted into geometric shapes, with glittering, curved lucite backs as smooth as polished marble; bright orange wall-to-wall carpeting as luxuriant as a field of ripening wheat, the pile hiding the furniture's feet so that the chairs seemed rooted there, sprung flowers of extraterrestrial origin, the science fiction garden of a World's Fair exhibit; three of its walls a flat and spotless white, and bare except for a series of evenly spaced paintings which in an ordered progression grew from the size of a postage stamp on the first wall to a three-foot square on the third. The paintings were formless swatches and splashes of color, reds and oranges, and they reminded the Detective of his own mind, an eruption of thoughts, boiling and swirling like lava, seeking the bottom ground, the cooling ocean, inert and settled form. A stainless steel mobile hung from the center of the ceiling; in constant chaotic motion, its individual parts, shiny metallic propellers, spun against each other—a separate mechanical universe with its own complex of rules and conflicts whose unfolding gave the Detective a headache.

But more disconcerting to him, the strangest aspect of all, was the room's shape. A triangle whose top had been sliced off, its walls joined at oblique angles, each chair situated so that it had at least a three-quarter frontal view of the triangle's wide base, the fourth wall, that wall made of a single sheet of glass—not a picture window, but a full wall of glass. And stretching behind it, as if some vacationer's snapshot, a mammoth color slide flashed upon the wall, were the cliff, the promontory rock, the cove, the orange metal walkway leading to them all, and beyond, as far as the eye could see, the ocean. The scene of the crime, frozen there before their eyes. Only the gulls and terns seemed alive, arching, swooping, diving into the funneled depths of the cove, then rising effortlessly on invisible thrusts of wind, arrogant and free. Toy-sized in the distance, a Coast Guard cutter rocked in the cove's mouth, searching for the body.

"Let's go through it one more time, all right, Mrs. Klein?"

The police chief spoke slowly; he was exhausted and on the edge of exasperation, yet still polite. The Detective tried to brush out the others from his sight—Charlie Wriggins, Officer Truax, the eyewitness called Dexter—and concentrated on the Chief and Mrs. Klein. This review was for his sake, he knew, and he was conscious of intruding into another man's case, a feeling difficult to erase with Officer Truax glaring at him from the corner.

"All right," the police chief said again, the Detective noting his heavy-lidded and expressionless face, "let's start from the top then. Last night, at about five o'clock, Dexter here, coming back into dock, saw a body fall into the cove. He also saw someone else standing at the top of the cliff, near to the point from where—he assumed—the body must have fallen." The Chief paused, breathed deeply as if the sentence had been too complex and mentally exhausting for him. "Unfortunately, though, due to the distance and poor light, he couldn't recognize either of the two people. Have I got that right, Dexter?"

Dexter, rail-thin, stood in the center of the room, his feet buried in the rug pile like a pier post at low tide. His hair was a salt-bleached gray, his face a parched red; his eyes, tiny and black, clung above his cheeks like barnacle shells. A crucifix of defiance, he stared straight ahead as he spoke.

"I saw what I saw," he said.

"All right. So what we have, then, are two nameless people, one presumably dead and one who presumably saw him die but for some unknown reason failed to report it to the Coast Guard or the police. Now the logical thing to do would be to try to identify who those two people were, starting with the presumed deceased. Dexter couldn't find the body last night and, as of this moment anyway, the Coast Guard hasn't had any luck either. So, what we're left with, then, is the process of elimination. Now Officer Truax and myself know all the full-time residents of this area and it didn't take long to ascertain that none were missing. That left the part-time residents such as Mr. and Mrs. Klein. Now Officer Truax and myself keep a list of phone numbers where those part-time residents can be reached in case of theft or damage to their property up here. So we called those numbers, last night and all this morning, and as of right now, the only person not accounted for is Mr. Klein. Am I right on that, Officer Truax?"

A clipped nod. "Right."

"All right. So what we have is this. Either the person who fell last night from the cliff into the cove was Mr. Klein or it was someone who had no business being up here. Now this *is* Mr. Klein's property; he *does* have business being up here."

The Chief inhaled laboriously. He leaned forward in his stainless steel chair, focusing on Mrs. Klein, and the Detective sensed in him then something of the law itself—plodding, implacable, relentlessly inhumanly patient.

"Mrs. Klein," he said, "where is your husband?"

Mrs. Klein sat in one of the room's obliquely angled corners beside the wall of glass, dwarfed by the dimensions of the coastal setting. And for a moment, the Detective's mind seemed to expand, embracing that contrast between the size of the woman and the immensity of the world she had been born into; it seemed to stretch, groping toward some concept bigger than the person and the scene inspiring it, a concept tagged with words like "folly," "awe," "futility." But now no longer alone in his study, no longer merely biding time, the Detective resisted the philosophizing which had begun to dominate his mental life, those drifting, irrational sequences he secretly found compelling but feared were a sign of encroaching senility and death. Instead, he shrunk the borders of his vision, focusing not on what this woman meant, but on who she was—this could-be widow, this suspect.

He guessed that she was in her fifties, her hair cropped short and fully gray, her clothing—dark stockings, short plaid skirt, a fisherman's turtleneck sweater—campus style. Her eyes were white-rimmed and protuberant, hyperthyroidal; they cast about the room in an endless, jittery search of the floor as if she had lost her wedding ring there. Perhaps she had. The Detective saw no ring on either hand, but found little significance in that fact.

Traditions, the old symbols, meant nothing anymore, especially to the sort of people who built stainless steel and glass living rooms. Sadie, the Detective remembered, immediately trying to squelch the memory, had never removed her wedding ring, that thin gold band melding with her skin; she'd been buried with it on. And he sees her now, framed in mahogany, a plush silken background, the scent of flowers so overwhelmingly sweet that he feels he may vomit from it, her cheeks so pale that the mortician's rouge can't cover their lifelessness—as he bends, now and forever slowly bending, and removing his ring, drops it on her chest. The Detective stared at his left hand; the ring finger, freckled, swollen, showed no sign of the band he had worn there for nearly fifty years. No, the old symbols meant nothing anymore—maybe they never had—but he'd ask Mrs. Klein about it later anyway. "A case," he hears himself lecture over and over, words in amber, "is solved with details."

"Mrs. Klein," the Chief repeated after receiving no answer. *"Where* is your husband?"

"I, I don't know. I just don't know." She frowned, surprised at herself, as if she were perplexed by her own lack of knowledge.

"Were you here at the house last night?"

"Yes. Here."

"Well, was your husband with you then?"

Mrs. Klein said nothing; refused even to lift her head, her eyes still involved in their frantic searching, like . . . like REMs, the Detective suddenly thought, rapid eye movements that signified dreaming during sleep, as if although awake, she were still living in last night's dream.

"Mrs. Klein," the police chief said. He sighed. "Mrs. Klein, now that's a simple question. Your husband—was he or was he not with you last night?"

"I . . . I don't know. He might have been. It seems to me that, that . . ." She picked at short, silver strands of hair that covered her ear; her voice dropped: "He might have been."

There was an uneasy pause. Then, Dexter, the eyewitness, his gaze directed at no one in particular, broke in, reminding them that he considered the entire procedure an attack on his honor.

"I saw what I saw," he said again.

Mrs. Klein looked up quickly. "I don't doubt that," she said. "I don't doubt that at all. You saw what you saw; see what you see; will see what you will see—when you see it. I don't doubt that at all."

She stared at Dexter for a moment, her eyes finally focused, steady, but when he refused to acknowledge her, she panicked, glancing quickly around the room far confirmation. Out of the corner of his eye, the Detective noticed Charlie Wriggins gesturing to him, an I-told-you-so expression on his face.

"Yes," the Chief said at last. "Well." He stood up. "Why don't you freshen yourself up a bit, Mrs. Klein? I realize all of this has been quite a trial for you."

Without giving her a chance to respond, the Chief crossed the room and gently lifted her by the elbow from her seat. He led her to the door, the others watching her unsteady, bewildered, sleepwalk shuffle—all but the Detective who, taking advantage of that short moment of privacy, gradually straightened his left leg. (He mustn't let them see how lame he was.) By the time the Chief had returned to the living room, the Detective was standing, his secret concealed, the pain in his leg a dull and bearable ache, no longer visible on his face. Charlie Wriggins, notebook in hand, and Officer Truax had risen too, and the four of them huddled there in the center of the room beneath the twisting stainless steel propellers of the mobile. Only Dexter stood apart.

"Well," the Chief said, his eyes neutral, conceding nothing, "what do you think?"

"Is she always like that?" the Detective asked.

"No one up here seems to know. Her husband did most of the errands around town. They didn't spend much time up here anyway—their second home. Mainly in the summer."

"It could be from shock," the Detective said. "But the question is, shock from what? From being informed that her husband might be dead? From having seen him die? From having killed him?—You don't have any physical evidence that Mr. Klein was up here last night?"

The Chief shook his head. "That's the strange thing. No food in the cabinets; no garbage. For Christsake, we even had to turn the water on. It's just as if the house had been closed up for the winter, as if neither of them had been here in months. There's not even a car in the garage. Now how the hell did she get up here, I keep asking myself. I already checked the one taxi in the area—no fares to the Klein house since September, the driver says. One more thing for whatever it's worth. These drapes were open when we came in; it was the only sign that the house was occupied—besides Mrs. Klein herself, that is."

"There's men's clothing in the closets," Officer Truax said.

The Chief shook his head. "Means nothing. They're all summer clothes. When you're as rich as the Kleins, you don't bother carrying wardrobes around with you. You just keep full closets in all your houses."

The Detective thought a moment and then said, "What's his size?"

Officer Truax, stung by the Chief's dismissal, laughed sarcastically. "What, you want his hand-me-downs?"

"Truax," the Chief said. He sighed, then looked up to the ceiling, seemed to study the intricate motions of the mobile.

How patient he is, the Detective thought, how controlled. "Truax, he's talking about the man, not his clothes." The Chief turned to the Detective. "He was a big one all right, bigger than you. But that doesn't eliminate Mrs. Klein as a suspect; she still could have pushed him, tiny as she is. Just take a look at that walkway out there; it was built with the view, not safety, in mind."

The three of them, all but Dexter, followed the Chief's pointed hand and stared through the glass wall to the cove. The Coast Guard cutter was half blocked from view by the promontory rock; the sky, as gray as the cutter's hull, was so overcast that the time of day was indiscernible.

"The body," the Detective said, "is there much chance of recovery?"

The Chief shook his head. "No, and that means, unfortunately, that even if she did do it . . ."

The Detective nodded, completing the thought for him. "No corpse, no crime," he said.

Charlie Wriggins broke in: "But you've got a witness."

The Chief glanced at Dexter. "Who witnessed a falling body, not someone pushing that body. We'd never even make it to court on his testimony. Not without a confession. Well, any suggestions?"

The Detective hesitated: the Chief's eyes still veiled his mood, his motives, but there was no time left for stalling. Tact, the Detective lectured himself, be tactful, courteous; no swaggering, no arrogance.

"It does occur to me that a woman in Mrs. Klein's condition . . . well, that she might be frightened, confused by so many people."

He paused. The Chief stared at him—a cop's stare, suspicious, penetrating. "You want to speak to her alone?"

"It might be helpful. Someone out of uniform. Give her a chance to relax; a simple conversation instead of an interrogation."

The Chief said nothing, and the Detective watched him as he made up his mind, sympathizing with him, knowing from experience the painful conflict he was going through: duty versus personal pride. To have invited the Detective in as a consultant was excusable, but to leave him alone with the major suspect was to concede his own failure and to permit the possibility of the crime being solved without his own participation.

The Chief sighed. "All right. It can't hurt. I'll leave Truax outside in the patrol car to guard the place and relay any messages. Charlie here will give Dexter and me a ride back to town. It's what, three o'clock now? I'll give you till six or so unless something comes up in the meantime."

Charlie broke in to protest his exclusion from the questioning. The Chief listened to him briefly, a slight ironic smile on his face, the first sign of emotion he had displayed since the Detective's arrival.

"Right, Charlie," he said. "Just what we need to calm her down— a reporter recording every word out of her mouth. No, you go with the rest of us. And besides, we need the ride, don't we, Dexter?"

Dexter said nothing. A moment later, Mrs. Klein reentered the room, freezing the conversation in its silence. She stopped in front of the glass wall and stared out to the cove.

"I better let her know what's going on," the Chief said softly. "The rest of you get going. I'll be out in a minute."

Dexter, Truax, and Charlie Wriggins grabbed their coats and silently left the house. The Detective stood to the side and watched the Chief, a man of formidable bulk and presence in his dark blue uniform, as with hat in hand he lowered himself to Mrs. Klein's level and explained to her gently that he would return in a few hours. The Detective admired the Chief then, admired his patience and gentleness, the character it had taken to let the case out of his personal control; and he reexperienced through his admiration the sense of common mission which had always enhanced his love of detection, felt again that sense of higher duty, of belonging to a whole, a whole which, extending beyond the individual self, was defined by a devotion to one shared goal: solving the crime. The good ones always knew it. The prizes and medals, the media attention, none of that mattered; the one-man-against-the-multitude-of-evil image, the Sherlock Holmes syndrome, was the province of fictional romance, not reality. That the Detective understood and accepted this was both the source of his sincere humility and, to a degree, the secret of his professional success. He knew that individuals in and of themselves could rarely solve a case. It was the backing of a team, the consolidated effort, the combined and therefore relentless pressure of society's law that crushed the sordid and private mystery of a crime. The good detective merely directed the mass, discovered the pressure point where the weight of the law, once applied, would be irresistible.

The Chief had finished with Mrs. Klein. He walked with the Detective to the front door where he stopped, turned, and, after a pause, accepted the Detective's hand, shaking it with quick, vigorous jerks. A professional exchange; not friendship but respect—teammates.

"Chief," the Detective said, finally dropping his hand. "I've been meaning to ask you about Dexter."

"Oh, yes, Dexter. Well, he's reliable, if that's what you mean. You'll have to take my word on that for now, and you'll have to know the people around here a little better to understand it. They may not make much of a living or break any records for friendliness, but they do make great witnesses. Oh yeah, I believe him. It happened, all right . . ."

The police chief paused, placed his hat on his head and, staring past the Detective to Mrs. Klein and her glass-wall view of the promontory point, said:

". . . whatever 'it' is."

————————

The Detective sat in the living room and attempted without success to adapt his sagging, aging body to the inflexible curves of his steel and lucite chair. Mrs. Klein, her back to him, stood ten feet away, silently staring through the glass wall toward the cove, her arms clasped from cold or fear—a fisherman's wife keeping an uneasy vigil, waiting for her husband's return from the sea.

"Are you feeling any better?" the Detective said. "I could make some coffee if you'd like."

"We have no coffee." She spoke without turning her head, an emotionless fact, a truism. "We don't believe in coffee."

"I'm afraid I don't understand."

"We don't believe in artificial stimulation."

"Oh—bad for the heart, I suppose. Actually, I shouldn't have any myself; just decaffeinated."

"Bad for the mind."

"What's that?"

"We believe it's bad for the mind. We believe artificial stimulation is unnecessary, excessive. We believe the brain is biochemically sufficient without the addition of artificial stimulants."

"Oh." The Detective frowned, as puzzled by the delivery as by the words themselves. There was something about her insistence on the plural, there was something about her emphasis of that "we" that made him wonder if she were being bitter or ironic; but without seeing her face, he couldn't be sure.

"Yes, well, when you get to be my age you begin to wonder. Nothing in your body seems sufficient by itself."

"You don't have to reach your age . . ." Mrs. Klein said; she paused and then added, as if she only grudgingly accepted a responsibility to be more than cryptic, ". . . to wonder."

"I understand," the Detective said, although he wasn't certain that he did. "It's the waiting. It's the not knowing. Don't worry—something should turn up soon; something definite."

Mrs. Klein faced him for the first time; she turned, tilting her head, her arms clasped beneath her breasts. Her protuberant eyes were steady now, attentive and yet distracting still, their transformation from boredom to interest too sudden and complete.

"Is that what you think—that it's the not knowing?" She walked to a chair and sat down in it. "But then, you're a detective, aren't you?"

"Yes."

"And it's your job—to know, I mean; to come up with something definite."

"In a manner of speaking."

"My husband's a detective in a manner of speaking."

"Yes, I was told that he was a scientist." The Detective flinched at his use of the past tense, but Mrs. Klein didn't appear to notice it. "A physicist, they said."

"Yes, a physicist, but a detective nevertheless, a detective in a manner of speaking. Not knowing bothers him too; coming up with something definite is his job too. Matter in motion, that's his field, pieces of matter so small that they can never be seen by the human eye. He worked on the atomic bomb."

"Yes, I believe someone mentioned that."

"Aren't you going to ask if we feel guilty about it—the atomic bomb, I mean?"

"I don't think . . ."

"We don't believe in guilt. Oh, it exists, but we don't believe in its importance other than as a corrective adjustment for future behavior. We believe guilt is a feedback mechanism."

The Detective shifted in his chair. There was no doubt in his mind now; he saw bitterness in her face, heard sarcasm in her words—the overemphasis on the "we," the mock blank expression—and instinctively he began to think of motive. Sarcasm negated meaning: "We don't believe in guilt" enunciated that way meant that she *did* believe in guilt, that she felt guilty. Or at least that she disliked her husband's lack of guilt. But ideas do not motives make, the Detective told himself. Wives do not kill their husbands because they worked on the atomic bomb; it was always more petty, irrational, personal. Murder was a personal act, the Detective had come to learn, though often rationalized by grander notions. Perhaps Mrs. Klein had convinced herself otherwise; but if she had killed Mr. Klein, the true motive would lie in the slough of their everyday lives, the balance of power between husband and wife, the subtle shades of emotional betrayal, the knifeglances and abused intimacies, the resenting of someone who knew her too well.

"And you," Mrs. Klein said, her eyes growing wider, circular and white-rimmed, "do you believe in guilt?"

A frame, blurred frame, discolored from age (what day, what year, which moment, or is it many moments recomposed into one?); in it a chair, shapeless and unclear (which chair? whose chair? try to remember, to focus the picture but all that appears is *the chair*, an abstraction, an idea); Sadie in the chair, Sadie not abstract, Sadie now and forever a face in a moment, a profile turning toward him, pride smoldering in silence . . . all her accusing glances merged into one: "The Motive?" "The Motives?"

"But of course," she said, "you're the detective, the criminal investigator, and the detective must believe in the assignment of guilt—first degree and second degree, felony and misdemeanor. That's your job, after all."

"No, that's not my job." The Detective sat up, a sore point struck, an argument he had fought time and time again. "Guilt is subjective; it's assigned by the judge, by the jury. I, I just . . ."

"You detect."

"Yes, I detect. I tell them what happened."

"The objective truth."

"The objective truth; as close as I can come to it."

"Your subjective view of the objective truth."

The Detective watched Mrs. Klein, uncertain of her intent, unable to enter a rhythm of conversation because he didn't know what to anticipate next. She sat five feet from him, legs and arms crossed, a knot of intensity, her shorn head stretched forward in expectation of an answer from him—sincere, too sincere; serious, too serious; and above all, too logical, the supralogic of the insane. Her eyes were drawn into a stare too focused to sustain, the Detective waiting uneasily for them to jerk into their jittery searching again. Beyond all this, though, beyond the facts before his eyes, her physical presence, was the suspicion that she was acting, this entire conversation a contemptuous deception, the murderess's self-defense. But a suspicion based on what—what besides the paranoia he had absorbed from Sally lately? The Detective wasn't sure, and sitting within the Klein living room, that oddly antiseptic opening to the stark Maine coast, he felt himself trapped in some visual conundrum, the impossible metaphor of his own confusion, poised at a fulcrum where paired opposites met—time and timelessness, nature and artifice, pity and suspiciousness, all coming full circle and fusing at a border as paradoxical as glass.

"No answer for me, Descartes?" Mrs. Klein said. "Too confused to answer?—It's the not knowing, isn't it? It's the not knowing that upsets you so. Don't worry, Descartes; something should turn up soon. Something definite."

Sarcastic and yet pitying, contemptuous and yet compassionate—the Detective couldn't be sure. Although they were not at all alike physically, in some illogical way that he couldn't quite conceptualize, this strange woman, this murder suspect, reminded him of his wife; aroused in him a similar complex of conflicting emotions, a frustrating urge both to accuse and embrace, to punish and console. Yes, that was it; Mrs. Klein was right, the Detective suddenly understood; it *was* the not knowing that bothered him so, the lack of certainty that paralyzed him with second thoughts and indecision. If he knew, if only he knew which were true: grieving widow or deceiving murderess; loving, loyal wife or . . . The Detective thought of Sally; missed her. She would be in the kitchen now, at the table or at the stove, on the phone, keeping informed while making supper, a vigilant ear for incipient trouble; and he could almost hear spoons striking pots, the familiar tattoo of her knife against the cutting board, the way those sounds eased into consciousness as he lay half-asleep in his shuttered study. That was his reality now; not crime or detection, not the intimate dance of interrogation, but the muffled preparation of the bourgeois dinner—soft, safe, distant.

"I say that to Andy," Mrs. Klein said. "I've said it for years now. It's a joke, an in-joke. You know, the sort of silly thing that couples share?"

The Detective nodded. He knew; he knows: the wine mispronounced on their first wedding anniversary is mispronounced on the second, and on the third, and on the tenth, is forever mispronounced, and no one else may mispronounce it, an exclusive right of Sadie's and his, giving shape to their marriage, to their special, secret life together—now and forever.

"Whenever he's stumped, whenever he's reached a dead end in his work, whenever those tiny pieces of matter in motion have confused him so much that he begins to despair of ever finding out the truth about them, I say to him, 'Don't worry, Descartes, something will turn up.' It's an in-joke now, one of those little rituals that make up a marriage, one of those little boosts that sustain our momentum. It keeps him going, he says. I'm his in-spiration, he says. His accomplice."

"His accomplice?"

Mrs. Klein ignored his question. "Should I do that for you—be your in-spiration, help you to discover something definite? Should I become your accomplice?"

"About your husband," the Detective said, trying to initiate the inter-rogation.

"Yes, about my husband. Do you think he's dead?"

The Detective blinked, his hands fumbling with his pocket notebook; stunned, he stared at her for a moment. The question had been normal, but the manner of its asking, incredible—intellectual curiosity, as if she were working on some academic problem.

"I'm . . . well, I'm skeptical, let's put it that way. What about you?"

"Yes," Mrs. Klein said, "that makes sense. You're skeptical—the definite knower, the objective truth-seeker, the detective. Andy, who is a detective in a manner of speaking, has always promoted skepticism. We be-lieve in it."

"Yes, Mrs. Klein, but your husband, right now: do you think that he's dead or alive?"

Mrs. Klein looked away from him, her sarcasm suddenly failing her, her eyes gone manic again, caught up in their waking dream, searching, search-ing. Her loss of control frightened the Detective, but excited him too, his blood-instinct aroused by her sudden vulnerability, by the appearance of a pressure point that he could use.

"At this moment, Mrs. Klein, at this exact moment, is your husband dead or alive?"

The Detective tried to lean forward in his chair, to press home the question with his physical presence, his body resisting with its inertial pain, Mrs. Klein avoiding his insistent stare.

"Why must you know? Why do you have to keep on the trail? What if I told you that whatever happened, it was for the best—couldn't you just leave it at that?"

She knew; she did know. "Dead or alive, Mrs. Klein?"

Mrs. Klein hid her face in her hands. "I," she began, "I believe . . ." She paused, measuring her breaths, gaining control by degrees. She dropped her hands, lifting her face to meet his stare; yes, she nodded to herself, yes. Her eyes had begun to steady themselves.

"We believe he's alive."

She had slipped away from him; he had allowed her to slip away, into her sarcasm or her pretense of sarcasm, out of her vulnerability, the pressure point so visible just a moment before suddenly gone. The Detective was tired, felt a tepid disgust for his own inadequacy. Fact: he was losing his touch. He no longer had the mental tenacity, the will required to force the connections—he didn't really want to. Something was missing, a subtraction of old age, some basic drive dried up, that insatiable desire for solution. But he must try; if only to keep his life coherent, if only out of allegiance to his old self-image, he must try to finish it. And so he stalled, staring at the blank pages of his notebook, twisting his feet in the orange carpet, as he tried to organize his thoughts.

"Mrs. Klein, when did you arrive here? Exactly how long have you been up here?"

"Always."

"You've always been up here—with no food or water."

"In a manner of speaking."

"I'm not interested in manners of speaking. I'm interested in facts, times of arrival and departure, confirmed and witnessed events; facts concerning your husband's disappearance."

"I don't doubt that," she said. "I don't doubt that at all. It makes perfect sense that you should. You're the detective and the detective believes in facts; the detective sees what he sees."

"Well, then, perhaps you'd like to give me some facts to believe in. For example, was your husband here at the house last night?"

"Yes."

"He was here?"

"He's always here."

"He's not here now, Mrs. Klein; that's a fact I believe in."

"You see what you see when you see it." She tilted her head, considered him. "You *do* think he's dead, don't you? That's your subjective view of the objective truth."

Curiosity again; the wrong mood at the wrong time—always. The Detective watched her helplessly and felt that she was toying with him, that she had become the interrogator and he the suspect.

"Perhaps," he said.

"And perhaps you believe that I killed him. But then, you can't be sure about that, can you? You must be skeptical, mustn't you?"

The Detective sighed—no, he hadn't the endurance any longer; the mockery, the convolutions of their conversation exhausted and confused him, made him impatient. His bad leg, stationary since the others had left, its already poor circulation pinched by the hard edge of his lucite chair, had gone numb, radiating needles of pain. He winced from it, cried out from its suddenness and surprise, reaching down with both hands and squeezing his thigh just above the knee. Mrs. Klein leaped from her chair in a panic of concern and hovered over him, a confusing form on the periphery of his attention, for he could only focus on the pain, the pain and the fear that his heart, erratically racing, would burst or simply stop, too exhausted to go on. Slowly, though, as the pain ebbed, as his heart regained a steadier rhythm, the Detective became aware of her presence above him: her fingers, weightless spots of cold, touched his brow in a healer's gesture, a priest's blessing; her voice lapped over him, gentle waves of some deep, embracing calm.

"Don't worry, Descartes," she said over and over again. "Something will turn up. Don't worry, Descartes, your accomplice is here."

The Detective straightened up, releasing his thigh, drawing his forehead away from her icy touch while avoiding her eyes. His frailty fully revealed now, he was ashamed and afraid, feeling that their relationship had changed, sensing that a kind of equality had been reached, a parity of pain: widow and widower, teammates in suffering, caught up in this mystery by the fact of their survival; lost together. And for the first time, he believed her without qualification; accepted the sincerity of her offer without understanding its meaning.

"I'll help you," she said. "I'll be your accomplice."

There was a pause; she waited there silently above him—for confirmation, he knew, for a commitment on his part, some visible sign of his willing participation. The Detective waited, too; and then, without understanding why, he felt himself nod.

"All right," Mrs. Klein said, her sarcasm instantly returning, mockery of the Chief's methodical style, "let's start from the top." She turned and began pacing. "Last night at about five o'clock, a local fisherman named Dexter saw what he saw. And what he saw was a body falling from the promontory point into the cove. Now who could this body be, we ask ourselves? The property from which said body fell belonged to a Mr. and Mrs. Andrew Klein, Nobel prize-winning physicist and obscure medieval historian respectively, and a thorough check has revealed that Mr. Klein, despite his Nobel prize, is missing. Tentative conclusion: Mr. Klein is what the local fisherman named Dexter saw when he saw what he saw. Am I right so far?"

The Detective nodded.

"So the question is, how do we proceed from here? Now what would Andy do, I ask myself? How would Andy, who has been a detective in a manner of speaking all his life, approach the problem of the disappearance of one Andrew Klein?"

"Possibilities," the Detective said. "List all the possibilities and then analyze them, eliminating the unlikely ones."

"That's it, that's what Andy would do: proceed scientifically. We believe in the scientific method. The possibilities . . ."

"Accident, murder, suicide, fake death," the Detective interrupted, seeing his hand trace the letters on a smudged slate blackboard.

Mrs. Klein sat down abruptly, crossed her legs, folded her arms, her head craned forward—wound energy about to explode. "But surely you've forgotten one."

The Detective shook his head. "I don't think . . ."

"Sacrifice, what about a sacrifice?"

"I don't understand,"

"A human sacrifice. An appeasement to the gods, to nature. Diving into the volcano's mouth in order to prevent the catastrophe. A symbolic act. A ritual of penance. An atonement."

"An atonement for what?"

"For going where he was forbidden to go; for knowing what he was forbidden to know; for killing what he cared about most without even being aware of it. For hubris. A man who has violated the secrets of those tiny pieces of matter in motion, a man who has worked on the atomic bomb, has a great deal to atone for, wouldn't you say?"

The Detective didn't reply, endured her sarcasm as it reached a peak of purity and then surpassed it, becoming anger. Her voice shook, dropped to a husky, wavering accusation.

"But no, no, you're the detective, aren't you? You're one of us and we don't believe in guilt, do we? It's subjective; we leave atonement for the judges and juries to decide. All we care about is what happened, something definite, the objective truth. We see what we see when we see it, and nothing more, don't we?"

"No, I don't think that's true," the Detective said. "We wouldn't know very much if it were—only ourselves, only our own lives. We can deduce, we can listen to others, we can make educated guesses. We can from our past experience suggest possibilities and then analyze them." The Detective paused, tempted, excited by the ideas, drawn once again into the impulse to philosophize; but he resisted it, this desire to generalize, to expand and connect, and instead began to dissect.

"For example, the fake death possibility. Its motive is almost always an escape: from debt, from an unhappy marriage, from punishment for a crime already committed; sometimes it's accompanied by a large life insurance policy, and the benefactor is his accomplice. But does that scenario fit the facts? Does it fit the particular features of this particular case? One advantage to this possibility: it does explain the second person, the one who the eyewitness saw at the railing. If a dummy had been thrown off the promontory point, that other person could have been Mr. Klein himself. And that, in turn, would explain the absence of a car here—Mr. Klein drove away in it after faking his own death. But then we turn to the liabilities. In order to fake a death, in order to convince police officials and insurance investigators, he would need a witness, someone he had fooled into thinking that he had actually died. True, we do have Dexter, but Dexter was in a boat a thousand yards away or more, in poor light. There's no way Mr. Klein could have assumed that Dexter would even be looking in the right direction at the right moment. Not unless Dexter is his accomplice, which, on the surface at least, would seem highly unlikely."

The Detective felt himself expanding, a lifetime of intelligent work, of specialized thinking, unfolding from him effortlessly. And he began to feel as well that controlled joy of mastery, that self-consciousness of one's own competence in the midst of the action itself, which had propelled him into case after case and had kept him preoccupied, despite the hours, the fatigue—despite his wife and child.

"So what we have, then, is a possibility, but an unlikely one. So we push that to the side for a moment. We don't eliminate it. We still check on insurance policies and personal debts; we still make sure that Dexter hasn't come into a sudden fortune. But for the moment, we push it to the side and look for a more probable solution. Are you with me so far?"

"Yes," Mrs. Klein said, her voice suddenly gone flat again. "Probability. We proceed according to probability; that makes perfect sense."

"Okay. We have three other possibilities then: accident, suicide, murder. But if we look at the facts—the facts, Mrs. Klein, the few pieces of information available to us—if we consider them, letting our minds stretch to meet their implications, one specific fact stands out from all the others; seems to tell us more, to hint at a solution. And do you know which fact that is, Mrs. Klein?"

Mrs. Klein didn't look at him, seemed to have lost her interest in the case. "The other person," she said in a monotone, "the one at the railing."

"That's right, Mrs. Klein. Fact: the person seen at the railing did not report the fall. Now if it had been an accident or suicide, why wouldn't the person have called the Coast Guard or the police or run to a neighbor's house? There are possibilities, of course, but are they likely ones, are they probable? Do you see what I mean, Mrs. Klein?"

"So you think it's murder; that's your subjective view of the objective truth."

No sarcasm this time, but no real interest either—just a tepid curiosity. The Detective was disappointed; yes, it was his tentative view of the facts that they seemed to point to murder, but he realized suddenly that the conclusion itself wasn't what mattered to him. Instead, he had wanted to prove the philosophical point; had wanted to demonstrate that we can know more than what we see, extending ourselves beyond the moment of our experience. No, more than that, he had wanted to defend a state of mind, a way of thinking, his profession, his life in fact; had wanted her to withdraw the accusing glances and sarcasm, and then, acceptance won, to stand over her, victorious in his detective's competence—vindicated. And when he realized this, when he realized that he cared more about Mrs. Klein's opinion of himself than he cared about the case, more about his own guilt or innocence than hers, all of his professional enthusiasm seemed nothing more than a plea for . . . for what—affirmation? An old man begging someone he barely knew, a murder suspect, to tell him that his life had been worthwhile?

Years ago, before her death, only Sadie's opinion had mattered to the Detective; and now, as he stared at Mrs. Klein's emotionless profile, he was reminded again of his wife. How often he had tried to convince her; how often he had tried to have her openly affirm his life, his career, and she, too, would deny him victory with the same silent elusiveness: losing every argument but never submitting; letting him talk on but never agreeing, just sitting there quietly in her passive, feminine indomitability. And he sees her now: the high cheeks, the blank stare, the black eyes averted and brushing him out, now and forever brushing him out; the impenetrable veil of her physical silence protecting some secret self which she had always denied him, that self untouched—by him, by anyone . . . or was there someone? The *letters*. The Detective rubbed his legs and turned slightly in his chair toward the gray spray of sky, its spiraling gulls.

"You'd be surprised," he started to say. His voice seemed far away from him and small, as if a muted cry for help from beyond the glass, from that opposite world. "You'd be surprised what can be deduced from just a few facts."

There was no reply; silent, they waited, trapped in their separate worlds—Mrs. Klein hidden behind a lifeless exterior, all emotions withdrawn; the Detective slumped in his chair and drained of will. The mobile spun above them, a chaotic clockwork of twisting wire and speeding propellers, a manic unwinding of a hundred separate time frames all at once, while outside the room, the ocean, caught in its tide, and the sky, rotating through the filtered sunlight, changed in degrees too immense and gradual to be discerned.

"You believe," Mrs. Klein finally said, "you *believe* it's murder, but can you be sure?" She nodded to herself. "Yes, how can you be sure? It might be an accident, or a suicide, or even a little of them all. Yes, that's right, a little of them all, 33.33 percent of each. Perhaps all murders are accidents . . . and suicides, too. Perhaps each murder victim is, to a degree, a co-conspirator, an accomplice in his own death. A man walks the city streets late at night and is killed by a thief, and who's to say—does he himself even know—if he chose to walk those streets because he secretly wished it to happen? And how many times, at the last crucial moment, have people hesitated to rescue themselves from some accidental or murderous danger—isn't that suicide, too?"

"There's the law," the Detective said.

"Oh yes, the law. We believe in the law, don't we? First degree and second degree; felony and misdemeanor; murder, suicide, and accidental death. The coroner's inquest. The declaration. But tell me this—does the law ever say, 'We don't know; it's a mystery and we simply don't know'? Not our law. We can't abide an unsolved mystery, can we? We don't believe in it so we make a declaration anyway: first degree or second degree; murder, suicide, or accident. But does the declaration make it so? Can every death be summed up by just one of three words? Does legal terminology, a court's declaration, tell you what actually happened—ever? Is it ever equal to the event itself?"

The Detective said nothing, but he sympathized with the idea, understood it implicitly—that organic quality, the formal beauty he found in every crime, a wholeness that could not be defined, only sensed viscerally. He had always tried to sketch that organism, that almost living form that was the crime, a form which, in some amoral way, he could appreciate aesthetically. The law, though, devoured subtlety, his complex sketch, his solution, with its ambiguities and shadings, with its own formal beauty, inevitably reduced into crude categories of guilt or innocence. There had been times when he had resented it, this profaning of his art; times when he would have agreed with Mrs. Klein's argument—but he wasn't about to admit that now. Not while still trying to solve the case, not while she mocked his life-long profession.

"For example," Mrs. Klein said, "what if . . . what if the body that Dexter saw when he saw what he saw, the body we have tentatively identified as Andrew Klein, what if its fall were the result of not one of the possibilities, but all three? What if the body . . ."

"Mr. Klein?" the Detective suggested.

"All right. What if Mr. Klein were to a degree, but only to a degree, a participant in his own demise? Let's assume . . . yes, let's assume that at the time under question, about five o'clock yesterday evening, Mr. Andrew Klein, sitting in his living room, was suddenly struck by the notion that he'd like to take a walk. And who can say why? Perhaps his legs were stiff; perhaps he felt too warm in the living room or wished to watch the sea birds more closely, a particularly passionate hobby of his; perhaps he had a difficult problem to consider and needed to walk it out. Or perhaps it was just a whim, nothing more than the need to do something, anything, and with the cove before him, a walk was the first thing to come to mind. It could have been any of those reasons or a combination of some or all of them, or something else entirely, and very probably Mr. Klein himself couldn't say for sure. Perhaps it was simply an accident that he should have decided to take a walk, but regardless of our ignorance of his exact motivation, let's assume that Andrew Klein did decide to take that walk. And let's further assume that he took someone along with him, someone close to him, someone who understood him as well as, and perhaps better than, he understood himself."

"His wife perhaps?" the Detective said.

He watched her closely now, sensed a change in her manner—an uneasiness, a tension—the first step perhaps on the road to confession. It was true, he well knew, what they said about criminals wanting to confess; lying by its very nature created a state of anxiety that begged for release. The interrogator, then, was merely guide, midwife, to a natural event; his job at all times to offer up peace of mind in exchange for the truth: the detective as priest.

Mrs. Klein stared at him. "Perhaps," she said. "Perhaps it was his wife."

"Let's assume that it was, shall we?"

She hesitated, tugging nervously on the border of her fisherman's sweater. "All right," she finally said. "For the sake of the detective, we will assume that it was his wife . . . Mr. and Mrs. Klein strolling along the walkway of their dream house in Maine, their country retreat, chatting about this and about that as they approached the promontory point overlooking the cove. Who can say what a Nobel prize-winning physicist and his medieval historian wife would talk about on such a walk on such a day? The weather, perhaps? The Uncertainty Principle? The death of the American novel?" She stood up and turned her back to him, facing the cove. "Divorce, perhaps?"

The Detective twisted in his chair, struggling to get a view of her face; every nuance was crucial now, every subtle facial expression could qualify the meaning of her words. But she rotated away from him and hid herself until the moment had passed.

"Just a middle-aged couple strolling along the edge of the cove's cliff, their cove, their cliff; they are silly enough to think that they own them. Just a middle-aged couple chatting about this and about that. It's a January day in Maine, a cold and windy day as all January days in Maine are; there's a blustery wind, fickle, now pushing, now pulling, a challenge to their balance as they walk along the cliff's edge, ernes rising from within the cove helplessly, inevitably, like air trapped in water. A blustery January day in Maine, a middle-aged couple, a promontory point rimmed by a walkway and its railing—do you get the picture?"

The Detective momentarily glanced out through the glass wall, then turned back to Mrs. Klein. "Yes," he said.

"All right, then. Mr. and Mrs. Klein are standing at the promontory point within the walkway's cul-de-sac, leaning right against the railing there, a low railing really, waist high so that it doesn't obstruct the view. And then it happens, the provocation: a gust of wind perhaps, a slip of the foot, some accidental agent; the precipitator, pushing them into this moment, pushing him against the railing and over it, Andrew Klein dangling for an instant on a fulcrum, back arched over the railing, hands cast into the air, balanced, time suspended . . ."

"And Mrs. Klein?"

"And Mrs. Klein facing him, watching him, this man, her husband, her

... her accomplice, this man she knows better than he knows himself, this man balanced far an instant between the solid ground and the distant ocean, between life and death. And perhaps, just perhaps, she sees in his eyes a plea; not the plea we take for granted, but its opposite, a plea to be left alone, a plea to let this accident happen, a sign that he wishes it to happen, has always wished but never had the courage on his own. She sees this conjectured plea, Mrs. Klein does, and because she knows him better than he knows himself, knows that he wants, has always wanted, this accident to happen, because she is his accomplice in all things in spite of herself, she lets him drop—like the ernes in reverse, she lets him drop, helplessly, inevitably away from her and into the ocean. And what is that? Not legally but really, not in court but in life—an accident? a suicide? a murder?"

Her voice died away as if it, too, were falling into the cove, and turning toward the ocean as it disappeared into silence, she stared into the distance, arms folded, the fisherman's wife keeping her anxious vigil again.

"Perhaps," the Detective said, "just perhaps in this moment we're talking about, Mrs. Klein sees a different plea in her husband's eyes; perhaps she does see the plea we take for granted: the plea for life. And perhaps as she sees this plea, she realizes suddenly that *she* wants, that *she* has always wanted this accident to take place, and realizing this, she lets him fall. A possibility, is it not?"

"Yes," she said softly, still staring toward the cove. "Yes, a possibility."

"And perhaps she not only lets him fall. Perhaps in that moment of realization that she wants, has always wanted, this accident to take place, perhaps she decides to help it take place. Perhaps she disturbs the balance, tips the fulcrum, helps the accident along . . ."

Mrs. Klein turned toward him, her eyes, though, directed above and beyond him, preternaturally still. "Perhaps," she said in a whisper.

The Detective studied her, oblivious to everything but her face, to everything but the case which had distilled itself into this face in this moment—his detective's instinct which carried him now, which controlled him, which became him in this moment, sensing the pressure point, her need to confess.

"Did she, Mrs. Klein?" the Detective asked gently. "Did Mrs. Klein push her husband off the cliff?"

He waited, watching her silently as she dropped her gaze gradually, lowering her line of vision to the chair where he sat: a slow focusing, a curious stare, as though she had just noticed his presence there. Her skin was ghost-white, her hands at her sides; her fingers pinched the nap of her skirt.

"Do you know about Descartes?" she said. "Shall I tell you about Descartes? Shall I give you the lecture, a lesson in history from the medieval scholar?"

"Descartes?"

"Did you know that a historian is a detective too, that a historian seeks something definite too, that just like you I'm in the business of reconstructing crime, the crime of our past? I do that. I collect evidence; sift through the clues, the artifacts; examine motives, relationships, culpability—yes, culpability, too. And there's where we differ, you and I, Andy and I, because I assign blame. It's a historian's most sacred duty, even if only a feedback mechanism for the generations to come, even if it's just a corrective adjustment for the social gyroscope. I assign blame, declare it aloud. Descartes, I say, Descartes: guilty as charged."

"What are you talking about?"

"How could it happen, I ask myself? How could such shortsightedness exist, such self-delusion? The man was a Catholic, a religious man, schooled by Jesuits. His Catholicism mattered to him; they say that as an adult he always asked himself how the Jesuits at La Flèche would receive his work. He refused to see it, though; he refused to admit to it; became indignant at the mention of it. It's just hypothetical, he would say, my work is hypothetical; it isn't necessarily applicable. My work is theoretical, so it can't be a threat. And because he could say that to himself, because he could fool himself with that rationalization, he kept on with his work. This Catholic, this religious man, kept right on destroying the very world he relied on, the very beliefs which gave him comfort and purpose. He turned heaven into a clockwork; he turned God into an idea; he robbed them of meaning; he robbed them of mystery. Descartes killed for all those who came after him what he himself valued most. He was the true end of the Middle Ages; he was the real father of the Modern Age: the first man who could destroy his own world and call it theoretical.

"Are you with me so far? Has my fellow detective kept up with me? Because I'm going to leave you behind now; I'm going to make the leap of faith. I'm going to take up the historian's prerogative and say: guilty, Descartes, guilty as charged."

"Guilty of what?"

"Murder, fellow detective. Descartes killed God."

Mrs. Klein paced in front of the Detective, an absent-minded, irregular path across the thick orange rug; he focused on her face, tried to concentrate and force the connections, but nothing made sense. The feeling, though, was still there, the instinct of the detective, the belief that this was all part of the confession, a need to reduce tension, a gradual, perhaps allegorical revelation of her involvement—if only he could decipher it.

"What are we talking about, Mrs. Klein?"

"The motive, of course. We're talking about the motive for the murder . . ." She paused, a wan and bitter smile flickering across her features. "I mean, of course, the *hypothetical* murder of Andrew Klein."

"And what would that motive be?"

"Revenge. Revenge for the death of God."

"You mean to say that Mrs. Klein killed Mr. Klein because Mr. Klein killed God?"

"Let's say that he was an accomplice in the death of God. It's a possibility, isn't it?"

The Detective shook his head.

"You don't believe it?"

"I believe that Mrs. Klein believes it, but . . ."

"But it's subjective, is that it? It's not the objective truth? It's not what the detective sees when he sees what he sees? Of course not. How stupid of me even to suggest it. The detective, a son of Descartes in a manner of speaking, doesn't believe in God alive *or* dead, does he?"

"Not as a motive for murder, he doesn't."

"No, no—of course not. We'll have to try something different then, won't we?" She paced silently for a moment, her face a caricature of concentration, mimed sarcasm; then, as if inspired suddenly, she turned to him. "Has the detective ever been in love? Has he ever been married?"

The Detective hesitated, shades of his earlier suspicion reappearing, his distrust of her, his reluctance to be exposed personally. But it was much too late to worry about involvement; he had already lost his professional distance, and, too, he still believed they were nearing an answer, that just beyond one of these bends in their meandering conversation, the solution awaited him.

"Yes," he said, "I've been married."

"Good. We'll start from there then; we'll start from the top. It's always a good idea to start from what you believe in, and since the detective believes in marriage, marriage it is—the motive for the murder, the hypothetical murder of Andrew Klein."

"Marriage is the motive?"

"No, revenge is still the motive, but revenge for the death of a marriage instead of revenge for the death of God. You do believe in the death of a marriage, don't you? The detective can see that, can't he? It is a possibility, is it not?"

The Detective said nothing, felt the conversation turning again—on him, out of his control, like his leg, like his heart, like the last two years of his life, a man adrift in a current he no longer had the strength to resist, a man afraid. And Mrs. Klein seemed to feed on his weakness as she probed him with her bulging eyes.

"Yes, I can see that he does; he believes in its possibility. But let's analyze it, shall we? Let's take the possibility and analyze it for its likelihood, stretching our minds to meet its implications. We need to flesh it out a bit, this motive; we need something a little more specific. An etiology of a murder, a history of causes, if you will. How about . . ." She nodded to herself. "Yes, how about infidelity—infidelity on the part of the victim's wife?"

"Infidelity?" the Detective said; his voice was no longer his, behind the glass again, far away from him.

"Yes, infidelity; adultery; cheating on one's mate. You do believe in it? It is a possibility?"

The white, feminine-fancy stationery, the rubber band, the slanting curls of Sadie's script . . . it is late, night, and spotlit, stage center, the woman sits. I'm keeping a diary, she says. The man nods, accepts, but now and forever the Detective wanders, peering into, peering from, the blurred and darkened corners, the edges of vision, superimposing new transparencies, analyzing possibilities—but who can tell now, who can tell . . . ?

"Yes," Mrs. Klein said, "yes, I can see that he does. The detective believes it's a possibility. However, let's assume a further motive, a motive for the infidelity, a motive for the motive. All causes are external, says Descartes, every cause has a cause. Hypothetical murder is caused by hypothetical infidelity which, in turn, is caused by the hypothetical death of a marriage. Now what is it, I ask myself as a historian, as a detective in a manner of speaking, what is it that caused this hypothetical death of a marriage? What's the cause of the cause of the cause, I ask myself as a believer in the scientific method? Are you with me, Descartes?"

The Detective felt himself nod.

"All right. So how could it happen, how could this marriage, which started out so wonderfully, die? The man was not unkind. The man was loving and considerate in his own way. His marriage mattered to him; it was the bedrock of his life, in fact. His work, however, was changing him, was beginning to obsess him. He refused to see it, though, refused to admit to it; he became indignant at the mention of it. And because he refused to admit to it, he got worse, became more and more obsessed with his work (which was hypothetical to a degree, which was theoretical), and it was killing his marriage, killing what mattered to him most. Can you see that? Are you with me so far? Is that a possibility for the detective—that someone, without knowing it, could kill what mattered to him most?"

"The absent husband," the Detective said softly. He wet his lips. "The empty vessel."

"Yes," Mrs. Klein said. "Absent. Empty."

"Perhaps, perhaps she didn't let him know. Perhaps if he had only been told . . ."

"Perhaps he couldn't be told. Perhaps no matter how hard she tried, he wouldn't admit to it."

They were silent for a moment. Mrs. Klein retreated to her chair, stepping backward, never taking her eyes from the Detective's.

"Yes," she said, "he couldn't be told. He became obsessed with his work and wouldn't admit to it. And there we have the cause, the hypothetical cause of the death of a marriage. But what's the cause of the cause, I ask myself? I do that. I keep asking myself why he became so obsessed with his work—gruesome, cold work, with awful implications. How could he fool himself with those rationalizations? How could he let his work kill what mattered to him most? Can you tell me that, can my fellow detective please come up with the solution to that? . . . Because I can't."

"Perhaps," the Detective said; he shook his head. She waited, pinioned him with her protuberant stare, with its sincerity. "Perhaps," he began again, "she never understood. Perhaps if she had become involved herself, if she had had the gift herself . . . those moments when he was completely engaged, those moments when in the middle of a problem, he felt at peace with himself, carried by something bigger than himself, perhaps if she had felt them too?" He faltered. "Perhaps she never understood."

"No," Mrs. Klein said softly, eyes averted, "no, she never understood."

"So she . . . ?" The Detective hesitated, hoping Mrs. Klein would complete the question; but instead, she only prompted him.

"So she?"

"She was . . . unfaithful?"

"Perhaps—it is a possibility, is it not? But you see, that's what *he* never understood. He never admitted to himself that it was a possibility. Oh, he believed in possibilities, all right, but his possibilities were always hypothetical, theoretical. He never in his heart believed that it could actually take place."

There was a pause, a natural lull, this part of the interrogation brought to a close. Helpless, the Detective stared at Mrs. Klein—she knew, she did know something, about the case, about infidelity—and his glance was a plea for her to stop her teasing, to end the ambiguities and tell him something . . . something definite. For a moment, she seemed to relent, her face gone sad, hidden in her hands, rubbing her eyes with her fingertips; but then, recharged, she surfaced quickly, an actress again, exuding energy—merciless.

"And there we have it; Descartes himself couldn't have done better. Our etiology, our history of causes: his obsession with his work led to the death of their marriage which, in turn, led to her infidelity which, in turn, served as the motive for his murder. All hypothetical, of course. All theoretical."

Mrs. Klein rose from her stainless steel chair and stepped toward the wide glass wall to her left. Behind her hung a canvas, the room's largest,

riotous with color; beyond her the sky, still uniformly overcast, had darkened gradually into a premature nightfall, the evening smothered by
fuliginous shadows that clung like lichens to the mist-topped, brine-soaked
rocks. No gulls or terns crossed the sky now and the Coast Guard cutter
had disappeared from view. The dull green of the ocean was gone too; all
of the cove, the scene of the crime, framed by the shrieking orange of
the drapes, had been bled of its color, merging into shades of the approaching night, toward one black frame, impenetrably opaque. The Detective
watched Mrs. Klein as she stared at the cove. She seemed trapped to him
then, out of place in the room, a creature indigenous to the outside world,
this violent seascape he was forced to call home, but which frightened
him, overwhelmed him now with its blunt indifference to human forms; a
world he had ignored all his life until Sadie had died, leaving him the
letters to open his eyes; a world beyond rooms, beyond measure, baroque
with complexity, whose secrets defied his powers of detection, and which,
alien and immense, had begun to cloud his mind with alien thoughts. He
had tried to hide from those thoughts, their suspicions, their ever expanding, spiraling implications, afraid that he would lose himself in their cold
immensity, a mote of matter in infinite space. But then Mrs. Klein had appeared, those thoughts, that world given an advocate, a face and voice for
their mysteriousness; and, too, with her sarcastic probing, her relentless in-
trusion into his private self, an instrument of that world's steel-stark justice:
its detective.

A world, a woman, he feared; a crime he could not comprehend; a life
he could no longer with confidence justify, although an end, the end, was
drawing near. Fact, he told himself, fact: you're dying. It was Mrs. Klein
who reminded him.

"It's about five," Mrs. Klein finally said, "wouldn't you say?"

"Yes—about five."

"It's about time, then, wouldn't you say?" She turned to him, her face
passionless; a scale-bearer, implacable Justice. "Time to test the hypothesis."

The Detective swallowed, turned away; Sally would be in the kitchen
now, his study—down the hall and around the corner—warm and safe.
Looking up again, he shrugged his shoulders, shook his head.

"Oh yes you do," Mrs. Klein said. "You know what I mean—you may not want to, but you do. It's time, Descartes, time for the real detective to take over; time to reenact the crime, test the hypothesis. You *do* understand that the time has come?"

Adrift in the current, unable to turn away, he watched her. Freeze-frame the crime, he has said, says, hears himself say over and over, the words in amber, the climax of detection. Freeze-frame the crime; enter its world; reenact, relive the moment of its occurrence—but if the crime's your life, when the crime's your life . . . ? The Detective turned toward the cove, an alien world darkening: the scene of the crime, the death of Mr. Klein, or just another seaside postcard setting?

"It's a little before five," she said again. "It's time," he heard her say to him.

He didn't move, the mobile spinning above him, the sun—hidden somewhere behind the house, the clouds—dropping faster now, light fading, sight fading. He had thought himself a good husband, a good father . . . The Detective felt a hand tugging gently on his sleeve. Mrs. Klein bent over him; seemed, he thought to whisper to him, a voice from beyond the glass: "I'll help you, Descartes. I'll be your accomplice."

The Detective stood, felt himself stand, silently led to the corner of the room; a slow procession, priestess and penitent, seeress and initiate, seekers after truth in a ritual reenactment—detectives, too, in a manner of speaking. There, at the brink, the oblique angle where glass and plaster met, Mrs. Klein deserted him, slipping behind a strand of drapery, the Detective alone again and staring out . . . at the scene of the crime, the wormwood wilderness of his enforced retirement, this dimmed Maine coast. He reached out, touched the glass, tested its illusions, the cool hard sheen of its sentinel surface, his own image, a wraithlike visage, cast back at him— "pass no further!" Always stopped; always between the see-er and the seen, this cruel exclusion, a glass partition; this permanent exile, the limits of knowledge: Moses, the old man, brought to the top of the mountain and shown where he can never go; Moses, forever dying in the land of Moab, on the other side of what he wished to know. But then, against his skin, the breath of the wilderness, a cold wind penetrating; the pulse of the surf, like the hushed promise of the burning bush, drawing him forward; the drapes thrown open; and there, in the corner, the Red Sea miraculously parting: a door.

The Detective passes through.

———————

A promontory point on the northern coast of Maine. Its rock worn smooth, washed by wind and rain, perpetually damp—always the salt spray, always the fog rolling off the North Atlantic and condensing on its abraded, undulating face. Daylight asphyxiates; no sun, no stars, no moon, a time when all things become their shadows, when ernes turn invisible and, bodiless, screech from within the cove, a resonating cry muted by the rhythmic rush of the tide, a water-soaked echo. A metallic walkway, raffish orange, arrives at the point from two directions, merges into a cul-de-sac, a low-railed rim around the promontory's edge; and there, sealed in by the fetid ceiling of a sky, framed by the railing and by time, the couple stand face to face. A man, a woman, a promontory point, a moment. The North Atlantic—white-capped, rock-torn—five hundred feet below.

Fact: now and forever it is January.

A man and a woman in a moment. Living, relived, they stand stage center, spotlit by the Detective's eye as he peers into, peers from, the blurred and darkened corners of the crime. Note how the man is propped against the railing; note the arms cast into the air, struggling for balance; note the arched back, the bowed thighs, the heels raised from the ground, toes begging for a hold. Note the face, try to focus on the face—its desperation or surprise, mouth dropping and eyes gone wide, yet focused on the other face. Yes, note the man's face, an expression there, a message, silent because words take time, a plea, but which plea: to live? to die? Note the woman, how she faces the man, close, so close, an arm's length away. Note how their positions balance, how she mimics him in reverse, her shoulders pulled back, arms drawn to her side—a flinch perhaps, a reflex, the body's wisdom beating time? And the face, her face, is there a message there too, a plea? a denial? Note the scene, its formal beauty, its unity, the organic quality appreciated by the aesthetician's eye, and then sketched by him, entitled: "The Fall"? "The Crime"?

A man and a woman in a moment. But there is no title, there is no meaning without movement—and no movement without meaning. In the cove, tide-tossed, Dexter waits, not knowing that he waits; in the bedroom, Sadie waits, pen in hand, not knowing that she waits. For the new scene. The new moment. For another miracle, another door to the world beyond.

It happens; now and forever it happens, one moment into the next, one frame into the other, movement and meaning. She reaches, has reached, is always reaching, her hand on his chest; frozen there at the fulcrum, the critical moment, a time when the world demands an accomplice—everything possible still. In the cove, Dexter waits; in the kitchen, Sally waits, always waiting. Somewhere below a lone gull cries and, time suspended, echoes again and again its crying, waiting for the sound to die, as her hand rests on his chest: to push or to pull? to save or to kill?

The Detective peers into, peers from, the blurred and darkened corners. Note the face, her face, fate's accomplice; the sketch is incomplete, the solution elusive, without understanding that face. But there is only one angle of vision, one point in time and space that can provide the solution. Truth always a risk, to know or not to know—only he can decide.

It happens; now and forever it happens, one frame into another; he too becomes fate's accomplice, taking a step into the world beyond. The Detective becomes, has become, is always becoming a man in a moment, a man at a railing, back arched, arms cast into the air, heels raised from the ground, toes begging for a hold—the North Atlantic, rock-torn, five hundred feet below. The Detective becomes this man in this moment, the man at the fulcrum, his wife's hand on his chest, and who can say, does he himself even know for sure, which plea is in his own eyes? But note the face now, her face in this moment, the key to the solution—the protuberant eyes, the pride smoldering in silence. Is the jittery search over? Is the dream at its climax? Have all the accusing glances been merged into one?

A man, a woman, a promontory point, a moment. Helplessly, Descartes awaits the judgment of history; passively Moses, the sentence of God. Helplessly, passively, with her hand on his chest, the truth-seeker, the detective, awaits the solution; the absent husband, the declaration: to be pushed or to be pulled? affirmation at last or guilty as charged?

But does it happen—now or ever? objectively or in a manner of speaking? And who can say, does she herself even know for sure, the declaration, the final answer? No, she fails him; no longer an accomplice, she withdraws her hand; no longer his inspiration, she withdraws into mystery, into movement whose meaning can never be spoken, whose essence can never be frozen. No, the moment fails him; hypothetical, it is a possibility never to be born. And answerless, he waits; judgment ever suspended, he waits, while somewhere below them, the gull's cry dies and dissolves within the wash of the tide.

They sat silently in the living room before the glass wall. Brine dampened the Detective's forehead and salted his lips, and he dabbed at it slowly with his handkerchief as he emitted a series of involuntary sighs. His heart wasn't racing, the pain in his leg bearable, but weighed down by an exhaustion so complete that even gravity seemed palpable, sucking at every muscle and drawing him down into death, he suddenly threw back his head and stretched for air, gasped like a whale at the surface, trying to inflate himself with life. Mrs. Klein sat close to him, her face blood-drained and expressionless, her short gray hair, wet along its edges, hanging in water-darkened points across her forehead like a crown of thorns. She seemed to shrink before him, a change from menacing interrogator to plausible widow, and attempting to pace his recovery with hers, the Detective watched her closely, waiting for signs. But ever a mystery, she hid from him, hid behind the glass shell of her excluding silences, and unable to break through, too tired to speak, to think, he waited as night obscured the cove and darkened the room.

She shivered; the Detective watched her shiver, a sudden disruptive shuddering which caught him by surprise, her arms and legs twitching, chest shaking. Amazed, he thought: "Her feet barely touch the ground." She was motionless for a moment, as if in that one violent exorcism, she had expelled some core of coldness she had absorbed from the out-of-doors; but then, the shaking began again, her hands thrown up to her face, her fingers quaking, muffling sounds—were those sobs he heard?

The Detective fought to stand, struggling out of his chair, out of his bone-drenched exhaustion and onto his feet, all motion a compromise now between speed and pain. The room reeled as the weight of his body shifted to his feet, became an extension of its own decor—the swirling paintings and spinning mobile—until the Detective steadied himself, his hand grasping the arm of the chair. Limping, he slowly crossed the room and stood beside her, staring down at her sobbing body. At a loss for a moment, indecisive, his hand fumbled like a clumsy lover's until, finally, it found its object, settling softly on the back of her head. There, in some lullaby of comfort, of gentle caring, he caressed her hair.

"It's all right," he said.

He waited there above her, a watchful father, until her crying had spent itself and her shuddering had receded to a slumped, still calm. Then, when she reached up and softly touched his hand—an expression of gratitude, a sign of recovery—he returned to his chair and sat down again. They remained there in their chairs, in their silence, in the dark, the room's meager light scattered around them like the firefly memories of an old man's childhood. He could just barely discern her face across from him; no longer blank or bitterly ironic, it mourned now—a solemn, passive grief, a glowing ember of pain, slow-burning and eternal. There was a purity to her suffering, a depth beyond feeling, a breadth beyond personality which awed the Detective, made him feel responsible, as though he were sole witness to a sacred ritual. He needed no words from her now; the power of her grief was eloquence enough, and he wished only to remain there forever, a quiet mirror to her sad surrender.

But then, the sound of tires biting into gravel, of car doors slamming and approaching voices, drew him out of that calm, reminding him that the Chief would be returning any moment, reminding him that he had a case before him, a case still unsolved—he had been alone with Mrs. Klein for over three hours and still didn't know if there had been a crime. Pride, fear of failure, allegiance to the old self-image, panicked him; he had to have something far them, something definite. And so, ashamed of himself but helpless to act upon it, he heard himself violate their perfect silence.

"Mrs. Klein?"

She turned toward him. Although only five feet away, she seemed removed from him, as distant as death from life; beyond the glass again, as if she had never returned. She watched him, waited.

"Did you . . . ?" he started to say, but suddenly incapable of completing the question, of profaning her mourning, he stopped. He knew what he should ask, what a detective should want to know, but his time with her nearly over, he sensed that there was another, more important and personal question to ask, one that only Mrs. Klein could answer for him, if he just knew how to phrase it. Desperate, he struggled after it, a form for his need, words slipping through his fingers, though, failing him. "Did you . . . ?" he began again, but again he faltered; his hands, pleading with her, kneaded the air.

Mrs. Klein nodded. The Detective watched her nod to him and felt relief—teammates, they understood each other; teammates, they completed each other; she would give him what he needed to know.

"I loved him," Mrs. Klein said.

The Detective leaned forward; her voice, soft, receding, drew him toward her, and he paused in expectation as she held her breath. She closed her eyes, and her face, radiant with pain, seemed to float before him, to drift on the exhalation of her whispered answer.

"I love him."

The Detective sat motionless and silent, a dumb and stunned supplicant before the priestess, weighing her oracle, unsure of its meaning. Footsteps outside the room finally broke the spell, twisting him in his chair; her voice, though, followed him there, refusing to let him go.

"I'll tell you," she said.

He turned back to her. She nodded to herself, opening her eyes.

"If you must, if you must know, come back to me—I'll tell you then. But for now, I can only give you this: whatever happened, it was for the best."

The Detective stared at her, trying to freeze-frame the face, to draw it out of the darkness and fixate on it, extracting from it the meaning of her words—a friend's promise or the last obfuscation of a desperate defense? Incredibly, he thought he saw a shade of a smile appear there, not quite mockery and certainly not joy, something of sadness endured, of survival, but he couldn't be sure: there was too little light, too little time to consider, the door creaking open, a surprised silence following the first steps in.

"Hello?" the Chief finally called out into the darkened room.

They didn't answer; the Detective refused even to turn in his seat, his eyes locked on hers. The smile dissolved. He saw her nod to him once (the last line of her message or just another meaningless gesture?) before she disappeared into the glare of the room's struck lights. And then, by the time his eyes had recovered, he found a different woman sitting before him, the one he sought withdrawn again, her face as cold and featureless as glass.

"There you are," the Chief said as he walked toward them, Officer Truax trailing behind. Mrs. Klein immediately rose from her chair and, without a word, left the room. The Chief let her go, waiting until she had disappeared behind a closed door before sitting in her chair. There, he unzipped his official coat and placed his hat on his knee. He turned toward the Detective.

"For a moment there I was afraid I'd lost two more people."

"You haven't found him yet?"

"I haven't; the city cops where he teaches haven't; the Coast Guard hasn't. And that leads us right back here to you.

The Detective ignored the implied question, instead staring at the door where Mrs. Klein had stood just moments before. "She's a strange woman," he said.

"Can't disagree with you on that. And to be honest with you, it's comforting to hear someone else say it. After a full morning of interrogating her, I was beginning to wonder if *I* wasn't a little strange. She's a challenge, all right." The Chief paused, struggling to be polite, to maintain his patient composure. "Well?" he finally asked.

The Detective shrugged.

"Come up empty-handed?" Officer Truax said; standing beside the Chief, he smiled sarcastically.

"I don't know."

"He don't know," Truax said to the Chief.

"I got ears, Truax." The Chief leaned forward. "You don't sound too sure about that," he said to the Detective. "You sound like you just might have something."

The Detective was silent; he sensed suddenly the widening gap between already divergent loyalties, afraid then of betraying either side. He looked to the glass wall for a moment, but it was full night now and the cove, the ocean, the sky were nearly indistinguishable.

"I don't know. I'll have to think about it."

"Yes," the Chief said; he looked toward the ceiling. "Yes, why don't you do that. Tried it myself this afternoon—sat alone and tried to sort out the facts, to get some distance on it. Didn't have much luck, frankly, but maybe you'll do better. Just give me a call if you come up with anything."

"I'll do that."

The Chief stood. "I had to chase Charlie Wriggins away from here. He was parked down the road, waiting to ambush you for the inside scoop, killing himself from carbon monoxide poisoning. I figured you'd want to avoid him for awhile anyway; he can be a real pain in the neck when he gets like this. I'll have Truax here drop you off at your home."

The Detective rose slowly; he accepted the Chief's hand and shook it.

"I appreciate it," the Chief said, "I appreciate you coming over here and taking a shot at it."

The Detective nodded; felt again the camaraderie, the bond of common work. You're a good man, he wanted to say; you're one of the good ones, one of the professionals. A good man not to have acknowledged my failure, to have remained a gentleman in spite of your job—not many do; Sadie had been right about that. But he didn't say it; instead, he reached out with his second hand and grasped the Chief's more firmly. Wavering from fatigue after a moment, though, he fumbled for support.

"Are you all right?" the Chief said. "Do you want to lie down for a few minutes?"

The Detective steadied himself, keeping his eyes off the mobile's spinning blades, its clockwork universe machinations. "No, no, I'm okay—but I better get home. My daughter will have supper waiting for me."

3

The Detective sat in his study's easy chair, his eyes closed, his feet resting on the cracked leather ottoman, time suspended, body suspended; only the wave of heat pressing against his cheek from the fireplace beside him and the warmth radiating from the food in his belly reminded him that he was alive, a reminder as casual and pleasant as the sound of rain against a roof at night, or the first shovel's scraping on a snow-bound morning. The best times in an old man's life were when, free of pain, he could forget his body—times of rest, of slow recollection. The old rested well; they practiced their dying. Perhaps it won't be so terrible, after all, the Detective thought; but then, suddenly frightened, irrational: perhaps it's happening now. The Detective stirred his legs; they talked back to him with their pain, their angry exhaustion, telling him that he was alive. For now, he thought, for this moment, one more night. And what would it be like? A serene, sleepy withdrawal from consciousness like a wave from the shore? Or painful, an awful wrenching, something torn from your chest, from your mind; a separation, you from your life? You die alone. An old man was forced to suffer too many separations as it was, a parade of goodbyes, subtractions of the vital stuff—people he loved, a way of life. The Detective thought of Sadie then, ached for her, and not just her words or the sight of her, and not even her touch in the night, but a knowledge beyond the senses, a feeling he had had when lying beside her, a wordless and secure belief in her life. This much we owe each other, the Detective thought, the assurance that someone will be beside you, a human hand for your head when you're crying, dying . . . . He shouldn't have left Mrs. Klein alone.

From the next room, the Detective heard his granddaughter Nan's laughter, girlish still, flirting with his consciousness, obscured by the crackling of burst wood fiber and the hot exhale of the fire. How reassuring that laughter was, reminding him of how Sadie had smiled at Sally's childhood laughter, and of how he had smiled at the two of them, his family frame-frozen in a happy moment. Etiology, Mrs. Klein had called it, the cause of the cause: her laughter caused her smile caused his smile, a case history for the cure to his loneliness—not hypothetical, but simply gone. Did Mrs. Klein have children and grandchildren, he wondered, or was her husband all that she had? And how could that ever be for the best—to be deserted on that rock overlooking the ocean, that desolate point? The city, though, was not much better, the Detective suddenly remembered. During those first few weeks after the funeral, there were a million hands to stroke his head, but no one had touched him. Perhaps no one could.

Nan's laughter disappeared now, and the Detective struggled to find it; tried to will its existence out of the busy respiration of the fire; pleaded to hear it, a lifeline to the world beyond his solipsistic study, beyond his time. They had sneaked Nan into the hospital the week before Sadie had died, he remembered. Sadie herself had begged them to break the rules, asking time and time again until, guilt-ridden, they were forced to give in. Ten years old then, Nan had been unselfconscious and energetic, bouncing around the room and from subject to subject, first offering to recite a poem she had learned, but then forgetting about it, caught up in relating the outrage of a schoolgirl betrayal. How Sadie had smiled at Nan that day, radiant, content for the first time since she had been told there could be no cure, a smile miraculously defying her pain and the stuporous drugging to kill it. The Detective had been jealous of his own granddaughter then, jealous of her effortless ability to bring happiness to Sadie, happiness that should have been his to give.

But now as he strained to hear Nan's laughter once again, as he pleaded for her presence in the room, the Detective felt that jealousy leave him. Now, for the first time, he sensed fully what Nan had given Sadie that day a week before her death; understood the importance of having someone beside you in time as well as in space—no emptiness to touch you; everywhere, in every direction, every dimension, past and future too, a familiar loving face, part of yourself, to greet you. Now at the edge himself, near the end himself, he could no longer rue any happiness for anyone, any escape from loneliness, and certainly not for Sadie, the one he cared about most, the one he cared about even now, as if she were still alive, a form stirring in his mind, begging for comfort. Too late. He couldn't help her now; nor she, him.

The Detective suddenly remembered the letters. The pure thought, unsuppressed; the clarified image projected before him: the white, feminine-fancy stationery, the rubber band, two lines of Sadie's script. And he waited—for the racing heart, for his body, his thoughts to leap out of rhythm, for the uncontrolled anger and jealousy, the paralyzing fear. But they never came, in their place a sadness so profound, so all-consuming, that he was past crying; and in his mind's eye, he saw Mrs. Klein again, her passive grief as they had sat alone in her living room, but this time she was

his mirror, the image of *his* lonely survival. The letters, their physical existence, their presence in the desk drawer beside him; the letters, his soul's
metronome, his every dream's question, the one sure key to his unsolved
case. The letters. Now that he could remain calm in the face of them, now
that he could consider them without his body erupting, they seemed to fill
him up with the simple fact of their existence, seemed the very word and
substance of the sadness he felt, and an accusation in themselves.

Before, and until now, that accusation had always been directed at
Sadie, a flush of incredulous anger at her potential betrayal. But now that
he could consider the letters more passively, analyzing them the way a detective should, he went one step further, searched for the cause of the cause,
and began to shift the blame onto himself. The Detective had failed his
wife, failed to make her happy—as with Nan in the hospital, when in need,
Sadie had turned to someone else. The Detective couldn't bear that; even
now he wondered if he could bear the realization that she had been forced
to go outside of him for comfort, that he hadn't been enough. And helpless,
he saw her once again lying on her death bed: Sadie, his Sadie, her flesh
stripped and eroded by a pain so insistent that it couldn't be dismissed—no
false hopes, no lasting relief—the finality of its meaning undeniable. And
he wondered about the other, earlier pains, the ones he might have eased,
the aches and hurts hidden behind her silent, uncomplaining face, her
plea-less pride. Too late now. He had failed to soothe those more subtle
pains when it had been possible; he hadn't even been aware of their existence, hiding them from himself. If only he had known, if only he had
forced himself to see, if only he had been aware when he could have made a
difference . . . if only he could comfort her now, to make her happy now
would bring him peace.

He couldn't bear it; even now the Detective couldn't bear the thought
of her in pain: Sadie on her death bed; Sadie's emaciated face; Sadie's eyes,
frightened, searching his for peace. But there was no comfort for an agony
so real, so unhypothetical—only an end. He couldn't help her, not now,
not then; able only to watch, a dumb witness to the death of his happiness.
It was painless in the end, the doctor had told him; it was painless in the
end, the doctor had tried to console. Painless for whom, the Detective had
wanted to scream as he watched Sally sob in her husband's arms, Nan cling-

ing to her coat. I died, I died then, too, he had told himself time and time again; but he knew now that it wasn't true. You die alone.

The Detective heard the phone ringing in the hallway. He opened his eyes, startled by its sound, an alarm retrieving him to another world, the present tense, the here and now. The call was for him, he suddenly knew with clairvoyant surety, Charlie Wriggins or the Chief; either way an inquiry into the case, pressure to decide whose side he would take. If you must, if you must know, Mrs. Klein had told him, come back. But would she really tell him? First degree or second degree; murder, suicide, or accidental death, they weren't the language of her version of the truth, but it was the only language that Charlie Wriggins and the Chief—that the law—could accept. The law, he had served it all his life; could he turn his back on it now by ignoring a solution? could he betray his allegiance to the lifelong cause, to his own self-image? The Detective wondered if the old ideas mattered to him anymore. People, though, he knew, did matter; loyalty to a man meant more than allegiance to an idea, and he felt bound to the Chief. To ignore the possibility of an answer was to betray the Chief—not literally, not legally perhaps, but in fact; there was no escaping that. Just as there was no escaping the bond he felt to Mrs. Klein, the marriage of their common grief, his desire, his need to comfort and protect.

The Detective heard his daughter's footsteps in the hall and then (he imagined them in his mind just before they occurred) three sharp knocks on his study door. He closed his eyes when, after a pause, the door swung open.

"Dad," he heard Sally call softly.

He didn't move; he breathed through his nose; his belly rose and fell slowly as he sensed her drawing closer.

"Dad," she said softly, "it's for you."

The Detective sat motionless, time suspended, body suspended; he didn't need to open his eyes to see his daughter now. They were so close, so interdependent, that he knew her face better than he knew his own: the pinched concern, the constant conflict between fear and caring; always the struggle to do the right thing, features flexed in perpetual moral crisis. She was at that age when one thought one ran the world, when one assumed responsibility for it, a middle-aged martyrdom. It seemed so silly, so sad to him now, the Sea Gull Sallys striving to save us all, and for an instant he thought he might sit up and tell her: "Leave it alone, Sally; it will happen on its own." But time suspended, body suspended, he didn't move; knew at last that he wouldn't, couldn't tell her. That was what old age was for—you had to feel it in your bones before you could believe that it was true.

The room seemed so calm, his body so painless and peaceful, that the Detective felt as if he could wait there forever with his breath held. Only the fire was impatient, busily consuming itself, a hushed but relentless rustling beside him. He knew that his daughter still hovered above him, indecisive and concerned, and he knew too, in another feat of detection, that she would call out to him one more time—out of guilt for having hung up earlier in the afternoon, out of concern for his, her father's feelings; because she cared about him, because despite her worrying and her need to maintain control, she would do what she thought would make him happy as best she could. And when she did that, when she leaned closer and once again called softly just above the steady pant of the fire, "Dad," he wanted to reach up and hug her for her effort. She tried so hard, her struggling ascent out of the pith of her own failures into kindness was so desperately human that he was moved to recognize it, to let her know that he knew. But by the time he could arouse his inert body—raise his head and open his eyes—the study door was closing, her back disappearing behind it.

Too late, again too late to give comfort to his family. The Detective straightened up in his chair and conversed with his body, the language of old age, the paradox of suffering; reminding him that he was, at the same time, both alive and dying; arousing a fear that he would die before Sally would return again, before he could show her how much she mattered to him—a curse-prayer-promise tossed out into the night begging his survival for just that much longer. There seemed no end to this business of living, only to life itself; always a few more facts needed to settle the issue, solve the case. Death seemed to lack resolution; he put it off with these pleas for reprieve because he had too many things to do, a lifetime of loose ends to tie up. At the end, one should be able to gather all of the accomplices in one's life into a single room as at the climax of a murder mystery story, and there resolve one's relationships with them; explain every false lead and missed connection, reveal the alibis and extenuating circumstances; and then, after assigning guilt, bestow and receive forgiveness in an ordered, happy finale. If only he could see Sally just one more time before he died, one more chance to explain his feelings; if only he could have seen his father one more time, held his hand as he was dying; and Sadie, above all Sadie, if only she had told him, if only she had understood . . . . My gift, the Detective thought, was detection, a miraculous gift that appeared as if from nowhere, that wasn't even mine except to cherish and protect, that will leave me like a soul when I die, that seems to have deserted me already, the vessel empty, a prelude to the end. Detection was my gift and I wasn't very good at anything else; but I tried, Sadie, I did try, he wanted to tell her. I hope you knew, I hope you felt it somewhere behind the silence I so rarely broke through—how much you mattered, how much I would have sacrificed for you if I had only known how. To ease your suffering, to quiet your pain, I would have absorbed it all myself. I hope you knew, I hope you know that I'd accept, that I'd embrace even this awful loneliness if it brought you peace.

The Detective suddenly remembered Mrs. Klein, felt again the shaking of her shoulders beneath his hand, heard again the palm-stifled sounds of her crying. And he was reminded of the endless and multiform suffering of all the men and women in his life, pain's many faces: his daughter sobbing in a hospital waiting room, Sadie's searching eyes, the Chief's perplexed exhaustion. Even Dexter's rigid mask couldn't hide from him now the shared anxiety in them all, the quiet, constant fear best expressed by Sally's need to intervene, her lack of faith: *life dies when you close your eyes—better not blink!* He would have reduced them all if he could have, compressed them into the quaking form of Mrs. Klein; and there he would have reached out and touched them, a benediction for the tired and frightened; there he would have told them, all the suffering survivors: "It's all right."

But could he say that to himself? Where was the source of peace in the world for an old man past his time? Could one offer comfort, forgiveness to oneself? There were moments when he had sensed a peace in Mrs. Klein, moments when he had believed she was tapping its secret source, moments when, as she had probed him, he had felt her to be his teacher and guide, possessor of a strange wisdom he had only begun to understand. She seemed then to beckon to him, to bring him closer. But in the end, she had only been human; in the end she had cried like everyone else, lonely like everyone else, just another of pain's many faces, although her suffering and isolation had seemed more perfectly complete, more fully understood—but was that because they were self-induced? I'll tell you, she had promised him at the day's end, two survivors grieving in the dark. Come back and I'll let you know. Would she, though?

The Detective felt buoyant, expanding suddenly with that old sensation of dispossession, of time suspension, that instinctual belief preceding the infallible solution—his gift returning. But now, for the first time in his life, the gift frightened him; seemed now to have been infected by his philosophizing, by the uncertainty of those strange thoughts which had afflicted the last years of his life, bringing him not an answer unquestionable, not a solution, but another question in itself. And that question wasn't, would she tell him, but rather, could she? Did even Mrs. Klein know for sure? Would her answer, if she provided one, be anything more than a pro forma gesture to satisfy the law? Would it be anything more than an act of friendship, a reciprocal kindness to the Detective, giving him only what he wanted, what he felt he had to know, rather than the truth? And could he now, after his day alone with her, after those moments at the promontory point, could he himself accept any of the definite answers? Was there ever, the Detective suddenly thought, terrified by the thought, was there ever a solution? Not to satisfy the law, but for him, for her, for any man or woman? Was there ever an etiology, a chain of facts to be relied upon? Could one ever close one's eyes while at the brink, on the edge, and still be sure? I'll tell you, she had said. If you must know, if you must . . .

The Detective rose, felt himself rise, above his chair, above his pain and exhaustion, the accrued erosion of a hard day, a hard life; and carried by his concentration, only the case to be solved on his mind, he walked past the fire to the desk beside him. Bending, one hand propped against the writing top for balance, he opened a drawer and removed a pack of letters, raising them then before his eyes.

A pause then, a lingering sensation—tantalizing, frightening—of proximity in time and space to a conclusion, a crisis. Now unavoidably fate's accomplice, he feared his freedom, the weight of the impending decision, forced complicity in life—he alone to decide. The Detective's mind reeled for a moment, spinning memories of Sadie, a multitude of images from the days of their lives, all the framed scenes, the stored immortalities, the secured niches where she still lived in his mind, and all illuminated it seemed at the same time, an explosion of her being inside him. Sadie as his fiancée, Sadie as his wife, Sadie as a mother, breastfeeding their child, Sadie a thousand different times, tagged by a thousand different titles, and appearing so rapidly that they began to blur in his mind, becoming not one picture, not many pictures, but beyond them all, until he could no longer see her face or hear her voice, but just accept and believe in her life.

A thought occurred to the Detective then, appearing in its entirety as if by magic. Perhaps he had read it somewhere or overheard it in conversation, but having lost the mental tenacity to force the connections, he couldn't recall its source, only the thought itself: "Identity is more than just content." He would leave it to the Sallys, to the new generation of detectives, to chart the etiologies, to trace it back to its origins; he was through with that now. Instead, he held onto the thought, to the feeling it described, to Sadie's presence, so real to him now that he believed her by his side: the reprieve granted at last, a little more life; one last chance to show her that she mattered, to break through the silence, to ease her pain and earn his own peace by it; one last chance to prove that he loved her. His choice now. His freedom to decide.

The Detective stands, has stood, is always standing, a man in a moment, a man in his study, a study middle class in all respects, Victorian Yankee. Its leather easy chair, oxblood red; the slotted cupboard of its roll-top desk; its bookshelves, inset, their contents arranged by subject; its Tiffany reading lamp illuminating the hung emblems of success, Latin-graved plaques and framed newspaper print—all evoke the bourgeois faith in order, in justice: that wild hope-belief in the eventual redress of effort with reward. A flagstone hearth and carved wooden mantel, memento-adorned with a Sherlock Holmes hat and luridly gleaming, fake gold statuettes, frame the fireplace, whose controlled destruction, a slow explosion of heat and light, hypnotizes this old man, this detective. Gravity-bent, he stands there, an arm outstretched, a pack of letters balanced on his palm. Flames, searing yellow against the black-charred brick, leap chaotically beneath his hand.

Fact: he is alone.

A man in a moment, a man in a crisis, the Detective peers into, peers from, the blurred and darkened corners of his life—for sense, for shape, for the sure means to decide, the sure lines. But there is no frame to the frame when you're in it; there is no meaning without movement and no movement without dying. Everything grows tentative, vaporous, murky, his life undefined, its borders stretching beyond the limits of his eyes, his mind. For him, no safe enclosure; just empty space, black infinity, the unknown to hold him.

The Detective stands, has stood, is always standing, a man in this moment, a man at a fire, the letters balanced on his palm, he alone to decide— to forgive, forget? to let the question die? Living, relived, Mrs. Klein waits, hoping as she waits. Living, relived, Sadie waits, hoping as she waits, the unseen silent presence by his side. Helplessly, passively, with his hand on her chest, the murderess, the unfaithful wife, await the declaration, guilt or redemption, while outside the study a girl is heard laughing, and time suspended, is always heard laughing above the coarse, rasping voice of the fire.

But does it happen—now or ever? objectively or in a manner of speaking? Can it really come to this: destruction of the evidence? Can it really be a case of "no corpse, no crime"? No, ignorance fails him; now and forever he knows that it fails him, forgetfulness too hypothetical to be born. Forgiveness is not to forget what he can never forget, but is instead to live the question, to suffer and survive it, to know always that he will never know and to accept that. Forgiveness is to sacrifice the old self-image, to deny his gift of detection, is to leave, now and forever, the case unsolved . . . because he loved her. Because he loves her.

The Detective stands, has stood, is always standing. Always a hand on his chest; always poised at the fulcrum, on the cutting edge of paradox where opposites meet: judged and judging, alive and dying in the same moment—suffering. And waiting, always waiting for the miracle, for a reprieve he must believe in from a sentence he must take on faith alone as well. Always a man with the unknown before him; always alone at the end. But in spite of that, it happens; now and forever, he makes it happen; the sufferer, the survivor, he alone decides—becomes fate's accomplice, an accessory to the crime. He leans; he steps; he moves yet closer, daring even to close his eyes. And love spills from his palm, an old man's affirmation, into the purging flames, the purifying ocean, from one moment to the next, from one frame to another, the miracle: life.

THIEF

Robley Wilson

He is waiting at the airline ticket counter when he first notices the young woman. She has glossy black hair pulled tightly into a knot at the back of her head—the man imagines it loosed and cascading to the small of her back—and carries over the shoulder of her leather coat a heavy black purse. She wears black boots of soft leather. He struggles to see her face— she is ahead of him in line—but it is not until she has bought her ticket and turns to walk away that he realizes her beauty, which is pale and dark-eyed and full-mouthed, and which quickens his heartbeat. She seems aware that he is staring at her and lowers her gaze abruptly.

The airline clerk interrupts. The man gives up looking at the woman —he thinks she may be about twenty-five—and buys a round-trip, coach class ticket to an eastern city.

His flight leaves in an hour. To kill time, the man steps into one of the airport cocktail bars and orders a scotch and water. While he sips it he watches the flow of travelers through the terminal—including a remarkable number, he thinks, of unattached pretty women dressed in fashion magazine clothes—until he catches sight of the black-haired girl in the leather coat. She is standing near a Travelers Aid counter, deep in conversation with a second girl, a blonde in a cloth coat trimmed with gray fur. He wants somehow to attract the brunette's attention, to invite her to have a drink with him before her own flight leaves for wherever she is traveling, but even though he believes for a moment she is looking his way he cannot catch her eye from out of the shadows of the bar. In another instant the two women separate; neither of their directions is toward him. He orders a second scotch and water.

When next he sees her he is buying a magazine to read during the flight and becomes aware that someone is jostling him. At first he is startled that anyone would be so close as to touch him, but when he sees who it is he musters a smile.

"Busy place," he says.

She looks up at him—Is she blushing?—and an odd grimace crosses her mouth and vanishes. She moves away from him and joins the crowds in the terminal.

The man is at the counter with his magazine, but when he reaches into his back pocket for his wallet the pocket is empty. *Where could I have lost it?* he thinks. His mind begins enumerating the credit cards, the currency, the membership and identification cards; his stomach churns with something very like fear. *The girl who was so near to me*, he thinks—and all at once he understands that she has picked his pocket.

What is he to do? He still has his ticket, safely tucked inside his suitcoat—he reaches into the jacket to feel the envelope, to make sure. He can take the flight, call someone to pick him up at his destination—since he cannot even afford bus fare—conduct his business and fly home. But in the meantime he will have to do something about the lost credit cards—call home, have his wife get the numbers out of the top desk drawer, phone the card companies—so difficult a process, the whole thing suffocating. What shall he do?

First: Find a policeman, tell what has happened, describe the young woman; damn her, he thinks, for seeming to be attentive to him, to let herself stand so close to him, to blush prettily when he spoke—and all the time she wanted only to steal from him. And her blush was not shyness but the anxiety of being caught; that was most disturbing of all. *Damned deceitful creatures.* He will spare the policeman the details—just tell what she has done, what is in the wallet. He grits his teeth. He will probably never see his wallet again.

He is trying to decide if he should save time by talking to a guard near the X-ray machines when he is appalled—and elated—to see the black-haired girl. (*Ebony-Tressed Thief,* the newspapers will say.) She is seated against a front window of the terminal, taxis and private cars moving slug-gishly beyond her in the gathering darkness; she seems engrossed in a book. A seat beside her is empty, and the man occupies it.

"I've been looking for you," he says.

She glances at him with no sort of recognition. "I don't know you," she says.

"Sure you do."

She sighs and puts the book aside. "Is this all you characters think about?—picking up girls like we were stray animals? What do you think I am?"

"You lifted my wallet," he says. He is pleased to have said "lifted," thinking it sounds more worldly than *stole* or *took* or even *ripped off.*

"I beg your pardon?" the girl says.

"I know you did—at the magazine counter. If you'll just give it back, we can forget the whole thing. If you don't, then I'll hand you over to the police."

She studies him, her face serious. "All right," she says. She pulls the black bag onto her lap, reaches into it and draws out a wallet.

He takes it from her. "Wait a minute," he says. "This isn't mine."

The girl runs; he bolts after her. It is like a scene in a movie—bystand-ers scattering, the girl zig-zagging to avoid collisions, the sound of his own breathing reminding him how old he is—until he hears a woman's voice behind him:

"Stop, thief! Stop that man!"

Ahead of him the brunette disappears around a corner and in the same moment a young man in a marine uniform puts out a foot to trip him up. He falls hard, banging knee and elbow on the tile floor of the terminal, but manages to hang on to the wallet which is not his.

The wallet is a woman's, fat with money and credit cards from places like Saks and I. Magnin and Lord & Taylor, and it belongs to the blonde in the fur-trimmed coat—the blonde he has earlier seen in conversation with the criminal brunette. She, too, is breathless, as is the policeman with her.

"That's him," the blonde girl says. "He lifted my billfold."

It occurs to the man that he cannot even prove his own identity to the policeman.

———

Two weeks later—the embarrassment and rage have diminished, the family lawyer has been paid, the confusion in his household has receded— the wallet turns up without explanation in one morning's mail. It is intact, no money is missing, all the cards are in place. Though he is relieved, the man thinks that for the rest of his life he will feel guilty around policemen, and ashamed in the presence of women.

FRANKENSTEIN MEETS
THE ANT PEOPLE

Jonathan Penner

They lay curled in their chaise lounges; the ocean foamed at the island dunes like milk. Perry and his wife were sharing a cottage with another couple. On the darkest nights, when the island seemed to slip its moorings, he sometimes liked to tell about his father and Jasmine.

He had been twelve, he could remember this distinctly. His father had come home on a Friday, impatiently fingered through the mail, lit a burner under the waiting potatoes that Mrs. Lawrence always peeled and sliced, mixed mayonnaise into the carrots that Mrs. Lawrence invariably shredded, and asked—he'd been a widower since Perry was two—"What would you think of my getting married?"

But the question was how Perry, a shrimp with an old man's cane and built-up shoe, no brother or sister, no money or lawyer, no understanding of guns, could prevent it. The woman would share his father's bedroom, where Perry would have to knock before entering. He could foresee the complete loss of his own privacy, and a shortage of closet space. In his own closet were collections and toys not touched for years, things that would seem babyish today, lifted out into the light.

"Who to," he asked.

For a long time his father had dated a woman like those in movie previews—that was how Perry still thought of them, because the movies themselves, his father had said, would be dull as hell for them both. The woman was thin, with huge mobile eyes, the whites too large for the irises, the irises too small for the pupils. Her perfume was stupefying, and she gave Perry stale sticks of gum from her purse when his father wasn't looking. When his father took him to baseball games she often came too, cheered at the wrong times, and incited Perry to plead for a cupped slush both of them loved, one that (his father shouted) destroyed the teeth, then the jaw.

But the woman whose name his father now pronounced, as neutrally as the time of day—"Jasmine Cook"—a partner in his architectural firm, didn't chew gum and couldn't possibly have ever cheered at anything. Her eyes were dead as marbles. All her expression was in her dark abundant hair, on which she must have spent half her life, transforming herself every day or two: poodles and ponytails, bunches and bangs, severe parts and sumptuous waves.

Vanity? Boredom? An architect's hobby? You'd see her head chained in braids, which it seemed to burst overnight, appearing the next morning in shock waves of fluff. For years, Perry hadn't understood that her manifestations were all of one person. She looked built to the scale of his father, the biggest guy in line at any ticket window. Her skin was so unblemished that it seemed to have just come from the store. Except for her unpredictable hair, she might have been a newly bought refrigerator, and it was that, her seeming not human, that always made Perry feel creepy after he had seen her.

"I don't know," he said.

Now his father was sprinkling paprika on the four chicken breasts, eaten five nights a week and endlessly reincarnated, that Mrs. Lawrence eternally skinned. In two minutes his father would turn on the radio for five minutes of six o'clock news. Then they would both sit at the kitchen table, reading, eating applesauce, while the potatoes boiled and the chicken filled the house with its sharpening aroma. Nothing would be the same: Perry felt a suffocating rage.

"I don't think you should," he said. Then he turned his chair around, away from the table, and sat squeezing both his soft upper arms. He knew that his father knew he was crying, but that they could continue the conversation as long as his father didn't see his face. If that happened he would find himself swinging through the air onto his father's lap, held between his father's arms and beating chest, inhaling the smell of his father's clothes and body; and if *that* happened he wouldn't be sure why he was crying, or whether he could stop.

His trouble, he would say in years to come, out for napoleons after the movies, masked and perspiring at Halloween parties—his trouble, he explained at poolside barbecues, standing chest-deep with a can of beer (he barely swam but loved the weightlessness)—his trouble had been that he never had a plan, because even thinking about Jasmine hurt so much he had to stop.

The Saturday after his father told him, Jasmine came over so they could all (said his father) discuss it reasonably. But none of them discussed anything. His father mowed the lawn at furious speed while Jasmine, her hair back in a kerchief, edged and swept the walks. Perry sat on the grass with his cane and radio and canteen of grape juice, now and then pulling weeds from the flowerbed border, feeling the house and lawn shift their loyalty from himself to her. When the mail came he hurried to get it—he didn't think he could even touch it if Jasmine touched it first. His father stopped and straightened, pressing both hands into the small of his back, arching so that his belly protruded in a way Perry found disgusting, then wrung out his sweatband and asked, "Anything good?"

And there was. The brown-wrapped box was marked KEEP FROM EXTREMES OF HEAT AND COLD. Perry took it inside and opened it at the kitchen table.

This was one of those times when the world surprised him with its fairness. It was months before that he'd ordered an Ant City from an illustrated ad in *Boy's Life* magazine, the drawing a closeup of two huge ants conversing in a cross-sectioned tunnel. Please Allow Six Weeks For Delivery—that seemed excessive, shameless, and he'd been pessimistic from the start, drawing less hope from the "Please" each time he reread the clipping. He came to sense the ant merchant's sneering triumph: here was a crippled twelve-year-old whose father didn't want ants anyway, the kind of kid you could do anything you wanted to.

But here was the package, and inside a manual—*Enjoying Your Ants*—and what looked like a little double windowpane, the space between its two glass panels half-way filled with sand—and a thumb-sized cardboard tube marked "LIVE ANTS!" His father and Jasmine had come into the kitchen behind him. "Lemonade?" his father asked, rattling ice from a tray of cubes. Jasmine pulled up a chair next to Perry's. He could smell her unfamiliar sweat, sweeter than his father's, somehow damper.

"How fascinating," she said.

Sweeping a dripping hand an inch above the swimming pool's surface, or, supine on webbed plaid plastic, thoughtfully patting his baking belly, Perry would try to convey to his listeners exactly how Jasmine talked. "How fascinating"—as though it were boring, and elementary, and sad. That was her only tone of voice, the pitch of defeated wisdom. No matter what she was saying, she said endurance was all there was.

She was turning rapidly through *Enjoying Your Ants*—even his father couldn't read that fast, and Perry guessed she was faking. "First drip some water into the city," she said. "May I help?" She brought the thing shaped like a double windowpane over to the sink, then back to the table. "Why don't I hold it," she said, "and you be the one to put them in."

"I'm not a four-year-old," said Perry.

"What?"

He began peeling off the tape that secured the cap of the tube. Of all times, he wished she were not here now, but with his father looming up at his other side, glugging and sighing at a tall glass of lemonade, there was nothing he could say. He pulled off the cap and peered inside—a slowly churning tangle of black. Excited, he gently began tapping them from the tube down into their waiting city.

There were far fewer than he had expected, no more than fifteen or twenty, but they were enormous ones, and Perry could see that this was going to be wonderful. They would always be in sight: their city was sliced so thin that their tunnels and rooms would have walls of glass. When the tube was empty he told Jasmine, "Put the top on." She reached to close the city. Then she made a peculiar sound, as though she had been suddenly squeezed.

A single ant had somehow not gone in and was clinging to the top rim of the city, its antennae twiddling the air. "*Wait*," said Perry. But she was already coming down, her face averted as though the ant might jump at her. She caught him between the city and its top, and he hung out by one leg, his other legs working furiously. Perry grabbed the city, freed the ant, and dropped him in. The trapped leg detached itself and fell to the kitchen table.

"Hate them," Jasmine said, backing slowly away from the table, her hands spread like pitchforks against her thighs. Her face was still expressionless. Perry's father, wetting a fingertip, picked up the severed leg at once and took it outside, from where came the clang of the garbage can lid. "If you marry her," Perry screamed into the wall, but ended in humiliating silence—what could he even threaten?—stopped as suddenly as though his canetip had entered a crevasse.

––––––––––

"I want you at the wedding," said his father.

The ants milled slowly, apparently helpless, atop their sandwich of sand, and when Perry went to bed that night he expected to find them dead in the morning. But again, to his surprise and somehow his worry, the world was working as advertised. The little guys had gotten themselves organized and made a start on tunnel construction, piling what they excavated, so that the building went up as well as down.

"I want you at the wedding," said his father.

After that they did a lot of their work in the daytime, and Perry watched as the network of tunnels grew brilliantly, stupidly, intricate. The ants seemed to have no sense of how constricted they were, or how few. Did they think they could raise their young in those tunnels? *Enjoying Your Ants* said all of them were workers—shipping queens was against the law. How did they expect to reproduce, or what else were they building for? He fed them a cornflake every day, watered them, and waited for the first deaths: the dead, said *Enjoying Your Ants*, would be buried in a graveyard at the top of the city. But even Fiveleg—the only one Perry could identify—was haul-ing his grains of sand with what seemed inexhaustible vigor.

"I want you at the wedding," said his father. "Have some faith in me." He crossed his legs on the footrest of his reclining chair. "I've known her a long time. We work well together."

"Do you—" Perry attempted a knowing expression that a moment later he felt was ridiculous. Do you love her, he had thought he would ask, but the words seemed too silly.

Nevertheless his father understood. "Not like I love you. This is dif-ferent."

"You haven't justified it, Dad."

His father looked at him closely. "I want you to be my best man." Then his father stared down at his huge slippered feet, pinching his cheeks with one hand so that his lips protruded. Finally he said, with an anger that startled Perry, "*If* it's a mistake I can *make* a mistake."

Perry felt unfairly beaten. How could you argue with something like that? "I won't live here," he said. Suddenly his life with his father seemed laminated into the past—even right now, stretched on the carpet next to the big chair, doing homework while his father rustled and snapped through newspapers, the smell of his father's socks coming through his cracked black slippers: strange! He wished he could tell his father what it was like—remembering the present.

("That's obscure," his wife would remind him years later, hearing the story again, with friends in a bar about to close—"Get to the car horns," she would tell him, stranded in a foreign airport.)

"I want you to be my best man," said his father. Perry saw himself in the wedding procession, walking alone in his great shoe, tilting over his cane. "I want you to hand me the ring."

Later, Jasmine came to his room, to see the ants, she said. Perry pointed to where their city stood on his dresser, next to his clock and Jacques Cousteau bathyscaphe. The bathyscaphe was a masterpiece—the only sur-vivor from his years of building models. Now, seeing Jasmine's eyes flick past it, he knew he would throw it out as soon as she left the room.

"They're amazing," she said. "Why don't those tunnels collapse?" It sounded as though she wished they would.

"This is my room," said Perry.

Jasmine had begun to lower herself to the floor, but now she stood up straight, huger than ever next to Perry's little dresser, near his child-sized desk and chair. Her hair was styled like a helmet, as though she'd come from another planet. "Why don't you like me?" she asked, expressionless.

He would never be able to bear her as long as he lived, that was all he knew, no more than Jacques Cousteau could swim free of his brilliant chamber. "Because you're ugly."

"That's so." She seemed relieved, as though something hard had turned out to be simple. "When I was little, everyone thought so." And to Perry's amazement she began to clap her hands above her head, sidestepping around him in a little circle, while he rotated to watch her as she chanted: "Jasmine is a friend of mine, She resembles Frankenstein, I forget the something line, She resembles Frankenstein."

("Of course," said the girl who would soon become Perry's wife, as they lay through summer weekends in her vacationing parents' bed—"Of course," she said, stroking the hair back from his forehead, or kissing his foot that had never fully formed, "you knew it was yielding your father that you hated, not that poor lady." Jasmine had been something he loathed, not hated—a disfiguring illness—and though his heart was now quiet, the mark was there. Perry didn't reply, because he badly needed this girl. And in a minute she held his head against her breasts, or sat up in bed cross-legged, or brought fresh ice cubes for their coffee cups of wine, and asked him to tell her again.)

The morning of the wedding, while his father was out getting his hair cut, Perry stuffed some clothes into his school briefcase and caught a bus downtown. He had emptied his bank account the day before.

But at the Greyhound station, nauseous with diesel fumes, the throb of engines muttering from its tiled walls, all he did was sit on a bench ornate with obscenities, watching people depart and arrive. And it was as though Jasmine had infected everyone, because none of them looked human to him. Even children younger than himself—aliens in plastic skins.

Every few minutes a new bus delivered more, and others left. On one wall was a Greyhound route map like a vast anthill seen in cross-section. Perry saw how it was. The world was crawling with them.

He walked all the way home. The sun was high by the time he arrived. He wanted to be so tired he wouldn't think, but what he felt was only his regular walking pain and a terrible thirst.

At first he thought he'd mistaken the house. There were strange cars and a van in front. Inside, he found people in uniform: a fat woman in the kitchen, two waitresses setting out trays of half-dollar-sized sandwiches, and a white-jacketed bartender who quickly gave him a ginger ale. "Nice home," the bartender told him. "Those your ants? Pretty nifty setup."

"Your father was *sick*," said the fat woman, watching him gulp his ginger ale.

"Sick?"

"Just *sick*. I told him this is *his* day. Do you know he almost called it *off?* I told him absolutely *not*."

She bowled away back to the kitchen. The bartender, looking after her, made one hand into a flapping, quacking jaw. Then he fixed another ginger ale, this time with cherries. Burping, Perry took it to his room. But now the room hardly seemed his, he'd thrown out so many things he couldn't bear for Jasmine to see—books with print that was childishly large, walkie-talkies with dead batteries, board games missing most of their cards, old snapshots of himself: in a sandbox, in a crib, riding on his father's back.

––––––––––

In later years a time came when Perry had to enter the hospital. He was to have tests for cancer, possibly an operation. While he was waiting to find out, his wife sat with him every day. Their friends from the city came, friends from the shore, until the room was like a florist's shop, and the nurses' aides laughed and brought more chairs, and people had to leave so new ones could sit, chewing each other's chocolates.

The man who shared his hospital room had no visitors at all. He could not speak; the doctors had taken his larynx. The cancer was still active in him. After visiting hours, when Perry's wife and friends had gone in a flurry of careful hugs, the mute loved for the curtains between their beds to be drawn back, and for Perry to talk. He lay on his side, listening, bright-eyed. It helped him go longer without his shot.

Perry told him the story of his father and Jasmine—how on the day of their wedding he had almost run away. How, coming home, he lay on his bed with the tingle of ginger ale in his nostrils, and realized, when he saw something move, that it was time to get rid of them, too.

He brought their city to his bed. Stretched on his stomach, his eyes inches from the glass, he watched their mindless scramble and rush. They couldn't know he existed, or even that they themselves did. And this, *Enjoying Your Ants* had claimed, was educational for the entire family. The ants knew nothing, Perry tried to explain—only what the whole world knew, the same imperative that held the oceans in their beds and hurled apart the stars. The mute, his cheek flat against his sheet, gave a horizontal nod. He was beginning to sweat.

At the end of the most remote tunnel an ant was lying still, and lay still as Perry continued to watch, even when he shook the city slightly. It was Fiveleg, apparently dead. Contrary to what *Enjoying Your Ants* had promised, he had not been removed to a cemetery. The other ants were just letting him lie there.

Perry had been expecting death—how long could these creatures continue?—and wasn't surprised that Fiveleg was the first to go. It was actually a relief. He got a tweezers from the bathroom and reached into the city, collapsing Fiveleg's tunnel, to pull him out and flush him away. Reaching into the air between the high hospital beds, he pantomimed the operation of tweezers, while the man with no larynx stared and nodded.

But Perry saw with horror that now, crushed in the grip of the tweezers, Fiveleg was spasmodically moving. "Reflex action," he explained to the mute, who crinkled his eyes in doubt. And in fact Perry wasn't sure that he hadn't killed Fiveleg himself, or even that the ant had been finally dead. He got rid of him in the toilet, then washed the tweezers and scrubbed his hands until they hurt.

Back at the city, he felt better to see that several others looked feeble. It was obviously time for them to go. He carried the city out to the back yard, to a spot that was mostly bare dirt, and dumped them. They wandered blindly, lost.

Church bells, he told the mute—who was now sopping with sweat, his hand wandering toward his call button in swimming gestures—the sudden pealing of bells was probably an invention of memory. But something had made him wonder whether he still had time to get to the church and hand his father the thin gold ring. He knew where the church was. He felt certain he could walk that far.

But he was still there in the back yard, retying his shoelaces, brushing dirt from the knees and seat of his pants, cleaning his hands and face at the garden hose and slicking down his hair, when he heard (to hear it again was why he liked to tell this story) the approaching joyous clamor of many cars blowing their horns.

THE LUCKIEST MAN IN THE WORLD

Randall Silvis

When Emiliano Fortunato returned to Torrentino after being wounded in the war, he found his small village still in mourning. Of the twenty-eight men who had marched off happily a month earlier, vowing to destroy the oppressive federal regime, only Emiliano, a thin, hazel-eyed youth of seventeen, survived his outfit's first encounter with the enemy. Ironically, the men of Torrentino had suffered no previous oppression at the hands of the government. So remote and insignificant was their mountain village that most of the inhabitants could not even name the politicians then in power. But the revolutionary soldier who happened into Torrentino had told such eloquent stories of repression and taxation, such tales of brutality, of rape, torture, and decapitation, that the men of Torrentino felt a long-neglected national pride stirring deep within them, and all were subsequently moved to march against the faceless capitalist tyranny that was threatening to usurp their birthrights.

That their birthrights consisted of little more than a dusty garden plot and an earthen-floored shack for each of them did not seem to deter their enthusiasm. Any opportunity to escape the monotony of Torrentino was welcomed. And as a consequence, every Torrentino male between the ages of thirteen and sixty-five was wiped out. Only Emiliano Fortunato survived. Perched thirty feet up in a treetop, he had been acting as lookout for his regiment but fell asleep cradled in the fork of two branches. He awoke to the sound of gunfire, only to discover that federal troops had already passed beneath his perch and were swarming over the resting revolutionaries. The men who were taken prisoner were lined up almost immediately and shot. The entire encounter could not have lasted more than fifteen minutes. Emiliano huddled in his treetop cradle, weeping and vomiting, and watched as the federal soldiers tossed his dead neighbors into a shallow ravine and covered them with a few shovelsful of dirt.

When the soldiers departed Emiliano attempted to climb down out of the tree. But so weakened and dizzied was he by what he had witnessed that he lost his footing and tumbled down through the branches, shearing off limbs as he fell. Landing on his right side, he struck the earth with a heavy thud and lay unconscious for several minutes. Finally he staggered to his feet. To his amazement Emiliano discovered that a twig approximately an inch in diameter had been rammed through the triceps muscle of his right arm. There was no pain, though he could see clearly where the skin closed around the twig at its point of entry, sealing the wound, and where, on the other side of his arm, the twig's sharp point distended the skin.

As though in a dream Emiliano watched a trickle of blood drip from his arm. Then, regaining some of his senses, he removed from around his neck the green bandana, symbol of the Regimiento Torrentino, and tied it tightly around his upper arm, tugging at the bandana end with his teeth. He then walked in wide circles around the battlefield for several hours, pivoting in a daze past the pit in which his slain neighbors lay like fishing worms in a tin can. Toward nightfall his legs gave out, and he fell asleep beneath an huisache tree. Inhaling the rich fragrance of its yellow flowers he lapsed into unconsciousness. For the next eighteen hours he slept, his sleep haunted by mocking, accusative visits from his dead neighbors.

Early the next morning Emiliano awoke, his arm throbbing and burning, swollen to three times its normal size. After breaking off the protruding twig so that only a fragment extended outside the skin, he began the long hike back up the mountain to Torrentino. He was afraid to go home, but at the same time afraid to go anywhere else. For the first time in his life, he was alone. As the only child of his widowed mother, Emiliano had been coddled and pampered, and at seventeen was still very much a boy.

He filled the tedious walk with self-denigration and chastisement. He called himself a coward, a little girl, a shivering puppy. On the third day he reached the depths of self-humiliation and stood on the rim of a high rock ledge, wanting to jump. But he could not force himself over the edge. Aloud he prayed: "Dear God, I am a gnat, a mere pimple on the face of the earth. I don't deserve to live. If You will give me a little push I won't in any way attempt to hold myself back. Send me hurtling down into purgatory where I belong. I am ready to die and am awaiting your assistance."

But although Emiliano stood poised on the ledge for a full ten minutes, not once did he feel the hand of God upon his shoulder, giving him that necessary shove. No dark wind came sweeping down upon him to carry him off into space. There was not so much as a breeze to ripple his torn shirt.

Emiliano stepped away from the edge and sat down in the dirt. Apparently God did not want him dead. Maybe, Emiliano thought, it was not by accident that he had been perched in a treetop while his neighbors were dropping like flies. Maybe it was more than chance that had landed him on his shoulder rather than his head when he tumbled out of that tree. The sharp twig could as easily have pierced his heart, couldn't it? But no, it had been directed into the muscle of his right arm, to an out-of-the-way place that would not prove to be life-threatening.

Maybe God had plans for Emiliano Fortunato. He certainly had not gone to all the trouble of keeping the boy alive only to help him kill himself in a fit of self-loathing.

Reasoning thus, Emiliano quickly overcame his depression and turned his attention to his wounded arm. The arm had, thankfully, ceased its intolerable burning. Emiliano took this as a sign that God was looking after him from moment to moment. The only discomfort Emiliano now felt, aside from his hunger, was an occasional prickliness in the tips of his fingers and a bothersome itch around the mouth of the wound itself. Throughout the rest of his arm he felt nothing. It dangled from his shoulder like a wet cloth.

On the fourth day after the battle Emiliano staggered into a small village in which there was a doctor. Dr. Sevilla was a slight, heavily perspiring man who lived in a large white house, its screened porch alone as big as the house Emiliano shared with his mother. The doctor appeared quite touched by Emiliano's wound. He even stroked the boy's chest reassuringly while, between strokes, he gingerly removed Emiliano's shirt.

"You don't have to be so careful," Emiliano told him, affecting the stoicism of a hardened warrior. "My arm no longer hurts. In fact I can't feel a thing."

Dr. Sevilla cut away the green bandana and exposed the arm. "Oh, you poor beautiful child," he said, and he actually began to weep. "Who tied this scarf around your arm like that?"

"I tied it myself," Emiliano said, a bit too proudly.

"But much too tightly," the doctor said. "And you never loosened it to let the blood flow, did you? The wound itself wasn't serious; the muscle would have healed in time. But you cut off all the circulation to your arm. Oh, my poor stupid child."

Emiliano did not quite understand. Wasn't the purpose of a tourniquet to prevent the blood from flowing? Nor was he certain just what Sevilla had in mind when he prepared a hypodermic syringe and then swabbed Emiliano's shoulder with alcohol.

"Will that help my arm to heal?" Emiliano asked.

"Your arm is no longer an arm," Sevilla said, shaking his head and not bothering to wipe away the tears as they trickled down his cheeks. "It's just a tail on a chicken now. It's just an old snot rag that you used to wipe your nose on."

Emiliano was confused, but he said nothing. Without feeling he watched as the syringe needle punctured his skin, as the clear fluid in the hypodermic was gradually injected into his shoulder.

"You never even tried to clean the wound, did you?" Sevilla asked. He placed some frightening-looking instruments in an enameled basin, then poured over them a full bottle of alcohol.

"Do you know what gangrene is?" Sevilla asked.

Emiliano shook his head. He was beginning to feel very sleepy.

"Oh, you poor child," Sevilla said. After preparing his instruments he came back to sit beside Emiliano and to hold the boy's good hand, his thin fingers stroking Emiliano's wrist.

After a few minutes Emiliano slumped forward into the doctor's arms. Sevilla held him upright, his smooth-shaven cheek against the boy's as he caressed the back of Emiliano's neck. Then very gently he eased the boy down on the table. He lifted Emiliano's dangling wounded arm, truly as lifeless as a wet cloth and as useless as a tail on a chicken, and laid it flat on the table. Then he went to the enameled basin to retrieve his instruments. He came back to the table and spread out the instruments in a row. Then, weeping softly each time he looked into Emiliano's handsome, youthful face, he began to saw off the arm.

———————

For three weeks Emiliano recuperated in the doctor's comfortable home. He wore Sevilla's clothing, slept in Sevilla's bed, ate at Sevilla's table. The doctor pleaded with him to remain permanently, to become, Sevilla said, his assistant. But Emiliano did not feel at ease in the huge empty house. The servants looked at him snidely, and he had the feeling they talked about him behind his back. Also, Sevilla was constantly wanting to touch him—under the pretext of examination, of course. But sometimes in places which, the boy thought, could not have anything to do with his amputated arm.

One day when Sevilla was attending to another patient, Emiliano gathered a bag of food from the doctor's kitchen and resumed his journey home to Torrentino. His village was approximately a five-hour hike away, situated on a remote mountainside well off the main-traveled roads. He walked half the distance that first afternoon, and then, still weakened by his operation and three weeks of inactivity, spent the night beside a shallow, fast-running stream. He slept until noon the next day, and in mid-afternoon finally caught sight of the low buildings of Torrentino.

The villagers of Torrentino, all of whom were now women or children or very old men, were preparing for their siesta when one of them looked down the road to see Emiliano trudging toward them from fifty yards away. From that distance he appeared lopsided and hazy, his body seeming to shimmer in the heat. As soon as his face was recognized, the assumption was made that Emiliano, thought to have been killed with all of the other village men, was a ghost.

Argentina Neruda, a wrinkled, shrunken, and smelly old woman who practiced Aztec shamanism, chanted and shook a small leather pouch of animal teeth at the approaching figure. She warned her neighbors to remember the federal soldier who had come to gleefully announce that the entire Regimiento Torrentino had been killed, snuffed out like a weak candle flame in a windstorm. The pathetic little rebellion had been squashed, the messenger had said. Ground like a tarantula beneath the boot heels of the magnificent General Cruz. He had spoken as eloquently as the revolutionary who had earlier led all of the men to their deaths. How could they not believe him?

The villagers gathered in the dusty street in front of Father Vallarte's Mother of the Holy Infant church and watched Emiliano approaching. As he came nearer they stood their ground but huddled closer together. Father Vallarte, his glaucoma-plagued eyes squinting to make out the hazy figure, feebly made the sign of the cross and began to mumble the Lord's Prayer. Halfway through the prayer he lost his place and was forced to clear his throat and begin again. Argentina Neruda chanted ancient indictments and rattled her pouch of animal teeth.

What could the ghost of a seventeen-year-old boy want of them? the villagers asked themselves. Hadn't they been lighting their votive candles nightly for the souls of the departed? Hadn't they been reciting their novenas and attending religiously to their mournful thoughts? Why was this specter coming to haunt and grieve them even more?

Emiliano Fortunato approached the villagers and stopped just five feet short of their huddled group. A layer of reddish brown road dust clung to his eyebrows and lashes. His face was streaked with dirt, his hair tangled and uncombed. The clothes he wore, clothes that had once belonged to Dr. Sevilla, were a bit too small for him and made him appear as though, swollen with death, he had grown a few inches. The clothes too were painted with a fine veneer of brown dust. Overall he looked as though he had only recently climbed up out of his grave. His beautiful hazel eyes were dulled and cloudy with fatigue, and he had only one arm.

Teresa Fortunato, Emiliano's mother, stepped out of the crowd and faced her son. Before marching off to war he had been her only source of comfort, her reason for enduring a hard life. She did not recognize the clothes he wore, but as he stood there, slouching and unwashed, Teresa thought she saw in his tired smile a true-to-life vestige of her son.

"Emiliano," she said hesitantly, almost afraid to open her mouth to speak. "Is that really you, or are you a ghost?"

Standing lopsided, smiling crookedly, Emiliano answered, "What would a ghost be doing with only one arm?"

His mother rushed forward to embrace him.

In the ensuing weeks it became all too easy for Emiliano to lapse into an infantile laziness. His mother tended to his every need: she washed his hair and scrubbed his back and shoulders when he bathed; at times she even fed him like a baby while he reclined against a thin mattress propped up in the shade of the gabled roof against the outside wall of their house.

To answer the barrage of questions with which his return to the village was met, Emiliano fabricated an elaborate story about being left for dead on the battlefield, about later regaining consciousness only to discover all of his comrades slain. He had dragged himself from body to body, he said, saying a prayer over each man and gathering some small memento to carry home to the grieving family. From Juan Volutad he had recovered the tiny penknife with the mother-of-pearl handle. Hadn't he watched Juan on innumerable occasions use that very knife to carve up a piece of fruit, and didn't he know how much the return of such a souvenir would mean to Juan's bereaved wife and children?

From Carlos Gutiérrez he had secured the gold coin with the hole punched into it so that it could be hung from a string and worn about the neck as a good-luck piece. And from Pablo Márquez, the devout, soft-spoken Pablo, he had recovered a medal of the Blessed Mother.

From each of the twenty-seven men, Emiliano said, he had salvaged some memento certain to bring comfort in the empty days ahead. All of these treasures he had wrapped carefully in his green bandana to carry home to the grief-stricken families. Unfortunately he had been accosted by bandits along the way, beaten and robbed.

When he told this story he bowed his head and wept and begged forgiveness for his failure. All but a few of the villagers comforted him when he grew sad or recounted for them his nightmares peopled with specters of slaughter and death. Argentina Neruda and a few other bitter old women wondered aloud why Emiliano Fortunato alone had been saved, why a skinny, lazy boy had been returned to them while good men with large families had been struck down.

All but these few women paid a certain deference to the boy. This was especially true of those women aged approximately fifteen to thirty-five. More than once Teresa Fortunato was forced to shoo away a crowd of women who with their solicitous attention threatened to smother her son. What thick dark hair he had! they told him, each wanting to run their fingers over his head. What beautiful and sad hazel eyes! they cooed. How he must have suffered from the loss of his arm! How truly brave he was! What a good brave husband he would make one of these days!

Emiliano, of course, did nothing to discourage such kindliness. He luxuriated in the attention as a well-fed cat luxuriates in the warmth of the sun. He teased playfully and even stole a kiss or two when no one was looking. Late at night he would sometimes slip out his bedroom window and not return until dawn was already creeping up the mountainside. This latter activity became so habitual, in fact, that by the time Emiliano had been home for only twelve days his mother was remarking how wan and lethargic he had become.

"Don't you sleep well at night, my little soldier?" she asked.

"I am haunted by dreams," he told her while lying on his mattress propped up against the outside wall of their home.

"Dreams of the battle?" she asked.

"You will never know, mama, how horrible it was for me. You will never know how bravely I fought. And all to no avail. I sometimes wish I had not been successful in keeping myself alive."

"You must never say such things," she warned. "It's a mockery of God's will."

"If only I could forget how terrible it was.

His mother clicked her tongue sympathetically. "Such awful scenes you must have witnessed."

"They are etched into my memory," he replied. "Even my arm, shot off as it was at the very height of the battle, even it will not allow me to forget. Each night it burns and pains as though it were still attached. Consequently I am forced to crawl out of bed to take long walks through the darkness, hoping to wear myself out sufficiently to snatch an hour or two of rest throughout the day."

Emiliano quickly discovered that such wounded-hero posturing was very effective in eliciting his mother's sympathies, and equally effective on many of the widows he visited covertly each night. This self-pitying attitude was best with the older women, women who had lost sons of their own, while the braggadocious swagger could be counted on to produce the desired effect in the younger girls.

One warm afternoon Emiliano awoke from his siesta to realize what a fortunate man he was. He may have lost an arm, but in many respects he was truly blessed. He had a loving mother who doted on him, who dragged his spare mattress back and forth, who placed herself at his beck and call. And there were several warm, lovely women who each night waited anxiously for him, waited naked and eager beneath soft sheets, their hearts fluttering like tiny birds learning to fly. And there were several other women who, while not quite lovely by the light of day, were soft and solicitous and whose murmurs in the thick syrup of darkness were just as sweet as those of the prettier ones.

There were, of course, those few women who could not bear the sight of Emiliano Fortunato. To see him lounging on his mattress reminded them that their husbands or lovers or sons, once as virile and handsome in their eyes as was this boy, were now dead. Why couldn't Emiliano be dead and the lost husband or lover or son here in his place? The women who entertained such thoughts frequently gathered together in the evenings to condemn the boy. Argentina Neruda encouraged their enmity; she cracked eggs and pointed to the spoor of blood, she read viscera and threw her bones and regularly pronounced Emiliano an evil spirit raised from the battlefield to haunt their village. After all, hadn't he been spotted more than once slinking between the small houses in the dead of the night, slithering through the shadows like a thief? And didn't it seem that he had cast some kind of spell over the younger women, so that they fondled and caressed and cooed over him as though he were a newborn baby? He was behaving as though he was Christ Incarnate, and not just a lazy, shifty-eyed boy with one arm and a huge supply of sexual energy.

Emiliano knew very little of the machinations of his detractors. He ate well and was well looked-after and was practically lionized by three-quarters of the women in town. He slept throughout the day and indulged himself sumptuously each night. He had participated in a raging battle and had managed to escape with the loss of only one arm. As far as Emiliano Fortunato was concerned, he was indeed the luckiest man in the world.

Nearly a month had passed when Dr. Sevilla came riding into Torrentino on horseback. He sat stiffly astride his well-lathered gelding, jouncing along like a small boy on a merry-go-round. He wore leather riding breeches and a pink silk shirt, and over the shirt a rebozo of handwoven wool. The first person he met was Argentina Neruda, who, when Sevilla came riding down the narrow street into the village, was returning from her daily scouring of the mountainside for dead wood for her oven.

"Which is the house of Emiliano Fortunato?" the doctor asked, reining back his horse and peering down at the wrinkled old woman. She had a face like an ancient cat's, small and round and suspicious as she squinted up at him.

"Who are you?" she asked, her arms full of dead branches and twigs.

"My name is Dr. Sevilla. Emiliano is a patient of mine."

Argentina did not like this man with the thin face, hawk's nose, and large, piercing eyes. Why would a man in a pink silk shirt—she had caught a glimpse of the shirt when the doctor raised his hand to shield his eyes from the sun—come all the way to Torrentino to see a patient who could not afford to pay him more than a compliment? Besides, what right did he have to sit there peering down at her so disdainfully, as though she were some kind of an animal, a bug he would like to step on and squash?

"Six houses down," she finally told him. "On your right. You'll find him where he always is—sleeping on a mattress outside his house."

The doctor nodded his thanks, shook the reins, and urged the tired horse forward.

The clopping of a horse's hooves against the dry earth stirred Emiliano out of his slumber. Shielding his eyes he peered up the street, uncertain of what he was seeing until the doctor grinned happily and waved.

Now Emiliano stood and went inside the house. His mother, surprised to see her son moving so quickly in the middle of the day, asked him what was wrong. He did not answer. Hurrying into his bedroom he pulled the already lowered shades down over the windowsill, then sat on the edge of the bed in the tepid dimness.

Out front, Dr. Sevilla introduced himself to Teresa Fortunato. A few minutes later he lifted aside the blanket that hung across Emiliano's doorway and, like a prairie dog peeking out of its hole, poked his head into the bedroom.

"Emiliano," Sevilla said, holding back his emotions for the sake of the boy's mother in the next room, "I've come to have a look at your arm."

"There is no arm to look at," Emiliano said dryly.

Now the doctor came into the room and sat on the bed beside the boy. He laid his medical bag and another small package against the pillow.

"May I unbutton your shirt and take a look at your arm?" Sevilla spoke softly, his voice timid and almost whining.

"Everything is fine," Emiliano told him. "If you've come all this way just to examine me, you've wasted a trip."

"Please let me look at you," the doctor said. He raised his hand to Emiliano's shirt and undid the top button. Emiliano seized the doctor's hand.

"I have to examine you," Sevilla said, speaking firmly now, "in order to determine that the wound is healing properly, that there is no infection, and that I got all the gangrenous flesh. Now please don't be a stupid boy. You don't want to have another operation, do you?"

Hearing this, Emiliano submitted and allowed Sevilla to unbutton the shirt. Afterwards Sevilla raised the window shade, then turned the boy by his shoulders so that the amputation faced the inward-slanting shaft of sunlight.

"It's healing nicely," Sevilla said, probing the scar tissue. "All the pus is drained out, isn't it? That's what I like about you young boys; you all heal so quickly."

The doctor's hand slid from Emiliano's shoulder down across his chest and over his waist. "You've put on a little weight, haven't you?" Sevilla said. "Somebody must be taking very good care of you."

Emiliano reached for his shirt and draped it over his right shoulder, then drew his left arm through the sleeve and began to fasten the buttons. Quickly the doctor stood again and lowered the shades. He sat lightly on the bed, leaned toward Emiliano, and slid his damp palm beneath the boy's shirt.

"My poor dear boy," Sevilla whispered. "Why did you sneak away from my house the way you did? You know you broke my heart, don't you? I couldn't see any patients for a week, I felt so miserable without you."

Emiliano tried to stand but Dr. Sevilla grasped him by the belt and held him firmly. "Please don't walk out on me," Sevilla said. "I came so far just to see your beautiful face again." He sniffed, his own face held close to the boy's, his breath smelling of cloves. Sobbing quietly, he massaged Emiliano 's wrist.

"If you'll only come back with me you can have everything you want. You'll have new clothes and a fine big house to live in. Why would you want to stay here when I can give you all that?"

"This is my home," Emiliano said archly. "This is where I belong."

"Who is to say where each of us belongs? And what makes you think you belong here, in a village full of women, rather than in my village living in a handsome white house? What can you accomplish here? From what I have heard, you do nothing all day long but lounge in the shade on your mattress."

Emiliano drew himself up straight. "I sleep in the day because my services are so much in demand at night."

Now the doctor understood. "So that's what keeps you here, is it? No wonder you're acting like a rooster in a henhouse. But how long do you think this can last before you tire of it?"

"I will never tire of it. When I don't have it I spend all my time thinking about it."

Dr. Sevilla emitted a soft click from the back of his throat. A pout formed on his lips and he looked as though he might weep again. Then he turned and reached for the small brown package that lay on the bed. He stripped off the paper and handed the contents, a neatly pressed and folded pink silk shirt, to Emiliano.

"It's just like the one I'm wearing," Sevilla told him, and lifted his shawl in evidence. "Touch it; feel how smooth it is. Your skin is so delicate, especially here, at the amputation; you should have a material that will caress and soothe your skin instead of chafing it. What woman here could give you a shirt like this?"

Emiliano held the shirt in his lap and fingered the cloth. It was as slick and sensual as the skin of a woman's breast. Emiliano was only remotely aware that, while he stroked the soft cloth, Sevilla had slid his hand along the inside of Emiliano's thigh.

"I will give you a whole closetful of shirts like this," the doctor whispered. "As well as silk trousers and silk socks and silk pajamas. And silk sheets to sleep on every night."

Emiliano ran his finger over the shirt collar. He felt each of the small pearl-like buttons. While the cloth had the texture of a woman's skin, smooth and slightly cool as when you first touch it before it becomes flushed with excitement, the buttons reminded him of the small hard nipples of María Castaneda's breasts.

It was this analogy that finally convinced Emiliano to lay the shirt aside. "I'm staying here," he announced. "This is where I'm needed."

"It would be easy enough to inform your admirers of the truth about your injury," Sevilla said. "I remember well how you wept when you told me, knowing that you alone were responsible for the slaughter of your neighbors."

Emiliano's eyes narrowed. "And it would be easy enough to inform your patients of what a maricón you are."

The doctor drew his hand away as though it had been slapped. He stood and snatched his medical bag off the bed. "You'll get tired of them," he said. "You'll get tired of the way they moan and the way they smell. You'll get tired of their flabby breasts and their soft stomachs. And sooner or later, with only one young man in town, there's bound to be trouble, isn't there?"

"What kind of trouble?" Emiliano asked.

The doctor only looked at him, smiled as though he knew a secret, and sniffed. "Keep the shirt," he said. "It's my gift to a poor stupid boy. Maybe in a month or so I'll return to see how you're coming along."

Emiliano found the doctor's jealousy amusing. "Stay a while," he said consolingly. "My mother can make you something to eat before you go."

After Sevilla's departure Emiliano returned to his bedroom. Prostrate on his bed, he wondered if there could be any truth to Sevilla's prediction of inevitable trouble. It was something he did not wish to think about, but Sevilla's words kept returning to him. On the other hand, Sevilla was a capon, so how could he guess what a village full of women might or might not do?

To put the doctor's warning out of his mind, Emiliano turned his head toward the wall and watched a spider constructing a web in the corner of the room. Emiliano had always been fascinated by spiders. They never seemed to rest. They suspended their delicate doilies in out-of-the-way places, then crouched unobtrusively like dustballs and awaited their lunch. But why did spiders never get entangled in their own webs, Emiliano wondered. Because they knew where to step, how to tiptoe around trouble. Just like me, Emiliano told himself. Even so, there was something about the subtle horror of the spider's anticipation that filled Emiliano with a vague unease.

Later in the evening his mother looked in on him to inquire if everything was all right. He answered that the doctor had given him some medicine that made him sleepy, and would she please not disturb him again? He lay on his back and draped the pink silk shirt over his face and imagined it to be the perfumed hair of María Castaneda. So aroused did he become by his fantasy that he was barely able to wait for the fall of darkness so that he could climb through his bedroom window and, wearing his new silk shirt, hurry to María's house.

María Castaneda was only nineteen years old, but she lived alone because her husband, to whom she had been married just two short weeks, had been a member of the Regimiento Torrentino. Before being married she had acquired a reputation as a bold and adventuresome girl. Now she was just another widow, younger than most, but one of the many who prayed fervently each night that Emiliano would choose her window or door to come tapping upon.

This night Emiliano was barely into her bed, his new pink shirt hung carefully over the back of a chair, before María accused him of neglecting her.

"It's been four days since you were here last," she complained. "Do you expect me to be satisfied with that when you promised you would be back the very next night?"

"I'm sorry, I couldn't make it," he said, and allowed his hand to explore the firm fullness of her breasts, the slope of her stomach, and the warm gentle curve of her thighs.

"As you know, María, I have many other things to attend to."

"Things?" she said. "Is that what we are to you? I get awfully tired of waiting here by myself five nights a week while you attend to your other things. I'm a young woman and I need more attention than you've been giving me. Didn't you mean it when you said that I was your favorite?"

"Please, María," he said, snuggling up to her, her jealousy more than a little bit pleasing. "Believe me, I do everything I can to get to you sooner. I'm working myself to the bone."

She giggled at this and allowed him to move his hand in playful circles over her belly. Then she pushed his hand away. "Do you have more fun with any of the others?" she asked.

"Not half as much as with you," he answered honestly. "They all seem to take it too seriously. Some of them even pray afterward. They get down on their knees when they think I've fallen asleep and ask God to forgive them for their sins."

"But one of them gives you silk shirts."

"I have only one silk shirt so far," he told her. "But I've been promised a closetful."

"Who in this village can afford to give you a closetful of silk shirts? Is it Constancia Volutad? Or maybe that old hag, Alissa Márquez? I don't know how you can stand to be with her."

"She's barely thirty years old, María. Besides, when she prays it's not to ask forgiveness for her sins, but to ask for the opportunity to sin even more."

"Then she's the one? She gave you the silk shirt?"

"No," he teased. "But it's someone who likes me very much."

"How can I compete with someone who gives you silk shirts?" she asked angrily, and struck him so hard on the chest that he drew back, stunned, and blinking in the dimness stared down at her angry face. She had struck him as hard as she could with the ball of her fist, her clenched hand thudding against his sternum and causing him to lose his breath for a moment. He was torn between being flattered by her jealousy and wanting to slap her for having dared to strike him. But after a few moments he concluded to himself that her possessiveness was amusing, in fact satisfying; and above all else, it was understandable.

"I pay more attention to you than to any of the others," he told her. He stroked her hair and lowered his head to hers so that his lips brushed against her neck. "I have been with some of them only twice since I returned from the war, and then only because of my sense of civic duty. But I have been with you ten times so far."

"Only nine," she told him. "Counting tonight."

"Everyone knows that I think you're the prettiest," he said. He lowered his head to kiss her breasts. "Just the thought of you brings me running to you."

"So you've thought of me only nine times in over a month?"

"That's not what I meant. Sometimes I have other commitments. But it's always you I'm thinking of, María. When we lie in bed together like this you remind me of a cat, so sleek and graceful, the way you purr and rub yourself against me. And then there's that glint in your eye that reminds me that, like all beautiful cats, you are essentially untamable and perhaps even a little bit dangerous. The truth is, María, I am fascinated by you. I always have been. And no matter who I am with, I always close my eyes and pretend it is you lying beneath me."

"If that's true, she said, sliding her hand between their bodies to grip him firmly between the legs, "it shouldn't be such a hardship for you to marry me."

Her grip on him was slightly too secure to be pleasurable. Before answering he squirmed and tried to wriggle free, but she tightened her grip even more, lifted her leg over his hip, and rolled against him.

Afraid of what she might do to him in such a position, Emiliano chose his words carefully. "Marriage," he said, "would be best with a woman like you, María. But these are not ordinary circumstances. God has reached out and plucked me from the hand of Death. Obviously He has guided me home to Torrentino because He wants me to perform my special duty, whatever it might be, surrounded by my family and friends."

"I don't give a damn what God wants," María Castaneda said. Her face was so close to Emiliano's that he could feel her lips move. His own face felt as though he had accidentally put it into a spider's web, and María's moving lips and tongue were the spider's feathery crawl.

But now her entire body seemed to enfold him as she held open her legs and pulled him tight against her. He felt the slick warmth between her legs and the immediate surge of his own desire. Guiding him into her she slid her hands around his back and gripped his buttocks.

"This is what it's like to be mine," she whispered, her hands crawling up his spine, fingernails raking his vertebrae. "No one else can make you feel like this." Leaning heavily into him she rolled him onto his back, she rolling with him and coming up astride his pelvis, one palm pushing hard against his chest while the other reached behind her own buttocks and pulled on his testicles.

Emiliano closed his eyes and allowed his body to ride on the swell of darkness. He cupped her breast in his hand and tried to visualize other women, other lovers, but it was only María's image he could summon forth, only María's breast to fill his palm, the nipple as hard as a pearl button.

Moaning involuntarily beneath her, arching his pelvis toward the ceiling, he felt her hips grind down atop him and heard her voice asking again if he would marry her. He tried not to answer, to hold back all sounds. But just as he began to shudder and convulse, just as he felt his limbs explode, his arms and legs ricocheting off into space, the yes burst from him so much like a scream that María pressed her mouth to his to swallow the sound. Moments later he felt his exploded body gathering together again, hollow and weak, feeling almost tiny beneath the smiling girl and the sweetly purring darkness.

———

"I wanted you to say you would marry me," María told him later as they lay side by side, Emiliano's head resting sleepily on her arm, "before I told you about the gift I have for you."

Emiliano opened one eye and looked at her.

"It's not a silk shirt," she teased.

"What is it?"

"You try to guess. It's something that only a woman can give to a man."

"Just give it to me," he said, closing his eye. "I'm too sleepy to guess."

"I can't give it to you yet," she told him, and took his hand and laid it upon her lower abdomen, "because it's still in here."

"Oh, sweet Jesus," Emiliano groaned, and turned his face into the pillow.

"Actually, it's far too soon to be certain. But a woman always knows."

"But sweet Jesus, María, I'm only seventeen years old."

"Apparently that's old enough," she answered sarcastically. "I haven't been sleeping with Father Vallarte or any of the other dried-up old men in town, and I haven't yet attempted to seduce any of the little boys, so by all indications seventeen is a sufficient age to become a father."

Emiliano, who in his half-sleep had been considering ways to break his agreement to marry María, now merely groaned again and opened his mouth to bite the pillow.

"It hurts me that you're not as happy about this as I am," María said, though to Emiliano she did not sound especially hurt. "Of course I will allow you a certain amount of freedom; I would expect the same myself if the situation were reversed. And with you being used to having so many women, and the women used to having you, it's the most sensible thing for me to do. I don't want people accusing me of being unreasonable. One night a week to do as you please should be enough to keep everyone satisfied."

Emiliano wished that he were at home asleep in his mother's house.

"But now finally I'll have a little prestige of my own in this stinking little town," María said. "Constancia Volutad might be the only woman in town with a sewing machine, and Alissa Márquez might have the only talking parrot in a huge wrought-iron cage, but before long I'll be the only woman in Torrentino under sixty years old with a husband. And when the baby is born all of the women will gather around me and coo and murmur and be jealous of what I have. If you truly love me, Emiliano, you'd be happy for me. I'm giving you one night a week for which you won't have to make any excuses. It's more than any other woman in my position would do."

Emiliano, who was far too numbed by shock to think effectively, had already resigned himself to his fate. Half-heartedly he mumbled, "Two nights a week would be better."

María gave him her breast to suckle and answered, "It's time you started acting like a husband and a father."

––––––––

Accustomed to waking before dawn, Emiliano did so once again to creep from María's bed to his own in his mother's house. Just before falling asleep he remembered vaguely his conversation with María and, thinking it a dream, smiled to himself. But when he awoke around noon to find his mother measuring him for his wedding suit, he shuddered involuntarily and groaned. He had the feeling of being measured for his own burial.

Seeing his eyes flutter open, Teresa Fortunato flung herself upon her son and embraced him. "My Emiliano," she cried. "My little soldier. I'm so happy for you! You don't know how I've worried about you since your return, how I've worried about your sleepless nights and the lost, troubled look on your face. You don't know how I've feared that the loss of your arm might turn you into a bitter, brooding man and prevent you from ever marrying and giving me grandchildren. But God has blessed us, hasn't He, my son? Maybe in her youth María Castaneda was a little wild, but who isn't wild in her youth? She'll make a good wife for you, and you will be an excellent husband. Now straighten your legs so that I can measure you for your trousers. I think your father's suit is going to fit you nicely without having to be cut down."

All that day Emiliano lay awake in the shaded dusk of his room, feeling sorry for himself and cursing this cruel twist of fate. Maybe he should run away and take up residence in another village. But where in the world would he find another village comprised almost entirely of amorous women? Maybe it wouldn't be so bad being a father and a husband. What duties did a father and husband in Torrentino have, especially a father with one arm who would be excused from working in the garden, and who certainly could not be expected to do such woman's work as feeding the chickens or gathering grain or hauling wood for cooking? Maybe family life wouldn't be so distasteful after all. He would still have that one night a week María had promised him. And how happy the women would be to see him on that one night! How richly he would be received! It seemed that a few of the women had been growing bored with him lately, saying that he was impatient and selfish, an unsatisfying lover. But they would have to change their tune now or he would strike them off his schedule altogether. To tell the truth, he had of late been growing a little tired of the incessant bedhopping. It was almost a relief to he able to curtail his activities.

Emiliano weighed in his mind the pros and cons of being married to María Castaneda. But throughout the day his thoughts were frequently interrupted by the sound of female voices raised in argument in the front room or outside the house. Young and middle-aged women, upon hearing of Emiliano's impending marriage, came to assault him with their vehement disapproval, came to demand a denial. But Teresa Fortunato, surprised by her son's popularity, turned them all away. The desperate women, however, did not give up so easily. Alone, or sometimes in groups of two or three, they huddled outside Emiliano's bedroom window and cursed him. One of the women even broke the glass in the windowpane and rattled the shade.

"I still have one night a week," he whispered, hoping to placate them. "I promise to visit you first. You won't be forgotten. You know you're my favorite."

"You're the one who will not be forgotten," was the hissed reply.

Emiliano cowered on his bed. Just when he had convinced himself that marriage might not be so bad after all, something like this had to happen. The ferocity of these women, women he had known to be solicitous and gentle, soft-spoken and passionate, surprised and frightened him. He lay on his bed and stared dazedly at the spider web in the corner. The spider, a long-legged, hairy, black-bodied creature with a triangular green marking, had trapped a fly in its web and was in the process of methodically devouring it. Emiliano was horrified and yet intrigued by the silent spectacle. He felt his skin itch and imagined he could hear the spider's jaws crunching up and down on the doomed fly, its wings crinkling like stiff paper.

Later Teresa Fortunato dragged in the spare mattress which Emiliano used to lie on outside in the shade. "Look what somebody did," she said, and pointed to the knife slashings that crisscrossed the thin mattress and caused the stuffing to spill out.

"Who would do such a thing?" she asked him. "And why?"

Emiliano shrugged and sighed deeply. He rolled over and pushed his face into the pillow. Maybe being safely married to María was not such a bad idea after all.

———

María and Emiliano quickly settled into a comfortable routine. After the marriage they lived together in María's house, where Emiliano was treated by his new wife with much the same deference as he had received from his mother. When María was in a surly mood, troubled with morning sickness or some other temporary ailment, all Emiliano had to do was to walk down the dusty street to his mother's house. Teresa would fuss unsparingly over her son, inquire of his happiness, his state of health. She would fry tortillas and eggs for him, and sometimes even boil a scrawny chicken. Well fed and pampered, Emiliano would a few hours later return to his wife, who by then would remember what a valuable asset her husband was and would welcome him home with open arms.

Every Friday night Emiliano was free to go wherever he wished, to do as he pleased with no excuses or explanations. María had judiciously allotted him this night because on Friday nights Father Vallarte heard confessions in the small adobe church at the end of the street. María suspected, and not without some justification, that given the choice of consorting with a married man or receiving absolution of sins, at least some of the women would choose the latter. For although María wished to be fair to her husband and the women of Torrentino, she did not want Emiliano wearing himself thin. She reasoned that the women would not blame her if they failed to enjoy Emiliano's favors on a Friday night, but would recognize the responsibility in their own choice of absolution over sin. And to a certain degree her reasoning was valid. Father Vallarte, however, began to note late each Friday night that two or three women would appear successively for confession each with the musky scent of the bedroom still smelling on them as fresh as the scent of a newly plucked rose.

At the same time, Emiliano was noticing a different trend. An increasingly larger number of women chose to cross the street whenever he approached rather than pass him face to face. Sometimes it would even be one of the women with whom he had recently lain. Their doors, he discovered, might still be open to him on Friday nights, their pillows fluffed and their sheets still perfumed, but some of these same women, in the light of day, gave him wide berth, or simply turned downcast eyes at his flirtatious wink.

Some he spotted more frequently in the company of Argentina Neruda, who, it was rumored, was now regularly conducting public displays of her rituals in her home. Emiliano heard reports that her campaign to expose him as an evil spirit was now more vigorous than ever.

One morning he walked outside to find Argentina Neruda dragging a dead chicken around his house, the chicken's head digging a shallow furrow in the dust to complete a wide circle. While doing this Argentina Neruda puffed frantically on a fat cigar, keeping a cloud of smoke around her head in order to cleanse the air of evil influences.

Emiliano laughed and called her a demented old bag of bones. Snatching the dead chicken from her he flung it back into her face. He then walked off down the street to visit his mother, leaving the old sorceress huffing and puffing on her cigar.

Despite these diversions, it was not long before Emiliano began to feel that his life was assuming an unpleasant odor of sameness. He had been married for less than three months, and yet already he found his daily routine boring. No longer was it exciting to lie in bed all day and dream of María's ripe young body, a body which recently had begun to hint of the bloated appearance of being overly ripe. Nor did the anticipation of sneaking out for a night of stolen pleasure fill him with nervous arousal anymore. His Friday night schedule was widely known, perhaps by everyone in the village except his mother. And to vary from this schedule was, at least as the women saw it, unconscionable; María was being more than generous with her husband, and the other women in town, no matter how much they secretly wished to, would not dishonor the limits of her generosity.

Even sitting in the late morning hours on the shaded steps of Father Vallarte's church with a handful of old men soon became a tiresome routine for Emiliano. At first he regaled these old men with tales of the battle, of whizzing bullets and clashing sabers. But how many times could you tell the same story to the same assemblage of wrinkled faces and rheumy eyes and manage to retain even your own enthusiasm? He took to entertaining them with ribald descriptions of the attributes of each of the young women in town, remarking how this one's tongue was as long and as active as a lizard's, how that one had an almond-colored birthmark in a certain place which, when you kissed it, had the same effect as touching a lighted match to a string of firecrackers.

Though stories such as these would for a moment bring erect posture back to each of the old men, would perhaps even cause them to shudder once or twice with the expulsion of a melancholic tear, more often than not Father Vallarte joined the men there on the steps, in which case the talk turned to the weather, to unanswered, indifferent speculations of whether or not the distant revolution still lived. All too often the men spoke of nothing at all, but sat and watched a threadbare dog sitting in the dust and licking himself, watched a tarantula being harassed by a chicken, or watched an occasional breeze push an occasional cloud across the sky.

So Emiliano Fortunato was not altogether displeased when once again he heard the clopping of horse's hooves and looked up from his seat on the church steps to see Dr. Sevilla, astride his dusty gelding, come jouncing down the street. In fact the alacrity with which he hurried out to greet Sevilla convinced the old men that the doctor and the boy were friends of long standing.

After exchanging perfunctory greetings with Sevilla, Emiliano took the horse's reins and led the animal, with Sevilla still astride it and grinning like a little boy on a carnival ride, to Teresa Fortunato's house. There the doctor and the boy went into Emiliano's former bedroom for a brief examination, Sevilla explained to Teresa. After assuring himself and Emiliano that the wound was completely healed, Dr. Sevilla lowered the shades and then sat on the bed very close to the boy.

"So," Sevilla said, unable to conceal his happiness, "by the way you greeted me I would guess that you're finally ready to leave this God-forsaken place and come home with me."

Emiliano shook his head. "I'm a married man now," he explained. "My wife is going to have a baby."

Dr. Sevilla looked as though he had been kicked in the groin. His eyes brimmed with tears and he emitted a soft clicking noise from the back of his throat.

"My poor stupid boy," he said when he recovered enough to speak. He laid his hand on Emiliano's thigh. "Don't say such a thing if it isn't true. If all you want is to drive me away again, please don't tell such an awful lie."

"It's not a lie," Emiliano said. "Though sometimes I wish it were. I married María Castaneda because such a thing is a man's responsibility. She's just beginning her fourth month."

Sevilla slumped forward, his head falling into Emiliano's lap, and wept. "It's my fault," the doctor moaned. "I shouldn't have stayed away so long. I thought it best to give you time to get thoroughly fed up with this place. But you're just a poor stupid boy and I gave you too much time, and now look what's become of you."

Emiliano felt a curious twinge of sympathy for the doctor, and stroked Sevilla's hair.

"Before you go," Emiliano said to Sevilla as they stood outside Teresa Fortunato's home, "would you mind taking a look at my wife? Just to make certain that the baby is healthy and that María is in no danger."

They walked together, Emiliano leading the horse, to María's house. María was very happy to be examined by a bona fide doctor; she had been worried lately of Argentina Neruda's resentment of her, and to be tended by a midwife with such primitive beliefs and prejudices did not instill in María the soundest of confidences.

Dr. Sevilla, his superciliousness lost on María, laid his palm on her rounded belly, put his ear to her abdomen and listened for the fetal heartbeat, palpated her breasts, peered at the pupils of her eyes, inquired of her diet, and finally pronounced her as healthy as a cornfed sow.

Though she did not care for the analogy nor for what she mistook as

Sevilla's cold professional manner, María was grateful for the diagnosis. She offered him coffee, and he, smiling snidely at Emiliano, accepted. While María was preparing the coffee Sevilla went outside and removed a package from his saddlebags.

Seated again beside Emiliano in the tiny living room, María still busy with her back to them in the kitchen, Dr. Sevilla handed the package to Emiliano and whispered, "After the way you've behaved, I don't know why I'm even bothering to give this to you. You should be ashamed of what you've done to me."

But Emiliano felt no shame. Upon seeing the two silk shirts inside the package, one bright yellow and the other a deep lavender, he felt a familiar twinge of arousal as he ran his forefinger over a smooth collar, as he crushed a silky sleeve against his cheek and felt the cool, hard pearl buttons upon his skin.

Emiliano looked up to see María standing in front of him. She stared at him quizzically, holding Sevilla's cup of coffee in her right hand.

"Well, give him his drink," Emiliano scolded her. "Or do you expect him to come and lap it up out of your hand?"

María handed Sevilla the cup. He accepted it, she thought, with an almost lordly air, as though to convey to her what a great favor he was doing by drinking her coffee.

"Look at the gifts Dr. Sevilla brought," Emiliano said, and held the shirts up by their collars. María grasped the tail of each shirt between a finger and thumb and silently admired their color and texture. Then it occurred to her that Emiliano already had one silk shirt, a pink one whose origins he had never explained.

Now Emiliano saw the way his wife glanced back and forth from himself to the doctor, and became suddenly aware of the implications of Sevilla's gift.

"One of them is for you," Emiliano quickly explained. "They are Dr. Sevilla's wedding gift to us. Take your pick. One is for you and one is for me."

"Both are the same size," María said, thinking out loud. "Either one will be too large for me."

"Wasn't it smart of Dr. Sevilla to bring one that will fit over your new belly?" Emiliano's hands had begun to perspire, and there was a band of beaded moisture forming on his upper lip.

María looked at the doctor. "How did you know I was pregnant?"

Sevilla smiled and took a sip of coffee.

He has a smile like an egg-stealing fox, María thought.

Emiliano laughed nervously. "What new wife isn't pregnant within a month or two? And after the child is born you can cut the shirt down to fit you more snugly, or just keep it until you become pregnant again. It's a beautiful gift, isn't it? How many women in Torrentino own a silk shirt? Take whichever one you want, María. Personally, I think you would look best in the purple one, don't you, Dr. Sevilla?"

The doctor merely smiled at María, his piercing hawk eyes unblinking. Taking the yellow shirt from her husband's hand, María threw it over her shoulder, said "Thank you very much for the lovely gift," then turned and went into the bedroom.

"Why didn't you help me?" Emiliano whispered to the doctor.

Now Sevilla turned his smile on the boy. "Did you ask for my help in getting her pregnant? Did you accept my help when I offered you a home? You're just a poor stupid boy, Emiliano, and from now on when you get yourself in a tight spot, I'm just going to sit back and watch you squirm the way you've been making me squirm."

Saying this, the doctor set down his cup and stood to leave. Emiliano walked him to the door. He was trying frantically to think of some way to detain the doctor, to get him to stay for a day or two without leading him to any unwanted conclusions. Having someone besides women and tired old men to talk with for a while had been a treat for Emiliano, and he knew that, given time, he and the doctor might discover many interests in common. The truth was that, in the midst of a crowd, Emiliano had begun to feel quite lonely. It was like having nothing to drink meal after meal except sweet wine. Eventually you would begin to thirst for a sip of water.

But before Emiliano could think of anything to deter the doctor, Sevilla pulled open the door to stride outside. Blocking his progress, however, were five young women.

"We heard there was a doctor here," the first one said. Her name was

Rosarita Calderón, a pretty, unmarried girl of sixteen with whom Emiliano had spent many pleasurable hours. Her bedroom was separated from her mother's (another room which Emiliano had occasionally visited) by only a thin wall of plasterboard, and when Emiliano was with Rosarita she would hold her pillow over her face so as not to awaken her mother with the uncontrollable squeals of ecstasy she made.

Also in the group were others whose bedroom windows Emiliano had squeezed through at one time or another. In fact, looking over the faces, he saw with horror that there was not one among them he had not known in an intimate manner.

"If it's not too much to ask," Rosarita continued, "we would be extremely grateful if the doctor would consent to take a look at us. Each of us has been troubled lately with a minor ailment, and it would put our minds to rest if we could each receive a brief examination."

With a questioning arch of his eyebrows Sevilla turned to look at the boy. Emiliano had already begun to sweat profusely, and at the same time to shiver. He stumbled back into the house and, like a timid child, watched from around the doorjamb as Rosarita Calderón led the doctor away, the other women following quietly behind.

Throughout that day Emiliano observed from his doorway as Dr. Sevilla was led at intervals of a half hour or so from one house to the next. Darkness fell and Emiliano tended to the gelding tethered outside. María, as she prepared her husband's dinner, wore her new yellow silk shirt, the long tails flaring out over her skirt, the sleeves rolled up and pinned at the wrist.

Emiliano was too nervous to eat. He only picked at his food. "Aren't you feeling well?" María asked. He stared blankly as though he failed to recognize her. María cleared away the dishes and hummed to herself, making Emiliano wonder what it was that made her so cheerful.

Eventually Emiliano's nervousness got the better of him. He went outside and ran down the street to his mother's house. "I just want to be alone for a while," he told Teresa, and headed for the sanctuary of his former bedroom. "Please don't disturb me or allow any other woman to disturb me tonight."

Lying on his bed Emiliano anxiously massaged the stump of his amputated arm. What did all those women want with Dr. Sevilla? He knew by the way his amputated arm throbbed that he was somehow involved. Maybe he even knew what "minor ailment" troubled the women, but he would not allow the thought to take concrete form in his mind.

It was nearly midnight when Dr. Sevilla finally stumbled in and fell on the bed beside Emiliano. Emiliano, wide awake, lay as still as a corpse.

Finally Sevilla heaved a heavy sigh and sat up. "You've been a busy little rooster, haven't you?" he asked.

Emiliano groaned.

"What a horrible day this has been," Sevilla said. "Nearly every woman in town has tried to seduce me." He patted Emiliano affectionately on the rump. "But don't worry, not one of them succeeded. My virtue remains intact."

Emiliano felt a glimmer of hope. "That's all they wanted of you?" he asked, rolling over to face the doctor. "To get you into bed?"

"Not quite," Sevilla answered. "It seems that seven women in this village, not counting your wife, of course, will within five to eight months have little Emilianos clinging to their bosoms."

Emiliano felt a surge of nausea overtake him. He jumped up, ran to the window and pushed it open, hoping to steady himself with deep drafts of fresh air. But when he leaned out over the windowsill he saw a young girl, her slender body barely showing the first buds of womanhood, standing not far away, staring moon-eyed at his window while she hugged herself suggestively and rocked on her heels. He ducked inside again, pulled shut the window and yanked down the shade. Fearing that he might soon pass out from dizziness, he flung himself face down on his bed.

Dr. Sevilla regarded him with a mixture of amusement and disdain. "How could you have been so stupid?" he asked. "Didn't it ever occur to you where all of your whorish rutting might lead? Didn't you ever once stop to think that if it could happen to María it could happen to the other women as well?"

Emiliano was seized by a fit of shivering, and began to sob.

"There, there," Sevilla said, and stroked Emiliano's back. "The damage is done, you might as well face up to it. But you needn't worry, I'm not going to abandon you now. I've decided to be godfather to your children. I'll make certain they all come into this godforsaken world red-faced and healthy."

Emiliano could not bring himself to roll over or even to mumble his thanks to the doctor. Sevilla seemed almost to revel in this latest misfortune. Emiliano lay with one eye pressed to the pillow, the other eye staring dully at the dusty spider web in the corner in which the dried and empty shell of a fly was irrevocably trapped.

"Imagine," Dr. Sevilla said, softly chuckling as he ran his hand up and down the back of Emiliano's leg, "a poor, stupid one-armed boy such as yourself, valiantly assuming the task of repopulating a devastated village. It's too bad you don't have a newspaper in this town, Emiliano. What a wonderful story this would make."

———————

In the morning Emiliano viewed Torrentino through new eyes. He had returned to his own home the previous night to a fitful, agitated sleep, leaving Sevilla snoring comfortably in Teresa Fortunato's house. Shortly after sunup Sevilla came by for his horse and found Emiliano standing a few feet back in his open doorway, peering out with the temerity of a man afraid of the sun.

Sevilla laughed. "How do you like your little garden of Eden this morning?" he asked.

"Shhhh!" Emiliano said. María was still asleep and Emiliano dreaded facing her, dreaded her reaction when the awful news of his profligacy became known. "I thought you promised to stick by me now," he said.

Sevilla looked happier than Emiliano had seen him in a long time. "You really need me now, don't you?" Sevilla said. He tightened up the cinches on his saddle, put his foot in the stirrup and climbed atop the gelding. "I didn't make arrangements for a prolonged visit," he explained, "so first I have to return home for a while. But don't worry, little papa. I'll be back soon to see how your family is coming along."

Leaning over the saddlehorn then, clasping the gelding's sleek neck, Sevilla whispered, "I'm only coming back as a favor to you, Emiliano. When this is all over with I expect the same consideration from you."

Emiliano nodded dully. Standing in the shadow of his doorway he watched Sevilla ride away.

When María awoke she put on her new silk shirt and came padding out to the kitchen in her bare feet. There she found her husband slumped forward with his head on the table. She gathered a few sticks of wood from the kindling box and built a small fire in the stove. After setting on the morning coffee she turned to Emiliano and said, "You were late coming home last night."

He lifted his head, lifting it slowly, as though it were either extremely fragile or extremely heavy. "I was with Dr. Sevilla," he explained.

María nodded. "Just so you weren't somewhere you shouldn't have been." There was a strange quality to her voice, a teasing lightness that puzzled Emiliano. "It isn't Friday night yet, you know."

"There will be no more Friday nights," Emiliano said.

"What are you talking about?" She scooped flour from an earthen crock into a deep bowl and added a half-ladle of water from a covered bucket beside the stove. Working the dough with her strong fingers she shaped it into a ball, pulled off a chunk, and flattened it expertly between her palms. She tossed the tortilla into a skillet in which there was hot lard. The smell of the tortilla frying made Emiliano nauseous.

"I said," María repeated, "what are you talking about? What do you mean there will be no more Fridays?"

"Never mind," Emiliano said. He stood up and went out the door.

Almost reflexively Emiliano headed for his mother's house. But three-quarters of the way there he realized that even that sanctuary would be closed to him now. How could he face such a loving and trusting woman, only to tell her that she would soon be grandmother not only to María's child but to seven squealing bastards as well?

Hurrying past his mother's house Emiliano wished that Sevilla had not ridden off so early. Now that Emiliano had his senses about him, he might be inclined to join the doctor, if only to escape for the time being the unpleasantness about to befall him. Within a matter of hours the entire town would know of his sexual extravagance. For the sake of his own skin, he thought it best that he get away somewhere for a while.

Standing at the end of the unpaved street, at that point where the narrow street tapered off to little more than a rutted goat path, with the village of Torrentino behind him and nothing but the side of the mountain ahead,

Emiliano came to a halt. Where could he run? Where would he be safe for a few hours from the wrath of his wife, his mother's humiliation, the villagers' scorn? Dear God, Emiliano prayed, if you truly saved me from the battle, if you see me standing down here now as confused as a dog that's been kicked in the head by its master, please forgive the lies I have told and the wasteful life I have been living. I will right all of these wrongs, dear God, if you will forgive me and save me one last time and show me some small sign that all of this senselessness is your divine will.

On Emiliano's right the door of the Mother of the Holy Infant church swung open. Father Vallarte shuffled out of the door and, looking even too feeble to push the straw broom he clung to, began to sweep the dust from the steps. Soon the other old men of the village would be gathering there to watch the day pass. Emiliano turned, raced across the street and bounded up the steps.

"Father," Emiliano said, "I need urgently to talk with you. It is very important. A matter of life and death."

Father Vallarte looked first at Emiliano, then at the straw broom in his own gnarled hands. For fifty years now he had been sweeping the steps of the Mother of the Holy Infant church at precisely this hour each morning. After sweeping the steps he would go inside and run a dampened cloth over the pews and the altar table. If he finished these chores in time he would then return outside to sit with the other old men for an hour or so. Then he would prepare for himself a light lunch, and then lie down for his siesta. After the siesta came a brief period of unscheduled time during which he read his Bible or played a few hands of solitaire.

But these young Indians, he thought, have no respect for the value of a daily schedule. Upset one aspect and you upset the entire schedule. He suggested that Emiliano return in the evening, and then resumed his sweeping of the steps.

Emiliano glanced up the street just in time to see Rosarita Calderón going into his wife's house. Groaning audibly, he pushed his way past Father Vallarte and fled inside the church.

Father Vallarte methodically swept all of the dust off the four church steps. He swept from left to right, from the top step to the bottom. Afterwards, inside the church, he set the broom in a corner, lifted the square of woolen cloth from the nail in the wall on which it hung, dampened the cloth with water from the holy water fount, and began to wipe off the seats and backrests of the single row of pews. He worked from the rear to the front, from the left side of the pew to the right. On the fifth pew from the rear he was forced to pause momentarily while Emiliano, who had been lying curled like a frightened caterpillar on the seat, crawled out of the way.

Emiliano crept to the door and peered out. Already a few old men were lounging on the church steps. They were leaning forward and craning their necks to see up the street. Outside Emiliano's house, several women stood in a group. Emiliano recognized María's face among them. He ducked back inside the church and hid himself in the confessional.

When Father Vallarte finished wiping off the pews he wiped off the rickety scarred desk that served as his altar. Then he shook out and straightened the altar cloth. He rinsed out the soiled cleaning rag in a bucket of water, emptied the bucket in the street, and came back inside to hang the cloth to dry on its nail in the wall. Afterward he returned outside to sit for a while with the old men and to wonder with them about what was happening up the street at Emiliano Fortunato's house.

———

Emiliano had no idea how long he remained in the cramped confessional. It seemed as though he had been there for an entire day. In his mind he had watched the sun travel across the sky to sink far below the mountain. So when María came and led him away by the hand, out of the church and back up the street, he was more than a little surprised to view the sun nearly directly overhead, the old men not yet adjourned from their seats on the church steps.

What punishment, Emiliano wondered, did María have in store for him? When she came and took him by the hand she had said very little, only "What are you doing in here? Come on, I've been looking for you." And now, leading him up the street, she actually smiled, as though whatever punishment she had in mind was going to bring her great satisfaction.

Emiliano prayed that María would remember that it was she who had proposed the Friday night schedule. For himself, he would have been content to act the role of the faithful husband, to do what every other faithful husband did and sneak away now and then for a little stolen love in the moonlight. But no; María had coerced him into a strict routine, a well-supervised schedule of infidelity. When thought of in that way, there could be no doubt that all of this baby-making business was María's fault.

"It's all your fault," he told her.

She pulled him along and said nothing. From behind the windows and doors that they passed, women peered out and smiled at him. Had they conspired on some devious retribution, some sinister plan of punishment that made each of them giggle with a perverse glee? He could have broken away and run, could have knocked María down and barricaded himself in his own house. But he felt weak and dizzy and was barely able to keep his feet beneath him. He shuffled along through the dust and felt like a schoolboy being led away to be spanked.

María pushed open the door to her house and then stood aside so that Emiliano could enter first. He slouched across the room, expecting to be berated and assaulted, maybe even to have María pounce on him from behind and box his ears. Instead he saw the kitchen table stacked high with gifts. A recently plucked chicken curled like a fetus in a clay bowl, and in another bowl were a half-dozen delicate quail eggs. Beside this was a jar of amaranth seeds, and hung over the back of a chair an ochre-colored handwoven vest called a xicholi. There were tiny cakes molded in the shape of animals, a clay pot filled with ripened coffee beans, a large yellow gourd heavy with intoxicating pulque, a pair of men's bedroom slippers, slightly worn, and two complete spools of blue thread.

Emiliano felt María's hand at the back of his neck, her fingers affectionately twirling his hair. He shivered. What did she have up her sleeve?

"From now on we're going to live like a king and queen," María said.

Dizzy with confusion, Emiliano asked, "What is all this?"

"Tokens of respect from the mothers of your children," she said. "And later there are bound to be even more. Constancia Volutad has promised that I can use her sewing machine any time I wish. And look in here in the bedroom; see what I managed to coax from Alissa Márquez."

In the corner of the bedroom, beneath the window, sat a huge black wrought-iron birdcage. It was four feet wide by four feet long, shaped like a Chinese pagoda and with a center height of at least three and a half feet. Perched on a swinging bar near the top of the cage and returning Emiliano's unblinking gaze was a green and white parrot. The bird and its elaborate cage had been Alissa Márquez's wedding gift from her husband eleven years earlier, hauled from Orizaba and up the mountainside on the back of a burro. It had been Alissa's pride and joy ever since, openly coveted not only by María but by many of the other villagers as well, and Emiliano was amazed that his wife had been able to talk Alissa into parting with it.

"Is Alissa . . . ?" he managed to say, nearly choking on his words.

"Not yet. But I had to promise that you will pay special attention to her from now on. She wants a baby so badly. I didn't have the heart to refuse her."

Emiliano wondered if this was some kind of a trick. "You're not angry with me?" he asked.

"Why would I be angry? Because you've made me the richest woman in town? How could something like this not happen, with you visiting two or three women every Friday night? Didn't you realize it was inevitable? My only concern was that I should be the first to bear a child, which I shall be, but only by a few weeks judging from the looks of Rosarita Calderón's belly. And I admit that I was a little worried at first that one of the younger girls might steal you away from me, that you might fall in love with someone else. But that hasn't happened, has it? And just look what we have now! And who knows—in a month or so there might be more mothers-to-be to shower us with gifts. There are at least a half-dozen women who have come to me expressing their desire to have a child. With no husbands, what other hope for a comfortable old age do the women in this village have? I promised them that you will continue with the Friday night schedule. I think it best that we do this on an orderly, limited basis. If we are careful and plan effectively, we can assure ourselves of ten children a year for the next several years."

Emiliano felt his legs go rubbery. He groped for a kitchen chair, pulled it away from the table, and slumped into it.

"And as those children grow older," María continued, speaking more to herself than to her dazed husband, "they will all come to you for advice and guidance. I, of course, will be their godmother, and I too will exert a considerable influence over their lives. We're going to be the king and queen of Torrentino," she said, and hugged Emiliano's head against her swollen breasts.

"God spared you from death on the battlefield and brought you home to me for just this purpose. From Torrentino your seed will spill down over the mountain and into a hundred other villages. In years to come your name will be more famous than those of Moctezuma, Zapata, or even King Solomon!"

The table upon which Emiliano's hands rested began to sway beneath him. His vision blurred and the room began to spin. Emiliano felt his head rolling back and forth on his neck. He was going to be a national hero, a one-armed Biblical legend? Emiliano Fortunato slumped forward and passed out.

———————

Teresa Fortunato, though initially shocked by the news that her hazel-eyed son had become "papacito grande," soon discovered that, as mother of the village progenitor, she too enjoyed a sudden elevation of social status. Young women whose bellies had not yet even begun to bulge with life came to confer with her about the tailoring of baby clothes, about how a child should be raised so as to grow into a brave and unselfish adult like papacito grande himself. Women who yearned for motherhood begged Teresa's advice on how to prepare her son's favorite food, how best to attract his attention, if only for an hour at a time. Older women beyond the age of child-bearing came to sit with her, hoping that by proximity they might also be referred to as grandmother and treated with respect. All listened reverentially to stories about how Emiliano even as an infant displayed signs of greatness. The fact that their recollections of Emiliano as a child were not consistent with Teresa's did not seem to disturb them.

Emiliano himself, after recovering from his dizzy spell, quickly adapted to the role of papacito grande and found it to be not at all a disagreeable role. His wife accorded him a newfound courtesy, his mother an almost obsequious deference. Each day he was courted by young women who wanted nothing more than the honor of laundering his shirts or combing out his hair. From the old men who gathered daily on the steps of the Mother of the Holy Infant church he was awarded the uppermost step. The deteriorating old men huddled at his feet as though he were a Zen master who possessed the secret of eternal youth.

Only two sour notes were sounded during this happiest of times for Emiliano. The first came, of course, from Argentina Neruda, who frightened the young women by announcing that their babies were actually reincarnated souls of their slaughtered husbands and fathers and brothers and boyfriends, returning to Torrentino to seek revenge against the liar and coward Emiliano Fortunato, a man with whom they had each consorted and who was probably an evil spirit himself.

The second disparagement, though not as sour as the first, came at the hands of Father Vallarte. Troubled by the questionable propriety of Emiliano's patriarchal status, the old priest nightly searched his heart and petitioned the Lord for some evidence that this epidemic of pregnancies was God's will and not Satan's. Receiving no such evidence, Father Vallarte would every now and then studiously regard Emiliano as he sat on the church steps, and even on occasion inquire seriously of the boy, "But how can we be certain that this is a good thing?"

Emiliano assumed that the old man had finally lost his senses, and subsequently told everyone, including Father Vallarte himself, exactly that.

In this manner the remote village of Torrentino, perched on the side of a mountain, watched another three months pass. At the end of March Dr. Sevilla came riding into town on his dusty, tired gelding. After examining ten pregnant women, the doctor returned to the house of Emiliano and María Fortunato.

"You should give some thought to moving permanently to Torrentino," Emiliano told the doctor. "What's happening in this village could someday make you nearly as famous as me."

The doctor thought Emiliano's tone of voice more than a little condescending, and promptly told him so.

"You were a great help to me once," Emiliano said. "And I realize that no man attains greatness without the aid of several smaller, less important people. I simply want to do a little favor for you in return. Do you have something against seeing your name inscribed in the annals of history?"

Sitting in Emiliano's living room, a room now lavishly decorated with all manner of gifts—fans and baskets woven of straw, hand-woven tapestries, colorful pictures torn from two-year-old magazines and mounted on boards—Dr. Sevilla found the change that had overcome his former patient hard to believe. Emiliano seemed nearly as bloated as his wife, as arrogant as a retired fighting cock. When María, now fat as a heifer ready for the slaughterhouse, excused herself and went off to bed, Sevilla told Emiliano, "I had planned to stay for a while, though not permanently. You seem to have forgotten the agreement we made. So now I think I'll stay just long enough to watch this illusory world of yours come crashing down atop you."

"The world I have created is no illusion," Emiliano said.

"You poor stupid boy. You've been so gorged on stories of your own importance that you've actually come to believe them, haven't you? Don't you realize that these women don't value *you*, they value the output of your glands. Who in this village really loves you for yourself—or perhaps I should say in spite of yourself? Probably no one but me. You're just a poor stupid boy with one arm and the only ready supply of sperm in town."

Emiliano flushed with anger. The veins in his neck bulged and his eyes flew open. Leaping to his feet he flung open the door. "Cabrón!" Emiliano shouted, clenching his fist. "Choirboy! Get out of my house and don't ever come back!"

Dr. Sevilla emitted a soft click from the back of his throat. Chuckling softly, he stood and went outside. Emiliano slammed the door shut behind him. Sevilla walked down the street and spent a comfortable night at the home of Teresa Fortunato in the childhood bed of her son, the illustrious stud.

———

Teresa Fortunato became Dr. Sevilla's assistant. When young girls came for an examination, it was Teresa who met them at the door, who counseled the mother-to-be on how best to care for her unborn child, which foods and activities should be avoided and which could be indulged. She exacted payment from each patient, insisting that even the briefest of visits be paid for, if only with a warm brown egg or a handful of coffee beans. She considered it an honor to have the esteemed Dr. Sevilla as her houseguest, even if he rejected the women's advances, and when Emiliano reproached her for boarding Sevilla she defended herself philosophically.

"If you had been slain on the battlefield with all of your brave neigh-bors," she said, "what would I now have, Emiliano? Would I be looked up to and respected by all the other women, or would I be just another childless mother rotting with grief? Are you going to deny me my one opportunity to hold my head up high? Do you think it was mere chance that first led you to Dr. Sevilla? Do you think it was chance that directed the bullet into your arm and not into your heart? Don't you know, my son, that everything is for a purpose? Even here in Torrentino, in this tiny village made of straw and sun-baked mud, even here we are cradled in the palm of God's hand. If Dr. Sevilla has come to live in my house it is because God has directed him to do so. You have become a great man, Emiliano, but are you so great as to believe that God no longer exerts an influence upon your life?"

Emiliano shook his head in disgust and walked away. If his mother wanted to house that clove-sucking cabrón, then he would not try to stop her. But she must be as crazy as Vallarte to believe that God had deliber-ately sent Sevilla to them. That God had given them Emiliano to raise Torrentino from the dust there could be no doubt. But a clove-sucking, silk-shirt-wearing girl-faced cabrón of a doctor like Sevilla? Ha! There was about as much chance of that being true as there was of Emiliano losing his kingdom.

———————

As the days passed, Argentina Neruda sat in her darkened hut and brooded. Even the handful of women who a few months earlier had joined in her ritual anathematizing of Emiliano had now abandoned her. Why could no one see that devil of a boy as she saw him?

Seated at her kitchen table Argentina Neruda stared down at the con-tents of the bowl in front of her. Into the clay bowl she had spilled the vis-cera of a wild duck. By the undulations and alignment of the viscera she could read the will of Huitzilopochtli, the stern and exacting hummingbird god. Argentina had come upon the wild duck yesterday on her daily trip to gather wood for her stove and herbs for her incantations. The duck, its wing broken as it lay on the bank of a small pond, was nearly dead when she found it. She had carried the duck home, fed it a mash of ground maize and water, and this morning put a sharp knife to its belly and spilled its vis-cera into the enameled bowl.

She studied the viscera for a long time, employing the same skills of intuition once employed by powerful Aztec priests. Finally she was satisfied that she saw in them confirmation of Emiliano's evil. Afterward she prayed to Huitzilopochtli and thanked him for his message of truth. Then, without bothering to remove the duck's head or webbed feet, she boiled the plucked fowl in a pot of steaming water. The intestines she deep-fried in lard until they puffed up crisp and brown. A side dish of delicate water-fly eggs completed her afternoon meal.

When María Fortunato went into labor, Emiliano forgot for the moment that he had not spoken to Dr. Sevilla for several weeks and went running down the street shouting the doctor's name. It was ten in the morning and Sevilla was just finishing a breakfast of fried eggs topped with a spicy tomato and chili pepper relish, tortillas, and strong black coffee, which Teresa Fortunato had cheerfully prepared and served to him.

Hearing his name being shouted so urgently, and in Emiliano's voice, Sevilla smiled to himself. He wiped his mouth on his handkerchief, rose out of his chair, and met the boy at the door.

"María is having her baby!" Emiliano cried, breathless and redfaced, his hazel eyes wide with worry. Teresa Fortunato sighed happily and hurried out of the house.

"Hurry, please!" Emiliano urged the doctor.

Sevilla smiled calmly. "Why?" he asked.

"Why? Sweet Jesus, I told you; María is having her baby!"

"So?" Sevilla said.

"What do you mean, so? Aren't you coming? She needs you!"

"The midwife can attend to her."

"I don't want that old witch near María! Please, doctor, I know you're angry with me, but can't you forget about it for now? I'm sorry I said what I did. Won't you please come? María needs you!"

"You're sorry?" Sevilla asked.

"Yes, truly, a hundred times!"

Lifting his chin into the air, Sevilla smiled, satisfied. He went into the bedroom for his medical bag, then returned to follow Emiliano out of the house. Emiliano ran ahead of him up the street, shouting over his shoulder for the doctor to please hurry. Sevilla walked casually, humming to himself, enjoying the fullness of his belly and the warmth of the morning sun. From his shirt pocket he took a clove and popped it in his mouth.

After nineteen hours, at five the following morning, María Fortunato was still in labor. The baby was in a breech position and Dr. Sevilla could not get it turned around. The umbilical cord had wrapped itself around the infant and allowed no freedom of movement. Dr. Sevilla, at the end of those nineteen hours, was as distraught as Emiliano. His white silk shirt was splattered with blood, his face splotchy with perspiration.

María was so weak and near death herself that Sevilla had no option but to sever the umbilical and pull the infant out by its feet. He carried only weak anesthetics and lacked the proper instruments to perform a cesarean. With a pair of forceps he pulled the slack out of the umbilical cord and snipped it free. For the next ten minutes he struggled, María now unconscious, to get the infant out. The baby, a boy, was of course stillborn. Emiliano ran from the house screaming, pounding his fist against the side of his head. Teresa Fortunato put her face in her hands, chewed at the calloused flesh of her palms, and wept.

When the news of the stillborn child reached the crowd of women who had been standing vigil through the night outside Emiliano's house, Argentina Neruda burst into the house and hovered over the baby. She unwrapped the umbilical from around its neck and blew air into the baby's face. When this had no effect she seized Emiliano's sombrero off its peg in the wall and fanned the wide-brimmed hat over the infant. She fanned frantically, rocking back and forth, spitting out angry chants while Sevilla, shaking his head, slumped against the wall.

Finally Argentina Neruda too gave up and leaned back. She laid the sombrero aside and pronounced the baby in *miccatzintli*, the state of death. A few minutes later she told the women outside that, had she been permitted to preside at the birthing, she could have saved the child. But without the buffer of her presence, Huitzilopochtli had sought his revenge against the village through María. Emiliano had planted a seed of tragedy and Huitzilopochtli had caused that seed to sprout. The same seed, she predicted, grew inside every pregnant woman in town.

A pall fell over Torrentino. Though the pregnant women reassured themselves of the fallaciousness of Argentina Neruda's prediction, they lost their capacity for gaiety and spent their nights filling the front pews of the Mother of the Holy Infant church. Father Vallarte led them in somber prayers for the health of their unborn children. They each in turn made vows reaffirming their faith, and then lit candle after candle beseeching the souls of the dead to intervene on their behalves.

Upon Dr. Sevilla they descended daily. Sevilla cautioned them against shamanism and stupidity. The older women and those not yet pregnant, though they sympathized with María's tragic loss, studiously avoided the Fortunato home. Alissa Márquez made it known that she wanted her wrought-iron birdcage and parrot back, and were it not that she would have had to confront Emiliano himself, she would have demanded that it be returned to her. Many of the other women, as they had done earlier, now avoided looking Emiliano in the eye or passing too close to him on the street.

Emiliano did his best to console his wife, but he was little comfort to her. Her complexion remained pallid even two weeks after the tragedy. She had little appetite and slept fitfully. She sometimes walked in her sleep, sometimes screamed so loud in the middle of the night that the entire village sat up in their beds. Emiliano suspected that she was among the growing number of women who once again were surreptitiously seeking advice from Argentina Neruda, women who knelt and prayed with Father Vallarte and then ten minutes later requested that the sorceress rattle her pouch of animal teeth for them.

And each night, after the women had silently filed home from the Mother of the Holy Infant church, Emiliano himself stepped out of the shadows and up to the altar, where he lit a candle for the soul of his never-born son. He sought out Father Vallarte to ease the painful burning of his heart, but the timeworn chestnuts of consolation that the priest had to offer provided little solace.

More and more frequently Emiliano took his dinner at his mother's house with Dr. Sevilla. No longer did the pretty young girls call for Emiliano to tease and arouse him. No longer did he find their doors and windows flung open for him on a Friday night.

As each day passed it became more and more obvious to Emiliano that his wife was losing her senses. For hours at a time she would sit and stare at him, not even bothering to brush away the flies as they crawled across her face. When he could stand her gaze no longer he would jump up and bolt out of the house. More than once he awoke in the dead of night to find María leaning over him, eyes wide open, mouth snarling. She took to wearing a foul-smelling leather pouch hung on a string around her neck. She became so slovenly and unkempt that Emiliano could barely tolerate the sight and smell of her. And when she wasn't staring unblinkingly at Emiliano she was sitting cross-legged on her bedroom floor, watching with a catlike patience the green and white parrot in its pagoda-shaped cage.

Only Dr. Sevilla and Teresa Fortunato seemed willing to share Emiliano's company. But after only three weeks Sevilla announced that he would have to return temporarily to his own village. He would require additional medicines and equipment, he said, if he wished to prevent a similar tragedy in the future. Emiliano begged to be taken along. But Sevilla suffered a great deal of guilt over the death of María's child and her subsequent deterioration, and he insisted that Emiliano remain in Torrentino long enough to nurse his wife back to health.

"No matter what," Sevilla warned him, "don't touch another woman. I'll be back in a week or so to stay until your last child is born. And on that day you and I will ride off together and leave this cursed village behind like the pile of chicken dung it is."

Emiliano, nearly paralyzed with grief, could only nod quiescently.

Four mornings later Rosarita Calderón was spotted walking out of Torrentino, flanked on her right by María Fortunato, on her left by Argentina Neruda. Behind this solemn vanguard trailed ten or twelve other village women, a few of them, like Rosarita, pregnant young girls, the rest older widows, aunts and mothers and even a grandmother or two.

Teresa Fortunato watched with horror as this gloomy entourage filed past her house. It was barely nine in the morning; what could these women be up to? Argentina Neruda wore a red blouse with the design of a spider web stitched across its front, and of all the women in the crowd, only her face was void of fear and dread.

Rosarita Calderón, who was expecting her child any day now, walked with downcast eyes, practically dragging her feet through the dust. She walked awkwardly and with obvious discomfort, for as she walked she clutched a squealing piglet to her turgid breasts.

Hurrying back inside the house, Teresa Fortunato rushed to her son's bedroom to shake him awake. He had had a lot of pulque the night before and did not appreciate being disturbed. He cursed under his breath and tried to push her away. Finally Teresa had no choice but to grab him by the hair and yank him into a sitting position, holding him upright as he tried to pry her fingers loose. Undeterred, she described for him the scene she had witnessed and explained its implications. At last Emiliano understood. He rose and, still fully dressed from the night before, stumbled out of the house and ran after the women.

A few yards beyond the Mother of the Holy Infant church the women had turned off the street to ascend a narrow, winding mountain path. On a broad ledge of rock that stuck out of the side of the mountain like a tongue and overlooked the village, Emiliano caught up with them. He was out of breath and nauseous from the effort of running, his head throbbing as though a thunderstorm raged inside. Panting and heaving he made his way over the last hundred feet.

A half-circle of women stood grouped near the inner edge of the overhanging rock, partially obscuring Emiliano's view of Rosarita and María, who stood facing one another ceremoniously, the squealing piglet held by four hands against a flat pedestal of rock. Standing with her back to the outer rim of the ledge, Argentina Neruda faced these two women and, with a broad gleaming knife clutched in her right hand, raised her arms in supplication and loudly invoked the name of Huitzilopochtli.

Emiliano shoved his way through the half-circle of women and grabbed Rosarita by her hair. He yanked her around to face him, María struggling now to hold onto the piglet alone.

"What is this?" Emiliano demanded. "What are you doing here? You should be at home, lying in bed. Do you want to have your baby before Dr. Sevilla returns?"

Rosarita stared at him with a blank look. Her usually sparkling eyes were clouded and dull in a way he had never seen on her before.

"Huitzilopochtli must be appeased," she said. Her voice was peculiar, monotonic, so dreamlike that Emiliano felt certain that the old hag Argentina Neruda had fed her some herbal drug.

"If Huitzilopochtli doesn't have blood," Rosarita said, "my baby will end up like María's." For *blood* she said an ancient Nahuatl word, a word which in the Aztec language could also be interpreted as *flowers*. But with Argentina Neruda standing nearby, the morning sun glinting off her knife blade, there was no question as to the proper translation.

Emiliano was furious. Stepping up to María he yanked the piglet from her hands and, tossing it to the ground, set it free. The pig scurried away squealing, darting wildly back and forth until it found an opening through the groping hands of the women. Emiliano spun María around and kicked her rear end. "Get home!" he shouted at her. "Enough of this nonsense. Get home where you belong and start taking care of yourself!"

Both Rosarita and María turned to look back at the shrunken old woman who stood near the rim of the ledge, her back to Torrentino fifty feet below. "You old bag of bones," Emiliano hissed at her. He approached cautiously, keeping an eye on the knife she clutched and mentally calculating the extent of her reach.

Stopping at what he determined to be a safe distance, he said, "Why don't you sacrifice yourself, you pile of filth? You stinking old corpse. You walking excrescence. Why don't you slit your own throat and offer your own stinking blood to your stupid god?"

The wrinkled old woman, though angered by Emiliano's cruel epithets, was also extremely frightened. She did not say a word. She stood with the knife poised in front of her, just in case Emiliano decided to come any closer. Glancing over her shoulder at the buildings far below she had a chilling mental image of a body tumbling end over end to shatter on the hard ground. She clutched her knife with both hands and settled into a defensive crouch.

But Emiliano did not venture any closer. He drew back his head and, like a snake ejecting venom, spit a gob of phlegm in her face. Then he spun around and herded María and Rosarita side by side, shoving or kicking one and then the other as he pushed them past the other women and back down the mountain path.

At María's house he kicked open the door and roughly shoved his wife inside. "You stay put and don't go out!" he ordered, and slammed the door. From her window she watched as her husband escorted Rosarita up the street.

With Rosarita he was gentler. He spoke soothingly and guided her toward her house with his hand against the base of her spine.

"María's crazy," he told her, as though imparting a secret. "Her mind has been all stirred up like a sopa seca. We'll find another place for your mother to live and then I'll move in with you. We'll be the king and queen of Torrentino, guapa. You'll be the first mother and I will be papacito grande."

Rosarita said nothing. Her eyes remained dulled and troubled. Emiliano led her into her house and put her to bed, then lay beside her, knowing that her mother was still among the women gathered on the ledge.

Stretched out beside Rosarita, Emiliano nuzzled her neck and stroked her huge belly. "You don't need to worry about our baby," he told her. "It's going to be a strong and healthy boy. You wait and see. It was only because of María and her stupidity that we lost the first one. But I've been lucky all my life and I can feel in my bones that this baby is going to be fine. He'll grow up to be just as handsome and brave as his father."

Emiliano unbuttoned Rosarita's blouse and kissed her breasts. Suckling her right breast he tasted the sweet rich milk, too sweet at first but then warm and delicious.

"You're more beautiful than María," he told her. "And you're younger too. You have nothing to worry about. Stop letting those stupid women frighten you with their nonsense." He licked her breast and then ran his tongue over her stomach to her protruding navel. She lay unmoving, eyes open, palms flat on the bed.

"Even with your big belly," Emiliano said, kissing her stomach, "you still excite me. Right now I want you more than ever. Just forget about what that crazy old witch told you. Give me your hand and let me show you how much I want you. See how hard you make me by just letting me touch you."

He pressed her hand between his legs and moved against it. But when he released her hand to undo his trousers, her hand fell away from him, lifeless. Pushing himself to his knees he saw that she still regarded him with the same blank, unresisting expression. She looked, he thought, almost like an animal frozen in fear, a wounded deer lying on the ground and waiting fatalistically for the stroke of death.

"Jesus," he muttered, and crawled off the bed. "You women are all alike, you know that? You'd better just lie there and don't move until Sevilla gets back. Jesus, you're all so stupid that I can't believe it."

He went out of the house and slammed the door behind him. As he stalked down the street he saw coming toward him the small pack of women who had been on the mountain. Upon seeing him they all stopped in their tracks, and then, as a flock of birds suddenly wheels around in the sky with no apparent signal, they turned as a group and fled into the nearest house. Emiliano muttered angrily to himself and continued down the street to his mother's house. There he drank the last of the pulque and fell into a drunken, restless sleep.

––––––

At four in the afternoon, just when the heat of the day was beginning to relent, Emiliano was once again awakened by his mother's screaming. She shook him violently and, tugging him by the arm, dragged him off the bed. With his head still throbbing, feeling now as though a team of burros were kicking at his skull, he could not understand anything she said. She wailed hysterically and at the same time shouted and pleaded with him.

Emiliano allowed his mother to lead him by the hand outside, then down the street and behind the Volutad house. There the entire village had already gathered. They stood peering upward, necks craned to the over-hanging tongue of rock fifty feet above. On the edge of the rock stood Rosarita Calderón. She was dressed in her finest clothes, in an azure blue pleated skirt, black toeless shoes, and the lavender silk shirt Emiliano had given her.

From beneath the ledge a chorus of pleadings rose up to her. "Stay where you are!" some of the villagers shouted. "Don't move!" Others urged her to step back, away from the dangerous edge. But to all these remonstrations Rosarita seemed oblivious. She stared straight ahead, her palms resting flat against her swollen belly.

Argentina Neruda ordered that a pig or a chicken or even a scrawny dog be brought to be sacrificed on the spot, and two small children ran off to find an unlucky animal. María Fortunato, standing beside the old woman, stared silently up at the ledge, her face as expressionless as Rosarita's. Standing next to her, Father Vallarte fingered his rosary beads and mumbled a prayer. Halfway through he lost his place and was forced to begin again.

In the meantime Emiliano was running down the street toward the narrow path that ascended the mountainside. Having grown overweight and out of shape during the past months, he ran laboriously, out of breath, his lungs burning and his vision blurred by the throbbing pain inside his head. As he ran he mumbled aloud and tried to communicate telepathically with Rosarita. "Don't jump," he muttered. "Don't jump. Stay where you are, guapa, I'm coming, please stay where you are. Don't jump, don't jump, don't jump, *don't jump!*"

He struggled up the path, thinking with each stride that he could not go a step further. Finally he rounded the top and came within sight of the rock ledge. The ledge was empty, a flat platform leading to empty sky. Emiliano sank to his knees on the hard ground. He felt paralyzed, unable to move. He could not make himself crawl to the rim of the ledge and peer down. From below came a wailing of voices, a keening that filled his skull with a ballooning, cutting pain. He fell face forward onto the ground, determined never to rise again.

———

Only vaguely was Emiliano aware of the women approaching him. He knew that a great deal of time had passed since prostrating himself on the ground, for night had fallen more than an hour ago. At dusk he had listened to the screech of a white-breasted hawk, had even felt its shadow pass over him as the bird wheeled and circled through the sky. And now, more than an hour later, he heard the approaching footsteps of a dozen or more women. In his dazed, self-pitying state he imagined the sound to be the thumping of wings of a huge predatory bird, the women's sibilant whispers the rustle of wind across a hawk's feathers.

With his cheek to the ground Emiliano felt the women gathering around him. He smelled the fire from their torches of grease-soaked rags. He lay absolutely still for several minutes. Then it occurred to him that these women must be very worried about him, that to them he must appear dead. He pushed himself up on his elbow and turned his head to reassure them.

The first blow of a heavy stick caught Emiliano squarely between the shoulders. The sudden pain, flashing like lightning through his body and brain, immediately brought him back to full consciousness. Rolling away he curled like an armadillo, his arm protecting his head. A dozen other sticks came lashing down upon him.

"Diablo!" someone hissed, and kicked at his head. "Muerte!" said another, and rammed a thick club into his anus.

Emiliano tried to struggle to his feet but was struck successively on the head, the face, the groin, the stomach. "It wasn't my fault!" he tried to say. "It was the will of God! I'm not to blame!" But his protests were punctuated by his own involuntary yelps of pain, which rendered his words unintelligible.

Sticks broke across Emiliano's back. Rocks and boots tore at his clothing and bruised his skin. Emiliano rolled back and forth, squealing like a rabbit caught in the talons of an owl. For a moment he thought he was going to lose consciousness and felt a pleasant murky numbness spreading over him. But then a violent kick to his chest brought alertness back with a blinding flare of pain.

"*Aiyeeeeee!*" Emiliano screamed, and without knowing where the strength to do so came from, sprang to his feet. His scream was a wild, inhuman scream, the kind of shriek that could arise only from the festering depths of hell. Astonished and frightened, Emiliano's tormentors fell back. Blindly he plunged forward, arm over his face, and broke free of them. A sharp command from Argentina Neruda brought the women back to their senses, and they chased after him, cursing and bellowing.

Shielded in darkness, Emiliano ran without knowing what lay ahead. Rocks and sticks whizzed by his head. He tucked his neck into his shoulders and sprinted blindly, desperately. Within a matter of seconds he heard a difference in their voices, a rise of anger and a diminishment of power, and he knew that he had outdistanced them.

Settling into a comfortable trot, Emiliano ran for another fifty yards. Warm liquid trickled into his mouth and he tasted his own blood. His hand, broken at the wrist, dangled like the clapper of a bell. His spine felt twisted, cracked, wrenched into an impossible position. And yet, despite his discomfort, Emiliano felt exhilarated; he had beaten Death again. His luck still held.

Smiling through his pain, Emiliano slowed to a walk. The thought that he should stop advancing through the darkness and orient himself had just occurred to him when, with the next step, the earth fell away and he tumbled headfirst into a ravine.

———————

When Emiliano Fortunato regained consciousness, he felt himself to be lying on his side. His arm was tied behind his back to a rope that tightly encircled his waist. His broken wrist had been set and was immobilized by a splint wrapped heavily with cloth. His feet were bound at the ankles, and when he tried to stretch his legs he discovered some obstacle that would not permit full extension. A silky strip of cloth had been pulled between his lips and tied at the back of his head so that he could not speak. Everything was dark. Although he felt nothing covering his eyes, he could only assume, from the profundity of darkness, that his eyes had been masked.

By drawing his legs up beneath him, then leaning heavily on his shoulder and elbow and then jerking himself up, Emiliano worked himself into a sitting position. With his feet and head he determined the approximate perimeter of his cell. If he sat leaning slightly forward with his hips pushed against the rear wall he could stretch his legs out completely, the front wall then a mere two inches from the soles of his feet. His cell seemed to taper toward a point at the top, so that if he leaned too far forward or backward from the waist, he banged his head.

A bat, it seemed, had somehow gotten into his darkened cell. Every now and then Emiliano felt the flutter of its wings against the top of his head. He even felt the animal perch on his shoulder for a moment and take a bite out of his ear. He felt the sliminess of bat shit dripping onto his hand,

and by the stench of his cell assumed that a good supply of that commodity had already accumulated on the floor.

Only one name came to mind when Emiliano considered whom his captor might be. Apparently Argentina Neruda had dragged him from the ravine, had salvaged him from certain death for some devious and evil purpose all her own. Maybe she planned to publicly sacrifice him, or maybe to torture him by slow, excruciating degrees. Only she, that vile bag of bones, would be capable of such a thing.

Hearing noises coming from far away Emiliano sat very still, straining to hear. He recognized, or thought he did, the slow rhythmic cadence of a funeral drum. That, of course, would be for Rosarita Calderón. It meant also that night had passed, that it was probably mid-morning of the following day.

Picturing in his mind the funeral procession, Emiliano envisioned it proceeding solemnly down the street toward the cemetery behind the Mother of the Holy Infant church. Rosarita would not be allowed interment in consecrated ground, so a place would be made for her just outside the low cemetery fence. Father Vallarte would be standing at the graveside, mumbling an apology for Rosarita 's wasted life. He would lose his place and leaf haphazardly through the moth-eaten Bible, find his place, begin again, and then become distracted by the movements of a cloud or the spiraling flight of a hawk gliding on updrafts.

Emiliano even imagined that he could recognize his mother's weeping. After a long time he heard the villagers returning back up the street, muttering and sighing.

From not far away came several recognizable voices. The most important was that of Dr. Sevilla, who announced that in a week or two he would return to look in on the remaining mothers-to-be. But something in Sevilla's voice told Emiliano that the doctor would not be returning to Torrentino, that he fully intended now to turn his back on the village forever. What, he wondered, had they told the doctor about Emiliano's disappearance? That he had run off, unable to bear the guilt of Rosarita's sacrificial suicide? Or that Emiliano was a demon, an evil spirit who himself had thrown the hapless girl off the ledge and had then slithered back to his dark master?

Emiliano kicked at his cell. He rattled the walls and groaned through his gag in an attempt to be heard. But all he accomplished was to stir up his cellmate, who squawked and flew frantically from side to side, its wings lashing Emiliano's face and frightening him so thoroughly that he ceased his kicking and fell silent again.

Now the sounds Emiliano heard told him that the crowd was dispersing. He heard a door open and close, the latch click. Footsteps shuffled toward him. He heard the soft scrapings as someone knelt outside his cell. He heard excited breathing.

Emiliano wished the gag were not in his mouth so that he could spit in Argentina Neruda's face when she first showed herself.

After Rosarita's funeral, María Fortunato watched Dr. Sevilla riding away with tears in his eyes. Then she returned alone to her house. Once inside, she locked the front door, then crossed the room to the bedroom and the huge wrought-iron birdcage that sat now in the far corner. Lately Alissa Márquez had been asking to have her birdcage returned, but María would never part with it now. No, never. She would fight Alissa tooth and nail if necessary, but she would never give up the birdcage.

Kneeling in front of the enormous cage, María lifted off the heavy cover and smiled warmly at her two birds. The green and white parrot did not look very happy; it perched on a swinging bar near the top of the cage and stubbornly refused to face her. The newer bird, however, stared at her with wide hazel eyes. María laughed to herself: how Alissa Márquez would love to get her hands on this bird! In fact every woman in town would covet it if they learned of its existence. María would have to be very careful and discreet if she wished to keep this bird for herself. It was the kind of bird that would fly away forever if you did not clip its wings.

But what a handsome, valuable bird it was! María would have been content just to sit there in front of the cage, to sit for hours at a time with her demented catlike patience and merely stare at the bird's pretty face. Gingerly she stuck her hand through the wrought-iron bars and with her long ragged claws stroked the huge bird between its legs. The bird seemed to like that. Anyway, it was smart enough not to resist.

THE MAN WHO LOVED
LEVITTOWN

W. D. Wetherell

You realize what I had to do to get this place? It was thirty-odd years
ago come July. I'm just out of the Army. Two kids, twins on their way, a wife
who's younger than I am, just as naive, just as crazy hopeful. We're living in
the old neighborhood with my folks four to a room. All along I've got this
idea. Airplanes. P-40s, these great big 20s. We're slogging through Saipan,
they're flying over it. DiMaria, I tell myself, this war is going to end, when
it does that's where you want to be, up there in the blue not down here
in the brown. Ever since I'm a kid I'm good with machines, what I do
is figure I'll get a job making them. Grumman. Republic. Airborne. They're
all out there on Long Island. I tell Kathy to watch the kids, I'll be back tonight, wish me luck. I borrow the old man's Ford, out I go. Brooklyn Bridge,
Jamaica Avenue, Southern State, and I'm there.

Potato fields. Nothing but. French-fried heaven, not another car in
sight. I stop at a diner for coffee. Farmers inside look me over like I'm the
tax man come to collect. Bitter. Talking about how they were being run off

their places by these new housing developments you saw advertised in the paper, which made me mad because here I am a young guy just trying to get started, what were we supposed to do . . . live on East Thirteenth Street the rest of our lives? The being run off part was pure phooey anyhow, because they were making plenty on it, they never had it so good. But hearing them talk made me curious enough to drive around a little exploring.

Sure enough, here's this farmhouse all boarded up. Out in front is an ancient Chevy piled to the gunwales with old spring beds, pots and pans. Dust Bowl, Okies, *Grapes of Wrath* . . . just like that. I drive up to ask directions half expecting Marjorie Main. Instead there's this old man climbing up to the top of the pile. He's having a hell of a time getting up there. Once he does he stands with his hand shielding his eyes looking around the horizon like someone saying good-bye.

Maybe I'm just imagining it now but it seems to me it was so flat and smooth those days even from where I stood on the ground I could see just as far as he could . . . see the entire Island, right across the entire thing. Out to Montauk with waves breaking atop the rocks so green and bright they made me squint. Back this way over acres of pine trees, maybe one, maybe two lonely railroad tracks, nothing else except lots of ospreys which were still around those days. Then he turns, I turn, we look over to where the Jones Beach water tower is jutting up like the Leaning Tower of Pisa. Just this side of it the Great South Bay is wall-to-wall scallops and clams. You look left up the other way toward the North Shore there's these old ivy-covered mansions being torn down, pieces of confetti, broken champagne bottles all over the lawn. I have to squint a little now . . . I can just make out the shore of the Sound with all these sandy beaches that had "No Tres-passing" signs on them, only a man in a yellow vest is walking along now ripping them down . . . not two seconds later the beach is crowded with little kids splashing in the waves. Then after that we both look the other way back toward New York . . . the old man tottering up there in the breeze . . . over these abandoned hangars at Roosevelt Field where everybody took off to Europe alone from back in the twenties, then out toward where the skyscrapers are in the distance. I see the Empire State Building . . . for some crazy reason I wave. Then in a little closer over one or two small villages, acres of potato fields, and no matter which way you look . . . Sound side,

Bay side, South Shore, North Shore . . . there's the sound of hammers, the smell of sawdust, little houses going up in clusters, carpenters working bare-chested in the sun. The old man is looking all this over, then looks right at me, you know what he says? "I hope it poisons you!" With that he fell off the bundle, his son had to prop him back up, they drove away in a cloud of dust.

Fine. I drive down the road a little farther, here are these new houses up close. Small ones. Lots of mud. Old potatoes sticking out of it like dried-up turds. Broken blocks off two-by-fours. Nails, bits of shingle. In front of each house or half house or quarter house is a little lawn. Fuzzy green grass. Baby grass. At every corner is an empty post waiting for a street name to be fitted in the slot on top. A man comes along in a jeep, shuffles through the signs, scratches his head, sticks in one says LINDBERGH, drives off. Down the street is a Quonset hut with a long line of men waiting out in front, half of them still in uniform. Waiting for jobs I figure, like in the De-pression . . . here we go again. But here's what happens. A truck comes along, stops in front of the house, half a dozen men pile out . . . in fifteen minutes they've put in a bathroom. Pop! Off they go to the next house, just in time, too, because here comes another truck with the kitchen. Pop! In goes the kitchen. They move on one house, here comes the electricians. Pop! Pop! Pop! the house goes up.

There's no one around except this guy in overalls planting sticks in the little brown patches stamped out of the grass. "My name's DiMaria," I tell him. "What's yours?" "Bill Levitt," he says. "And what's the name of this place anyhow?" "Levittown." And then it finally dawns on me. What these men are lined up for isn't work, it's homes!

"How much does one of these babies cost?" I ask him casually.

He picks at his nose, leans his shovel against the tree. "Seven thou-sand," he says, looking right at me. "One hundred dollars down." "Oh yeah?" I say, still casual. But I kind of half turn, take out my wallet, take a peek inside. "I only have eighty-three." He looks me over. "You a veteran?" "You bet. Four years' worth, I don't miss it at all either." He calls over to a man helping with the sinks. "Hey, Johnson!" he yells. "Take this guy's money and let him pick out whichever one he wants. Mr. DiMaria," he says, shaking my hand. "You've just bought yourself a house."

I will never until the day I die forget the expression on Kathy's face when I got back that night. Not only have I bought a house but that same afternoon Grumman hires me at three bucks an hour plus overtime. "Honey, " I said, "get your things together, let's go, hubba, hubba, we're on our way home!"

————

I'm not saying it wasn't tough those first years. It was plenty tough. I worked to six most nights, sometimes seven. When I got home I fixed hamburgers for the kids since Kathy was out working herself. Minute she gets home, out I go pumping gas on the turnpike for mortgage money. Ten years we did that. But what made it seem easier was that everyone else on Lindbergh was more or less in the same boat. Young GIs from old parts of the city somewhere working at the big plants farther out. There were some pretty good men on that block. Scotty. Mike. Hank Zimmer. There wasn't anything we couldn't build or fix between us. I once figured out just among the guys on Lindbergh, let alone Hillcrest, we had enough talent to make ourselves an F-14. You know how complicated an F-14 is? Cabin cruisers, porches, garages . . . you name it, we built it. That's why this little boxes stuff was pure phooey. Sure they were little boxes when we first started. But what did we do? The minute we got our mitts on them we started remodeling them, adding stuff, changing them around.

There wasn't anything we wouldn't do for each other. Babysit, drive someone somewhere, maybe help out with a mortgage payment someone couldn't meet. You talk about Little League. Me and Mike are the ones *invented* it. We got the field for it, organized teams, umpired, managed, coached. Both my boys played; we once had a team to the national finals, we would have won if O'Brien's kid hadn't booted a grounder. But it was nice on summer nights to see dads knocking out flies to their kids, hearing the ball plop into gloves, see the wives sitting there on the lawns talking, maybe watering the lawn. The swimming pool up the block, the shops, the schools. It was nice all those things. People take them for granted nowadays, they had to start somewhere, right?

I'll never forget those years. The fifties. The early sixties. We were all going the same direction . . . thanks to Big Bill Levitt we all had a chance. You talk about dreams. Hell, we had ours. We had ours like nobody before or since ever had theirs. SEVEN THOUSAND BUCKS! ONE HUNDRED DOLLARS DOWN! We were cowboys out there. We were the pioneers.

I'll be damned if I know where the end came from. It was a little after the time I finished putting the sun roof over the porch. Kathy was in the living room yelling, trying to get my attention. "Tommy, come over here quick! Look out the window on Scotty's front lawn!" There planted right smack in the middle is a sign. FOR SALE! You know what my first reaction was? I was scared. Honest to God. I can't tell you why, but seeing that sign scared me. It scared me so much I ran into the bathroom, felt like being sick. Steady, DiMaria, I said. It's a joke like the time he put flounders under the hubcaps. Ginger needed a walk anyway, I snap a collar on her, out we go.

"So, Scotty, you kidding or what?" I say. Scotty just smiles. "We're pulling up, moving to Florida." "You mean you're taking a vacation down there? Whereabouts, Vero Beach?" He shakes his head. "Nope, Tommy. For good. I'm retiring. Twenty-five years of this is enough for anyone. The kids are on their own now. The house is too big for just the two of us. Carol and I are heading south. Thirty-nine thousand we're asking. Thirty-nine thousand! Whoever thought when we bought these shacks they would someday go for that?"

The twenty-five years part stunned me because it was like we'd all started yesterday as far as I was concerned. But the Florida part, that really killed me. Florida was someplace you got oranges from, where the Yanks spent March. But to actually move there?

"Come on, Scotty," I laugh. "You're kidding me, right?" "Nope. This guy is coming to look at the house this afternoon."

A guy named Mapes bought Scotty's place. A young kid worked for the county. I went over and introduced myself. "I've been here twenty-nine years," I said. "I knew Bill Levitt personally." "Who?" he asks. "Big Bill Levitt, the guy this town is named after." "Oh," he says, looking stupid. "I always thought that was an Indian name."

I should have known right there. But being the idiot I am, I take him out behind the house, show him the electricity meter. "Tell you a little secret," I whisper. "Got a screwdriver?"

I'd been helping myself to some surplus voltage ever since I got out there. Everyone on Lindbergh did. We were all practically engineers; when we moved in we couldn't believe it, all this electricity up there, all those phone lines going to waste. It was the land of milk and honey as far as we were concerned; all we had to do was plug in and help ourselves. I'm telling Mapes this but he's standing there looking dubious. "Uh, you sure this is okay?" "You kidding? There's plenty more where that came from. They'll never miss it. Twist that, jig this, weld that there, you're in business." "Oh yeah," he says, but you can tell he doesn't get it because when I hand him the screwdriver he drops it. "Oops!" he giggles. Meantime his bride comes along. Beads. Sandals. No, repeat, NO bra. "Jennifer," he says, "this is Mr. DiMaria from next door." "Call me Tommy, how are you?" The first words out of her mouth, you know what they are? "How many live in your house?" "Uh, two. My wife, myself." She looks me over, puffs on something I don't swear was a Winston. "That's not many for a whole house. If you ever decide to sell my kid sister's getting married. They need a place bad. Let me know next week, will yah?"

That was Mapes. Silver, the sheepherder took over O'Brien's, was even worse. "Hello, welcome to the neighborhood," I said walking across his lawn, my hand out. "That your dog?" he asks, pointing toward Ginger rolling in the pachysandra. "Yeah. Come here, Ginger. Shake the man's hand." "Dogs are supposed to be leashed, mister. If you don't get him off my property in five minutes, I'm calling the pound and having the animal destroyed." With that he walks away.

Welcome to Lindbergh Street.

———————

I'm not saying it was because of that but right about then a lot of old-timers put their houses on the market. It was sad because before, guys like Scotty could at least say they wanted to go to Florida, actually look forward to it. But now? Now the ones who ran out ran out because they were forced to. Taxes up, cost of living, heating oil, you name it. Here we'd had these homes for thirty years, broke our backs paying the mortgages off, you'd think it'd become easier for us now. Forget it. It was harder. It was *harder* keeping them than getting them.

What made it worse was the price everyone was getting. Forty thousand. Fifty thousand. The ones who stayed couldn't handle it anymore thinking they'd only paid seven. The real estate bastards dazzled them into selling even though they didn't want to. That was the sad part of it, seeing them try to convince themselves Florida would be nice. "We're getting a condominium," they'd say, the same somebody told you they were getting a valve bypass or a hysterectomy. "Well, I kind of like fishing," Mike said when he broke the news to me. "Don't they have good fishing down there?" "Sure they have good fishing, Mike," I told him. "Good fishing if you don't mind having your finger sucked by a water moccasin."

You think I'm exaggerating? You expect me to maybe say something good about the place? What if all your friends were taken away from you by coronaries, you wouldn't be too fond of heart disease, right? That's exactly the way I look at Florida. Guys like Buzz and Scotty think they're going to find Paradise down there, they're going to find mosquitoes, snakes, walking catfish, old people, that's it. This guy I know in the plant had his vacation down there. He thought it would be nice, no crime, no muggers. The first night there a Cuban breaks into his trailer, ties him up, rapes his wife, takes everything they had. Florida? You guys can have it. If Ponce de Leon were alive today he'd be living in Levittown.

But anyhow, nature hates a vacuum, the sheepherders moved in, started taking things over. You have to wonder about them to begin with. Here they are starting off where we finished, everything took us so long to get they have right away. They're sad more than anything . . . sadder than the old-timers moving south. You know what these kids who stayed on Long Island know? Shopping centers, that's it. If it's not in a mall they don't know nothing. And talk about dreams, they don't have any. A new stereo? A new Datsun? Call those dreams? Those aren't dreams, those are pacifiers. Popsicles. That's exactly what I feel like telling them. You find your own dream, pal, you're walking on mine. My generation survived the Depression, won the war, got Armstrong to the moon and back. And when I say *we* I'm talking about guys I know, not guys I read about. You think Grumman only makes F-14s? I *worked* on the landing module my last two years. Me, Tommy DiMaria. Nobody knows this but Scotty and me carved our initials on the facing under a transistor panel inside of the cabin. T.DM.S.S.H. right straight to the goddamn moon. But that's the kind of thing *we* did. What will the sheepherders be able to say they did when they get to be our age? . . . Evaded the draft. Bought a Cougar. Jogged.

It's like I told each of my kids when they were teenagers. "This town is where you grow up," I told them, "not where you *end* up." And they didn't either. They're scattered all over the place. I'm proud of them all. The only problem is like when Kathy got sick the last time it was a hell of a job getting everyone together. When I think about Kathy dying you know what I remember? Kennedy Airport. The TWA terminal. Going there to meet each of the kids, trying to figure out plane schedules, time zones, who I'm seeing off, who I'm meeting. The older I get the more I think what the real problem is in this country isn't *what* or *how* or *why* but *where. Where's* the question, the country's so goddamn big. Where in hell do you put yourself in it? Where?

Each of the kids wanted me to move in with them after Kathy died. Candy's a psychologist, she told me I was crazy to live by myself in the suburbs. If it was one thing people in suburbs couldn't stand it was to see someone living alone. It threatened them, they'd do anything to get rid of that reminder the world wasn't created in minimum denominations of two . . . that's the way she talks. But I told her no because the very last thing Kathy said was, Tommy, whatever you do don't give up the house. She was holding my hand, it was late, I was there all by myself not even a nurse. "Tommy, don't give up the house!" "Shh, Kathy," I whispered. "Rest now. I won't ever give it up." She squeezed my hand. I looked around to see if the nurse had come in, but it wasn't her, it was the lady in the next bed mumbling something in her sleep. "I'll never give it up, Kathy," I promised. I bent over. I kissed her. She smiled . . . she closed her eyes and it was like she had gone to sleep.

"Goodbye, Kathy," I said. "Sweet dreams, princess."

It was harder without her. I remember I'm in the back yard fixing up the garden for spring just like I would if she was still there, watching Ginger out of the corner of my eye, when Mapes's wife comes up the driveway. She stands there chewing gum. "I'm sorry about your wife, Mr. DiMaria," she says. "I guess you're going to sell your house now, huh? " When I told her no she acted mad. "We'll see about that!" she says.

Her little boy Ringo runs over to help me like he sometimes did. She pulls him away, stands there clutching him tight to her body like she's protecting him. "Never play with that dirty old man again!" she screams. "You old people think you can keep putting us down all the time! You think you can ask anything for a house we'll pay it on account of we're desperate! What's Janey supposed to do, live in Queens the rest of her life?" She's screaming, getting all worked up. Mapes comes over, looks embarrassed, tries to quiet her down . . . away they go.

A few days later I'm out there again, this time planting beans, when I hear voices coming from the porch. I'm just about to go inside to investigate when this guy in a suit comes around back with a young couple holding hands. "This is the yard!" he says, pointing. "It's a nice yard, good place for kids. Hello doggy, what's your name?" He walks around me like I'm not there, squeezes a tomato, leads them back around front. Ten minutes later they come out of the house. "You'll like it here, it's a good investment. Oh, hello," he says, "you must be the owner. I'm Mr. Charles from Stroud Realty, here's my card, these are the Canadays, they love your house." "Scram!" All three of them jump. "Go on, you heard me! Clear the hell out before I call the cops!" "But I'm showing the property!" the little guy squeaks. I had a hell of a time chasing them off of there.

The pressure really started after that. It was little ways at first. Kids that had been friendly before staying away because their mothers told them to. Finding my garbage can spilled across the lawn. Mail stolen, things like that. One morning there's a knock on the door, this pimple face is standing there holding a briefcase. "Mr. DiMaria?" "That's right, who are you?" "I'm from the county. We've come to assess your home." "It was assessed." He looks at his chart. "Yes, but twenty years ago. I'm sure it still can't be worth just four thousand now can it? Excuse me." He butts his way in, starts feeling the upholstery. He's there five minutes, he comes back to the door.

"Nice place you got here, Mr. DiMaria. I can see you put a lot of work into it since we were last here. Let's say forty thousand dollars' worth, shall we? Your taxes will be adjusted accordingly."

"You're crazy!" I yell. I'm about to lose my temper but then I remember something. "Hey, you know D'Amato down at the county executive's office? Him and me grew up together." "Never heard of him," pimple face says, shaking his head. "Well, how about Gus Louis in the sheriff's office?" "Oh, we don't have much to do with them these days I'm afraid." He starts to leave. "Well, you're probably going next door now, right?" "Oh, no," he says. "This is the only house on the block we're checking." "Wait a second!" I yell. "That's bullshit. You're going to Mapes, then Silver or I'm calling my congressman. Discrimination's a crime, pal!" His eyes finally light up. "You mean Mr. Silver? Hell of a nice guy. His brother is my boss. Goodbye, Mr. DiMaria. Have a nice day."

I don't want to give the impression I didn't fight back. I did, because if there's one thing I know about Levittown it's this. People are scared about blacks moving in, only nowadays it isn't blacks, it's drug treatment centers. It terrifies everyone. It terrifies them because all they think about when they're not shopping is property values. So what does DiMaria do? I wait until the next time these sweet Seventh Day whatever ladies come around selling their little pamphlets. I always give them a dime, no one else on the street ever gives them a penny . . . they think the world of me. They're always very polite, a bit crazy. What I did when they rang the doorbell was invite them into the house for some coffee. That was probably enough to give most of the sheepherders a good scare. It's Saturday, they're all out waxing their Camaros, here's two black ladies inside DiMaria's talking about God knows what, maybe thinking to buy it. But what I do is take them outside around back saying I wanted to show them my peach tree. These ladies are so sweet and polite, they're a bit deaf, besides they'll do anything I want.

I point to the side of the house. "This is where we'll put the rehabilitation room!" I say really loud. "Over here we'll have the methadone clinic!" The ladies are nodding, smiling, handing me new pamphlets, I'm slipping them fresh dimes. "AND OVER HERE'S THE ABORTION WING!"

I see Mapes and Silver staring at us all upset; if they had a gun they would have shot me.

————

What really kept me going, though, was Hank Zimmer. He was the last cowboy left besides me. Every once in a while I'd get discouraged, he'd cheer me up, then he'd get discouraged, I'd cheer him up . . . we'd both get discouraged, we'd take it out working on my new den, maybe his. What we used to talk about was how there were no hedges on Lindbergh in the old days, no fences, no locked doors. Everyone's home was your home; we all walked back and forth like it was one big yard.

That was long since done with now. You think the sheepherders would have anything to do with the other sheepherders? It was like the hedges we'd planted, the bushes and trees, had grown up so high they'd cut people off from each other. The only thing they wanted anymore was to pretend their neighbors weren't there.

I remember the last time he came over because it was just after I finished wallpapering the den. Ginger was whining to go out so I let her . . . that crap about leashes didn't bother me at all. Hank's telling me about school taxes going up again, how he didn't think he could pay his on social security, nothing else. "What we should do," he says, "is find other people in our position to organize a senior citizens' group to see if something can't be done." "Hank," I tell him, "no offense or anything, but all of that what you just said is pure phooey. You join one of those senior citizens' groups, women's groups, queer groups, right away you put yourself in a minority, you're stuck there. All these people running around wanting to be in a minority just so they can feel all nice and persecuted. Forget it! We're humans, that puts us in the *majority*! We're humans, we should demand to be treated like it."

Hank runs his hands up and down the wallpaper, admires the job. "Yeah, you're probably right," he says. Humans. He never thought of it that way before. We go into the kitchen for some coffee. "Now what my idea is, we find out where Big Bill Levitt is these days, we get a petition together telling him how things have gone wrong here, all these young people moving in, taxes going up, forcing us out. He'll find some way to make things right for us. I'd stake my life on it."

Hank nods, reaches for the cream. "By the way," he says. "You hear about Johnny Holmes over on Hillcrest? The guy who once broke his chin on the high board at the pool?" "What about him?" "He's moving to Fort Lauderdale, him and his wife. They bought this old house there. They're going to fix it up nice. Have a garden and all. He made it sound very appealing." "Oh, yeah?" I say. Then I remember myself. "Appealing, my ass. It'll collapse on him, he'll be back in a month. If you don't mind my saying so, Hank, change the subject before I throw up."

All of a sudden we hear this godawful roar from out front like a car accelerating at a drag strip, then brakes squealing, only I knew right away it wasn't brakes. "Ginger!" I jump up, knock the coffee over, run outside . . . There's this car fishtailing away up the street. In the middle of the pavement in a circle from the streetlight is poor Ginger. I run over, put her head in my lap, pet her, but it's too late, she's crying, kicking her legs up and down. Behind her head's nothing but blood. Hank's next to me nearly screaming himself . . . There's nothing to do but put her out of her pain with my bare hands because there's no other way. Then Hank's got his arm around me, I'm shivering, crying, cursing, all at the same time. He takes me back to the house, his wife comes over, they have me swallow something . . . the next thing I know it's morning, Hank's buried Ginger in the back near the birch tree she always liked to curl up against in the sun.

It was a while before I found out who did it. I kept on taking my walk around the block same as before, except I didn't have Ginger with me anymore. Maybe a month later I'm walking along past Silver's house, I see him out in his driveway with Mapes, a few other sheepherders. Silver is giggling. Mapes is standing to one side acting half-ashamed, but smirking, too. "Hey, DiMaria!" Silver yells. "How's your dog?"

I didn't do anything right away. We had a tradition in the old days, you had a score to settle you took your time. I waited for the first stormy night, went over there with two buckets of the cheapest red paint money could buy.

It was pretty late. I shined a flashlight at the lamppost which if you ever want to try it is enough to put one of those mercury vapor jobs out of commission for a while. Then I propped my ladder against the side of his house facing Mapes, went to work. The first cross stroke on the left was pretty easy, the upper right-hand one was tougher because I had to paint across a bay window O'Brien had put in years before. I was being careful not to drip any on the bushes. No matter what I thought of Silver I had a certain amount of respect for his shrubbery which had been planted by Big Bill Levitt back in the forties. It must have taken me two hours all told. I'm painting away humming to myself like it was something I did every night. When it was morning I woke up early, took my usual stroll past Silver's house, there on the side looking wet and shiny in the sun is the biggest, ugliest, coarsest swastika you ever saw, painted right across the side of his house big as life, the only thing bothered me was the upper right stroke was a bit crooked after all.

There were pictures of it in the paper, editorials saying Levittown had gone to hell which was true but for the wrong reasons. The entire Island's gone sour if you ask me. The Sound's gone sour, the ocean's gone sour, the dirt's gone sour. We used to grow enough tomatoes to last the winter, these great big red ones, now you're lucky if you get enough to feed the worms. Great South Bay? Sick clams, dead scallops, that's it. I remember it wasn't that long ago we used to catch stripers bigger than a man's arm, me and Scotty, right off Fire Island a twenty-minute drive away. I remember going there before dawn, cooking ourselves breakfast over a fire we made from driftwood, not seeing another soul on the beach . . . just Scotty, me, the sun, the stripers. Nowadays? Nowadays you can't even fish without getting your reel gummed up in oil; you're lucky to take one crap-choked blowfish let alone stripers.

Looking back what I think happened was that guys like Scotty, Buzz, Mike, and me had the right dream in the wrong place. Long Island's gone sour. Sometimes I remember the first day I came out here, a know-nothing kid, watching that farmer, that last old farmer up there on that overloaded Chevy looking around saying good-bye at the same time cursing it once for all. Other times I walk around the house looking for something to do. What I usually end up doing is put the record player on. Mitch Miller doing "Exodus." I put it on real loud. When they sing, "This land is mine, God gave this land to me," I start singing, too. Listening to it makes me feel stronger, so I keep turning it up, playing it again. After that I fix lunch for myself. Tuna fish, a cup of soup. After lunch I end up staring out the front window trying to figure out who lived where in the old days. Know something? It gets harder every year. O'Brien's and Scotty's are easy, but sometimes I get confused on the others.

It's like this morning I'm looking out across the street trying to remember if Buzz or Rich Ammons lived where this sheepherder name of Diaz lives now, when who do I see over on Zimmer's lawn but the same real estate bastard I chased off my place, Mr. Charles, with two young kids showing them around. This time I was really mad. I ran outside without even a coat, started screaming at them, telling them I'd call the cops, break every bone in his miserable little body if he didn't clear out and leave poor Hank alone. But what happened next was that Hank was outside, too. He was pleading with me to stop, but by then it was too late. Real estate man and kids are running into their car, locking the doors, racing away.

"Tommy!" Hank yelled, shaking his head. "They were going to pay me fifty-five thousand, Tommy!" "What are you talking about?" But now he looked away like he was ashamed. He took me inside the sun porch, sat me down on a lawn chair he unhooked from the wall.

"Tommy, we're moving south," he said. "Bullshit you are!" But he doesn't do anything, he just sits there. "We can't take it here anymore, Tommy, "he whispered. "The cold gets to Marge. The taxes are too much for me. All those kids, what do we have in common with them? We're going to Florida. Saint Pete. We bought a trailer."

It was probably the next to worst moment I ever had. "You can't do that, Hank," I said, just as quiet as him. "Not after what we've been through all these years. I was going to help you out with your den. Think of all the things we could do yet. There's another porch we could add on, we could add on a pool." But he was shaking his head again. "Let's face it, " he said. "You've got nothing left to work on, Tommy. The house is finished. You hear me? Finished! There's nothing left." He took out his wallet, showed me some pictures. "My grandkids. Terri and Shawn. They live down there now. We want to be close to them. That's the main reason, Tommy. We want to be close to them the years we have left."

By now I was getting mad. "Grandkids my ass!" I yelled. "You think your grandkids give a damn about you? Maybe at Christmastime, that's it.

To them you're an old smelly man they don't give a damn about they never will. Take it from me, I know." But then I looked at him . . . seeing him blink, cover his face with his hands, I got feeling ashamed of myself. "Hank," I said, "don't leave me alone like this. Please, Hank. Just hold on a little while more."

"Fifty-five thousand, Tommy. I can't turn it down."

"Listen, Hank. We'll call Big Bill Levitt up. I'll say, Mr. Levitt, my name is Tommy DiMaria, I live on Lindbergh Street, you probably don't remember but you once let me have a house for eighty-three dollars down instead of a hundred. Remember that, Mr. Levitt? Remember those days? Well, a lot of us old-timers are having trouble hanging on to our places you built for us. We wondered if maybe you could help us out. We'll call him up, Hank. We'll call him up just like that."

"You and your Levitt! I'm sick of hearing about him! What has Levitt ever done? He built these places and never looked back. He made his pile, then didn't want to know nothing. Levitt? You're so crazy about Levitt, let me ask you something. Where is Levitt now? Tell me that. Where is he now? Where is Levitt now?"

Like a dope, like the idiot I am, I shake my head, whisper, "I don't know, Hank. Where?"

"Florida!"

"Hank," I said, "I hope you fry."

When I got back to my place there was a panel truck in front, two men standing on the sidewalk watching me cross the street. At the same time Mapes's wife is on her lawn pointing at me, yelling "That's him, officer! That's your man!" One of the men came up to me the moment I reached the curb. "You Thomas A. DiMaria?" he said. "Beat it!" "You live at 155 Lindbergh?" "Beat it! You're trespassing on private property, pal!" "We're from the electric company. This is for you."

I'm feeling so tired by then I took the envelope, opened it up. Inside is a bill for $11,456.55. "You owe us for thirty-two years' worth," the man said. "If we want we can put you in jail. Stealing electricity is a crime." I looked back toward Mapes's house, sure enough there he is with that same half-ashamed smirk hiding behind his Cougar pretending he's polishing the roof.

"I'm not paying," I said. "Leave me alone." With that the other man, the one who hadn't said anything before, comes right up to me, waves a paper in my face. "You better pay, DiMaria!" he said with a sneer. "You don't, we take the house!"

I didn't waste any time after that. I went out to the tool shed, took a five-gallon can of gasoline, went back inside . . . took off the cap, taped a piece of cheesecloth over the spout, went into the den.

Sprinkle, sprinkle. Right over the desk. Sprinkle. Right over the wallpaper. Then after that I went into the bathroom. I remembered those men putting it in. I remembered redoing it with a bigger tub, new tiles, new cabinets. Sprinkle, sprinkle. Right over the cabinets. Right over the rugs. Next I went up the stairs I'd built with Scotty from lumber we helped ourselves to at a construction project on the turnpike . . . up to the dormer I'd added on for the kids. Their stuff was still there, all the kids' stuff, because they didn't want it, Kathy would never let me throw it away. There's a blue teddy bear called Navy, a brown one called Army. I took the can, poured some over their fur, propped them up in the corner, poured some over the bunk beds. I remembered the time Candy cried because she had the bottom one, she wanted the top. Thinking about that, thinking about the times I sat around the old DuMont watching Mickey Mouse Club with them waiting for Kathy to get home, almost made me stop right there.

I went downstairs, the can getting lighter, leaving a little trail behind me . . . into the twins' room where I sprinkled some on the curtains Kathy sewed, sprinkled some on the Davy Crockett hat Chris used to wear every time she came out of the bathtub. Then after that I went into the kitchen. The kitchen cabinets. The linoleum. Sprinkle, sprinkle. Out to the porch where we used to eat in summer, right over the bar I made from leftover knotty pine. I stood there for a while. I stood there remembering the party we had when we ripped the mortgage up, how Scotty got drunk and we had to carry him home only we carried him, dropped him in the pool instead. Sprinkle, sprinkle. Like watering plants. Like baptizing someone. Like starting a barbecue with lighter fluid, all the neighborhood there in my back yard. Into our bedroom, over the floor, the floor where the first night I brought Kathy home we had no bed yet so we lay there on the floor of what we still couldn't believe was our house, making love all night because we were so happy we didn't think we could stand it. Sprinkle. The fumes getting pretty bad now. Sprinkle. Outside to the carport, over the beams, over the tools, over everything. Sprinkle, sprinkle. Splash.

And that's where I am right now. The carport. The bill they handed me in one hand, a match in the other. I'm going to wait until Silver gets home first. I want to make sure everyone on the block gets to see what fifty-five thousand dollars, thirty-two years, looks like going up in smoke. A second more and it'll be like kids, neighbors, house, never happened, as if it all passed in a twinkling of an eye like they say. One half of me I feel ready to start all over again. I feel like I'm ready to find a new dream, raise a new family, the works. Nothing that's happened has made me change my mind. I'm ready to start again, just say the word. I feel stronger, more hopeful than ever . . . how many guys my age can say that? That's all I want, one more chance. For the time being I'm moving back to the old neighborhood to my sister's. After that, I don't know. Maybe I'll head down south where it's warmer, but not, I repeat NOT to Florida, maybe as far as Virginia, I'm not sure.

WEEDS

Rick DeMarinis

A black helicopter flapped out of the morning sun and dumped its sweet orange mist on our land instead of the Parley farm where it was intended. It was weedkiller, something strong enough to wipe out leafy spurge, knapweed and Canadian thistle, but it made us sick.

My father had a fatal stroke a week after that first spraying. I couldn't hold down solid food for nearly a month and went from 200 pounds to 170 in that time. Mama went to bed and slept for two days, and when she woke up she was not the same. She'd lost something of herself in that long sleep, and something that wasn't herself had replaced it.

Then it hit the animals. We didn't have much in the way of animals, but one by one they dropped. The chickens, the geese, the two old mules — Doc and Rex — and last of all, our only cow, Miss Milky, who was more or less the family pet.

Miss Milky was the only animal that didn't outright up and die. She just got sick. There was blood in her milk and her milk was thin. Her teats got so tender and brittle that she would try to mash me against the milk stall wall when I pulled at them. The white part of her eyes looked like fresh red meat. Her piss was so strong that the green grass wherever she stood died off. She got so bound up that when she'd lift her tail and bend with strain, only one black apple would drop. Her breath took on a burning sulphurous stink that would make you step back.

She also went crazy. She'd stare at me like she all at once had a desperate human mind and had never seen me before. Then she'd act as if she wanted to slip a horn under my ribs and peg me to the barn. She would drop her head and charge, blowing like a randy bull, and I would have to scramble out of the way. Several times I saw her gnaw on her hooves or stand stock-still in water up to her blistered teats. Or she would walk backward all day long, mewling like a lost cat that had been dropped off in a strange place. That mewling was enough to make you want to clap a set of noise dampers on your ears. The awful sound led Mama to say this: "It's the death song of the land, mark my words."

Mama never talked like that before in her life. She'd always been a cheerful woman who could never see the bad part of anything that was at least fifty percent good. But now she was dark and strange as a gypsy, and she would have spells of sheer derangement during which she'd make noises like a wild animal, or she'd play the part of another person—the sort of person she'd normally have nothing to do with at all. At Daddy's funeral, she got dressed up in an old and tattered evening gown the color of beet juice, her face painted and powdered like that of a barfly. And while the preacher told the onlookers what a fine man Daddy had been, Mama cupped her hands under her breasts and lifted them high, as if offering to appease a dangerous stranger. Then, ducking her head, she chortled, "Loo, loo, loo," her scared eyes scanning the trees for owls.

I was twenty-eight years old and my life had come to nothing. I'd had a girl but I'd lost her through neglect and a careless attitude that had spilled over into my personal life, souring it. I had no ambition to make something worthwhile of myself, and it nettled her. Toward the end, she began to parrot her mother: "You need to get yourself *established*, Jack," she would say. But I didn't want to get myself established. I was getting poorer and more aimless day by day, and I supposed she believed that "getting established" would put a stop to the downhill slide, but I had no desire to do whatever it took to accomplish that.

———————

Shortly after Daddy died, the tax man came to our door with a paper in his hand. "Inheritance tax," he said, handing me the paper.

"What do you mean?" I asked.

"It's the law," he said. "Your father died, you see. And that's going to cost you some. You should have made better plans." He tapped his forehead with his finger and winked. He had a way of expressing himself that made me think he was country born and raised but wanted to seem citified. Or maybe it was the other way around.

"I don't understand this," I mumbled. I felt the weight of a world I'd so far been able to avoid. It was out there, tight-assed and squinty-eyed, and it knew to the dollar and dime what it needed to keep itself in business.

"Simple," he said. "Pay or move off. The government is the government, and it can't bend a rule to accommodate the confused. It's your decision. Pay or the next step is litigation."

He smiled when he said good-bye. I closed the door against the weight of his smile, which was the weight of the world. I went to a window and watched him head back to his green government car. The window was open and I could hear him. He was singing loudly in a fine tenor voice. He raised his right hand to hush an invisible audience that had broken into uncontrolled applause. I could still hear him singing as he slipped the car into gear and idled away. He was singing "Red River Valley."

Even though the farm was all ours, paid up in full, we had to give the government $7,000 for the right to stay on it. The singing tax man said we had inherited the land from my father, and the law was sharp on the subject.

I didn't know where the money was going to come from. I didn't talk it over with Mama because even in her better moments she would talk in riddles. To a simple question such as, "Should I paint the barns this year, Mama?" she might answer, "I've no eyes for glitter, nor ears for their ridicule."

———————

One day I decided to load Miss Milky into the stock trailer and haul her into Saddle Butte where the vet, Doc Nevers, had his office. Normally, Doc Nevers would come out to your place, but he'd heard about the spraying that was going on and said he wouldn't come within three miles of our property until they were done.

The Parley farm was being sprayed regularly, for they grew an awful lot of wheat and almost as much corn, and they had the biggest haying operation in the county. Often, the helicopters they used were upwind from us and we were sprayed too. ("Don't complain," said Big Pete Parley when I called him up about it. "Think of it this way—you're getting your place weeded for *free!*" When I said I might have to dynamite some stumps on the property line and that he might get a barn or two blown away for free, he just laughed like hell, as if I had told one of the funniest jokes he'd ever heard.)

There was a good windbreak between our places, a thick grove of lombardy poplars, but the orange mist, sweet as a flower garden in full bloom, sifted through the trees and settled on our fields. Soon the poplars were mottled and dying. Some branches curled in an upward twist, as if flexed in pain, and others became soft and fibrous as if the wood were trying to turn itself into sponge.

With Miss Milky in the trailer, I sat in the truck sipping on a pint of Lewis and Clark bourbon and looking out across our unplanted fields. It was late—almost too late—to plant anything. Mama, in the state she was in, hadn't even noticed.

In the low hills on the north side of the property, some ugly looking things were growing. From the truck, they looked like white pimples on the smooth brown hill. Up close, they were big as melons. They were some kind of fungus, and they pushed up through the ground like the bald heads of fat babies. They gave off a rotten meat stink. I would get chillbumps just looking at them, and if I touched one, my stomach would rise. The bulbous heads had purple streaks on them that looked like blood vessels. I half expected to one day see human eyes clear the dirt and open. Big pale eyes that would see me and carry my image down to their deepest root. I was glad they seemed to prefer the hillside and bench and not the bottom land.

Justified or not, I blamed the growth of this fungus on the poison spray, just as I blamed it for the death of my father, the loss of our animals, and the strangeness of my mother. Now the land itself was becoming strange. And I thought, what about me? How am I being rearranged by that weedkiller?

I guess I should have gotten mad, but I didn't. Maybe I *had* been changed by the spray. Where once I had been a quick-to-take-offense hot-head, I was now docile and thoughtful. I could sit on a stump and think for hours, enjoying the slow and complicated intertwinings of my own thoughts. Even though I felt sure the cause of all our troubles had fallen out of the sky, I would hold arguments with myself, as if there were always two sides to every question. If I said to myself, "Big Pete Parley has poisoned my family and farm and my father is dead because of it," I would follow it up with, "But Daddy was old anyway, past seventy-five, and he always had high blood pressure. Anything could have set off his stroke, from a wasp bite to a sonic boom."

"And what about Mama?" I would ask. "Senile with grief," came the quick answer. "Furthermore, Daddy himself used poison in his time. Cyanide traps for coyotes, DDT for mosquito larvae, arsenic for rats."

My mind was always doubling back on itself in this way, and it would often leave me standing motionless in a field for hours, paralyzed with indecision, sighing like a moonstruck girl of twelve. I imagined myself mistaken by passersby for a scarecrow.

Sometimes I saw myself as a human weed, useless to other people in general and maybe harmful in some weedy way. The notion wasn't entirely unpleasant. Jack Hucklebone: a weed among the well-established money crops of life.

On my way to town with Miss Milky, I crossed over the irrigation ditch my father had fallen into with the stroke that killed him. I pulled over onto the shoulder and switched off the engine. It was a warm, insect-loud day in early June. A spray of grasshoppers clattered over the hood of the truck. June bugs ticked past the windows like little flying clocks. The thirteen-year locusts were back and raising a whirring hell. I was fifteen the last time they came, but I didn't remember them arriving in such numbers. I expected more helicopters to come flapping over with special sprays meant just for them, even though they would be around for only a few weeks and the damage they would do is not much more than measurable. But anything that looks like it might have an appetite for a money crop brings down the spraying choppers. I climbed out of the truck and looked up into the bright air. A lone jet, eastbound, too high to see or hear, left its neat chalk line across the top of the sky. The sky itself was like hot blue wax, north to south. A giant hammerhead sat on the west horizon as if it were a creamy oblong planet gone dangerously off-course.

There's where Daddy died. Up the ditch about fifty yards from here. I found him, buckled, white as paper, half under water. His one good eye, his right (he'd lost the left one thirty years ago when a tractor tire blew up in his face as he was filling it), was above water and wide open, staring at his hand as if it could focus on the thing it gripped. He was holding on to a root. He had big hands, strong, with fingers like thick hardwood dowels, but now they were soft and puffy, like the hands of a giant baby. Water bugs raced against the current toward him. His body blocked the ditch and little eddies swirled around it. The water bugs skated into the eddies and, fighting to hold themselves still in the roiling current, touched his face. They held still long enough to satisfy their curiosity, then slid back into the circular flow as if bemused by the strangeness of dead human flesh.

I started to cry, remembering it, thinking about him in the water, he had been so sure and strong, but then—true to my changed nature—I began to laugh at the memory, for his wide blue eye had had a puzzled cast to it, as if it had never before seen such a crazy thing as the ordinary root in his forceless hand. It was an expression he never wore in life.

"It was only a weed, Daddy," I said, wiping the tears from my face.

The amazed puzzlement stayed in his eye until I brushed down the lid.

Of course he had been dead beyond all talk and puzzlement. Dead when I found him, dead for hours, bloated dead. And this is how I've come to be—blame the spray or don't: the chores don't get done on time, the unplanted fields wait, Mama wanders in her mind, and yet I'll sit in the shade of my truck sipping on Lewis and Clark bourbon, inventing the thoughts of a stone-dead man.

———————

Time bent away from me like a tail-dancing rainbow. It was about to slip the hook. I wasn't trying to hold it. Try to hold it and it gets all the more slippery. Try to let it go and it sticks like a cocklebur to cotton. I was drifting somewhere between the two kinds of not trying: not trying to hold anything, not trying to let anything go.

Then he sat down next to me. The old man.

"You got something for me?" he said.

He was easily the homeliest man I had ever seen. His bald head was bullet-shaped and his lumpy nose was warty as a crookneck squash. His little, close-set eyes sat on either side of that nose like hard black beans. He had shaggy eyebrows that climbed upward in a white and wiry tangle. There was a blue lump in the middle of his forehead the size of a pullet's egg, and his hairy ear lobes touched his grimy collar. He was mumbling something, but it could have been the noise of the ditch water as it sluiced through the culvert under the road.

He stank of whiskey and dung, and looked like he'd been sleeping behind barns for weeks. His clothes were rags, and he was caked with dirt from fingernail to jaw. His shoes were held together with strips of burlap. He untied some of these strips and took off the shoes. Then he slid his gnarled, dirt-crusted feet into the water. His eyes fluttered shut and he let out a hissing moan of pleasure. His toes were long and twisted, the arthritic knuckles painfully bright. They reminded me of the surface roots of a stunted oak that had been trying to grow in hardpan. Though he was only about five feet tall, his feet were huge. Easy size twelves, wide as paddles.

He quit mumbling, cleared his throat, spit. "You got something for me?" he said.

I handed him my pint. He took it, then held it up to the sunlight and looked through the rusty booze as if testing for its quality.

"If it won't do," I said, "I could run into town to get something a little smoother for you. Maybe you'd like some Canadian Club or some twelve-year-old Scotch. I could run into town and be back in less than an hour. Maybe you'd like me to bring back a couple of fried chickens and a sack of buttered rolls." This was my old self talking, the hothead. But I didn't feel mad at him, and was just being mouthy out of habit.

"No need to do that," he said, as if my offer had been made in seriousness. He took a long pull off my pint. "This snake piss is just fine by me, son." He raised the bottle to the sunlight again, squinted through it.

I wandered down the ditch again to the place where Daddy died.

There was nothing there to suggest a recent dead man had blocked the current. Everything was as it always was. The water surged, the quick water bugs skated up and down, inspecting brown clumps of algae along the banks; underwater weeds waved like slim snakes whose tails had been staked to the mud. I looked for the thistle he'd grabbed on to. I guess he thought that he was going to save himself from drowning by hanging on to its root, not realizing that the killing flood was *inside* his head. But there were many roots along the bank and none of them seemed more special than any other.

Something silver glinted at me. It was a coin. I picked it out of the slime and polished it against my pants. It was a silver dollar, a real one. It could have been his. He carried a few of the old cartwheels around with him for luck. The heft and gleam of the old solid silver coin choked me up.

I walked back to the old man. He had stuffed his bindle under his head for a pillow and had dozed off. I uncapped the pint and finished it, then flipped it into the weeds. It hit a rock and popped. The old man grunted and his eyes snapped open. He let out a barking snort, and his black eyes darted around him fiercely, like the eyes of a burrow animal caught in a daylight trap. Then, remembering where he was, he calmed down.

"You got something for me?" he asked. He pushed himself up to a sitting position. It was a struggle for him.

"Not any more," I said. I sat down next to him. Then, from behind us, a deep groan cut loose. It sounded like siding being pried off an old barn with a crowbar. We both turned to look at whatever had complained so mightily.

It was Miss Milky, up in the trailer, venting her misery. I'd forgotten about her. Horseflies were biting her. Her red eyes peered sadly out at us through the bars. The corners of her eyes were swollen, giving her a Chinese look.

With no warning at all, a snapping hail fell on us. Only it wasn't hail. It was a moving cloud of thirteen-year locusts. They darkened the air and they covered us. The noise was like static on the radio, miles of static across the bug-peppered sky, static that could drown out all important talk and idle music, no matter how powerful the station.

The old man's face was covered with the bugs and he was saying something to me, but I couldn't make out what it was. His mouth opened and closed, opened and closed. When it opened, he'd have to brush away the locusts from his lips. They were like ordinary grasshoppers, only smaller, and they had big red eyes that seemed to glow with their own hellish light. Then, as fast as they had come, they were gone, scattered back into the fields. A few hopped here and there, but the main cloud had broken up.

I just sat there, brushing at the lingering feel of them on my skin and trying to readjust myself to uncluttered air, but my ears were still crackling with their racket.

The old man pulled at my sleeve, breaking me out of my daydream or trance. "You got something for me?" he asked.

I felt blue. Worse than blue. Sick. I felt incurable—ridden with the pointlessness of just about everything you could name. The farm struck me as a pointless wonder, and I found the idea depressing and fearsome. Pointless bugs lay waiting in the fields for the pointless crops as the pointless days and seasons ran on and on into the pointless forever.

"Shit," I said.

"I'll take that worthless cow off your hands, then," said the old man. "She's done for. All you have to do is look at her."

"No shit," I said.

He didn't seem so old or so wrecked to me now. He was younger and bigger, somehow, as if all his clocks had started spinning backwards, triggered by the locust cloud. He stood up. He looked thick across the shoulders like he'd done hard work all his life and could still do it. He showed me his right hand and it was yellow with hard calluses. His beady black eyes were quick and lively in their shallow sockets. The blue lump on his forehead glinted in the sun. It seemed deliberately polished, as if it were an ornament. He took a little silver bell out of his pocket and rang it for no reason at all.

"Let me have her," he said.

"You want Miss Milky?" I asked. I felt weak and childish. Maybe I was drunk. My scalp itched and I scratched it hard. He rang his little silver bell again. I wanted to have it, but he put it back into his pocket. Then he knelt down and opened his bindle. He took out a paper sack.

I looked inside. It was packed with seeds of some kind. I ran my fingers through them and did not feel foolish. I heard a helicopter putt-putting in the distance. In defense of what I did, let me say this much: I knew Miss Milky was done for. Doc Nevers would have told me to kill her. I don't think she was even good for hamburger. Old cow meat can sometimes make good hamburger, but Miss Milky looked wormy and lean. And I wouldn't have trusted her bones for soup. The poison that had wasted her flesh and ruined her udder had probably settled in her marrow.

And so I unloaded my dying cow. He took out his silver bell again and tied it to a piece of string. He tied the string around Miss Milky's neck. Then he led her away. She was docile and easy, as though this was exactly the way things were supposed to turn out.

My throat was dry. I felt too tired to move. I watched their slow progress down the path that ran along the ditch. They got smaller and smaller in the field until, against a dark hedge of box elders, they disappeared. I strained to see after them, but it was as if the earth had given them refuge, swallowing them into its deep, loamy, composting interior. The only sign that they still existed in the world was the tinkling of the silver bell he had tied around Miss Milky's neck. It was a pure sound, naked on the air.

Then a breeze opened a gap in the box elders and a long blade of sunlight pierced through them, illuminating and magnifying the old man and his cow, as if the air between us had formed itself into a giant lens. The breeze let up and the box elders shut off the sun again, and I couldn't see anything but a dense quiltwork of black and green shadows out of which a raven big as an eagle flapped. It cawed in raucous good humor as it veered over my head.

I went on into town anyway, cow or no cow, and hit some bars. I met a girl from the East in the Hobble who thought I was a cowboy and I didn't try to correct her mistaken impression, for it proved to be a free pass to good times.

When I got home, Mama had company. She was dressed up in her beet juice gown, and her face was powdered white. Her dark lips looked like a wine stain in snow. But her clear blue eyes were direct and calm. There was no distraction in them.

"Hi boy," said the visitor. It was Big Pete Parley. He was wearing a blue suit, new boots, a gray felt Stetson. He had a toothy grin on his fat red face.

I looked at Mama. "What's *he* want?" I asked.

"Mr. Parley is going to help us, Jackie," she said.

"What's going on, Mama?" I asked. Something was wrong. I could feel it but I couldn't see it. It was Mama, the way she was carrying herself maybe, or the look in her eyes and her whitened skin. Maybe she had gone all the way insane. She went over to Parley and sat next to him on the davenport. She had slit her gown and it fell away from her thigh, revealing the veiny flesh.

"We're going to be married," she said. "Pete's tired of being a widower. He wants a warm bed."

As if to confirm it was no fantasy dreamed up by her senile mind, Big Pete slipped his meaty hand into the slit dress and squeezed her thigh. He clicked his teeth and winked at me.

"Pete knows how to operate a farm," said Mama. "And you do not, Jackie." She didn't intend for it to sound mean or critical. It was just a statement of the way things were. I couldn't argue with her.

I went into the kitchen. Mama followed me in. I opened a beer. "I don't mean to hurt your feelings, Jackie," she said.

"He's scheming to get our land," I said. "He owns half the county, but it isn't enough."

"No," she said. "I'm the one who's scheming. I'm scheming for my boy who does not grasp the rudiments of the world."

I had the sack of seeds with me. I realized that I'd been rattling them nervously.

"What do you have there?" she asked, narrowing her eyes.

"Seeds," I said.

"Seeds? What seeds? Who gave you seeds? Where'd you get them?"

I thought it best not to mention where I'd gotten them. "Big Pete Parley doesn't want to marry *you*," I said. It was a mean thing to say, and I wanted to say it.

Mama sighed. "It doesn't matter what he wants, Jack. I'm dead anyway." She took the bag of seeds from me, picked some up, squinted at them.

"What is that supposed to mean?" I said, sarcastically.

She went to the window above the sink and stared out into the dark. Under the folds of her evening gown, I could see the ruined shape of her old body. "Dead, Jack," she said. "I've been dead for a while now. Maybe you didn't notice."

"No," I said. "I didn't."

"Well, you should have. I went to sleep shortly after your Daddy died and I had a dream. The dream got stronger and stronger as it went on until it was as vivid as real life itself. More vivid. When I woke up I knew that I had died. I also knew that nothing in the world would ever be as real to me as that dream."

I almost asked her what the dream was about, but I didn't, out of meanness. In the living room Big Pete Parley was whistling impatiently. The davenport was squeaking under his nervous weight.

"So, you see, Jackie," said Mama. "It doesn't matter if I marry Pete Parley or what his motives are in this matter. You are all that counts now. He will ensure your success in the world."

"I don't want to be a success, Mama," I said.

"Well, you have no choice. You cannot gainsay the dead."

She opened the window and dumped out the sack of seeds. Then Big Pete Parley came into the kitchen. "Let's go for a walk," he said. "It's too blame hot in this house."

They left by the kitchen door. I watched them walk across the yard and into the dark, unplanted field. Big Pete had his arm around Mama's shoulder. I wondered if he knew, or cared, that he was marrying a dead woman. Light from the half-moon painted their silhouettes for a while. Then the dark field absorbed them.

––––––––––

I went to bed and slept for what might have been days. In my long sleep I had a dream. I was canoeing down a whitewater river that ran sharply uphill. The farther up I got, the rougher the water became. Finally, I had to beach the canoe. I proceeded on foot until I came to a large gray house that had been built in a wilderness forest. The house was empty and quiet. I went in. It was clean and beautifully furnished. Nobody was home. I called out a few times before I understood that silence was a rule. I went from room to room, going deeper and deeper toward some dark interior place. I understood that I was involved in a search. The longer I searched, the more vivid the dream became.

When I woke up I was stiff and weak. Mama wasn't in the house. I made a pot of coffee and took a cup outside. Under the kitchen window there was a patch of green shoots that had not been there before. "You got something for me?" I said.

A week later that patch of green shoots had grown and spread. They were weeds. The worst kind of weeds I had ever seen. Thick, spiny weeds, with broad green leaves tough as leather. They rolled away from the house, out across the fields, in a viny carpet. Mean, deep-rooted weeds, too mean to uproot by hand. When I tried, I came away with a palm full of cuts.

In another week they were tall as corn. They were fast growers and I could not see where they ended. They covered everything in sight. A smothering blanket of deep green sucked the life out of every other growing thing. They crossed fences, irrigation ditches, and when they reached the trees of a windbreak, they became ropy crawlers that wrapped themselves around trunks and limbs.

When they reached the Parley farm, over which my dead mother now presided, they were attacked by squadrons of helicopters which drenched them in poisons, the best poisons chemical science knew how to brew. But the poisons only seemed to make the weeds grow faster, and after a spraying the new growths were tougher, thornier, and more determined than ever to dominate the land.

Some of the weeds sent up long woody stalks. On top of these stalks were heavy seedpods, fat as melons. The strong stalks pushed the pods high into the air.

The day the pods cracked, a heavy wind came up. The wind raised black clouds of seed in grainy spirals that reached the top of the sky, then scattered them, far and wide, across the entire nation.

AT ST. THERESA'S COLLEGE
FOR WOMEN

Ellen Hunnicutt

"I don't know who tunes the fiddles," says Sister Theophane.

"Fourteen?" I am only half listening.

"'They play the Bach Double Concerto but I don't think they can tune their own violins.'" She reads this information from a letter, refolds the page, looks into her coffee cup and finds it empty. One more betrayal.

"Perhaps they never go out of tune," I offer. "The Japanese can do anything these days." I am thinking about gardenias, my very first corsage, how my fingers ached to touch the soft ivory petals. *Any place you touch will turn brown.* This is my mother's voice. The fretful, rising tone is perfectly preserved in my memory, like the fingering pattern for an extended arpeggio that, once learned, lives on forever in the brain cells. "What ever happened to gardenias?" I ask Sister Theophane.

"Opal, please be serious. Success depends on seeing to details. I've spent half my budget on these children, half the budget for the entire series."

"I'll help you tune," I say, contrite. "What's fourteen fiddles? Even if you are putting me out of business."

Sister Theophane rises, takes both our cups for more coffee, hers in the left hand (sugar), mine in the right (black). "You have tenure, Opal." A gentle reprimand.

In the cafeteria at St. Theresa's College for Women, at four in the afternoon, it is 1949. I am eighteen and nothing has happened yet. It is a trick of the light, pale Chicago sun slanting through the high iron fence, bathing our simple buildings in a certain yellow glow that is inexpressibly sad. In many ways, St. Theresa's exists outside of time; many things have not changed since I was a student here. That is because nuns never wear anything out; and at St. Theresa's nobody vandalizes. Unscarred maple floor, golden oak dining tables, cool pink marble windowsills and, beyond the windows, the small sandstone chapel.

But I am not eighteen, and Sister Theophane in a neat blue dress, professor of music and my boss, thick-waisted and graying above the coffee cups is actually two years younger than I.

"I've decided to offer them ice cream," Theophane says, heartened by fresh coffee. "Lemonade might make them need the bathroom."

"They'll probably need the bathroom anyway."

"Opal, will you please stop it? You aren't helping. You really aren't."

"I'm sorry. I've just turned fifty. It's made me touchy."

Theophane considers, decides to say nothing, opens and reads again the letter from her friend, a nun in Indianapolis.

Why are joy and sadness so inextricably mixed? Memory and desire. I have a third-year student who is setting parts of *The Waste Land* to music for women's choir. She rehearses her singers in a basement room where someone is growing an ivy philodendron on a high windowsill. I listen to the voices, study the deep green of leaves spilling over the cool basement wall, and it seems to me there is some important thing I need to know, hidden in the voices of these young women.

One day last week I drove home by St. Luke's Hospital where nuns still wear habits. I paid a dollar to a parking attendant and sat quietly in the lobby of the hospital for an hour to watch the nuns. This recalled for me, oddly, not my childhood among teaching sisters but nuns in old films, moving across the landscape of faraway countries bringing succor to the needy. I saw a priest who looked like actor Barry Fitzgerald.

An hour later, moving through the glut of Chicago traffic, this experience lost all reality for me. I wondered if I had, indeed, been at St. Luke's. Sometimes this happens to me when I am teaching. I fancy a student will suddenly look at me and discover I am not a teacher at all, but an uncertain young woman like herself, masquerading in a middle-aged body. The two things are not precisely the same.

"Fifty," I say in the dark, moving close to Howie.

"I'm glad you're not fat," he says against my throat. It is the lopsided compliment too-thin women receive all of their lives. "Jack Webster's wife must be three feet across in the butt." He strokes my skinny butt gratefully.

"Howie, I need to know something."

"Okay."

"Do you think about girls? I want you to tell me."

"All the time," he answers promptly. "That's all I think about, naked girls standing in long lines, day and night."

"Please, I want to know. I'm not young anymore."

"Neither am I," says Howie, refusing to play games.

I do this to him almost daily, compulsively.

Theophane, my closest friend, is silent across the table. I wonder what her fantasies are, what nuns dream about.

Howie is an engineer, of the old school: get the work out. Georgia Tech, class of '51. He does not spend time planning utopias as many of the younger men do. Such things may come. Howie has no objection. But he isn't counting on it.

He flies to Boston (often) to supervise the installation of packaging machinery. In his pockets and in the expensive briefcase I gave him for Christmas he carries calipers, socket wrenches, locking pliers, a set of screwdrivers. Traveling, he is a walking hardware store. When he goes through airport security, he buzzes. Howie always buzzes. In an illogical, ridiculous way this pleases me. I'm glad I am married to a man who buzzes in airport security.

"Bring me something from Boston," I say petulantly.

Howie dutifully complies. At the end of the week he returns, bringing me two rolls of Lifesavers and a coffee mug. You can't shop in airports.

I thank him with a thin smile, set the mug on a kitchen shelf, serve dinner with cool, elaborate gestures, making it clear that I have been wounded.

At four in the morning I wake suddenly, gripped with remorse, gut-wrenching terror. Howie sleeping peacefully beside me is fifty-four, could die at any time. He has passed the age where people say, "What a tragedy, so young." They would say, "Howard Franklin? What did he have?" I slip from bed in the darkness, go to a hall closet and dig out the old air force jacket Howie wore in college, bury my face in it and weep piteously, seeing my husband in his grave and wondering what I should do with the second car. I have never learned to make out an automobile title. I determine to learn at once. This small decision calms me and I am glad Howie has not heard nor seen me. My hands release the jacket and I picture this calm, capable woman I have become: giving directions, signing papers, saying, "What, after all, is death? A change in mode from major to minor, a shift in tempo, a variation on a theme." All of our children are dead. Why not Howie? Why not me? Such things are easy. That's it, isn't it?

My mother never understood why all of our babies died. One two three four five. Like little Indians.

"Darling, people have one miscarriage," she said, visiting me at the hospital. "Everyone has one miscarriage. It's common." Somehow this was meant as instruction, like telling me to whip the fudge just until it loses its glossy sheen.

I swam up from a fuzzy sea of contradictions and drugs—scopolamine in those days—and pressed my fingertips against the outline of my uterus, a curious, swollen mass lying just beneath the skin of my abdomen. Then, for the one and only time in my life, I had a vision. I saw my mother going through supermarkets and department stores, making her private survey, stopping women with plump babies and curly-headed toddlers. All of them told her they had, indeed, had one miscarriage, between babies, probably a deformed fetus and all for the good. And mother, nodding, made check marks on a piece of paper that looked like a birth announcement. Scopolamine works on the mind.

Mother twisted her handkerchief, displayed courage, was admirable. Then bitter, shivery little sobs forced themselves from her throat. Against her will, she cried. Pushed past her limit, by me. Life until that time had been a trick done with mirrors; then the mirrors were snatched away.

This memory is self-serving. I savor the delicious tang of betrayal like rich dessert across my tongue, pity poor Theophane who has not suffered as I have, feel generous toward her because of this.

––––––

What, after all, is death? I know death the way I know a student composition. "Wait until you hear it!" cries the eager student. But I hear it already, just looking at the score. Epistemology of music notation.

––––––

After the fifth and final miscarriage, Howie and I lay side by side in the darkness, numb and shaken. "It's going to be all right," he said protectively, but with a hostile edge to his voice. Someone was to blame. Soon he would find the target for his anger. Any minute now. But he never did. Howie never got revenge. What he got was a promotion.

I got Robert, eleven years old, near-sighted. "Mrs. Franklin?" Robert's mother was an eager, huffy little voice in the telephone. "I understand you used to play violin with the symphony." When excited, she talked through her nose.

"I don't play any more. I don't teach."

"Robert isn't doing at all well in the class at school. We want private lessons for him with a skilled person." She came down hard on "skilled." Had she already interviewed and rejected a dozen teachers? Robert's mother was formidable. She did all of the right things for the wrong reasons, knew that any violinist who refused to teach her son had to be good. Damned good. "Don't give me an answer today, Mrs. Franklin." Robert's mother eventually found her true vocation, now sells insurance.

––––––

"Vibrate slowly," I said to Robert, "like an owl. Who-uh, who-uh, who-uh. After you smooth out the wiggle-waggle, you can speed up." Nobody had ever said this to Robert before and he didn't mind trying it. He was fascinated with a teacher who wore velvet pants and chain-smoked through the lesson.

"Can I ride in your Porsche?" he asked. At the end of the lesson, his mother handed me a five-dollar bill.

That night at dinner I showed the money to Howie. "I can buy my own cigarettes." He grinned, then he got up and put brandy in the coffee. I carried the bill folded in my wallet all week, and walked through shops looking at things that cost five dollars.

Incredibly, Robert liked me. He brought me sticks of Dentyne gum and told me jokes.

"To read a signature in sharps," I said to him "look at the last sharp on the right and go up one.

"Jesus, that's a neat trick," said Robert, who was just learning to swear.

I laid plans to steal Robert and flee to Australia. I'd call Howie from Brisbane and make him understand. Or maybe Canada. Howie could commute while the litigation dragged out.

Robert, who was ordinary, brought in his wake Clarissa, who was exceptional. Plain, stout, brilliant. Eyes as cool and clever as a leopard's. She was fifteen, and she hated me. Her vibrato was pure, no wiggle-waggle, and she knew it. She knew everything.

"All music imitates the human voice," I told her.

"I know that," said Clarissa.

"Sing the music as you play. When you're able to do that, you can just breathe with it. The length of one breath is the basis for all phrasing."

"I know that," said Clarissa, a reflex. She was an inch taller than I with powerful arms and hands and the perfect apple skin that plump little girls often carry into adolescence. When she is forty, I thought, she will be a handsome woman. She reminded me of pictures I had seen of Anna Freud. Except for the hatred in her face.

But she came back week after week, often with her lesson memorized. "Your instincts are good," I said to her. "Trust them. When the wispy little business starts in your head, don't cut it off. Nurture it." Her attack was masterly, a thick, brown bite, slightly bitter, understated, theatrical.

I wanted to steal her, run away to Argentina. "You'll like Buenos Aires," I'd say, and Clarissa would answer, "I know that."

I received the first phone call from her grandfather. Elderly, Russian-born, he called Leningrad St. Petersburg. He loved the violin the way some men love beautiful women. "The child sounds better. Thank you."

"She's doing it herself." Which was true.

"I am now prepared to buy her a better instrument." He named the amount he was willing to spend.

It caught me off guard. "You can't be serious." I stammered, gushed, sounded ridiculous. "For that money you could have a Guarnerius."

A Guarnerius, it seemed, was exactly what he had in mind. "What if she stops practicing?" I asked.

He chuckled. "She won't, and a fiddle is always an investment. I can't lose." Although he did not play himself, he had already owned a Stradivarius, sold it, now missed it. "I'd rather pay the finder's fee to you, Mrs. Franklin. You know the child best."

"Me," I told Howie.

"You can do it," he said. "Why not?"

"When he sees me he'll change his mind."

But the grandfather came over the following evening, shook my hand, and seemed satisfied. He smoked a cigar and drank Scotch with Howie. As a young student in Germany he had met Clara Schumann, heard her tell the wonderful stories about Brahms. I put it together—Clara, Clarissa. "Mrs. Franklin," he said, "Clarissa is modeling herself after you. She has purchased a pair of shoes exactly like the ones you are wearing."

"Clarissa?" It was news to me.

That night I dreamed I telephoned Clara Schumann and asked her to find a fiddle. She was barefoot, offered to trade a fiddle for a pair of shoes. In the dream I spoke fluent German, a language I do not know.

Actually, I called Altman, my own former teacher, retired in San Diego. "Opal!" he cried. "Bring Howie and come to California. We'll eat clams, just like the old days in Chicago. My wife died. Did you know that?"

Altman said, "Zenger's the best. In Cleveland. You call Zenger." Zenger said he'd talk to St. Louis and get back to me.

Clarissa's Guarnerius was in Amsterdam. A rich, winey beauty. With it, she caught fire, plunged into Paganini, Sarasate, Saint-Saëns, Wieniawski. I had to call Altman again. "She needs a teacher. She plays better than I do."

"Listen, Opal," said Altman, "I can get you into a quartet out here. It's hard today, very hard. The kids coming on are good. They show up knowing all the standard repertoire already. But I can get you in." He wanted to hear Clarissa play.

"On the telephone?"

"Yes."

But the grandfather found out and didn't like it. He bought airline tickets and sent Clarissa and me to California.

Flying terrified Clarissa. She clutched her fiddle case, fought nausea, turned white, bit her lips. And finally surrendered. "Mrs. Franklin, do you know why I hate you so much?" Her voice was a gray wisp, devoid of hope.

"Yes," I said. Gently, oh so gently. "Because I'm thin . . . and you think thin is beautiful."

Then her tears came, and small, bitter sobs. "I want to change. You'll help me . . . I know you will."

"Like hell I will," I said, capturing her in my arms. "You're a wonderful, marvelous person, just as you are." So I told her about the babies. I told her about Brisbane and Buenos Aires. I even told her about my mother and scopolamine.

"So nobody gets everything," said Clarissa, sniffling.

We landed, not healed, but holding hands. Eight years later, while on tour, Clarissa sent me a postcard from Buenos Aires: "Hey, I'm here! Come on down! Love always, Clarissa."

Altman said, "Juilliard."

"That's what I thought," I said, but the grandfather paid for everything and seemed pleased.

He met our return plane. "She'll need a high school equivalency," I told him.

"We'll get a tutor," he said. "Go ahead with her preparation."

When I got Clarissa past her auditions, the grandfather appeared at my door with roses and kissed my hand.

––––––––––

After Clarissa came Dwight, Stephen, Mary Ruth, Annette. Twin brothers who went into country music and still send me chocolates at Christmas. A quiet boy who loved Debussy and became a Lutheran minister. A gentle girl with white hands who, incredibly, committed suicide. More names than I can remember. But never another Clarissa.

––––––––––

In the same month, Altman died and St. Theresa's offered me a job. I received a call from Sister Mary Elizabeth. "Mrs. Franklin? Sister Theophane wants you for our music department." Mary Elizabeth is nothing like her fragile name. President of St. Theresa's, one hundred pounds of intensity, tough, formidable fund-raiser, frequenter of Chicago boardrooms.

"Sister, I'm afraid I'm not a very good Catholic."

"Who is these days? I wasn't proposing to hire you as a theologian. We already have a couple of those. We're looking for a violin teacher. You graduated from St. Theresa's, also studied privately, and played professionally. That combination makes you interesting to us. Come in and we'll talk about it."

"All right. Has everything changed?"

"Yes and no."

––––––––––

Sister Mary Elizabeth, wearing a gabardine suit, received me in her small, pleasant rooms: sliced cheese, poured cider. "We're putting together a music performance major. We've never offered it before. We've turned out school teachers, nurses, and secretaries."

"I can't imagine St. Theresa's changing. It looks the same."

"Read Father Newman, unfolding revelation. Our mission is to educate women. On any two successive days that means two different things, at least two."

"Ah!" Sister Theophane came in and settled into a chair. "If you're going to cite Father Newman then cite Prometheus as well."

Mary Elizabeth smiled. "Sister means we've been criticized, but that's nothing new. There's always been something a little illicit about educating people, especially women. For years our simplicity was protective coloration—cloisters, high walls, habits—to cover what we were really doing."

"Committing a crime?" Theophane asked cheerfully. "The first women composers were nuns. The orders sheltered them. And in the Middle Ages if you were fleeing an enemy you could run into a convent and claim sanctuary. And many people did. It's never been strawberries and cream, keeping the flame and all that."

And so the sisters took me in, and now I have that commodity above price: a place to get up in the morning and go to.

"Opal?"

"I'm sorry, Sister. What did you say?"

"I asked if you were going to eat dinner with me tonight."

"No, I'm going home to eat. Look, you've managed St. Theresa's Fine Arts Series for nine years, three programs a year, almost without a flaw. I really think everything will be all right."

Theophane is not convinced. "I think I'll close up my office and see you in the morning."

"And I'd better call my husband."

"Howie?"

"Hi."

"I'll be here another hour."

"No problem."

"Sister Theophane's upset. She's afraid the Suzuki kids will play out of tune."

Howie likes Theophane, immediately takes sides. "Do you believe this guy really has fourteen prodigies?"

"Suzuki? He claims they aren't prodigies, just ordinary children taught by his method."

"Baloney," says Howie loyally. "Does Suzuki come with them?"

"No, he's too old to travel. He sends his assistant. Guess what the assistant's name is."

"What?"

"Honda."

"You made that up."

At the far end of the cafeteria the serving line opens and the first boarding students drift in. At St. Theresa's the median age of students used to be nineteen. Today it is twenty-six. The numbers are weighted by part-time students, day students, evening students. Our oldest student is a woman of seventy-one who is studying art history.

———

"Opal, you're still here!" Winifred Orbison in blue jeans brings her brown bag dinner to my table. Thirty-seven, mother of two, political science major, she does not have time for music. "I can't get one damned person to picket O'Hare Saturday afternoon."

"O'Hare?"

"A military air show. I can usually count on at least ten people, but everybody's going to hear those Japanese kids play. Opal, I don't mean to be rude but what the hell is your music going to be worth if they drop the bombs?" She eats her sandwich without tasting it. "Try a cookie. My daughter made them. She's twelve."

"Delicious! Tell her I said so."

"She cooks all the time, even bakes bread. She's four times smarter than I ever was. You should hear her father brag about her. Opal, the bombs scare the hell out of me. I tell people just to walk down that hall and look in the day nursery, just look in at those children and think about it. Have you ever done that?"

"Yes."

"I have to run."

———

Our day nursery is under the direction of Sister Angela. She is small and rosy with fluttering hands. She never tires of children. She wears a black tunic and slacks, sits on the carpet with small boys and girls while their mothers study. She charges one dollar an hour and insists on being paid promptly.

———

My last student cannot come in until after work, tonight has been asked to work overtime. Betty. Bluff, bright, eager, she just wants to see if she can learn to play the violin. Last year she took a course in auto mechanics at the vocational school to see if she could learn to fix her own car. Betty has no sense of magic. "Count," I say to her. "Three-four time is a waltz. Do you dance?"

"Not the waltz."

I assign Beethoven's "Ode to Joy" in a student transcription, asking the music to do my job for me. "Five simple notes created the most glorious anthem the world has ever known."

"Can't I play a woman composer?"

"Yes . . . of course."

Cecile Chaminade's "Pas des Echarpes." She plays it mechanically, taking great care with the chromatics, as she takes great care with everything. I have four Bettys this year. The number is down slightly from last year.

The pleasant aromas of food drift through the room. Hannah passes. "Hi, Mrs. Franklin." A senior art student, she is graduating and being married in June. She has selected a china pattern, named her bridesmaids, asked me to play at her wedding.

"Hello, Mrs. Franklin." Marla is in music education. With her pleasant soprano voice she will teach school children to sing. Her parents' divorce has left her skittish about boys. She budgets her money carefully, sews her own clothes.

"Staying for dinner tonight, Mrs. Franklin?" Carol is twenty-two, an unmarried mother. Her parents care for her little boy while she studies nursing.

They come together, a line of bright flowers, all the modes of a scale, unique and yet related in an important and special way. They are the women I have always known, eager to laugh, nearly as eager to cry, filled with swift enthusiasm, sharp sorrow, enormous hope.

I rise, pass through the double doors, and bump squarely into Sister Theophane who is now smiling. "I read through everything again. Three teachers travel with them. They tune. Apparently my friend didn't know that."

"They don't need us, Sister. We're obsolete."

Theophane sighs. "I think you're teasing, but I will be so very glad when you get over this fifty business."

"Enjoy your dinner, Sister."

In the silent hallway my footsteps echo as in a cathedral, past deserted classrooms to my teaching studio. I think ahead to dinner, stopping on the way home for shrimp, Howie's favorite. At the doorway of the nursery I pause and look in at pale sunlight falling across soft carpeting, abandoned toys returned to bright shelves, silent walls. Five plush animals sit neatly on a windowsill: two bears, a rabbit, one soft cat, a perky dog. Misshapen from much hugging, inexpressibly sad. It is a trick of the light, the pale Chicago light that will be gone in a moment.

"Mrs. Franklin! I'm so sorry I'm late. Are you coming?"

"Yes. Yes, I'm coming."

UNCLE MOUSTAPHA'S ECLIPSE

Reginald McKnight

Idi, my very best friend here in Senegal, was suffering from a very strange eye malady. He didn't know precisely what had caused his usually quick, pebble eyes to swell, yellow, tear, and itch so. He'd gone to both doctors and *marabous* and they didn't know either. "All that I can say," said Idi, "is that my eye sickness remind me very much of my Uncle Moustapha's eye sickness." And at that he proceeded to tell me the story of his Uncle Moustapha M'Baye's eye "sickness":

"This was a long, long time ago, Marcus. Before I even was born. My uncle live in a small, small village along the Gambian river near to Bassi Santa Su, call Sakaam. It is too, too hot there. You would not believe it, my friend. The sunshine is so heavy there that a man can reach his hand into the hot air and squeeze the sunshine like wet clay. The mosquito there can only walk and the baboons move like old men, in Sakaam.

"It was there my Uncle Moustapha live and work with his three wives and seven children. He, it is say, was the finest peanut farmer in his whole village. He hardly never had a bad crop. When even there was too much rain, his crop was fair, and other farmers' much worse. And when the rains were thin, Uncle Moustapha always have plenty of rice for he save from the good years. This mean he was a very careful man. He was a hard worker, and very lucky. He had strong juju and was also a good Muslim.

"His only problem in life was that always, always he think about Death. He always think about Death most deeply on the night before his birthday. Now, you must understand, Marcus, that even when I was born thirty years ago, people did not know their birthdays. But Uncle Moustapha was very fond of many things in white culture. He like chocolate and watches, books and French bread. He like birthdays too, because my father tell me, he was a proud man and like the idea of having a personal day of celebration. So he begin keeping a birthday from the day his seventh child was born. He begin at the age of forty, and every year for twenty years, he keep the day of June seven as his birthday. This only add to his worry, for as we say here, Marcus, Death is birth and birth is Death.

"So on the eve night of his sixtieth birthday, he think about his death and he could not sleep. He lay in his hot room and no sound came to his ears. He wait with a numb heart for Death to enter any minute. He focus on nothing but the door, knowing that his final moments were upon him. He expect that soon, soon, a long, white hand would push the door open with no sound; that Death's face would be reveal to him and that he would be taken. He was not really afraid to die. Only he was very worry that his lazy brothers would not take good care of his wives and children. 'The moment I see this door open,' he say, 'I shall light a cigarette and smile at the old fool.' He feel for his cigarette and his matches. Upon coming into contact with both, he let his hand rest on them and say in a loud voice, 'How do you do, Death? Do you care for a smoke? No, no we have time, you and I; have one . . . yes, yes, of course. I have plenty left. Have one with me . . . indeed, master, sit anywhere. . . . So how are you? Been busy lately?' This make him laugh, you see, but only for a brief moment. He choke back his laughter when he notice that he cause his wife to wake. 'Why do you wake me?' she say.

"'I wait for Death,' he say, 'as always. My birthday is tomorrow, you re-member.'

"'Ah, you crazy man,' my Auntie say. 'These whiteman ways make you too, too silly. To talk and laugh with yourself is madness. Madness, you hear? If you have no birthday, you have no fear of Death.'

"'I do not have . . .'

"'First it is chocolate which make you sick always. Then it is watch which make your wrist turn green. Then it is birthday which make you fear Death and ignore the courage that Allah give you. Then it is foolishness about sun . . .'

"'It is eclipse, you old 'ooman. Eclipse. And it is true. There are a thou-sand of white men in Bassi Santa Su who wait for it. They say the sun shall disappear and I believe them. It will be tomorrow on my birthday. You shall see.'

"'Dugga doff tropp,' she say, which mean my Uncle Mousse was a very crazy man. Auntie Fatima was my uncle's favorite wife, but not because she was always sweet to him, but because she always tell him the truth. His other wives always would smile at all his curious doings and hold out their hands for the *xallis*. Fatima love him the most, and she did not care for a man with a lot of *xallis*. She say when he was first having birthdays she did not mind much. She used to even sit up with him each night before his birthday and humor him. But through the many years, as you say, Marcus, no dice. It make her angry.

"So she say, 'Dugga doff tropp,' to him and turn away to sleep. Uncle Moustapha only shrug, get up from bed and cross the room to where his clothes were. He reach into the pocket of his boubou and remove his watch. It was some minutes after midnight. He lay the watch on the floor and then say his prayers, thanking Allah with all his heart.

"'Get up, old man' say Auntie Fatima. 'Get up, I say.' It was morning. Uncle Moustapha open his eyes, but seem to see nothing as he always did in the mornings. His old bones were sore. He look about himself with his blind eyes and say, 'Fatima, it is dark, yet. Why do you wake me?' Auntie Fatima look at him and say, '*Wyyo!* Did you not ask me to wake you at cock-crow? It is you who ask me to do this so that you may see this Sun foolishness.'

"'Where did I put my watch?'

"'I do not know where is this watch,' say Auntie and she leave the room.

"Uncle Moustapha leap from his bed and find his watch. It was six o'clock and some minutes in the morning. There was still plenty of time for him to get to Bassi Santa Su before the eclipse. He wash his body, had a breakfast of bread and bitter black coffee, and put on his best boubou. 'Fati!' he say. Auntie Fatima return to the bedroom. 'Fatima,' he say, 'I will take my lunch in town today.'

"'There is someone to see you, Mousse,' say Auntie.

"'Why did you say nothing to me?'

"'He came only this moment.'

"'Who is this who comes here?' say my uncle, very angry. You see, he want no one to interfere with his trip to town on this most important day. 'It is a white man' my Auntie say, 'with many strange machines.'

"'The name is Madison,' say the white man. And it seem he was a scientist interest in renting some of Uncle Moustapha's land to set up his machines and telescopes on. Uncle Mousse's land is green, green and beautiful as heaven. It is call the jewel of Sakaam, and I would not be surprise if Madison the white man want to stay at there because of its beauty, but he say instead that it was the perfect scientific place for him to view the eclipse because of all these scientific reasons. 'How much may I give you, Mr. M'Baye?' say Madison. And he reach to his pocket for some money. Uncle Moustapha stop the white man's hand and say, 'Wait, wait, wait! I want no money from you.' This shock Madison to make his green eyes stick out and his face turn red, red.

"'But your land is perfect,' he say. 'I need it. I will pay you any price.' Uncle Moustapha say no. This make Madison even more shock for he have never seen a black man refuse money, you see. 'But I do not want this money,' say Uncle Mousse. 'Please allow kindly, Mr. Madison, for me to view the eclipse with your machines.' Uncle Moustapha explain, that because it was his birthday, he must be allow to see this very special gift from Allah. Madison only shake my uncle's hand and smile a big, big smile.

"Time move slow, slow for the two men. The eclipse begin at eight o'clock and some minutes in the morning, and all the land and sky change to a mysterious, curious haze. Like a pearl. Many people stay in their homes because this cloudless sky was becoming darker and darker. Uncle Mousse was singing and dancing inside himself because it was his personal day and a very strange important thing was happening. But like a true Wolof man, he was quiet and serious outside. He help Madison the white man assemble his equipment as Madison explain to him many things about telescopes, eclipses, etcetera. The sky grew darker. It became empty of birds and the land was quiet and golden green.

"Every few moments Uncle Mousse would turn his eyes up to the sky of haze to look at the Sun, but when Madison one time saw this, he say, 'Mr. M'Baye, you must not look at the Sun. It is too dangerous. One could go blind from such a thing.' Uncle Moustapha say nothing, but he did as Madison say.

"When the machinery was prepare, my uncle and the white man take turns viewing the sun. Uncle Moustapha was astonish. Never did he see something like this in his life. Finally, the sky was as dark as early evening. 'Happy birthday, Mr. M'Baye,' say Mr. Madison. My uncle was overjoy. This was his gift from Allah, a present from his ancestors. He shake Madison's hand and walk away very quickly to his home with the memory of the orange-black moonsun deep in his mind. 'Fati,' he yell, 'Fati! You must come go with me to our baobab tree.' This shock and surprise Auntie because Uncle Mousse never had interest in baobab tree or in the spirits of the old ones, though he respect them.

"So, anyway, he take Auntie Fatima and tell her all he saw and all what Madison had say him. They walk in the semidark to the great baobab tree of the M'Baye family. The baobab tree, as you must know, Marcus, is the great and huge upside-down tree in which, it is say, live the spirits of the village. The tree that belong to Sakaam (perhap you have seen it when we were there together) sits on the great knoll on the edge of the village very close to the river. It stands alone there; more alone than any tree or shrub or twig in the entire environs. The most remarkable thing about this baobab is the curious way it bows to the east. It resembles a faithful servant of Allah.

"Uncle move as if he were pull to the tree. He ran the last few meters, pulling Auntie along with him. Then he let go of her hand and threw himself at the base of the tree. He say a silent prayer to himself and with his hands, grasp the enormous roots. Auntie Fati say it is as if the very touch of the tree make him feel a sudden power of the spirit, and cleaning of his heart and mind. He seem to empty his heart on the red soil under him as he begin to sing the ancient song of our ancestors.

> Oh fathers. Oh Mother
> Welcome to our hearts
> You will bring us comfort
> At the setting of the Sun.

"Of course, this strange behavior in my uncle did not too much surprise my Auntie Fatima because, as I say, she love him so much. She fall to her knees and say a prayer too. Then she rise when Uncle Moustapha rise and kiss him and say to him in English, 'Fine birthday to you, crazy old man.'

"Ahh and then, Marcus, my uncle's senses at this moment became strongly, powerfully alive. His ears heard like a bat. He smelt the river and the earth and the rustling grass, the sweet, hot air. The smells about him were as strong as the smells of the ocean or a steaming bowl of *tjebugin*. His eyes took in everything—everything. He view each individual stalk of yellow-green grass, every twig, every pebble that sat on the ground. The twigs had made the earth look like to be an enormous patchwork boubou. The soft air touch him delicately as a smile. He turn slowly around—seeing, smelling, hearing everything no matter how small, small or subtle or obscure. And with not one moment of hesitation, he lift his face to the sky and stare directly into the eclipse with his both eyes wide open. He stand staring, unblinking, unflinching.

"He saw it all in supreme detail, as if his eye beams were like Madison's telescopes. He watch the burning moonsun, his birthday present from Allah, and Auntie Fatima watch his eyes knowing somehow that she must not disturb him. Uncle Mousse could see the eclipse more clearly, he later say to Auntie, than he could see them in Madison's machines. It was, you see, his eclipse. His eclipse!

"'Mousse,' say Auntie to him. 'Hey! Mousse. You say the white man say it is dangerous to look at this thing. Hey, Mousse. This is too dangerous.' She lead him to the bottom of the knoll. 'Mousse,' say Auntie, 'are you fine?' Uncle Moustapha's eyes were close. He sense that it would be unwise to open them straightaway, though he knew that he could still see. The image of the eclipse was yet in his eyes. It became a lemon, now an emerald, now a circle of evening sky—deep blue, now a violet, a rose and then it fade into darkness. 'Did you see it?' he whisper. 'Did you see my eclipse?'

"'No,' say Auntie. 'You tell me on the way here to not look at it. Anyway, it is your gift, you crazy old man. Are you fine? Can you see?'

"'What does it matter? I saw it. My own eclipse.'

"'We must go, old man. You are hungry.'

"So, Marcus, they walk away from the hill. They did not look back. Soon, Moustapha open his eyes and look about him. The whole world was more beautiful to him than ever before. He tell his wife of all that he have seen before, during, and after the eclipse as they walk home. He was happy that he did not obey Madison.

"When they get to the family compound they saw Madison packing his equipment into his suitcases and Auntie ran to him and speak very fast, but he did not understand. He spoke no Wolof, you see. 'Don't worry about my 'ooman, Mr. Madison,' say Uncle Mousse. 'She is afraid for I look into the eclipse.' Madison almost pull out his hairs when my uncle say this for, as you know, my friend, it was dangerous. 'You crazy man!' say Madison, 'I say not to do this, but you do this. Why?'

"'But I am not blind, Mr. Madison.'

"'One does not have any difficulty seeing after looking directly at an eclipse for a few hours, or even days. You must go see a doctor.' But Uncle Mousse smile only and light a cigarette. He spoke to Madison in the manner of a great imam. 'I will,' he say, 'see today, tomorrow, and always. I have seen what no other living soul have seen today. No, Mr. Madison, no doctor for me.' So Madison finish packing his things, slip some money to Auntie Fatima and went away.

"'What did he say to you?' ask my aunt.

"'He say foolishness,' say Uncle Mousse. 'He tell me to go to the doctor, but I will not. No, I do not care to—.' But he stop short. 'Did you,' he say to Auntie Fatima, 'see a big, black thing fly by to the left of us?'

"'No,' say Auntie.

"'I thought I saw a black shadow fly by us.'

"'Mousse, Mousse, you are going blind. Oyo! Oyo! Ndeysahn. I think I must—.'

"'Fati, stop this. I know what you will say. You old 'ooman, you . . .' But he was silence again by the dark spot that fly by his vision. It move slower this time and he turn quick to the left to see it, but was gone. 'You saw it again, didn't you, Mousse?' my aunt say with almost crying in her voice.

"'Yes, old 'ooman. Perhap I have make myself blind, indeed. Perhap I should see a doctor.' Auntie insist that Uncle Mousse go to see one of our own marabous because it was the white magic that put him in this situation. Of course, my friend, as you have perhap already guess, Uncle Mousse decide to see a European doctor. He got on the bus to Bassi Santa Su.

"The doctor find Mousse's story incredulous, for he find nothing wrong at all with my uncle's eyes. Nevertheless, Mousse saw the black constantly almost. It flick on and off, on and off in the corner of his left eye. At first it irritate him almost to vexation, but he soon got use to it. The doctor say to him over and over, 'This I don't believe. Your eyesight is excellent except for a slight asti'matism on your left eye.

"'This I have for years, Doctor Blake. This you already have tell me. Listen, I do not know why I see this little black spot out the corner of my eye; I can still see as before.' He would have say more, but he notice that Dr. Blake was beginning to become too red and his lips look like the lips of a baboon. Very thin and tight. My uncle look at the doctor's eye chart for a moment and then he say, 'Must I return to you?'

"'Yes,' say the doctor. 'I will see you two times more. Come on the tenth and the twentieth, please.'

"'Very good,' say Uncle Moustapha, and he went away.

"Upon arriving to home, Uncle Mousse explain to his wife what the doctor say and ate his lunch with a satisfy smile. Then he retire to his room for his nap. The little black spot follow him to his room like an English lady's dog follow her through town. The room was too warm so he open the window. With the door close and his reading lamp on (my uncle was the first in Sakaam to have electricity and running water in his house), he spread out his mat on the floor and take his Koran to begin his prayer and study before the nap. Everything was silent and still. His heart must have been at peace.

"As he begin to read, he notice that the dark spot no longer flash on and off, but it remain there, hanging in the air. It begin to grow. He was afraid to notice this growing blackness, because he fear it would disappear before he could turn. Or worse yet, would take completely his sight. A sudden chill touch him as the spot grew larger. He spin around violently. His heart pound as he fix his eyes on the giant, black image before him. Without thinking he fumble in his pocket for his cigarettes, offer one to the white hand of his guest, light his own and say to him, 'Been busy lately?'"

"Quite a story," I said to my friend Idi. "And you say it's true?"

"Who knows?" said Idi, lighting a Craven. "You must keep an eye on story-telling Africans."

ARIADNE IN EXILE

Maya Sonenberg

From the sea, there rise innumerable hilly islands, each densely for-
ested with pines and ringed with palms and juniper bushes. They break
through the ocean like scabs, their shores like scrollwork. On some, only a
few trees spring slantwise from the rocks; others support villages, a cluster of
churches, an airstrip with orange windsock flopping at the end. Around
each island, the yellow sand and pink rocks slide down the steep sides of the
hills and out under the taut blue-green surface of the water. When the wind
shifts to the north and clears the haze from the horizon, waves glint far into
the distance toward the mainland where, above a wall of white cliffs, fields
spread to the purple mountains, broken only by a grid of dirt roads that lead
from one port city to another. Pilots fly from these cities that are never,
themselves, visible, bringing washing machines and medicine, record players, newsprint, and presses. They dart down in planes with blue stripes
across the tails and leave as quickly. On the islands, people pretend to have
forgotten that their own ancestors fought their way from the mainland to

these spots of color on the sea; they prefer to believe they've always lived here, that the islands are their past. Ships rarely travel so far anymore although transistor radios pick up country music stations rocking across the water during the still nights in the middle of summer, and when the moon shines, making it seem that city lights are bouncing off the clouds in the east, old men draw the children to them and tell stories about someone who came to live on an island not so very long ago. They sit on the damp grass with children circling them like diamonds around the emerald in a brooch. On the islands, this is all anyone knows of the mainland: distance, technology, stories, a few sounds.

What did the girl do alone on the island?

Summer: she stretched sandaled foot from stone to stone, skirt fluttering above her ankles like the dirty foam that slid off the waves at shore. Poised between steps, she twisted her head, squinted, sniffed at the sea as the wind rode across her skull and spread her hair like a dark stain toward the crumbling styrofoam cups above the high-water mark. She stopped because she saw sails, movement out on the water. No: between the islands, the water was bare, flat as the broad side of a sword. The sun hurt her eyes.

Out the door of her cabin in the morning, she trampled the light into the thick layer of pine needles, then followed the shore to town. Halfway there, she sat between the boulders, scratched hot sand into the soft backs of her knees and let it slide away. The heat prickled, the other islands floated on a shimmer of silver. Like the echo of feet on floorboards, her brother pranced across her mind, making delicate indentations. Every afternoon, Mother would hold the attic door open, hand braced on her hip, chin in the air. She filled the small landing. "Come, come love. Bring that here." Her voice clanked down the stairs while the girl brought the tray from the kitchen, loaded with heavy green dishes, flatware, food. Through the fanlight, sun came and bleached the hall carpet. Outdoors, the farm land dropped suddenly, cleanly, and the sea stretched into the west. She might stop to look out the strip of windows on either side of the front door. "Calm," she might catch herself thinking. But her brother would be hungry, pacing, his hands darting through his hair. At the end of the long second flight, the keys to his room glinted between Mother's fingers like the waves cutting between the rocks at the water's edge. Sun in her eyes, she scanned for those sails and the man manning the tiller. She called him: Theseus, lover, savior, sailor. She rose, her head spinning from the heat.

When she turned from the sea, it was with the knowledge that he'd be standing at the top of the next rise, spread against the trees. She saw him leap like a wall of fire, his arms swinging wide, battling space, to reach her, to lift her. She blinked: gone. Above the green hills, only the white church steeples fingered the blue—the Galilean Gospel Temple, St. Brendan's Episcopal, St. Andrew's Lutheran, St. Mary Star of the Sea. She walked by on Sunday once when the central doors were braced open, and a few people turned white faces to watch her as she stared into a hymn swelling from the dark.

There—the first house with a widow's walk like a cage on top, flowers the color of blood in all the window boxes. A screen door whistled before it slammed and she jumped, started to walk quickly toward the center of town. The sound of the sea curled over the red and black tile roofs like a wave.

He could be in any of the buildings, watching her from behind a ruffled curtain, waiting to be found if only she weren't so hesitant, knocked on doors, asked questions. She let herself dawdle, scuff the gravel between the gas station and the clothing store where the yellow slickers stood disembodied in the bay window, past the pottery shop where the potter sat outside astride a chair. He called out hello and gave her a new name every day: Elsie, Jane, Prudence, Patience, Hope. It had become a joke they both smiled at after she'd gone by.

In the grocery store she floated past the cashier, holding her skirt gingerly between fingers and thumb. Her hair fell loose from pins, her eyes wide. Softly, slowly, she stopped by the back counter.

"What would you like, dear?" the shopkeeper asked, lifting her chin to see over the case. Her mottled hands slid over the shiny skins of the fish in their trays of ice behind the glass.

"Haddock," the girl said, dragging her voice over the first syllable as she did with the vowels of her own name, then took the cool package wrapped in wax paper and dropped it into her basket.

She walked down to the pier where piles of netting rotted, ropes frayed and stiff with salt. People treated her gently in town, she thought. They understood her loss though she had no memory of telling them anything. They understood the waiting made her attentive, silent. Perhaps the women got her story first and repeated it to their men once she was out of hearing, shaking their heads all the while. Perhaps he'd talked to the men before he left, told them to watch out for her. The boards sagged where she walked. In the harbor each float bobbed empty of its boat: midday, all at work far from shore or in the next cove, beyond the convolutions of the land. She watched the water come toward her, fought the breeze that picked up her skirt as if it were trying to dance.

———————

How did the girl come to be alone on the island?

Very simple: she awoke. Through an open door, she saw a slice of blue and no boat on it, no purple sail furled around the boom like dead skin. She'd never seen a sea so empty. At home there were always white yachts in the harbor and trawlers out beyond the breakers. And on their zigzag course from island to island, she'd always woken with the sail between her and the sky, the man's breath sliding down her neck—where was he?

She sat up into the dank air. One tiny room. No windows, just the open door and the sun guided in along its edge. Across from the bed there was a rocking chair and next to it, a table. Naked, she stood in the doorway, careful of the splintered boards. Under the low green branches of the pines, the sun scooted up from an inlet that curved into the hills, the same as on all the islands they'd seen, shorelines twisted back on themselves like paths in a maze. To the east the horizon was blank, as if home had never existed. But she saw the white cliffs the way they looked from sea—red in the sunset.

The previous afternoon they had landed at a village dock and walked up a hill, leaning into each other, laughing she remembered, arms linked. They passed the teetering houses and arrived at the square—churches, post office, library, and school placed around a rectangle of green. While he went off to look for food and rope, she sat down near a monument to the war dead with red geraniums planted at its granite base, grass mowed closely around it. The fine hairs were a golden net on his arms as he walked away, and she slumped, curled on her side, and slept. In the morning, she woke to the dark room, triangle of empty water.

Her toes curled on the doorsill. Watery reflections quivered on the tree trunks, but around her, all was quiet, warm, dead. The day she'd opened the door for him the morning glory vines had hung their pink flowers on the air as if on a still lake. He stood in the path looking down at her, his eyes pale opaque blue, the whites as pure as sugar. He smelled clean and cool although the summer dust should have settled on his shoulders. It hadn't rained for months.

"I hear your father wants someone to work in exchange for food and a place to sleep," he said, his voice rich, his vowels flat as the land around them. He hadn't looked as if he needed this job. "They told me all about it in town," he said. "They said he's had trouble keeping people on." Around his head midges spotted the air, and behind them the white buildings on the other side of the bay cast blue shadows against the cliffs.

"Yes, that's right," she said, "to help manage the farm. Mother's lands stretch all the way to there." She pointed to the houses on the outskirts of town. "And there," she said, pointing now to the hills that were only a smudge of violet from where they stood. She thought how she would continue just like this once the estate was her brother's, coming out from the dark house occasionally to stand on the narrow front step and explain the lie of the land to a stranger, looking out over this brightness.

The young man looked away from the fields and up at the house. She had never seen him before, not in town or on any of the neighboring farms; it was not a sailor's face either but something new, blank and beautiful, hiding nothing, his skin absolutely smooth. When he smiled, only one side of his mouth moved and she saw a glimmer as if he knew something he wasn't letting on. It must have been the shadows changing, though, as he turned toward a sound—her brother's laughter rolling from the attic—so familiar she didn't hear it at first, forgetting that someone else might find it strange here—that whooping and hollering—where the fields lay planted with artichokes and cabbages, the farmhands bending over the plants with their short hoes. Smiling to reassure him, she stepped aside and pulled her collar tightly around her throat.

In the parlor the golden hands on the clock, shaped like two pointing fingers, had barely moved since she left the room. Mother turned, tilting her head, and patted the plump sofa cushion for the young man to sit on. By the round mahogany table, Father still dozed with his fingers laced through his beard, his feet planted wide on either side of his chair. She watched the young man, how the pink flushed his cheeks and his eyes floated in the sockets, turning from Father to Mother and back again. He hesitated.

"Sir?" he said and handed over a slip of paper. Father grunted, but before he could say anything her brother snorted and hissed. She felt the dull creak of the walls and floors under his clumsy weight, the dark storm of sound muffling everything else. Father's eyes were slits of glass.

When the noise stopped, Mother leaned forward so that her pink blouse dipped open, exposing pale skin. "You can go dear." She smiled and nodded encouragingly as if the girl were too young to understand her words. "Go look to him. I'll call you when it's time to show this young man around." There was no doubt that he would be hired. Mother touched him, her hand like knotted wood on his. "Don't mind," she said to him. "You'll get used to it." When the young man looked puzzled, she added, "Our son. He has his own apartments upstairs. He's a bit difficult; we never know when he'll go off like that." She shook her head and the silver earrings rattled. She didn't take her hand off his.

Father was nodding, muttering, trying to conceal his sighs, to disguise his pained expression. "I see you've come about the work," he said finally, waving the slip of paper. "You come highly recommended. You can start right away if you like. It'll be supervising the work in the fields mostly, some other things too. My wife's just bought some more land and it's getting to be a bit too much for me to handle alone." He glanced over at Mother and she nodded absently, staring at the back of the young man's head.

The young man fumbled with his white duck bag. "Thank you, sir. I'm anxious to start."

At the cabin door the trees blocked her view—just a narrow path with the green water pounding the rocks at its end. Where was he? His voice? The burst of expelled air when he held her up over him? She had shown him the dark passage to the barn and the stairs up to the room Mother had assigned to him. Perhaps he went back to town. She bent to see under the branches and fidgeted, her fingers squeezing each other. The sun sprang from the rocks at shore. Her brother didn't like bright light. The one time she'd brought a lantern with her, he'd jumped up, arms wider than she was tall. His screams had sliced the air, his feet a shiny black whir as he pawed the floor. Her heart beat in her throat, hands stiff and useless until she thought to blow out the flame. After, she'd always tended him at dawn or in the dusty, murky noontime haze. She'd had all the attic windows boarded up.

She turned back inside. At the table she slipped her dress over her head; it still smelled of salt. He'd left all her clothes. Why? Her sandals, other dress, warm cloak for winter—the one they'd wrapped themselves in that first night on the water before they'd managed to break into the cubby and pull free two rough blankets. He'd left a sack of groceries, a plastic jug of water, money. She counted it, bills so soft they could be made of cloth, so much money he must mean to be gone a long time. She folded it smaller and smaller until it was just a dense square of paper.

Beneath her the bed was hard, but he'd provided sheets, a thin pillow, several woolen blankets folded at the foot. Perhaps he planned on being back after the first leaves had fallen. Still, that was months and months away. Why? Through the door the sun fell straight. She flung her arm across her eyes and slid down close to the wall. Hard hands, pink cheeks, tan feet branded by the straps of his sandals, hair like chains, thighs that held hers like irons—she'd wish him back, wish back the curl of his lip, the tendons distended in his hand as he held the sails through a storm, knuckles white as the waves kicked up around the boat. He'd taken her away from the farmhouse with its long hallways and twisting stairs and out onto the sea. Deceptive: from her window at home, the water had always been the tight silver surface of a plate, not a puzzle of currents and undertow. After tacking between the islands he'd finally brought her here: one dark room and the tortuous coastline outside the door. Why? She pulled her legs up close to her body. He'd said little about his past, nothing about where they were going. She hadn't cared. He'd held rakes like spears, dinner plates like shields. Suddenly he'd opened his arms, asked her to go.

For months she'd lain awake waiting for her alarm clock to ring and wondering if he were already up at the other end of the house, pulling on his pants, rubbing his wet face with a towel. As he carried the garbage away from the attic, she watched the lamplight disappear from his back, then climbed, grabbing the dusty rail, to make up her brother's bed and groom him with the silver comb Mother had provided in its own suede pouch. As she fought the snarls, she thought of these new possibilities — that there were people in the world she'd never met, places she'd never been. She thought of the jet trails the young man had pointed out to her, far above the house.

At night they met again. Her back against the wall, she couldn't swallow, took quick shallow breaths until he had walked down the hallway toward his room. She could turn then, let a rat loose in her brother's apartments as she did every night, stamping so it would run the tunnel of passages to the bedroom. In the morning, there was always a spattering of blood around her brother's mouth to clean; it was dry, brown, and he let her pull it free with her fingernails, grumbling a little.

Silence reminded her where she was. The birds had stopped singing. Under the sheet it seemed grayer, as if the sky had clouded over or the sun moved behind the house. A rough weave, the cloth let in thorns of light. Had she not been pretty enough for him, full-fleshed? But in the boat he'd often called her his beauty. Had she not responded quickly to his touch? Did she sing too much during the day? Or had she failed to chant him to sleep? She'd never complained that she could remember, but perhaps she'd been found wanting in fortitude. Perhaps she'd recited a poem more than once, boring him.

His shirt stretched tightly across his chest. Every afternoon her father had gone to find him outside. She saw them standing just where the dry grass gave way to the green irrigated rows of vegetables. Both men bent their heads as they talked, their caps tipped low over their eyes, and the younger man always tapped the ground with a stick as if considering what the other had to say but unsure whether he agreed. If he saw her watching from behind the stiff parlor curtains, he gave her a half-smile and then turned so she could not see his lips move. Father gestured toward the house, speaking fervently, pointing in turn to the servants' wing, the dark green shades of Mother's boudoir, her own bedroom, and then up to the roof.

Later, she leaned on the dining room table with the heels of her hands and looked out the window behind the young man's blond head. "I can't leave my brother," she said. "You know that. No one else can care for him." She thought of her brother listening for her step as though the chores were done automatically by a body, her body, which somehow could not be replaced. She saw herself going upstairs, charmed, unable to stop, and all her feelings left on the landing.

He reached over the table toward her. "Let's go tonight," he said again, pleading, nervous. "Let them fight it out themselves. It'll be better that way, you'll see."

"What do you mean, fight it out?"

"Just come with me. If you want to come back, you'll be able to, later."

"I can't," she whispered until her refusal was the song of all their meetings, the silent refrain while they sat at supper with her parents and talked about the crops, weather, politics in town. "I can't say why," she said later, the china bowl she held stained magenta from the beets they'd eaten. "I'd feel too guilty. He'd be alone."

Outside, the young man worked, the sky spread about like a quilt.

"Give me a little more time," she'd said. Inside, something gnawed at her—to climb a mountain and breathe the thin air at its peak, to step into a boat and sail to the edge of the world—but she couldn't agree.

"Time won't change anything," he mumbled, and a fine network of lines formed on his forehead. "We can't wait any longer." He grunted as he struck the spade into the earth, wouldn't turn around again even after she'd reached the house. He didn't speak to her for days, and she'd found him closeted more often with her father, found them whispering in the hayloft, the grainfield, and in the corner behind the stairs.

Unable to dissuade him, she'd stood on the landing, her lantern sending a thread of light after him through the partially open door. He'd broken her down; he'd been relentless. "It's too late for me to spare you now so you might as well help me. At least show me the way." How hard had she tried in the end? She couldn't even grab his arm to hold him back. Her brother—splashing and clawing as she bathed him, willing to eat only after he'd tossed his food to the floor and made her scoop it up again—was harder to control than this young man would have been. She could have stopped him with one word, said yes. Instead, she stood in the dark, the house silent, and thought how this year, all ties broken, her days would lighten, have a slow rhythm all their own. She would not have to lead her brother downstairs on his birthday, clean and combed. She would not have to watch him drink whiskey with the girls from town while they sat on his lap, fed him cake and ice cream, braided the hair on his massive chest and left the pink marks of their lipstick in it. They tickled his ears with straw until he, playfully, swatted at them, tossed one over his shoulder and carried her upstairs, the others following. For the rest of the evening, Father sat in a corner with a glass and a decanter of brandy, and she sat on the arm of his chair with her sweater wrapped tightly around her, afraid of any noise, waiting to see if all the girls came down again near dawn and how much money her mother slipped into their palms. She would not have to care for him at all; someone else would do it.

The young man had disappeared. He'd begged her, pleaded. Once, tears had even come to his eyes which he wiped away with his fingers. Still, she'd perversely said no. Now she followed him in her mind, heard the slab of oak rasp the floor, felt the rough wooden attic walls as he slid his hand along them, making his way toward the bedroom where a few rays of moonlight came through the shutters. She followed, all his blond hair gone black; together they anticipated the narrow opening where the darkness grayed a little. Her brother would be sleeping on his straw in the corner, but at the sound of feet approaching he would wake, stand on hairy legs, tilt his head around the doorway, and sniff with his flat nose to discover who was coming.

The time she had, so unwisely, brought a lamp at night, she'd found him like that—neck craned, watching, a savage look in his eyes. Once she'd put the lantern down, the shadow of his square head and shoulders slanted up the walls and ceiling. He'd leapt, ears twitching, crushed her to him and ripped her dress. He'd bent to lick her face, neck, breasts with his thick tongue as if to lick all the salt off her. He held her tighter, scratched his stiff white hair into the slime he'd left. Rubbing his body against hers, he spread his hand between her thighs. His sharp hooves trod her feet. When she screamed, he only snorted and blew damp breath, clutching her tighter still. Finally, her father had freed her with his whip, yanked her from the attic and, hushing her so she wouldn't disturb her mother, brought her down to the black quiet of her room where he left her, warning her never to say anything about the episode.

She shivered, remembering, but part of her entertained the thought that things might change now. The land could be hers, not her brother's. She'd tear down this house and build a new one—spacious rooms, no halls, immense windows—but the vision was shattered by a volley of curses from the hall behind the almost closed door, screeching, echoing. She shook, and the patterned wallpaper flickered as she swung the lantern. She had imagined a silent meeting, not this which would surely wake the house and bring her mother stumbling up the stairs. She had seen the young man stare her brother down, subduing him with those bright eyes and thought then —what? She didn't know. There'd been a blank space. The screams grew louder, nearer, and a hollow thump-thump-thump followed them. She sent a sliver of yellow light through the door, calling to the man, listening to him run lightly toward her and to her brother trot unevenly, slowly, wheezing deeply, fall. The man burst through the door and slammed it behind him.

She never asked how the pursuit had ended, stood frozen in surprise as the silence gathered again. He'd stumbled through the door and swept her down the stairs—the first time he'd touched her, hot steel. He'd stepped through the door, stripped off his drenched shirt, and pressed her to his smooth chest, his cold skin. Awkwardly, she'd held the lantern aside. Not a scratch on him but his white shirt was red with blood. What weapon had he taken? In the yellow light his eyes shone purple, but by the time he helped her into the boat they were the same calm blue as always.

And he'd taken her away, quick note left on the sideboard, dark sail under the moon. Although the night was warm she shivered beneath her cloak, numb, looked back and saw lights come on in the house, awake, a vigil. She imagined her mother's hysterics, pounding the floor with her fists, Father comforting her roughly.

"You are glad you came with me, aren't you?"

She dipped her hand into the water without answering.

"You wouldn't want to be back there now. There's everything in front of us, the whole world."

He'd thrown off his shirt in a wide, grand motion, and left it on the stairs. His chest had tasted salty.

"I wanted to come," she said at last and went to sit next to him. "Of course I did. There was never any question about that."

Until the points of light on shore were no larger or brighter than stars, everything was silent.

"I've never killed anyone . . . ," he started, rubbing his palms together. She reached out and stuck her hand between his to silence him.

They spent their nights in the bottom of the boat, swells pressing against the hull, one swell and then another until she wasn't sure whether the rocking was the sea's movement or their own wild tumbling in that sharp space. The halyard tink-tink-tinked against the mast. She slept most of the day too, curled in the sun, and when she woke up, reached for him. His fingers were a drug of forgetfulness; she thought they were crossing Lethe.

How did the girl spend her time on the island?

Winter: she went into town less frequently, following the road when she did, a strip of white on white. The houses lay back in the landscape, sucked up by snow. Around them the pines were black, the palms dauntlessly green. Out over the water the fog twisted around the islands like scarves around a throat.

At home she arranged and rearranged her few belongings, lining up jars on the shelf, folding blankets into squares of the same size, opening and refolding them more precisely. She sat by the table and knit, leaving the door open to smell the snow because the snow smelled of salt. She positioned her chair so that, when she looked up, she could see through the falling snow to the water, waiting for a flash of purple. She looked up often; jittery, she couldn't sit still. When she felt the cold on her ankles, she swept the snow out the door and closed it, then pulled her chair closer to the stove where the water boiled for the tea she drank constantly. The liquid warmed her. Cold comfort her mother taught her to knit—the thin tough hands had held her own around the needles, clumsy stiff movements. Her mother's hands fought to keep her fingers moving correctly. Together they made wide ribbons for her brother who tied the colors around his head.

When one of her hairs fell free, she wrapped it with her needles, knotted herself in. The material dropped to the floor, spread under the table, chair, bed, the color of the winter sea, gray-green. She had an idea that if she knit a net fine enough and wide enough, she could cast it over the waves, entangle him and draw him back. Through the winter she worked on it. Once before she had pulled him free, blond hair shining suddenly, from the dark, but then, of course, he'd wanted to come. In the spring, she thought, she'd stand on the promontory, fling her net out and reel him in, the pattern of her fabric embossed into his clean, red, salty skin. He'd turn and turn in the waves, his body rising in the swell, and the water would shine around the dark form she could see from shore. She floated, her breath lifting her body.

He might be lost at sea and pining for her. In which case, once he found his way back to the island, they would make the cabin their home, cut windows in the walls to let in the light, order pots and pans from a catalog and bed sheets in bright colors. She smiled, saw him tapping his fingers impatiently against the gunwale.

He might be dead, a skeleton, a web of bones in the stern of the boat. A tremor started in her stomach and spread; she couldn't stop shaking. The stench of his rotting flesh was everywhere. Still, at least she'd know, sail up or down, mast gone, anchor ripped loose or pulled into the boat. She'd know how he died: thin bone-hands pressed under his cheek as he slept, the shape of a child.

He could be eight hundred miles away in her sister's arms saying, "Poor girl. I miss her so. I cried for days when she disappeared overboard." He licked her sister's neck and she tweaked his earlobes with dainty baby hands. Such treachery! The image slid across her knitting, but she didn't know where it came from as she didn't have a sister. She stared at their body parts magnified, distorted by the rippling cloth, twining and relaxing. Her fingers slowed, she enjoyed the sour taste, the stiffness of her mouth. She didn't care; she would get him back, she could do anything. Rising, she tossed her knitting to the floor and strode the length of the cabin—stove to door, table to bed. When she looked outside, the storm was a blur of white. She let the fire burn out.

Once, in a gale, the potter came from town to make sure she had wood and food to last out the storm and found the cabin door propped open. He stood thinking how he should have come sooner, until the sound came up from the inlet on the wind, and he saw her on the ledge howling—the only name for that noise—with her arms thrust behind her and her skirt plastered to her thighs. When he took her hand, she came quietly but as if she didn't know what was happening to her.

The weather cleared and she wandered into town, her mass of tangled hair tucked under a black knit cap. At the pottery shop the precise semicircles of earthenware and porcelain in the windows drew her inside. She studied bowls and cups like a bride intent on choosing a pattern, picked up vases and platters to follow the scenes painted on them, the bright glazes smooth against her palms. When the floor sounded under her heavy boots, the potter opened the curtains at the back of the room and stepped through. He beckoned to her, a short dark man, beard straggling across his face. "Come," he said, putting a gray, clayey hand on her arm. "It's warm in the back."

As he looked at her, she thought to say, "No. Leave me by the light. I'm waiting for someone." It wouldn't have been a lie, but she followed him into the other room where he took her bulky winter coat and pressed her into the corner of a couch, its chintz greasy and faded.

"I'll show you my new ones," he said and brought them from the cluttered shelves. "My animal plates."

She was aware of his gaze, how he hovered behind the couch and then in front of it, aware of how his forehead furrowed and unfurrowed in complex and changing patterns as she tried to feel the line where one color became the next, foreground became background, where on one plate the white bull's horns lay bonded to the green.

"You like them," he said. "I can tell."

The animals were caught behind the glassy surface, staring past her blankly. They scared her; she could not say whether she liked that feeling or not. "They remind me of things. Is that why you made them? Do they remind you of things too?"

"I don't think so," he said. "I just made them, that's all. I don't remember much." He sat down, squeezing between her and the corner of the couch, his thigh surprisingly hot, put his hand on her knee. He was whispering so that she had to lean very very close to hear.

What did the girl think of her past?

Through the fall and winter she thought that she had been saved and then abandoned; she didn't know why. She thought her father, the king, was the son of a girl kidnapped and raped by a god in the form of a bull; her mother was the daughter of the sun and moon; her brother, with his thick tongue, the frenzied eyes of a man in pain, the wispy hairs at the end of his tail, was the fruit of their mother's monstrous passions. She believed she would be delivered again, soon. As the snow continued to pile up beneath the trees, her taste for isolation wore thin and she wanted to go back to the knife-slice coast of the mainland, the turrets of her childhood home. She refused to let herself think how not even the charm of royalty had saved her family from the meanderings of the heart.

Once, when she was four, she saw her mother ravaged by a bull after climbing inside the wooden cow a carpenter had fashioned for her. He finished the beast, sanding the rump smooth, while she sat under the table and Mother paced impatiently between the work bench and the window, clutching the front of her dress and stirring the sawdust with her toes. Outside, the bull trotted, white against the green east meadow, and then stopped, chewing, his jaw sliding sideways, tufts of hair springing from the ears behind the curved horns. When the real animal mounted the wooden one in the courtyard, she ran toward them, screeching. The pine creaked and groaned, and the carpenter swept her up before she even reached the open air, closing the door, covering her eyes and mouth, pressing her to his leather apron so that her body was bruised by the screwdrivers and chisels lined up in the pockets across his chest.

In the spring when she paced the narrow porch of her cabin, breaking the new forsythia twigs between her fingers, she recalled that all her years at home had been an imprisonment. The promise began outdoors where the straight rows of vegetables replaced the dark passageways and led to the sea. She felt her father's dread, heard her mother's imperious voice. She recalled how the house lights switched on as soon as they'd pulled away from shore as if someone had been waiting for her to leave, as if her father had woken her mother with one hand while he reached for the light cord with the other. She left because she thought her hand was forced, but that was no reason to return. She left because her young man had threatened and cajoled, because she had forced him into taking her away or, what amounted to the same thing, did not stop him from unlocking the heavy oak door to the attic, believing then that he was her only egress from fear and the pleasure she found in it.

————

Did the girl ever leave the island?

No. Under a worn brown blanket the potter's mattress held the indentations of their bodies like a cup. His little arms and legs sidled up against her. In summer they threw off the sheets. His kiss was different each time: violent, passionate, delicate, dry. She fought back, laughing, and they slept as if a saber lay between them.

He shaped dishes for her. Around the circumference of a plate, in the well of a bowl, she told the stories she'd only told herself before, reimagined now with black figures on red, red figures on black.

Theseus had shrunken, muscles like unraveling rope, hair thinning. He had drifted for over a year without a chart, under a reddened sky, unable to read the stars. All around the islands the sea had been flat and shiny as a ball gown's blue silk; the fishing boats on it, far and white. When she pulled him ashore, he was so weak that she had to carry him up the slope beneath the palm fronds and pines, his arms dangling to the ground, and he looked up at her in fear, as if she might be the angel of death. She flipped him into the air, tossing him, catching him, as she walked barefoot over the sharp stones.

In the morning all was silent. Her head ached, a dull throb like a memory: her brother, alone, crawled a complex of passages, visiting various rooms that all looked the same, one image of collapse after another; outside in the dark hall her parents passed without looking at each other, her father stroking his beard, Mother shriveling inside her black dress; then she saw them seated together at the dining room table, her brother in a black bow tie, using a knife and fork, all lifting glasses, clinking crystal loudly, drinking. Shadows, they stained her body, and she realized they'd taunt her always. She raked her fingers through her hair, lashed out, rolled her eyes, bellowed, had trouble telling one of her limbs from another until the man moved beside her, broke through with noise.

LIMBO RIVER

Rick Hillis

The bus trip took so long we felt like bugs trapped in a jar. It didn't seem like we were getting anywhere. The windows always framed the same rigid mountain wall, and the same highway unscrolled blackly before us like a river. I slept a lot. My mother awoke me as we passed Frank Slide, the horizon ruined by chunks of rock the size of houses.

"In the middle of the night," she whispered to me, "a mountain collapsed and buried the town that was here. There was only one survivor, a baby girl. Nobody knew anything about her, so they called her Frankie."

I pictured a mountain splintering like a rotten molar, a baby sitting in an ocean of rock and rubble. Rain was slanting into my window, making the same tinny sound as it had on the roof of our trailer back in Chilliwack. I pictured saucepans in the aisle catching the plink plink of falling rain.

"Nobody knew anything about her," my mother said. "Think about that. Total freedom!"

─────────

The first thing we set eyes on when the taxi dropped us off in front of the Alamo apartments was Marcel. He was sitting on one of three kitchen chairs set out on the lawn. The legs had been pounded into the ground like tent pegs so they wouldn't move, and the grass beneath them sprang up nearly to the seats. Even though it was about seventy-five degrees out, he had on a stained canvas parka with pockets huge enough to hide his beer bottle in.

My mother pretended to survey the area. Across the street was a park and a river that glistened like foil. The heads of some children bobbed offshore, and water-skiers slalomed around them, peeling off strips of brightness.

When it became clear Marcel wasn't going to help Mom with the two boxes of belongings she was carrying, she thumped them down on the sidewalk and lit a cigarette. When she was on the wagon she hated drinkers, but she chain-smoked.

Marcel said, "I don't blame them kids for playing hookey. School's just another prison."

Mom said flatly, "Kids belong in school."

"Why isn't he then?" Marcel was pointing at me.

"Good Lord, we just got into town." My mother looked down at Marcel. "Why aren't you at work?"

I thought he was sick; maybe that was why he had the parka on, but Marcel said simply: "I'm on welfare." And as if he read my thoughts: "This coat ain't warm as it looks."

My mother raised her chin as if about to sneeze, then patted down her skirt. "Unfortunately we are on welfare ourselves, but not for long. I think it damages the human spirit."

"Sure, but it beats working."

Mom was flabbergasted, "Work is what makes the world go around!"

"Work is prison," Marcel said, adding, "Give me welfare or give me death."

Her lips got hard as two bones. "Is that alcohol you're drinking out here in public?"

She knew darn well it was; she'd served enough of it in her day. But she was fed up, I could see it. This man perched on a kitchen chair on a lawn drinking beer in the middle of the afternoon had my numerous "uncles" written all over him. My mother had earned an aesthetician's diploma from beauty school, and wanted to make a fresh start away from the Marcels of this world. Problem was they were the only type of person who lived in the places we could afford.

"Is it?" she repeated.

"Why?" Marcel held the bottle out to her. "You want a swallow?"

"*Oh!*" Mom staggered inside with her boxes and Marcel said to me, "Who was that masked man?"

"Anita Sobchuck," I said. "She's my mother."

"Thank goodness," Marcel smiled, "for a minute there I thought she was mine."

Marcel swore he'd never done anything wrong in his lifetime. In fact the only reason he wound up in jail in the first place was for drunk driving.

"I drank for to get free," he told me, "and then I drove for to get free faster. Someday you'll know what I'm talking about." It was one of the few things Marcel ever told me that was true.

Crimped over street signs, squealed around corners up on two wheels, got into fenderbenders. Got his license taken away four times in six months, finally got a jail term.

"I went and nosed my car into a creek," he explained, sounding proud. "When the cops winched me out the next morning and made me blow, I *still* buried the needle!"

The pen was located out by where the blue vein of river wound through scrub prairie land. During exercise period, Marcel would hook his fingers through the chain link, look out over the river. It wasn't fair to be in there for just burning tire marks into lawns, etcetera, was it? Gusts of wind blew in off the river, pasted the hair to his head. The guards could tell he was shaking it rough, so they told an old con named Pope to go talk to him.

"Now the Pope," Marcel told me a few days after we'd moved into the Alamo, "was a recidivist criminal. B&Es, paperhanger, shanked a guard once . . . he'll die inside, but he's a smart cookie just the same. What he told me was to relax and roll with the punches.

"'But I didn't do nothing wrong though,' I told him. 'I don't even belong here!'

"'You and me both, pal.' Pope slapped me on the back and said we were here for a good time, not a long time."

Marcel and me were sitting on the chairs pounded into the lawn, watching the river. Marcel said he liked to watch it because every day was a different river. The current worked like a knife. Ghostly sandbars rose out of the water, and each night the current would rearrange them, carve them away, or sometimes build on long spines of silt.

"Here's what the Pope really said," Marcel told me, "and I pass it on to you, Sean, for your wisdom bank: 'Society don't like you and has kicked you out. That's why you're here. Take a look around,' he said, 'these ain't the first walls you been inside—'"

I looked over my shoulder at the Alamo, then back out at the river.

"'Get wise,' he told me, 'roll with the punches.' I'll never forget him telling me that."

————

My mom didn't like me hanging around with Marcel, but what else was there to do? Most of the other tenants were at the bar by the time I got home from school, and we didn't have a TV. For a while I swam in the river with the other kids, but then Mom found out they were metis and forbade it.

"Why?"

"They're half-breeds."

"So?"

"Ringworm, rickets, head lice," she said.

So it was me and Marcel. He told me "Limbo is good for the body and what's good for the body is good for the soul." Same went for smokey sausages, Player's sailor-cut cigarettes, whiskey, beer, and wine. He said, "In the old days when limbo was big and competitions were held all across the country, and the prizes were booze, nobody bought liquor when Marcel Gebege was in town."

And he limboed for me once in a while. Put a yardstick across the mouths of two forty-ounce whiskey bottles, spread his feet wide, and crab-walked underneath, hopping on the bolts of his ankles. I was only eight or nine at the time, and could bend like a pipe cleaner, but I couldn't get as low as Marcel. He got snakebelly low.

He told me how a cell is a bowl about the size of an empty head. That's how teeny his thinking got in jail. He said, "In jail, time is slow and quiet as a bowl of water. If you look into it you can see things. For instance, I sense your Mom doesn't really like me, does she?"

"I guess not."

"That's OK. Most people don't. Do you like me, Sean?"

"Yes."

"I thought you would. You remind me of myself at your age. A bit of a loner."

The reason Marcel drank at home instead of in one of the bars across the river was because he was having an affair with the woman who lived across the hall from him, Rhonda Bighead. I already knew plenty about hanky-panky, so it didn't take long to figure it out. When Rhonda's old man would go to the bar, Marcel would watch until he was on the far side of the bridge, then he'd peel his rear end off his kitchen chair and say: "Excuse me, I think I'll repair to my place for a nap."

Rhonda's old man's name was Ralph. He had arm muscles like big baloney rolls and his teeth were all punched out from bar brawls.

Mom was furious when she learned about Marcel and Rhonda. She was having a lot of trouble finding a job as an aesthetician and was smoking more than ever, which cost money.

"That bitch is using him!" she cried at me one night. Mom had gone down to the laundry room and saw Marcel's phone cord snaking out from under his door, across the hall carpet, disappearing under Rhonda's.

"She's just after him for his phone!" Mom insisted. I think she was jealous for not getting the idea first. Plus Marcel wasn't a bad catch. He was about fifty-five but he looked forty and seemed quite healthy for drinking all the time.

We didn't have a phone ourselves because we couldn't afford the deposit yet, and this made it hard for Mom to fill out applications for work. Another thing was, we didn't know anybody, and sometimes we felt stranded without a phone. It made Mom's blood boil to think of that slut Rhonda Bighead having a heart-to-heart with somebody on Marcel's phone when we didn't have a phone to use, or a soul to call up even if we did.

———————

The river started to drop. In some places it looked more like a highway than a river. Marcel told me when the ice goes off a river, it makes a sound like somebody standing behind a hill with a handgun.

"One of the stupidest things I ever did," Marcel told me, "was try to escape from the pen. I climbed the fence in the night and found myself on the river ice. It was April and the ice was breaking. It started to crack up and I was leaping floe to floe, ice swirling all around me like broken bottles of rye. I could have gone under at any time, the ice would have closed over me, and I would have drowned. But I'm lucky that way. I just keep pulling up aces. What's the stupidest thing you've done so far?"

I had taken money from my mom's purse and had shoplifted, but before I could answer, Marcel said, "Too many to pick from, huh? Well, let me tell you about the lowest I ever got. You got a minute?"

"Yes."

"Okay, listen and you might learn something. This was up in Fort Steele where I was working—last job I ever had. Anyways, one night I get this phone call. Come to Vancouver right away. Your son's been scalded. He was about two or three years old at the time. He'd be about your age now, I guess. Anyway, his mother'd put him in the tub to sleep and somehow he turned on the tap and scalded himself and drowned—"

He looked at me and wiped his mouth.

"—What was I supposed to do? I went to the airport, but they said: no seats left. *Lookit!*—I need to get back for my little boy's funeral *tomorrow!* Don't raise your voice at me, the ticket woman said, what a bitch. Anyways, so I go into the little lounge they got there at the airport, and I'm telling this story to the bartender when this lady at the bar—a real good looker, kind of looked like your mom—says I can have her seat.

"About two minutes later an announcement comes over the loudspeaker: *Seats available on flight to Vancouver, seats available.* So I don't need her ticket, but I'll be damned if me and this woman don't end up sitting beside each other on the flight. We have a few drinks, and when we land in Vancouver we go to a bar in Gastown, a real nice place. Anyways, we're not there half an hour when a brawl starts and I'm sucked into it. When the cops come to bust it up, they check my ID and it turns out I got a warrant out on me for not paying alimony, so they take me downtown and lock me up. Next morning I'm up before the judge. I say, 'Your honor, sir, I am a few months behind in alimony—true—but I have come for my little boy's funeral, and I have money to cover the alimony.' The judge looks at me for a minute. Then he says: '*Release this man. He should never have spent the night in jail. Take him out right now, and when he hits the front doors: immediate release!*'"

"Immediate release," I repeated dumbly. I wondered about the boy. Did he turn on the tap with his toes, or what?

"That's the kind of guy I am," Marcel said. "Lucky."

———

One night after school, I was in the laundry room folding shirts when I heard Ralph's voice booming through the wall.

"What do you care?" Rhonda screeched in return. "Marcel is your friend, too!"

Holy shit. I pressed my ear against the wall. Furniture was sliding across the floor, dishes shattering. I recognized the sound of somebody being thrown around and slapped the way Mom sometimes hit me for doing things that bugged her. She never meant to do it, but she got frustrated with my behavior sometimes. Later she would cry about it and say, "Let's forget that ever happened, OK Sean?" Sniffing back tears, hugging me. "Let's start fresh, OK honey?" And we would. For a while things would be fine, but it always happened again. So what?—I knew my mother loved me and never meant to hurt me.

I heard a terrible scream, then nothing.

It scared me so I ran upstairs, but I knew Mom wouldn't be home. I sat for a minute in the quiet apartment, then descended the steps and knocked on Rhonda's door.

"What do you want?" Ralph barked.

"This is Sean from upstairs?"

"You better come in here, man."

Rhonda's arm had been opened up with a butcher knife. Also her back from when she must have tried to get out the door. She was laying on her side on the floor, eyelids flickering like she'd been woken up and was trying to get back to sleep. I tried to back out the door, but Ralph started crying.

"What was I supposed to do?" he pleaded. "I love her." He was sitting on the couch staring into space. "You better call Diamond Cab." He pointed at Marcel's phone, on the carpet just inside the door.

They were piling into the cab to take Rhonda to the hospital when two police cruisers closed in front of the Alamo, cherries pulsing the dark river. Somebody else must have phoned them and there they were, cuffing Ralph, pushing him by the head into the back seat.

An ambulance blinked up and one of the attendants got out and snapped down the legs on a gurney. "Where's the victim at?"

A tall cop said, "What victim? The victim of history and circumstance or the one he just carved up?" He laughed.

Rhonda wheeled around, bandage on her arm bright. "Don't you fuck dare talk about him!"

In the rear of the cruiser, Ralph was swimming back and forth across the dark blue cage, slamming the windows, the wire mesh.

––––––––––

Marcel immersed himself in booze. He drank like a man taking off his clothes and getting into a pool of water. Floating the way a heart floats in a chest. That's how depressed he was.

"Rhonda's cut me off," he said to me, "but I still let her use my phone. What the hell. Know what I mean, Sean?"

"Kind of, I guess."

"Well if you don't, you will soon enough. You know what I just noticed about you?" Marcel said. "You're kind of quiet the way I was when I was a kid."

I never felt quiet. I just thought nobody ever listened to me.

"I'll tell you something you probably won't believe, but when I was your age—and this is just between you and me, OK?—I had a club foot that since has been repaired by surgery. Would you believe I spent every recess of my school life over by the playground fence, looking out at the street so I wouldn't get a soccer ball bounced off my face?"

"Really?"

"Absolutely." He patted his chest with the palms of his hands. "And look at me now. The sky's the limit. You'll see."

A few days later Marcel presented me with a bike, an expensive BMX. It wasn't new, but Marcel said it was even better than new since it had already been broken in. He'd found it in the river and used a solution to clean off the rust.

He said he was crossing the bridge on his way to the Shamrock bar when he caught something glittering in one of the pools. He couldn't believe it: a bicycle, the chrome rims glinting like a pair of eye glasses.

Maybe somebody stole it and threw it off the bridge when the water was high. Or maybe it happened during winter and had spent months on the ice covered in snow. Poor people were always going out onto the ice and falling through. They fell through cracks and were swept away by the current, never to be heard from again. The mounties didn't even bother to look for them until spring when they could drag the river. By then the victims were misshapen balloons hung up in debris after spending all winter locked in their frozen bodies under the ice.

That night, on his way home from the Shamrock, Marcel stumbled down to the river, over the sandbars, and waded the shallow water to the pool. He stripped off his shirt and pants and slipped in. He said he felt superhuman: doing it for me because a boy my age should have a bike.

He floated on the surface, looking down at the round lenses of the wheels. That's when he saw them—blue shapes darting, flashing in the blackness.

"Fish," Marcel told Mom and me, "maybe half a dozen of them. Big bottom feeders—carp or suckers. Maybe even sturgeon—"

I pictured shadowy blades hovering above the bicycle, facing into the slow current, mouths sucking up food.

"But the river's drying up," Mom said as Marcel oiled the chain of my BMX. "The water's so shallow—" she looked at the river, one hand in a salute against the sunset. "How are they supposed to get out?"

"They aren't," Marcel said. "That's the whole idea. It's nature's way."

The metis kids climbed up out of the river and crossed the park to ride my bike. They couldn't do it any better than me though. I guess they'd never had a bike before either. They wobbled up and down the street in front of the Alamo, weaving in and out of traffic until my mom put her foot down. She hated them and made me understand we weren't like them, we weren't.

————————

A few nights later I was entertaining myself by tightrope walking the rim of the fence that separated the Alamo from the chrome-and-glass condo next door when Mom clicked up the sidewalk in her high-heeled shoes. She brushed off the seat of a kitchen chair and sat down next to Marcel.

"You'll be pleased to know, Sean, that I begin work tomorrow at Beauty City—"

"Congratulations, Anita," Marcel said. "That calls for a toast." He hoisted his beer bottle into the air.

"Thank you, Mister Gebege." Mom took out a cigarette and Marcel held his lighter under it. "I see you are still supporting the breweries."

Marcel squinted: "Listen, I drink for to get free."

"No doubt," Mom laughed, adding that she had spent too many years working in the bar industry not to recognize a man living his life out of a bottle when she saw one.

Marcel looked wounded.

"I'm teasing," Mom said, smiling, blowing smoke out of her nostrils. I could tell she was feeling high, excited about the future. "Thank you again," she said, "for Sean's bike."

It was chained to the fence. In the dark it looked like a pair of sunglasses. I wasn't allowed to ride at night, but after school I loved to pedal through the streets above the Alamo. Some of the richest old homes in town were up there—pillared porches, yards full of big trees. As I sped by them it seemed likely that Mom and me would end up in one of those places. Good luck was just around the corner. At dusk I would ride home, following the gravel alley that descended steeply to the river. The yards on top had green swimming pools, but these quickly gave way to overgrown vegetation and broken-down cars. The yards near the bottom were hidden behind rickety unpainted fences, and big dogs threw themselves into the boards, barking loudly as I passed.

Marcel offered Mom a beer and this time she took it. "What the heck?" she said, and held it out as if toasting the river. "To new beginnings," though it was the same old beginning, same old snowball starting to roll.

"Don't look at me like that, Sean, I'm just celebrating. Can't I do that?"

"Your mother is allowed to have some fun too, isn't she, big guy?" Marcel punched me lightly on the shoulder and Mom giggled.

Somehow at that moment I knew I was in for another uncle. Which meant I would be losing both my mother and only friend in one fell swoop, but at least we'd have a phone.

I looked away, up at the flat purple streak above the river. I had patches on the knees of my pants and oversized Sally Ann runners on my feet. I started to feel sorry for myself, but then I thought of my bike, and my spirits soared a bit.

———————

Every day a different river. The water kept dropping until parts of it shrunk to a thin trickle like an overflowing sink. The skiers and kids moved upriver where the current still gouged the channel deep. In front of the Alamo, sandbars started to sprout grass.

A couple of days after Mom started making me call Marcel "Uncle Marcel," Ralph came to the door, slapping the fat end of a baseball bat into the palm of his hand. Rhonda wouldn't press charges, so he was on the street again.

"Where's Marcel, and no bullshit, OK? I got nothing against you, man, but I know your old lady's got a key to his place, and if you don't let me into it I'm going to have to club you." Even though I was only eight, he waved the bat in my face. I doubt he would have done anything to me, but I let him into Marcel's anyway. For a lot of reasons it seemed like the right thing to do.

Marcel wasn't in his apartment so Ralph commenced to smash things up. Caved in the aquarium so water gushed onto the carpet, then ground his heels on the little fish that flipped around on the floor. Punched a few holes in the gyprock. Brought the bat down over the top of the TV so the tube exploded across the carpet. He placed a few long-distance calls on the telephone, then hung up and splintered it with the bat. Then he tucked Marcel's toaster oven under his arm and left.

Marcel was sitting on our couch shaking when I got back upstairs.

"Did he at least leave me one beer?"

"You're lucky he didn't find you. He wanted to break your knees."

"Fuck him if he can't take a joke," Marcel said, grinning. Then he shook his head in amazement. "But you're right, I'm lucky. I just keep pulling up aces."

————

One of the metis kids drowned in the river, went down as if a weight was attached to his ankles.

A friend dove and dove for him, surfacing to fill his lungs, shaking his head. A grainy photo in the newspaper had the spray from his hair making a white flower on the water.

The mounties launched a small boat, dragged a grappling hook back and forth across the river. The water-skiers spiraled the area in their boat and a boy not much older than me sat on the prow, stabbing a paddle into the water.

The drowned boy's friends collapsed on shore, crying in disbelief. They had been swimming to the sandbar where the skiers partied, but they didn't make it. Their hands clutched the sand, their feet were in the river.

————

A few mornings later I went downstairs to go to school and found my BMX missing. I couldn't believe it. I thought I must have left it somewhere, but I knew I hadn't, and my next thought was, those fucking half-breeds had stolen it. Mom was right about them. All day in school I steamed. I pictured them climbing out of the water like mutant swamp monsters, taking what was mine. I almost totally forgot about the drowning. How could those hooky-playing sonofabitches steal my bike after I let them use it?

When I got home Uncle Marcel was sitting on one of the chairs. By now the grass was so long it draped over his lap like a luau skirt. He was pickled out of his mind.

"I have to show you something," he said.

"What?" I looked around excited, thinking he'd found my bike.

Marcel said, "Right there in front of you. The car." An old, bald-tired clunker was parked at the curb. "A friend owed me a favor so I got this off him for fifty bucks. What a steal, hey, Sean?"

A whistling started in my ears and I backed away. "You stole my bike," I said. *"Didn't you?"* The idea just flashed in my mind.

"Hey, you hold on! I didn't steal anything."

I glared at him. That bike was the best thing that ever happened to me. It was more than transportation, it *transported me*, changed the way I saw myself. When I was on it, skimming the streets, everything was possible. And now Marcel had taken it back.

"I didn't steal anything. It was my bike," Marcel said. "I found it and I let you use it and then I took it back. Actually I found the original owner and returned it to him."

"Liar!" I cried. I couldn't help it. Huge, wracking sobs shook my lungs and I thought I was going to drown from lack of air.

When Mom came home, she stormed into my room. "I told you to keep that damn bike locked!" Her breath smelled of booze. "If you don't look after your things you don't deserve them!"

"I did lock it! Marcel stole it!"

"Shut your dirty lying mouth!" my mom screamed at me, bringing her hand back to slap.

———————

Though it wasn't mentioned in so many words, I'm sure it was partly due to the bike episode, to smooth things over, that we went to the fair. Also, Marcel hadn't taken the clunker anywhere yet and wanted to feel the road beneath him. For my part I'd never seen a circus, zoo, marine world, or wax museum, much less a fair, and though I hated the idea of being bribed into being nice and civil again, I really wanted to go.

As we were pulling away, Rhonda Bighead and Ralph were reeling through the park on the way home from the Shamrock. Rhonda's gashes had healed nicely and she was holding a bouquet of white flowers Ralph had torn from a bed in the park. When they came to a patch of red flowers, he bent like a hero and ripped out a whole plant. Rhonda hugged it to her, roots dripping dirt. Then she lost her balance, staggered a few steps, and pitched over. Ralph tried to help her up, but toppled onto her, at which point she started yelling, slapping him on the head.

Marcel spewed some beer out of his nostrils, and Mom eyed him. She didn't mind him drinking, but drinking and driving didn't mix.

Marcel tooted the horn as we passed and Rhonda turned, cursing us, hurling flowers.

The clunker had a shot transmission, so we had to stop about every thirty miles for Marcel to add fluid. This was synchronized perfectly with his need to stop and water the ditch. It got dark and the pavement glistened like ice on a frozen river. For miles, it seemed, I could see the yellow Ferris wheel lights shining in the sky, and despite everything I got so excited I thought I could smell foot longs, corn dogs, and candy apples over the cigarette smoke in the car.

It was a bottom-of-the-barrel fair. Workers all tattooed up like a bad face; rides greasy, probably suffering from metal fatigue. The foot longs were about the length of your thumb and cost two bucks each. But so what? It was a fair! And the night was swept along in a blur of light and color, odor, sound.

Mom and Marcel rode the Death Trap, a bench chained to a giant arm that whirled around in the air like a propeller. Me, I flopped a rubber frog onto a lily pad with a huge tongue depressor and won a fly in a cube of clear plastic. Marcel limboed under a wooden rod set on bowling pins—passed through like he was kneeling on air—and won a stuffed snake he gave to Mom. Mom won a plaster sea gull for stumping the Guesser on what exactly she did at Beauty City.

"Hey boy," the Guesser said to me as we were leaving his booth, "I bet I know what you want to be when you grow up." A crowd of people had gathered to watch him perform, but nobody was investing in his act, so he was using me to drum up business. "Most kids want to be the same as their dad," he said. "It's genetic."

The crowd chuckled.

"Are you proud of your old dad?" The Guesser answered himself. "I bet you are." All the time his eyes were hunting the crowd for my father, a clue to my future. "Is your dad here with you?" he said finally.

I never knew my real father, but had no reason to suspect he would be any different from Marcel, so that's who I pointed at. The crowd turned to him and the smile dropped off Marcel's face. He looked down at his feet. For the first time I saw the guilt and shame that was probably always there, under the surface of the stories and drunken sprees. Marcel was King of the Alamo Apartments, but in the world of upright citizens he was just a drunken bum. That's what the murmuring crowd saw and I didn't blame them. How else could you judge the bulbous red nose, the gaps in his teeth, the creased map of his face?

Even the Guesser momentarily lost his composure, but he quickly regained it. "Kids like their teachers," he said, winking at me. "I bet you want to be a schoolteacher." This surprised me. I expected doctor or fireman. "But," the Guesser added, taking a plaster ornament off his shelf, "I'm not always a hundred percent right on, so here—" He offered me the ornament.

I glanced at Marcel who was still looking down. "No," I said, "you're right, I do want to be a teacher."

I refused the ornament, but the Guesser forced me to take it anyway, as though he didn't believe me. It was a figurine of a pointy-headed troll.

When we got away from there Marcel put one arm over my shoulder, the other over Mom's and said, "A teacher? Well why the hell not?" We all laughed.

Who knows what anybody is going to become? Maybe at one time Marcel envisioned something different for himself, but now life was just a river he was being swept down, and he was happy. My mother believed we could alter the course of our lives if we were strong and lucky enough, and if we had faith. One out of three isn't bad. In a way I think they were both right: nobody gets what they deserve, but in the end we all become who we want to be, deep down. I don't know.

At about midnight Marcel took me onto the Zipper.

It was a mesh cage that spun and orbited around a greasy hub like a planet around a star. There were broken bolts and nuts in the popcorn and cigarette butts scattered around the base, but we didn't care. "We're here for a good time, not a long time," Marcel laughed. And as he said this our cage jerked, lifted us into the night sky, and we spun upside down, and Marcel's change flew out of his pockets, whizzed past our ears like shrapnel. My heart tore free of my chest and I felt it in my mouth. We dove toward the ground, but at the last minute were scooped up, swirling through the blackness, me and Marcel, screaming at the stars between our shoes.

HAVE YOU SEEN ME?

Elizabeth Graver

Willa stood in the patch of light from the open freezer door and watched as the mist climbed in tendrils, swirled and rose. The milk carton in her hands was heavy, its surface smeared with yellowish cream—her mother had made more potato soup. Already the two tall freezers in the basement housed cartons and cartons of soup, enough to last them almost forever—carrot and broccoli soup, soup made of summer and acorn squash, rows of green and yellow frozen rectangles inside the cartons that had once held milk. And on the outsides of the cartons, rows of children—frozen too, their features stiff, their faces etched with frost. *Have You Seen Me? Do You Know Where I Am?* Each time Willa put the cartons in the freezers, she set up the children in pairs so they could have staring contests when she shut the door.

Go on, she thought to Kimberly Rachelle and David Michael, to Kristy-Ann and Tyrone. Stare each other down. She put them boy girl, boy girl, catalogued them by age. Some of the missing children were babies, and these she put on the shelf closest to the bottom. The ones who were eleven, her age, she gave special treatment, tracing their names in the wax coating of the milk cartons with her finger, dusting the frost from their eyes. She could recite their DOBs, their SEXs, HTs, WTs, and EYES, the color of their hair. Willa's mother didn't know about Willa's ordering of the cartons; she was upstairs cooking or painting child after child lined up like soldiers, serious kids in uniforms carrying weapons or naked, puzzled kids looking up at the sky.

Willa's mother expected the end of the world. She donated her paintings to three friends in the town twenty miles down the highway, and they turned them into posters which they hung in the public library and in the windows of the real estate agency that doubled as an art gallery. "You Can't Hug Your Child," they printed in fake child scrawl, "With Nuclear Arms."

Willa thought everyone was overreacting. Sure, there might be silos under the ground and blinking lights that could go off, and escape systems that would lead to nowhere, and broccoli and cauliflower that would grow big as trees afterwards, like in the paintings her mother made. There might be all that, but still what did they know about the end, for she was sure something would survive, making it really not the end at all—maybe only an insect or two, a shiny blind beetle or an ant like the ones in the ant farm her father had given her—some sort of creature, hard, black and shelled, rolling from the rubble like a bead.

She would not go with her mother to the rallies in Chicago and St. Louis, would not wear the buttons and T-shirts or lend her handwriting to the posters. In her room she hung photographs of animals instead of her mother's art work—slow sea turtles and emus with backs like the school janitor's dirty, wide broom. They came from the Bronx Zoo in New York City, the animals on the postcards. Willa's father sent them now and then.

Once a girl in one of her mother's paintings had looked just like Willa, small and dark and suspicious, with the same mess of curly hair. Then Willa had screamed and kicked.

"Take me out of your fucking painting, who said you could paint me? Just take me out!"

"Okay, now stop!" her mother had said, catching Willa by the shoulders. "Just stop screaming and don't go crazy on me. Listen to yourself—listen to yourself, would you just calm down?"

And she had squeezed a big wad of beige paint onto her palette, speared it with a paintbrush, and spread it over the painted Willa's face.

"It wasn't even you," she had said, but Willa had known it was, that her mother had put her there in that lineup of children with puzzled looks, had painted her empty-handed, naked, and puzzled next to an orange boy with wide shoulders and a bow and arrow in his hand.

"Just because I say 'fucking' doesn't mean you should," her mother had told her, but then she had kissed Willa's forehead and taken her far down the highway to McDonald's, where Willa ate two hamburgers and drank a thick chocolate shake while her mother drank water and tried not to look at the food.

Underneath their farmhouse was dirt, and underneath the dirt—if not directly underneath, then near enough, her mother seemed sure of it—were silos which were not really silos at all, but this was not Willa's problem. In a movie she saw once, a man drowned in the wheat of a silo, was smothered as the golden grain poured over him like sand, filling up his nostrils and his mouth. She told her mother about it afterwards, the danger of this silo filled with wheat. With *wheat*, Willa had said, which was what silos were supposed to hold.

"Actually silage," her mother had answered. "They're supposed to hold silage—fodder for cows and horses. It must have been a grain elevator."

No, said Willa. It was a silo. She saw it.

"I guess they could do what they wanted—it was only a movie," her mother had said, and then, more thoughtfully, "Hmmm, I suppose it probably happens now and then."

School was one thing, and home alone with her mother was another, and in between were her mother's three friends, who were thin and pretty like her mother and drove out to the house on weekends with bags full of magic markers, envelopes, and petitions that few people in the little town would sign. Sasha was a real estate agent and divorced, and Karen was married and taught kindergarten at Willa's school, and Willa didn't know what Melissa did, except stare sadly at her mother's paintings and say,

"Hello, Willa," as if Willa's name were a password or something deserving of the utmost seriousness. Willa's mother gave her three friends homemade bread and sketched their faces on napkins. Sometimes they drank vodka and orange juice and stayed up talking late into the night. When Willa came downstairs in the morning she would find the women sleeping on the couch and floor, still dressed, still wearing rings and necklaces and sometimes even shoes.

At night when no visitors shared the house, Willa's mother told her stories. This had been going on a long time. First it had been her father and mother together. He would say a sentence: "Once there was a truck who lived alone in the Sahara Desert," and her mother would add a sentence: "And he had no glass in his windows and at night the sand came blowing through, and he had no wheels," and her father would add on, and then her mother, each of them perched on Willa's bed, always touching part of her— her knee or her foot, her hand or the small of her back.

Then, when she was seven, her father went to live with a woman he said he had loved in high school, and Willa only saw him twice a year when he left his new family, she left her mother, and they stayed in a hotel in New York and went to museums and the zoo. She always got blisters on those trips from so much walking. After her father left, her mother came home with a whole stack of glossy children's books. Willa couldn't stand the pictures of fat, dimpled children and pets, the stories about going to the dentist, getting a pony, or cleaning up your room.

"*Tell* me one," she would say to her mother, and her mother would try, but she never knew how to start, and the stories stumbled along for a while until Willa grew bored and fell asleep. But over the years her mother improved, or else Willa just grew used to her way of telling. She gave her mother rules: no stories about zoo animals, vampires, or kids named Willa who lived on defunct farms. No stories about the end of the world. Instead, her mother told her more stories about objects—superballs looking for somewhere to bounce, a barn which threw up because of the smelly animals inside it, a snowflake in search of a twin. Sometimes her mother sat at the end of Willa's bed and leaned against the wooden railing. Other times she cupped herself against her daughter and talked right into her ear. Sometimes she slept there all night, squeezed onto the edge of the twin bed.

Willa didn't like this, found it sad and embarrassing, though she couldn't say why, but she wouldn't kick her mother out. In winter they stayed warm that way, like pioneers, for the farmhouse was big and drafty in the middle of its field, and the wind came howling round.

———————

After Willa filled the freezer with several loads of soup, she took her book on ants to the kitchen and settled by the wood stove. When the doorbell rang, she didn't look up, too busy with a glossy color photograph of a magnified ant with legs like shaggy black trees. But then her mother came back to the kitchen followed by a girl, or maybe a woman—to Willa the stranger looked young, though she carried a child who hid its face in her coat. Willa's mother showed the girl and baby to the living room, and then she returned to the kitchen and whispered to her daughter that this was a new friend, her name was Melody. They had met at a demonstration in St. Louis; Melody had worked in a nuclear power plant for four years, but now she had quit and was waitressing. She had come to the house for a lesson because she wanted to learn how to draw. Her son was blind and had just turned three.

"It should be fun for you," said her mother after she had called Melody and the child back in. "Isn't he awfully cute? Would you do us a big favor and watch him while we draw?"

Willa had watched the tiny, silent granddaughter of the farmer down the road while the farmer rode his tractor, but she had never babysat for a blind child, had never met anyone who was blind.

"I don't, I mean—" she said. "I don't really know—"

"Oh listen to you, you're just being modest," said her mother. She turned to Melody. "She's terrific with kids. Already she's babysitting at her age."

"He's pretty much like any other kid, aren't you, Tiger?" said Melody, readjusting the child buried in her arms. "Better, even—he's good as can be. If he wants anything, you can just give a holler. We'll be right upstairs. Or, if you want, we can take him with us."

"I'll watch him," said Willa, for her mother was giving her that look.

When they went up to the studio, her mother and Melody left the child sitting on Willa's baby quilt on the kitchen floor, his back to Willa.

For a while she hunched over her book and ignored the boy at her feet, but when she finished the section on carpenter ants, she lifted her head and stared at the child, who had settled on his stomach on the red and yellow quilt. As she stood and leaned over him, she saw that not only was he blind, but he had no eyes, just skin and a row of pale blond lashes where the eyes should have been.

Willa gasped and brought her hands up to her face, then stood for a moment peering into the darkness of her palms, trying to make herself look again. When she lowered her hands, she saw that the boy was sucking his thumb and using the end of his index finger to trace circles on his face. She stared. Did he have eyes under there, so that he wasn't actually blind at all, just confined to a view of his own pale skin? She moved closer to see if she could make out a bulge of eyeball above the fringe of lashes. The skin was smooth and flat like part of a back or stomach—as if nothing were missing, as if eyes had never been invented. Then the boy wrinkled his brow, seemed to be looking at her: Could he see through those eyeless eyes?

He could have been born that way, thought Willa. Not because his mother worked in a nuclear plant, but just because he was born that way. Paula, a fifth grader at school, claimed she had gone to a fair in Florida where they had people like this—Siamese twins joined at the head, children with flippers like dolphins and claws like lobsters, or as hairy as apes. Paula said she had seen the lobster family, three kids and two parents. They were ugly as anything, she said, but they loved each other, that family. They just stood there smiling like goons and holding claws.

As Willa leaned over the child, he reached a hand into the air.

"Ma?" he said.

And she said, "No."

"Can you talk?" she asked, kneeling by him. "What's your name?"

He was perhaps the palest, blondest boy she had ever seen, his hair like milkweed puffs standing straight up on his head, his skin so white you could see veins running underneath it, could see how his blood was blue. He wore a red turtleneck and pink flowered overalls that should have been for a girl. From the way he clenched his fingers to his palms, it seemed he must be angry, or else cold. He did not answer her. As she leaned closer, he reached up and grabbed a fistful of her hair.

"No," she said, starting to unclench his fist with her fingers, but he opened his palm and batted at her curls, swinging them back and forth.

"Girl," he said, and she nodded yes.

He lowered his hand, and she rocked on her heels and looked at him. She could stare and stare, tilt her head to examine him, and it wouldn't matter, for this boy had skin in the place of eyes. He reached out again.

"What?" she asked, backing up. His face grew red as if he might begin to cry, though she couldn't imagine where the tears would go.

"What?" repeated Willa, and the boy lifted his arms toward her, so she bent down and scooped him up. He was awkward in her arms, his legs dangling down, but surprisingly light. Willa was used to the house, wore four layers in winter, but this boy's whole body was shaking. With his arms tight around her neck as if he might pull her down, he began, quietly, to sob.

"Oh don't," she said, wanting to drop him and run." "Please don't cry. Don't cry—"

A thread of spittle ran down his chin; perhaps, she thought, his tears flowed like a waterfall down inside his head and out his mouth. She began to circle with him to warm him up, boosting him a little higher each time he threatened to fall.

"This is the kitchen," she told him, and he stopped crying as she went to a bag of onions on the counter and had him touch the brittle skins. She held an onion under his nose, and he batted her hand away. She went to the fridge and pressed his cheek against the side. "Listen," she told him, so he would hear it purr. She took him to the dining room where the table was covered with petitions, posters, and books.

"We don't eat here," she told him. "Usually we eat in the kitchen."

He touched the tabletop and ran his fingers over a copy of a drawing that a Japanese war child had made of its mother. The mother had bright swollen lips; the skin on her hands hung loose like rubber gloves. Willa hated those pictures, had seen that one before and read the caption: HIGASHI YAMAMOTO, MY MOTHER 53 YEARS OLD. Willa's mother had promised to keep them hidden, but sometimes she forgot and left one lying around the house.

"Not for you," said Willa, though she knew he couldn't see it, and she backed up.

She brought him to the front room where she used to sit with her mother and father counting trucks in the night, the lights coming toward them on the highway out of nowhere, the rush of sound, then everything growing smaller and smaller, less and less noisy, until it was quiet and they were just sitting there again. In summer they had watched from the porch, and then they could feel the wind of the passing trucks, like feeling the waves the motorboats made when she swam in Lake Michigan on vacations—more ripples than waves, really—and with the trucks it was not quite wind, but more a slight, brief wall of air. Her parents didn't argue when they sat there watching trucks. Her father didn't talk about his office, and her mother didn't talk about the rallies. It was the quietest time they had.

What a baby she'd been in her father's arms, thinking that under the ground was more ground, that in the silos was wheat, that her father would sit there forever in the green stuffed chair. She sat the boy down beside her in the creaking chair and told him to listen for trucks.

"Car," he said, and she said, "A truck is a big car."

"Plane," he said, and she thought of the ones she took to New York to visit her father. The flight attendants always gave her coloring books full of drawings of pilots and suitcases—books meant for much younger kids. Willa knew she should save them for her father's little children, but since he always took her to the hotel, never home, she left the books and crayons on the plane with a wonderful feeling of spite.

He had two children with his new wife, one who was just hers and one who was both of theirs. This meant that Willa had a half-sister and a stepbrother, which should have added up to something whole, but though she knew their names were Katherine and William, which was so close to Willa, she had never seen them, not even pictures, and part of her was not convinced they existed. The boy squirmed in her arms, so she put him down and took his hand, but he stumbled, groping at the air, so she picked him up and carried him again, making her way unsteadily to the ant farm in her room.

She couldn't show him, really. She could press his fingers to the glass, but that wouldn't tell him anything, so instead Willa read to him from a library book about army ants, though her ants were simple garden ants.

Army ants always moved in columns five ants wide, she told him, marching and marching for seventeen days; then they stopped and laid eggs until they were ready to march again. They had jaws like ice tongs and could eat a leopard, and almost all of them were female. The boy sat in her lap with a mild, interested expression on his face, so she told him about the replete ants who filled their abdomens with nectar until they swelled like grapes, then hung suspended from the ceiling of the nest. When the other ants were hungry, Willa said, they tapped on the mouth of the replete ant, and it spat out a drop of honeydew.

The boy looked a little bored, and he was still shivering, so she lugged him down to the basement where they could be close to the furnace's warmth. As he sat on the floor by the furnace, she kneeled beside him and lightly touched his hair, so like milkweed. How did he get to be so blond, she wondered; his mother had hair as dark as Willa's.

"Stand up, would you," she told him, and when he did she took both his hands and led him slowly across the room. "See, you're not a baby, you're a big boy. You walk fine."

"Fridge," said the boy when they stood before it, for he must have heard it humming, and he reached out and placed his palms flat against the large white door.

"Did you know some children don't live with their parents?" Willa told him. "Either the kids get taken away, kidnapped when they're still young and cute, or else they run away when they're a little older and no one wants them."

Holding the door ajar with her foot, she hoisted him up and guided his hand to the middle shelf of milk cartons. This was the shelf of the two to five year olds: Jason Mccaffrey with blue eyes and brown hair, Crystal Anne Sandors, DOB July 22, 1979, who was three and a half now, pouting like a brat and wearing tiny hoop earrings and pearls. Some of the children had been computer-aged, so that Billy, who was two when he disappeared from his aunt's shopping cart in Normal, Illinois, appeared three years later on the carton as a five year old, his face grainy and stretched-out, coated with wax.

To call those children missing, Willa knew, only meant they were missing for somebody, even though maybe they were found for someone else.

Just because they were not at home did not mean they were wandering the earth alone. There were too many of them, just look at all those cartons. First Crystal probably ran into Jeffrey, and then Crystal and Jeffrey ran into Vicki, and soon there were masses of them, whole underground networks. When she went to the supermarket with her mother she spotted them sometimes, kids poking holes in the bags of chocolate in the candy aisle or thumbing through a comic book—kids in matted gray parkas that once were white. They had large pupils and pale skin from living inside the earth.

They knew how to meet underground, these groups of children, knew how to tell a field with a hidden silo from a field of snow, how to comb through the stubble of old corn to find the way down, then slide behind the men in uniforms who guarded the silo like an enormous jewel. They could pass by the waiting dogs, for they were scentless from being frozen for so long. They were thin and coated with wax and could slide quite effortlessly through cracks. Underground they formed squads by age: the blue squad for the nine to eleven year olds, the brown squad for the babies who couldn't walk yet and were covered with mud and dirt. In the underground silos they found piles of wheat and hay left over from the days when the silos had been used on farms. They slept on the hay, woke in the morning with straw stuck in their hair. For breakfast they ground the wheat with stones, formed it into patties, cooked it into small round cakes.

The children knew Willa only as a sort of looming presence. They couldn't see her, but they could feel a shift in the atmosphere when she picked up their cartons, as if a cloud had cast its shadow or a truck swept by the house. They didn't understand how much she made them do; they thought they had their staring contests when they were bored, when really it was Willa pairing them up so they would stare into each other's eyes. Some of them she liked more than others, and these children received favors. The ones who had been there the longest got to sit at the front of the shelf. So far none of them had had to leave. This soup was not for eating. Her mother called it soup for a rainy day.

Someday Willa might have to join them. She did not know how to get there, exactly, but she knew she would figure out a way. Her mother would not be with her, or her father. The larger you were, the harder it was to survive; she could tell that from watching her ants. At eleven, Willa was still quite runty for her age, though her mother made her drink glass after glass of milk. She put the boy down, and then she took out the missing children and told him about each one, placing them in a large ring around him on the concrete floor, as if it were a birthday party and time for Duck Duck Goose. When she got to Craig Allen Denton, REPORTED MISSING FROM THE HOSPITAL ON THE DAY OF BIRTH, 9/11/80, she stopped and stared at him, then wiped the frost from his face with her cuff.

Craig Allen Denton had a shriveled face as white as milk and eyes screwed into slits. His mouth was open in a howl, his fist clenched in a tight ball by his cheek. Willa looked at him again, held him under the light, then turned and stared at the child in her basement. The baby in the picture, she saw, was the toddler on the floor. Melody must have stolen him, or maybe Melody's baby had been switched with him.

Before, Willa had thought the baby in the photo had closed his eyes because he was crying. Now she saw that he had no eyes.

Somewhere, to somebody, this eyeless boy was missing. Melody had a son, and the boy had a mother, but still something was wrong. Something was always wrong, no matter how right things seemed. Willa had known this for a while, but still it gave her a headache to think of it. She pulled the boy onto her lap and rubbed her forehead against his hair.

"What's your name?" she asked, but he only sneezed.

When she heard a creaking on the stairs, Willa assumed it was a cat. She was showing the boy how to run his fingernail along the side of a carton and gather tiny flakes of wax. She was telling him about Gail May Joliet, DOB 3/12/71, EYES hazel, Gail May who had been computer-aged so that the edges of her face were visible now as a series of small black dots like poppy seeds. "Computer-aged," said the print beneath, and in the wavery lines of her cheeks you could see how they had taken away Gail May's baby fat. Now she looked like a five year old whose cheeks had been carved away.

"She lives in the underground village," Willa told the boy. "She's a gymnast, you should see—she does back flips and balance beam and horse, and I think parallel bars. She's the head of the blue squad. Also she carves tunnels. She's two-and-a-half months older than me."

And she took his hand and placed it over Gail May's face.

Her mother must have been standing there watching from the stairs. She must have been staring at the ring Willa had made of all the soup, of all the milk cartons, arranged not by flavor but by child. She must have been looking at Willa and the boy sitting in the center of the ring. As Willa's eyes lighted on her mother and Melody two steps behind, she tightened her hold on the child.

"What on earth are you doing?" said her mother from the stairs.

Willa shrugged and touched the child's staticky hair. Her mother came toward them, kneeled outside the circle, let out a strained laugh.

"What are you doing with all the soup? It's melting, Willa. Will you just look at that? All my good soup is turning to mush."

She was right. Tiny puddles of water were collecting underneath each carton as the soup began to sweat. Her mother started to pick up a carton, but Willa leaned over the boy and swatted at her hand.

"Leave it, Mom, okay? I'll clean it up."

"I thought you were reading in your room," said her mother. "We heard you reading to him."

She stepped over the cartons, scooped the boy up, handed him up to Melody, and whispered something. Then Melody and the boy disappeared up the stairs. Outside the ring of cartons, Willa's mother crouched.

"Were you building a city?" she said. "There are blocks in the attic if you want to build with him. Why did you have to defrost all my soup?"

If she had felt like it, she could have explained things logically to her mother, how in an Emergency Situation the radiation would seep into the basement, inside the furnace, inside the canned goods, stacks of magazines, bottles of wine. How it would go right through the thick white insulation of the fridge, through the wax and cardboard of the milk cartons, through all those dotted faces to the soup.

But her mother knew that, and still she kept making soup.

Willa sighed. "I wasn't defrosting."

"What were you doing then?"

Her mother stepped over the cartons and kneeled by her side.

"Just playing."

"Well then," said her mother. "I'll put them away. I can't have all that soup melting. You can't refreeze, it doesn't work."

"I'll do it," said Willa, and as her mother sat cross-legged in the middle of the circle, she began collecting the cartons by age, by group, starting with the babies and moving up.

"Melody has potential as an artist," said her mother. She handed her daughter a carton, out of order.

"I'll do it. Let me do it." Willa peered at the carton—G. Phillip Stull, red squad—then put it back on the floor.

"Oh—oh I see," her mother said. "You were talking to him about these pictures, weren't you? You were telling Melody's baby about the children on the cartons."

Willa continued her ordering.

"I think a lot of it is media panic, honey," her mother said. "I mean, from what I've heard. A lot of these kids are with their divorced parents, or there's a custody problem, or they ran away. You'd be surprised. Most of them aren't actually missing at all."

Willa turned and began to collect the two to four year olds.

————

Upstairs, she went to Melody, who was cutting an apple into pieces in the kitchen, and stood by her side. In the living room she could hear her mother murmuring to the child.

"Hi there," said Melody, and Willa said hi.

"Your Mom said I could cut Jo-Jo an apple. Thanks for playing with him. Did he give you any trouble?"

Willa shook her head. Melody popped a slice of apple into her mouth and chewed.

"He's a good kid. All his babysitters love him, once they get used to him."

"Did he, I mean, was he—"

"He was born like that."

Willa nodded, and Melody squinted at her. "Has your mother been telling you stuff? About where I worked and all?"

Willa shook her head.

"Oh, okay. It's just that I've had a bunch of jobs, worked all over the place, but my last job was at that power plant down by Acton, and it's hard to say, about his eyes. You can never say for sure, but if your mother told you

I shouldn't take any more chances with that place, I can't argue. Too many funny things."

"What'd you think when he was born?"

Melody shook her head. "I had a C-section—you know, when they cut you open?" She traced a line down her stomach. "I was out cold."

"So you didn't see him."

"Oh sure, I saw him. They bring them in. I was real happy, seeing him there. I was—I guess I was so drugged out or something, but I just kept waiting for him to open up his eyes, you know?"

"He's got such blond hair," said Willa.

"His daddy's a towhead." Melody leaned toward Willa and whispered confidentially. "I'm blond, too, really," she said, lifting a lock of her dark hair, "but not white blond like him, more washed out, kind of dirty blond. Now you've got a real pretty color. That's all natural, huh?"

Willa nodded, and Melody smiled a crooked smile which almost looked sad. Then she touched the tip of Willa's nose with an outstretched finger.

"Lucky you. Hang onto that hair, okay?"

She scooped the rest of the cut apple into her hand, tossed the core into the garbage can, and walked away.

When Willa went to the living room, she saw Melody on the floor with the boy. They were playing the game where his mouth was a tunnel, the apple a chugging train. Jo-Jo was laughing and had his fingers splayed across his mother's face. Willa stood in the doorway, a sour feeling in her gut.

"I hate to say it, but we've got to get going," Melody said to her mother.

And her mother answered, her voice quick and concerned. "So soon, but you just got here. You hardly drew at all."

"They say the weather won't hold out." Melody looked up at the ceiling as if it were the sky. "We have a drive."

Willa's mother came and stood with her while Melody lay Jo-Jo on his back and zipped him into a snowsuit. Then she and her mother moved to the front door and watched Melody pick her way down the slippery stairs with the boy on one hip, a knapsack on her back, her drawings in a roll under her arm.

"You two take care now, okay?" said Melody, turning when she reached the bottom step, and Willa smiled a quavering, forced smile. Melody strapped Jo-Jo into a car seat that looked like an elaborate plastic bubble, slid into the driver's seat, and sat there a moment warming up. The car was blue and rusty, coughing as if the air were too much for it, but after a minute Melody waved. Then she and Jo-Jo drove away.

"Why couldn't they have stayed longer?" Willa asked after the car and then the sound of the car had disappeared. "I have nobody to play with."

"I don't know, honey," said her mother, and her voice sounded tired and disappointed. "People have things to do."

Willa went to her room and lifted the cardboard shield which tricked her ants into thinking they were underground. They froze for an instant, then saw it was just Willa and continued on. Their paths were so easy to follow; she could see through the glass on both sides and watch their every move. She would let them go, she decided. Not now, when the ground was frozen, but in spring when the earth grew soft and they could burrow down. She would take the farm outdoors, crack open its sides, and let the ants spill out like beads.

But then Willa remembered the Queen ant, the one who had broken off her own wings when she settled in the farm to lay her eggs, who lived off the energy of her useless flight muscles, leaving the broken wings in a corner of the farm. Auto-amputation was what they called it in *The Wonder World of Ants*. Willa had wanted to get rid of those wings, hated looking at them, but she couldn't reach them without dismantling the farm. The Queen couldn't fly, and she was too fat to walk. Out in the world, abandoned by her guards and workers, she would die.

Willa wished her ants were leafcutter ants, the kind who dragged bits of plants and caterpillar droppings to their underground nests and grew fungus on them, like farmers. Then they ate the fungus and fed it to their kids. That was practical—the leafcutters could live through almost anything, but Willa's ants were used to bread and honey and being fed by her. The missing children, the way she saw them, were more like leafcutter ants. Somehow they knew how to get by.

Ants had survived on this earth for more than a hundred million years. It didn't surprise her. The smaller you were, the better your chances. Her mother made her drink milk so she would grow big and strong and so there would be cartons for the soup. But big and strong was the wrong thing; small was what you had to be. She would not drink milk anymore. In the end, if it came to that, she would find a friend like Jo-Jo. Underground he would shine in his paleness like the fireflies in summer in the fields out back. Blind, Jo-Jo would be able to sense corners, the twisted workings of the paths, and if she took his hand, he would guide her far from the silos, deep into the insulated center of the earth.

DIRECTOR OF THE WORLD

Jane McCafferty

You can pretend when your father comes home from the war he's all right, same as he'll pretend same as your mother will pretend. First, the big supper!

She got in her apron, wore it like the miniskirt, tied the sash tight, put on nylons, high heels, nothing else, just the apron with the fruit that's the wrong color meaning oranges are grape and vice versa, someone's humor we don't need it.

He's with his keys, we don't know what they go to, there are fifty-two of them altogether, only I know because only I counted, it was night, they were over my head. All he wanted to do was cry, that was how it had to be. He said to her, you get out of bed so I can cry in peace. Get out of my dream. Out! Really loud, you would think to yourself, the neighbors.

Right over my head so on the gray couch looking at the ceiling I thought they might crash on through, would they be bare, I wouldn't want to see, I'm not like the others, especially the ones who do it, and they do it in the outdoors, for instance in a parking lot, even though I would say, "There's broken glass and you'll get cut." Once a girl said she likes it, the getting cut part, by the name of Yolanda Finch, not a lie.

You can still be a child, for instance, you can say no, I don't think I'll grow up yet, then you think it so hard, it works, and you go to a movie and get the child rate maybe all your life hunching.

And sometimes you can feel like saying to your mother that you don't like the world, so this way she'll say drink some milk, take a nap, or make a joke and say the world don't like you either but don't you already know that.

In the mornings you all sit at the white table, the kitchen seems full of fog, there should be a horn, she looks all right in her nightgown, he wears his underwear, calls them *drawers* and maybe his shoes on too, maybe even combat boots depending on his mood, you think to yourself I'm not inviting friends over anymore and your mother makes the joke, What friends?

There are all those times when you forget who you are. It can be like you're the impersonator and they're paying you, you can convince so many that you are yourself.

So she's standing at the stove frying eggs which he loves. So we think, when all the sudden he says "Tell me why you're cooking eggs." She turns around and says, For breakfast Silly, smiling but it's the crying tone now.

Also outside there is yelling. The bottle breaker likes the morning and to say Somebody Somebody. Like a rooster it could wake you, we're not on a farm, you can go to the windows press your forehead and see the bottles breaking. You might want to go to a farm for health, a little air. I could grow up and have a farmhouse, very quiet, I love nature and wouldn't need a car.

After he said "Breakfast, is that right?" he took the ring of fifty-two keys and examined it like a huge seaweed thing, it should be dripping wet. He shook it just a little, a little music in the kitchen, there goes the hole.

Important, he said. Important thing is to be a good *spy*. My mother turned around and said Come again?

Zenia, he said to me, Sometimes I look at you and think you're less than human. And I mean that as a compliment.

And my mother turned from the stove. Very lonely when she said nothing, and I said Why you got that look, it's a joke, he's funny, he's making a joke. Why are you looking so serious, spoiling everything! My father nods, then gives me the wink. Then says in the old voice: First we need raincoats.

That's right, I said, and then we laugh, do we know where we are? The nervous laughter, all those keys!

"Good-bye," I said to her. She folded her thin arms, that's all I can say, I wasn't interested in her eyes.

So we got into his car, which first he stood back, looked at smiling. This piece of shit, he said, it'll take us nowhere fast.

We got into the front seat, red like blood under my legs. Sun washed through the windshield so we squinted. I just clearly saw how I was, another person, and quiet in the piece of shit car.

We didn't look at each other, how could we. How do you say why you don't look. To get through it you stare straight ahead.

You miss me? How much? As much as you thought? and he asked me all three questions as usual before I even answered the first.

What did I say? Nothing! I loved him! I should've found my voice!

He started up the car, I was all right in his book he said. We drove, there was that sizzling sound, so the streets were wet. Tulip tree, he said, every time we passed one. And made an explosion sound. The trees were beautiful.

"Where's the raincoat store, honey?" he said, then looked over. I saw his eyes, you don't know how a hand can reach out of the pupil, which in him was then large, but I saw the hand reaching, maybe waving good-bye, maybe I wanted to say that too, good-bye! But you just look at each other anyway, it's a part of your life, your life and not to block things out.

"I don't know any raincoat stores," I said, talking in the tone of everything's fine. "Raincoat stores, hmmmm," I said, very cheerful since the silence. Then I said, "Can we turn on the radio?" and he said, "Radio?" and got a big smile on his face. "That's a fantastic idea!"

You thought I invented the radio!

When really, when I was small, it was us on the road listening to the radio, all the windows rolled down, that's how the years went by I think now, and then I was very happy. You can't imagine how many good songs there were. Every so often his hand reaching over and sitting on my head like a nice cap to keep my thoughts down.

You think about the hands you held once.

We sailed down the freeway like a speedboat. I could see the road was water going fast. He said, "Sears," and I nodded, very cheerful. There was green sky out the windows, and he had his keys on his lap like a small dog, that was the sad part. His hand smoothing them.

Before Sears there was a bar. I forget the name. The bartender told him No little girls and he said Little? Who's little? Then he said, Please, if she sits quiet on the end stool? The bartender shrugged. My father said he just wanted one drink and he'd be mighty quick.

He made it so quick my eyes didn't even get used to the dark. I was still blind from the daylight shining off the wet gray sidewalk. He put his finger up in the air and said, "To the raincoats!"

You can pretend people aren't gone, but really they are, that doesn't mean they're not them anymore. They're still blood.

In Sears he said for instance, "No we don't need any help" to the saleslady, and he said it so quiet, like a whisper, and his eyes fluttered, fluttered, froze.

He took us to the boy section. Girl raincoats aren't for spies, he said.

He picked out one real nice spy raincoat, size twelve, beige colored plain, dark lining.

Try it on, Zeen Queen.

That was the old name. It will tell you he had a sense of humor, also he made up songs for me and sang them when we drove. "Zeen-Queen, Zeen-Queen, what did the world mean."

In the spy coat I stood before the mirror and he gave a whistle. You know the whole Sears heard. "Beautiful!" he said, and asked a stranger, "Whatta you think, does she look like a spy?"

The stranger nodded very cheerful. Then we went to the men's section. He found a raincoat just like mine, three times as big and put it on. Handsome. I'm telling you.

He looked in the mirror, not at the front self but walking away he looked at the back of him, looking over his shoulder to see how he looked leaving.

"We're all set," he said.

"Sure Papa, what you say goes."

And then I snap my finger like the Three Stooges on the television, he used to watch with me on his shoulders. He used to be like that, a man watching television with a girl on his shoulders, four years old and smaller, before he saw them stick grenades up the village girls which he told us in his old voice in the other bar where the bartender didn't care how long I stayed. That was later in the night. We were in our spy coats. Let me go backwards.

He said at least he wasn't a Seal. They do things he couldn't imagine. The hardest things, he said. And black seals were slipping all over inside my head throwing red balls so when I told him, he had to say, "Not those kind of seals! Christ!" I was then blocking it out and seeing his hand on the pile of keys making him popular in the bar. They kept saying "Why all the keys? Why all the keys?" Laughing together against him.

There are so many people think it's a joke. Pick up your keys, we can leave the bar, I told him.

We were then back in the car. We drove in the dark playing spies. "There is so much to spy on," he kept saying. Beeped the horn. There in the Valiant the red front seat with the moon. It's dark enough. Both of us in our spy coats, he slides through the rich section, where I know people for instance from school. They look like magazines, very rich. He slid by in the car and we stared very hard at the houses. We spied on many things, the lit windows, the yellow flowers, the big lawns, we saw it all. A sprinkler, a sprinkler, shooting the air. An old man looking at the sky with a dog in his arms.

Then we spied on other things. The highway. We stared very hard at the other cars when they drove by us. Spying right on the driver, if they saw we didn't look away, kept spying.

Soon we were going so slow. We had a lane to ourself. Twenty miles an hour right on the freeway. He said he didn't care where his ass ended up. I remember his tone. We drove along.

"We could go spy on Supermarket," he said, he forgot the name. We did that, we drove slow by the window of Shop N' Save, all lit up and the shoppers inside with carts not knowing we were spying, and then he turned into the director.

"Keep shopping," he told them, don't stop. He nodded, he told them they were doing a good job. He was the director now. We were back on the freeway and he told the cars, "That's right, keep it up now, keep driving, that's right," and he nodded. He told them he was very proud of them, and also the light, he told it to change red so we could stop, then told the light it was very good, he was proud. We then passed a woman lit up in a glass telephone booth. "Insert the coin and make the call," he directed, and she did.

Also we went to the factory, leather I think, the one under the bridge, there was a big chain link fence, we spied through it, we saw the factory wall. Our shadows were there. How his hands were on the fence is very clear. He shook the fence. Then he put the collar of his spy coat up and told me to do the same. We looked at our black shadows on the wall and waved to them. Then, back to the car, and now the keys between us and also his hand patting them. Next.

We spied on sheep. They are downstate, way past Dover. We were flying, he directed the other cars, "Keep going, you're all doing fine, just keep driving." He directed the moon, he said, "Shine shine and don't fall down," and to the litter he pointed and said "Lie there and look awful" and we were going so fast the farmhouses float, float up off the land, he told them to. All the land was black and under the sheep. He pulled the car up and shined his lights on the sheep. We spied very long, he told them they were being good, doing a good job. He said stand there and look at us and they did. White wool bodies, black faces, pink ears and black legs. When they spoke the sound was men trapped inside.

Look at these poor animals, he said, they don't want to be here, they want to go to another planet, can't you tell? I kept looking at the sheep, just looking now, not spying. And they turned their faces, you could see the world turning away from you.

All the sheep were walking away and then he said "Your mother's in a dream world, a dream world all her own, and I don't know what's happening here." You kissed him as he cried like kissing him good-bye and hello at the same time you're not sure, push him away as hard as you can.

Very quiet. Back upstate. We drove and drove. Then we went down our street. It is very narrow, it never struck me how narrow our street was but then it did, that night, all the houses stuck together, we got claustrophobia. But he told the houses "Keep standing still in the moonlight." And then he parked right outside our house.

We spied from the car. Tears were running down. Already she was in the nightgown, roses on white. First she was in one window, her arms crossed. "You just stand there with your arms crossed," he said. "That's right. Then in another window. That's right," he said. "Walk from window to window in your roses." She then stood in the big window, lit a cigarette as he told her, "Light a cigarette. Now inhale. That's good, now smoke it." She smoked it, and he said "Perfect."

Let's go in please.

In the morning I woke up, he was gone. I could feel it, it's for good, maybe he went to another country. You don't hope for return.

My mother cried and didn't get dressed for some time. Then a new man came, one who brought me presents:

1 crossword books
2 red socks with light blue stars
3 underwater snow scene thing
4 china mouse with gray vest plus spectacles
5 poster of sea gull flying over ocean
6 notebook, pencils
7 a record by a fellow named B. B. King
8 several times, candy, including Baby Ruth, a personal favorite

A *very* nice man, nobody should complain, by the name of Everett and feels great sympathy for all the peoples of the earth. He and my mother sit at the white table now, two voices behind the wall, you can get the glass and press your ear. She said to him last night I'm like my father, and she can't help that damn it. Other people's husbands come back just fine, she said, in a way I'm glad he's gone. It's a big relief, she said. They were drinking hot water with lemon in it like they do with saltines.

To peel off my black leotards every night then to sleep, not under the blankets, they itch my skin, but under his spy coat, it smells like him, left behind on purpose, don't you think? and I clench my eyes shut and there is the sheep, every time, rising off the black land into the stars and inside the sheep's mind me pushing him away and his voice so clear in my head still directing. He tells the sheep *Fly* and they're already flying, so they fly.

WINTER HAVEN

Stewart O'Nan

My father calls about the grass. It's December, I'm trying to sell our place, and we've got a squatter jumping house to house down the beach, building fires on the marble floors.

"You said once a week," my father says, "it's more like once a month."

It's long distance—peak hours—and I pay no matter who calls. That's all going to change once Eileen gets the papers together. The market's depressed, and I'm eating Corn Flakes a lot.

"Look," I tell him, "I'll give him a call, all right?"

"I don't want to be a pain in the ass about it."

"You are being," I say, to let him know he isn't.

"So when are you coming down?"

"Christmas."

"When Christmas?"

"Things are crazy up here," I say, and end up telling him about Eileen.

"That's a shame," he says. "I bet you feel different now, don't you?"

"It's a collarbone."

"That's not the point," he says.

"All that's over," I say, "and I'm not going to talk about it." He shuts up to make me feel bad.

"I'll call the guy," I say.

I'm living in the guest room off the kitchen so Sandy the realtor can show the house looking nice. The furniture's here; Eileen only took the kids. I have the drapes open and the shades up, the rug's just been shampooed. I've taken down all the crosses except Dan's over my bed. I keep at the dishes, the counters. It's with the multiple listing; when I get off swing shift I find cards by the sink. I'll leave a few rounds on the dresser to give them a thrill.

"He's a detective," Sandy or Barb or Gerry will say. It sounds better than a plain cop, like the pay was really different.

The buyers'll give Dan's Jesus the eye, and depending on the sell, Sandy will or won't tell the story. I wonder what they think I'm going to do. I wonder if they have any suggestions.

Swing isn't as bad as graveyard. Everything's open, and you don't have to change the way you sleep. The day is basically the same, the meals and everything, you just call dinner lunch. You're never late for work.

I don't like to be in the house days. I'll drive down to the ocean and read the Psalms, which sometimes works. I have the department Blazer while I'm on the squatter. The waves come up the sand until they're under me.

> O Lord my God, in thee do I take refuge;
> save me from all my pursuers, and deliver me,
> lest like a lion they rend me,
> dragging me away, with none to rescue.

My father hates Winter Haven, the people always out. He says he wants to come back north now that my mother is gone. He doesn't have any friends in Florida, he misses the winter. When the spray is blowing and the gulls hover and the wind herds the trash barrels, I can see the attraction, but the old place is gone, and his friends are dead. But you can't tell him that.

"Any luck?" I ask Sandy.

"Things will pick up with the weather, it's just a buyer's market right now. One problem is people with children don't like breaking up the school year, and that's I think who we're looking for, a family with children. Unfortunately you know what the economy is like around here, I think that's keeping the market slowed down, but things will pick up I'm sure come March, it's just a slow time of year normally."

Eileen's face is coming along but she has to wear a sling, and I have a hard time stopping my sympathy. Once on a bust I fell into a boat and broke my hand. I hated her cutting my food; no matter what it was, halfway through it was cold.

"You want pizza five times a week?" she said. "You want hot dogs and hamburgers like a little kid?"

Our squatter dumps in the toilets but they're capped for the winter. It hits you a foot in the door, that and the smoke. He snips the alarms, even the big ADT systems, that's why Jimby thinks it's a pro. Jimby's from the city; to him if you can fix a car you're a genius. When I was a kid we used to do the same thing, that's why I'm swing and Jimby's days. Jimby comes in, there's an address on his desk, something-something Dune road, and by the time I get in it's pictures. A dried dump, charred ends of driftwood by a grand piano. I put on my duck gear and roam the dunes around the empty houses. Baymen say the sea talks if you listen, but I'm safe. God isn't like a star that can go out.

The grass guy says he's been there. "914 Clarendon," he says, "I got it right in front of me."

"What's the date?"

"Says Thursday."

"This Thursday."

"The Thursday just was."

"What about this Thursday?"

"It doesn't grow that fast."

"Then what, will you tell me, am I paying forty dollars a month for?"

"I'll go and do it again myself if you want."

"Please," I say.

I don't like talking on the phone with the kids. I don't know what she's said to them. "Your old man's not so bad," I say sometimes, but they don't bite. Jay wouldn't trust me even if things were normal; twelve's an ugly age. I expected some help from Dan, but he's gone quiet. It's a bad sign, I say to her, but she thinks I'm getting on her about the whole thing. "Maybe I should move back in," she says. "Sure. Give me a minute to pack everything up, OK?"

She doesn't bother to argue anymore. She'll hear it's me and hang up. She thinks the restraining order takes care of everything. Her sister's the one I feel bad for. Jenny's always liked me. "She's very confused right now," Jenny'll tell me outside. We both know it's not true but it makes leaving easier, and she watches me walk away from the porch like I'll be coming back.

I've got the profit figured at sixteen thousand, clear. When the car commercials come on, I think about walking into the dealer and dropping an envelope on the desk and just pointing to the one I want. Not that we're going to get close to what we're asking.

I like to four-wheel at night, rolling slow over the dunes. The surfcasters' fires hop out of the darkness, then black. A camper forms, battened down for the night. I've got the kids' mattresses in back, beef jerky on the dash, my basic ordnance. It's not going to be easy to go back to the Caprice. I send the spotlight out over the water; even at night, it is still coming.

> O Lord my God, if I have done this,
>   if there is wrong in my hands,
> if I have requited my friend with evil
>   or plundered my enemy without cause,
> let the enemy pursue me and overtake me,
>   and let him trample my life to the ground,
>   and lay my soul in the dust.

I don't have trouble sleeping, I just forget a lot lately. Jimby leaves me an empty pack of Salems, half-burnt, a blackened matchbook with JFK's face, and a pair of dead AA batteries. He has on a note card, "Menthol Crack Walkman?" I go down to the property room and get something to keep me going. I'm supposed to drop by the rest area past exit 66 and shine my light into the bushes, but when I get there I open the window and listen to the rustle of the men. When is love not evil?

The lights are on at Jenny's, the curtains drawn. Jay's bike lies on its side on the front lawn. I eat a stick of beef jerky and watch the shadows cross and recross the living room window.

Sandy calls and wakes me up to tell me we have a buyer. I'm in last night's camo and still going. My eyes are like tinfoil, my gums sweat. The offer is eighty-seven-five.

"That's not even close," I say.

"No one is getting list value out here right now. If I were in your position I'd think about a serious counteroffer."

"Things are going to pick up in a few months in the spring, is that right?"

"I can't predict the market," she says. "They're a good risk for a mortgage."

"One-oh-two."

"I don't think they'll like that."

My pump leans in the corner. Dan's Jesus bleeds down over me.

"Oh well," I say.

Jimby comments on my beard. "You're really getting into the part," he says, pointing at my hunting vest, my orange hat. They're my own clothes.

"So," I say, "how close are you?"

"Don't get wise," he says, "how're you holding up?"

"Aces, Jimby I'm living the life."

Jenny's husband, Howie, bowls Tuesdays and Thursdays in Hampton Bays. He rolls three strings then yuks it up in the bar, two pitchers max. The season is on a chart on the wall; it's not half over. This cheap crank makes me see funny, but it looks like Howie's the team's anchorman. Good for fucking you, Howie.

"Jay," I say.

"We're not supposed to talk to you," he says, and hangs up.

The men groan in the bushes. I go down to the beach and shine my fog lights into the houses, go home and sleep till noon. Sin is no enemy.

I've got to remember to eat more often, and then when I try to have cereal the milk is bad. I feed the cards into the disposal, pour the clotted milk in, and grind it all. The buyers are fuckheads.

"The grass," my father says, "no one came about it."

"I will take care of it," I say, "I swear if I have to come down there myself and cut it."

"I'm the only one here," he says. "You don't know what it's like."

"Do you want me to come down?"

"What about Eileen and the kids?"

"They're gone."

"That's a shame," he says. "Now don't worry about this thing with the grass. I know you've got problems."

"I'm absolutely fine," I say, "I'm just worried about you."

"Don't," he says, "I won't be in your hair much longer."

The guy at the grass place says there was nothing to cut but he ran the mower over it anyway. He gives me the address again. "Does your father have a problem with his memory maybe?"

"How much do I owe you total?" I say, "because I am sick of this bullshit."

Thursday our squatter's camped out at the Flamingo Club in the empty swimming pool and risks a fire because of the windchill. Jimby's coming back from a long lunch at the Crow's Nest and practically trips over the smoke. A local kid, what did I say? I get a change of shift day which takes me through the weekend, then Monday it's back to shaving.

I get down to the beach before sunset. The wind is up, the surf bucking. A few men in waders are letting fly. I've got the heater blasting, a cold six on the seat, my box of Flakes. I can't remember if I took the two I usually take around now, and take four to make sure. The sea never gets tired, never gives up.

> O let the evil of the wicked come to an end,
> but establish thou the righteous.

I fill up at a Hess and buy two of their Christmas tankers and drive over to Jenny's. They have a tree and presents under it, angels with pipe cleaner wings. Howie's into his second game. Either none of us or all of us are forgiven.

Jenny doesn't understand what I'm doing there. I hand her the tankers through the crack in the door and show her the gun.

"Ron," she says, but won't stop looking at it. I open the door and she steps back.

"Who is it?" Eileen calls from upstairs.

"It's me," I say.

She comes to the top of the stairs. "Jen, are you all right?"

"She's fine," I say.

"What do you want?" Eileen says.

"I wanted to say good-bye. I'm going to Florida. I brought these for the kids." I point to the tankers.

"Good-bye then," Eileen says.

"Good-bye," I say, and shoot her through the sling. She falls back instead of down the stairs so I can just see her feet, flopping. I figure the one's good enough.

I steer clear of the rest areas, sleep in the campgrounds. In the Carolinas everyone's friendly and has extra razors. Driving, I imagine a cop pulling me over, looking in my side while I pretend to get my registration. He'll figure I'm a regular guy and ask, "What's the lawnmower for?" and I'll say, "To cut grass with," and then who knows what will happen.

RISE

1994

Jennifer Cornell

This is a list of the things that went missing: half a metre of green nylon netting, a small quantity of stainless-steel gauze, a bolt of cheesecloth, two pairs of forceps, eight sheets of plywood and a box of syringes, half a dozen light bulbs, a spool of wire, a fret saw, a hammer, and a packet of needles.

It's that boy, my Uncle Vincent said. What did I tell you about that boy?

Now hold on a minute, my father said.

Hold on, nothing, my uncle answered. That's who's done it. And it's your own fault for taking in strays.

Alright, we'll go see him, my father said, but when we got to the house he wouldn't go in. Instead he went up to a man in his shirtsleeves who was leaning in a doorway on the other side of the street. The man straightened up when he saw us coming, and the girl on her knees in the hallway behind him sat back on her heels and set her brush down.

Michael Hagan, my father said. D'you know if he's in?

He is, the girl said. He's been in for a week.

He's sick, the man said.

Why, what's wrong with him?

That woman's what's wrong with him, the girl said. She took a sponge from the bucket beside her and slapped it down heavily onto the floor. Good bloody riddance if she has gone away.

They don't know what's wrong with him, the man said. He took sick last Sunday and he's been bad ever since.

Is it serious?

Could be, the man said. His mother's with him. A couple of times now she's sent for the priest.

A bad time to visit, then.

No, go on over, the girl said. She'll be glad of the company. It's been ten days now and he's not said a thing.

In the kitchen of the house we found a woman standing, her back towards us, making tea. Steam climbed from the mouth of the lidless kettle, but the woman's grip on its handle was bare. There were cakes on the table, a pile of cores and torn strips of peeling half-wrapped in newspaper on the edge of the sink, and the room was rich with the scent of cinnamon, the air just above the open oven still quivering with escaping heat.

Mrs. Hagan? my father said, and she turned.

Yes?

How is he?

Just the same. No change from this morning.

Is he eating?

Not a thing. I just took him soup but he wouldn't touch it. I tried porridge earlier but he left that, too.

And what about you, how are you doing?

Oh I'm alright, the woman said. I'm bearing up.

Have you sent for a doctor?

The woman looked at my father, at his tie and his spectacles, at the pen in his pocket and the briefcase in his hand.

Aren't you the doctor?

No, my father said, no. Just a friend.

From inside the cardboard box he carried came the fluttering sound of confetti falling, of raffle stubs tumbling before the draw. He offered the box like an explanation, and all of a sudden the woman's face cleared.

Oh, aye, sorry, she said. I do know you. You're the one who got him that job.

She led us up a narrow staircase, assisting each step with both hands on the rail. The woman's ankles were as thick as her calves, and I could hear the quick, uneven clouds of her breathing escape from her open mouth as she climbed.

That was awful good of you, she said on the landing. He liked that wee job.

Eight months before when my father found him—legs wide apart and fists on the table, staring down at a tray full of Bull's Eyes and Moon Moths my father had pinned the previous week—the jimmy he'd used to lever our window was in his back pocket, and the sack he'd brought to put things in was lying still empty at his feet. So what do you think of the royal family? he'd asked without warning. My father had spent the past forty-eight hours on a bench outside of Intensive Care; he'd stared at the boy in the black leather jacket, at his close-shaven head and the tattoos on his arms—trying to distinguish the uneven letters, to see in the purples and blues of the symbols an emblem he recognised, a slogan he'd heard—and said nothing. *Citheroniidae*, the boy had continued, they come from America. Only they're lumped in with the Saturnids now. Reclassified, my father had answered. That's right, the boy'd said. Seems they were silkworms, after all.

Michael, you have visitors, the woman said.

He was in a wooden chair by the window, and he didn't look up when we came in. Every flat surface—most of the floor, the desk and the dresser, the low wooden unit beside the bed—was cluttered with field guides and uncut labels, specimens in transparent envelopes, others on spreading boards, a few behind glass. My mind formed the names of the ones I could recognise—*Colias hyale*, the Pale Clouded Yellow, its wings and antennae outlined in lavender; *Lysandra coridon*, the Chalk Hill Blue; *Callophrys rubi*, the Green Hairstreak, fringed from wing tip to thorax in the softest of greys.

You should see it downstairs, the woman said. The kitchen's full of them. I couldn't believe my own eyes. Every drawer and closet in this house, every shelf, full of them, and not one crumb of food in sight. Just those things, everywhere.

We've brought him another one, I'm afraid, my father said. He handed the cardboard box to me. Go on, wee woman, you give it to him. He'll like it better, coming from you.

We had brought him a new imago, the first to complete the cycle that started with the eggs we'd discovered in the field Michael introduced to my father, one of the few laying patches he hadn't yet found. What do you look for? my father'd asked him. All morning they'd been comparing notes. Michael shrugged. Videos, mostly. TVs, if they're small. This was shortly before my father hired him, paying him out of his own benefit cheque. Sometimes Michael would let me help him, let me pass a pin through the tight coiled centre of a slender proboscis and draw it down into sugar water till the insect stopped struggling and started to feed. The trick was to see if we could get them all started before the first one finished and began to walk away, wings opening and closing with the tentative speed of untried machinery, taxiing slowly in preparation for flight. We'd managed it once, working together, till all around the room on greaseproof paper Apollos and Peacocks and Camberwell Beauties were swallowing nectar, while I watched their wing patterns shifting and thought about bedsheets with people underneath. Don't move, Michael said when the last one had finished and I'd just returned it to the breeding cage. His hand brushed my cheek as he reached past me, and I expected to see a string of silk handkerchieves, or the smooth removal of an egg from my ear. Close your eyes, Michael told me, and I'd felt its feet flailing, frantically scrambling to re-establish their grip; then its claws caught my skin with the tug of small anchors, and I thought of moored ships and hot air balloons in extravagant colours, tethered and straining against their cords. You can look now, Michael said, and there it was, a Great Spangled Fritillary, indignantly fanning, imagining itself bold and imposing when every tremor of its rust-coloured wings sent another shower of scales to my palm.

Look, Michael, I said.

It had made its way into an upper corner, had been testing the meeting of lid and wall there, when I opened the box. Placing one slender leg carefully after another until all six were pinching the rim, it climbed out, broad head first and wide-spaced antennae, then the short, stout body, wings flat at its sides—a butterfly, despite all the evidence, though even its flight was quick and erratic like a moth's. I felt the effort of its ascension just as I had when, with my father, I'd been a passenger in the plane he'd hired for an hour as a gift for my mother, who had always wanted to learn how to fly. . We'd stood by the fence which guarded the runway, watching other aircraft take off and land while the pilot pulled levers and adjusted dials and untied the cords that kept our plane bound. They all seemed to rise with the smooth, steady lift of geese leaving water; I'd never imagined the shuddering fuselage, the thrust and drag of my heart and stomach, or the way my own equilibrium wavered with each changing attitude of the plane. The land below us looked artificial, like the scenes behind glass in the museum at home, tiny figures of farmers and livestock grazing on velvet under parsley sprig trees: *Belfast and Surrounding Country, 1790–1801*. It bore no resemblance to what we'd seen of it when we'd taken the highway a few days before. We had come out of season, long after harvest, and well before blossoms hid the hunched, arthritic fingers of the peach trees again. The wizened phalanges of the apple orchards, the electrified carpals of the cherry trees we passed, the charred spinal columns of the naked vineyards, each with its singular pelvic twist—I could almost hear the startled hiss of them when our headlights swung round a corner and caught them unawares. Ah, look, my father'd said, slowing the car, and gradually my eyes did catch sight of them: Canada geese, two only at first, then three, then five, then a dozen or more, a whole flock of throats and bills and bandaged white jaws rising out of the mud and stubble of a cornfield in April in upstate New York. We'd intended to spend the day in Toronto, but Immigration had refused to let us in—something to do with our type of visa—so we were skirting the rim of Lake Ontario, hoping to see Canada on the opposite shore. But the weather was wet, and the lake barely visible; I could feel the mist on my face when we got out of the car—cool, like my mother's breath on my back as she slept behind me, all three of us together in a motel's queen-sized bed, and gentle, like the trick Michael taught me soon after she died. Give us your hand, he'd said, bending down, till I felt something lighter behind the touch of his hair, the insistence of eyelashes against my arm. Do you know what that is, missus? he'd said. That's what you call a butterfly kiss.

You see how it is, the woman said to my father. I've tried to get him to talk about it but he won't, at least not to me.

You don't know what's happened, then?

Not all of it, no, but I can guess. You know she'd gotten a job in England? Well, I thought she was fixing it so he'd have work, too. Three months go by and every day I'm thinking, He'll be off soon now, too, but then I hear she's home for a visit. I never saw her myself, but I know she saw him. The couple next door says she stayed for an hour, went away in a taxi and that was it. Then the milk bottles and papers started piling up. They knocked on the door but nobody answered. That's when they reckoned they'd better ring me.

I had no idea, my father said.

No, well, how could you? Sure he never said anything to anybody. She's found herself some fancy man, that's what I think, anyway. I don't know what she told him, but he's been like this ever since.

It's been awhile since we've seen him, right enough, my father said. But the weather's been nice, you know? I thought he might be collecting. See, what did I tell your Uncle Vincent? My brother-in-law thought he'd been stealing again.

It wouldn't surprise me, the woman said. But he's not been out of this room for a fortnight. Was it stuff of yours, aye? You're welcome to look for it. I couldn't tell you what's in this house.

No, my father said, I'm sure it's not Michael. It's been going on for awhile, see. A couple things disappear every day. I think it's me, to be honest. I misplace things. I don't know what I'm doing half the time anymore.

Well have a look anyway, the woman said. Sure, I'll make us a wee cup of tea while you do.

Thank you, my father said. You stay with Michael, daughter, alright? he told me. Try to get him to talk. I won't be long.

He was wearing pyjamas, his arms loose in the sleeves, each elbow at rest on an arm of the chair, and still I could see the inflated vessels altering the contours of his forearms and hands. I took hold of his wrist and turned it over, placed my two fingers at the heart of his palm and began to move up with a circular motion, crossing thin strands which began in confusion and later became conspicuous cords like the gradual gathering of slow drops of water, each bead jumping to join the stream till a single clear thread runs briefly down the length of a windshield or the cool face of a window, drains itself utterly and then is gone. Michael had taught me the game only recently, and the first time we'd played I'd fallen right into the trap, saying Now! There, stop! when his fingers were still a good two inches away from that tender hollow where an arm bends in, where the skin is creased even in infants, thin and defenseless behind the elbow's sharp bones. It's because of the way the nerves are laid out, Michael'd told me. It always feels like you've touched it before you do. But this time my fingers were well past the hollow and on toward that place near the armpit where all flesh turns smooth, in men as in women, regardless of age. I walked my two fingers onto his shoulder but he never responded, so I lay his hand back in its former position and smoothed his sleeves down.

You're awful pale, Michael, I said.

My mother had been white when the plane landed. She'd been sick for more than a year already, which is why my father had borrowed from usurers despite unemployment and the impossibility of ever paying them back, so she could visit her brother who now lived in America, having immigrated from Belfast some fifteen years before. But this time the illness refused to resettle, and a few days later we'd had to go home. What does it feel like, I'd asked her in hospital. Like you felt at Funderland last summer, she'd said—when I'd made myself sick on the main attraction, the one that replaced the Big Wheel that year. I forget the name of the ride now, but not the sensation. It began with the rise and tilt of the axis, then the floor fell away as we started to spin, the centrifugal force of lopsided rotation kept us pinned to the sides of the iron cylinder, the crush of the wind came from all directions, and against every warning I had opened my eyes. The bright colours of the cars and pedestrians on the Lisburn Road, of the shop fronts with their fruit stalls and displays of appliances, nearly new clothing and secondhand books, all tumbled towards me as if someone had lifted the asphalt at Shaftsbury Square and shook everything down towards the spot where I hung, the only solid the boy strapped opposite me, his own eyes shut across the bottomless space. I turned my head to look for my parents, standing by the ticket booth on the good ground below, and the skin of my face stretched tight as elastic, my flesh seemed to pass through the metal grille, and I thought of wax melting, of the disintegration of the Lundy's features that time on the Shankill when I'd watched him burn. I'd gone on a dare with a boy from Clonnard Gardens, had stood at the end of a row of old houses and watched the flames consume the effigy, thinking, How much wasted effort. I had an art teacher once who made models and drawings for illustration, to show us precisely why our own projects failed. With broad thumbs and fingers he'd bend and pinch the mysterious clay, or with quick charcoal sketches of femurs and vertebrae, he'd illustrate the error which had crippled our plan. When he'd finished he'd destroy the model or scratch out the drawing and say, Now you do it. I'd often wondered how that point could be reached, when I'd no longer be invested in every project, when a torn sketch wouldn't trouble me, when I could watch easily as they dismantled my armatures, as the screws were recycled, the wire unwound.

How do you feel, Michael? I asked, but he didn't answer. I followed his gaze out the open window, down the drainpipe at the edge of the sill to the patch of waste ground beside the house, where someone had dumped an old pot of tulips and some other horticultural rubbish in a tangle of weedroots and unwanted leaves. The lepidopterans of the floral world, my father once called them, and then tried to explain it to my cousin and me, how at every stage in a tulip's development it's transformed completely, how the final blossoming of the chaste, contoured petals was like the first full extension of a butterfly's wings. We'd spent the day looking for Painted Ladies, waist-deep and oblivious in the lush fluidity of the grass, and had come upon an inexplicable row of the flowers, paint-box bright, aloof and unblemished, in a rain-rutted pasture in County Down. The leaves look like cow's tongues, my cousin said, to be clever, though I could see the connection if I tried. I remembered a cow my uncle was supposed to have slaughtered; the animal had given him all kinds of trouble when he tried to drive it onto the truck. My uncle's cows were in Niagara County, on land which he left in the care of a neighbouring farmer a few months after we visited him there, so he and his wife and his son who was my age could be with us after my mother died. The cow's knees had been trembling badly and halfway up the ramp it'd balked, so three men were enlisted to help push it in. They stood side by side with their hands on its haunches, but their boots slid backwards over the gravel and damp diamonds of sweat appeared on their backs and under each arm. When they did finally get it into the back of the pickup, had pulled the ramp away and were raising the door, the cow's eyes turned white, its legs buckled beneath it, its tongue rolled out like a jubilee carpet, and the hard knob on its head where its horns would have been made the chassis ring as it fell. I don't understand it, my uncle'd said. She was great yesterday. The beast wants to live, Vincent, my mother'd said. Well if it does, my uncle'd answered, that's a strange way to show it. But he did phone the abattoir to say the cow was unhealthy—and that was the reason he kept on giving whenever the subject of slaughter came up, though every morning when we went out to look at her she was grazing serenely, her coat sleek, her belly enormous, her ears and eyes and hindquarters imperturbable, despite the relentless assault of flies.

Any luck? my father asked from the doorway.

I shook my head.

No, I wouldn't've thought so, the woman said. It's alright, luv. Don't you worry. He'll be right as rain again in a couple of days.

Listen, Mrs. Hagan, my father said, if there's anything I can do, you'll tell me, won't you?

What can anyone do? the woman answered. These things happen.

Well, if there is anything, you let me know.

You can catch that thing again, the woman said. It's over there.

The skipper had landed on a heavy curtain which hung in front of the closet instead of a door. My father approached cautiously, assessing the distance, then removed his coat to improve his reach, but still his hand missed its target. The skipper flashed once and vanished, then flashed again higher up; the half dozen tacks which had held the curtain popped like snaps on a raincoat and I heard their soft tinkle as they hit the floor, then the room overflowed with Sulphur and Brimstone, Magnificent Julias, True Lover's Knots. They came to rest on my sleeves like the dead skin of a bonfire, light and unsteady and easily dislodged—all the ones my father couldn't sell to collectors, all the ones whom the opposite gender ignored, all the outcasts who for some reason had hung incorrectly after eclosion and so had been able to inflate their wings fully or straighten their legs before the cuticle grew hard. Their flight made the sound of old wooden houses alone in the country, their floorboards and panelling resisting strong wind, and so many of them flew at my face on their way to the window that I had to close my eyes.

When I opened them again I looked for my father. He'd knelt down beside Michael, had the boy's hands in his, and they both were watching the steady exodus as even the most crippled among them struggled onto the sill and fell out, towards the light.

DANGEROUS MEN

Geoffrey Becker

Calvin, a drummer from Long Island who lived down the hall from us, wore jeans and tight, white T-shirts, smoked Lucky Strikes, and had eyes that nervously avoided contact. He was nineteen and skinny, but in a muscular way that reminded me of a greyhound. It was the summer of 1974, and my friend Ed and I shared a dorm room in what had once been a cheap hotel, but was now part of the Berklee College of Music. One Saturday night, Calvin came to our room and laid out ten little purple pills.

"Eat 'em up, gentlemen," he said.

I looked over at Ed, who was laboring to get his hair into a rubber band. Ed hadn't had a haircut in three years, and from behind, since he was short, you'd swear he was a girl.

"What are they?" Ed asked.

"Magic beans," Calvin said, punching my arm. "I traded the old lady's cow for them."

I picked one up, then placed it carefully back down. A little color came off on my fingertips.

"UFO," he went on. "Got 'em off a sax player I met on the elevator. Cat worked with Buddy *Rich*." Calvin had a thing about Buddy Rich.

"So?"

I glanced over at my homework. I'd been trying to write out a horn arrangement for "Satin Doll." After nearly two hours' work, I was still on the third measure, and I was pretty sure my trumpet part had wandered below the instrument's range anyway. Lili Arnot, the girl I loved, smiled down happily from where I'd taped her photo above my desk, tanned and lovely against the unhealthy green of the cracked plaster wall.

They were more like little barrels than tablets. Ed and I each had two, Calvin six. I watched with amazement as he placed them one after another into his mouth. They tasted bitter, no matter how fast you got them down.

———

It was the kind of night where your skin itches and the heat seems to sweat the street life right out of the city's pores. I gave a drunk with an English accent fifty cents and he croaked his thanks, but I sensed it might be a mistake in the long run, because the other drunks glowered at me, memorizing my face. Calvin led us past a trio of sullen hookers and over to TK's, a bar across the street where we could get served. Ed and I were both underage.

We ordered a pitcher of Black Label and listened to him.

"Let me tell you guys something," Calvin said. "I am dying here. At home, I get laid four times a day, I'm serious."

Ed nodded. He had a steady girlfriend back in New Jersey, Deborah, whose sexual appetite was enormous. I'd convinced him to come with me to Boston and do this summer program, and though we didn't talk about it much, we both knew what he'd given up. What he might, in fact, have given up permanently, given Deborah's obvious and immediate needs.

"You guys want to see a picture of my girl?" Calvin pulled out his wallet and unfolded a piece of paper that looked suspiciously as if it had been cut from a magazine. Ed looked at it first, then handed it to me.

"Nice," I said. It was a photo of a redhead, kneeling on a handwoven carpet, wearing an Indian headband and nothing else. I had to admit, if you were going to pick a girl to have delusions about, this was the one. Her eyes looked right out at you from the picture, not in a cheap way, or even a sexy one. It was more like she was studying you, as if she were seriously interested in who this person holding her in the flat of his hand might be.

When Calvin went to the bathroom, I asked Ed what he thought.

"I think that is one fucked-up individual, is what I think."

"He ate six," I said.

"We think he ate them. How can we be sure?"

"You think he tricked us?" The pills had begun to kick in, and whatever they were, they were cut with speed. I could feel myself tensing up. "Why would he trick us?"

"I don't know, man. The guy falls in love with magazine pictures."

"Maybe we're just paranoid."

"We're definitely paranoid. That doesn't mean we're wrong. Sometimes it's *smart* to be paranoid."

"We could just go," I said. "Go see a movie or something. He'd probably be OK by himself."

Ed stroked his chin. He'd taken his hair down again, and already he was turning into something gnomelike and medieval, a strangely proportioned face peering out from behind curtains. "The thing is, if he really did take six, we can't leave him alone. It wouldn't be right. Look at us. Now multiply this by three. Plus, the dude's a couple eggs short of a dozen as it is."

"Right," I said. "What do we do with him?"

"I don't know," said Ed. "Have some fun. Go out. What do we usually do?"

We drank another pitcher, then headed out into the evening. Ed and I wanted to see Andy Warhol's *Frankenstein,* which was rated X and in 3-D. Calvin told us he had something else in mind.

"There's this park not far away," he said. "Fags go there. I heard about it from one of the kitchen staff. They go and hang around in the bushes until some other fag comes along and then pair off."

This was a new concept to me. I knew there were homosexuals in the world, but I hadn't imagined them lurking about in bushes at night like zombies.

"What do you say we go kick some faggot butt?" asked Calvin.

We were standing in the shadow of a tall building smoking cigarettes, buzzing with the UFO, though some of that edge had been taken off nicely by the beer. It was cooler than it had been all day and my energy was high. I made a gallant attempt to run straight up the side of the building, but only ended up landing a good kick to the stone.

"Yeah," said Ed. "That sounds good."

I'd never really been in any fights, and I didn't know how I'd react. I'd never met a faggot, at least not to my knowledge, though there were some guys at school we had our doubts about. Beating them up had never crossed my mind. But Ed and Calvin seemed to have bonded on the issue. I figured I could just go along, see what happened.

We wandered through streets that seemed mirror images of themselves, angled and dark, the tall, brown faces of the row houses looking out at us with the calmness of age and location. The pavement was swollen and soft and the metal of the closely parked cars ticked with the day's heat. Stopping to admire a GTO, Calvin asked us which we'd rather have, a Goat or a T-bird, and when Ed said T-bird, Calvin told him he was full of shit.

"Goats *go*," he said, as if the sound of the words were themselves somehow proof.

For a while, I forgot about our purpose and tried to organize the arrhythmic thops of Ed's and Calvin's boots against the stone slabs of the sidewalk while I floated along behind, silent as a balloon. I could still see the blank staves of my music tablet, and now various rhythmic figures deported themselves for me, grouping and regrouping like children at a dance recital. Rhythm was my big weakness; I just couldn't translate what I heard to paper. That spring, I'd found a book in my parents' bedroom about people who'd made miraculous breakthroughs on LSD—an electrical engineer who'd suddenly understood how to solve a problem he'd been working on for ten years, a schizophrenic who'd managed to rid herself of the voices that had plagued her all her life—and now I wondered if I couldn't make a similar leap. As we walked, I experimented by plugging in time signatures:

4/4, 9/8, 5/8. With each change the dots would all shift. Though I doubted the accuracy of what I was seeing, I was definitely seeing something, and I was proud of my brain for being able to conjure answers so quickly, right or wrong. The more I thought about it, though, the more artificial the whole idea seemed. The world didn't divide up neatly, it fragmented in strange and unusual ways. It was only our need to make sense of it that made us believe in things like time signatures, or minutes and hours for that matter. Or days of the week, cities, states. Even countries.

We'd stopped moving and were waiting to cross a street. "The problem is limits," I said.

Calvin looked hard at me. "The problem is faggots."

Embarrassed, I bummed a cigarette from Ed, who was smoking Kools that summer, tearing the packs open at the bottom corner the way the black kids at our school did. I thought it was pretty affected, but I hadn't said anything to him about it. I was hoping he'd come around on his own.

"So where is this park?" It seemed to have grown a lot darker out. I didn't think I was having fun.

Calvin's face puckered with irritation. "Don't worry about it. We're close."

It occurred to me that probably, there was no park. There were no faggots. These things were as imaginary as the girl in his wallet.

In the distance, the CITGO sign hung in the air like a single, luminous eye, opening and closing with reptilian removal. Also there was, quite suddenly, music.

"We're near the water," said Ed.

On the grass by the Hatch shell, a festival was in progress. People beat on drums and blew saxophones and danced. Someone was shooting off medium-sized fireworks, and every few minutes there would be a whoosh followed by an explosion overhead, as red, green, silver, and gold flowers bloomed in the night sky. A woman with her face painted white wearing a clown wig and a Mr. Donut apron hurled handfuls of miniature glazed donuts up into the air. I asked her what was going on.

"You don't know?"

"No, I don't."

"The president resigned," she said.

"Who?"

"*Nixon!* Isn't it great?" She gave me a couple of donuts and I returned to my friends. Ed was doing push-ups, while Calvin tossed a small knife in the air, catching it each time by the blade end.

"It's Nixon," I reported. "He resigned."

Ed got to his feet, grinning, and slapped me five. It was like our team had won the Superbowl. I hadn't followed the specifics carefully, but I had watched with fascination the haggard images of the man that had appeared on TV over the past few months. There was no doubt in my mind the president had lost it, had become Humphrey Bogart in *The Caine Mutiny*, hollow eyed, intent on discovering who'd eaten his strawberries. I had only the vaguest memories of the Kennedy assassination. I'd been in summer camp for the moon landing, 150 of us squinting at one snowy TV screen that had been set up in the dining hall. Here was something I'd remember.

"Are you guys with me, or what?" Calvin asked. He didn't even look at the knife, just flipped it. He never missed, but even so, I kept thinking at any moment he was liable to lose a finger or two.

"What about the movie?" I suggested. In the flickering river-light, Calvin had become something of an old newsreel himself.

"Movie?" He toed the earth, kicking a small hunk of dirt to the side. "I want to kick some *ass*."

"You don't know where they are," I reminded him. "What have we been doing for the last hour?"

"I know where they are."

"Here," I said, distributing the donuts. Ed popped his in his mouth whole. Calvin slit his into pieces with his knife, dropping the sections to the ground.

"So, where are they?" I asked.

"What are you saying?"

I told him I wasn't saying anything. His eyes, I thought, had a peculiarly dead look to them, as if they'd been replaced with lug nuts.

"You think I'm shitting you? You think they aren't out there? This whole town is crawling with faggots." He looked around, as if some might be listening at this very moment.

"But *where?*" I asked. "This is all I want to know. Where are we going? You say we're going somewhere, and then we walk and walk, and we don't get there."

Calvin scratched at the side of his nose with his middle finger. He'd begun to glow a little, like something irradiated.

"Forget it," he said. "I don't need you guys. I'll do this alone."

"Hey," said Ed. "We're coming."

———————

We hadn't gone far when I saw that Ed was holding something. Calvin walked a few paces ahead of us, leading us back into the city; away from the water. It was a kitten.

"Where'd she come from?" I asked.

"In the park," he said. "I'm naming her Ella."

"What if she belongs to someone?"

"She belongs to me. She's a stray."

"But how do you *know* that? Maybe someone was just out playing with their kitten and she wandered off. Maybe they're out looking for her right now."

"Relax, man," said Ed. "You worry too much."

"I'm just saying it might not be a stray."

"It might not be a cat, either. They look like kittens, so we take them into our homes, then they tear us open while we're asleep, climb inside, and assume our bodies."

"All right, all right," I said. "But she's going to be your responsibility. Don't expect your father and me to feed her and change her litter box."

There was a screech of brakes up ahead, followed by a kind of thump sound, and I saw Calvin get tossed a few feet into the air backward, then fall hard to the ground. Ed and I ran to him. He was just lying there on his side. The guy driving the car was already out and on his knees.

"He walked right out in front of me," the guy said. "I think I killed him. Oh, lord, I think he's dead."

I knew he wasn't dead because I could see him breathing. "Calvin," I said. "Are you all right?" There was no answer.

"We ought to get the cops," said Ed.

"Maybe we could bypass that," said the man, uneasily. "I mean, I don't see that the cops are necessary here. Why don't we just get an ambulance?"

"Yeah," I said, remembering the hash pipe tucked in my pocket. "Let's bypass the cops."

"Out of nowhere," the guy was saying. He was older, a black guy, dressed in a suit, and while I was worried about Calvin, I felt bad for him, too. His car was a Cadillac, a new one. He'd just been minding his business, trying to get someplace. He didn't deserve us.

Ed helped Calvin to a sitting position. His eyes were open and he seemed to be able to see. "You blew it big time," he said to the guy. "My dad's a lawyer. I intend to own that car of yours."

"Don't mind him," said Ed. "He's not right in the head."

"Can you breathe?" I asked. "Can you move everything?"

"Well, I guess I'll be getting along," said the driver.

"Don't let him go anywhere," Calvin directed us. "Hold him." For a tense second or two, Ed and I looked at each other, waiting to see what the other would do. I didn't feel like grabbing anyone, though I wasn't sure about Ed. I sensed there might actually be a part of him that wanted to beat up strangers. The man edged away from us, got into his car and pulled away in a squealing of tires.

"Pussies," said Calvin.

"You're all right," I said after we'd all been silent for a little while. "Come on and let's head back to the dorm."

I tried to help him to his feet, but he shook off my hand and got up on his own. His jeans were torn down the side of one leg where he'd slid on the asphalt, and his arm was pretty scraped up, too. He brushed himself off and spat a couple of times.

"Amazing," said Ed. "You could be dead right now. You probably should be. What happened?"

"I don't know," he said. "I don't remember that much about it." His hands shook uncontrollably as he attempted to light a cigarette. After five matches, he got it going. "Where'd the cat come from?"

Ed put Ella up on his shoulder. "I found her."

Calvin took his cigarette and drew circles in the air in front of the kitten, who was fascinated. The orange ember left visible trails, like pinwheels in the dark.

The skinny, acned night desk guy was playing chess by himself and didn't even look up as we came in. The elevator stopped more or less at the fifth floor and we jumped down into the hallway, except for Calvin, who'd been limping slightly. He sat, dangled his legs, then stood. Outside our door we stopped as I hunted for the key. I was hoping Calvin would keep on going—I'd had enough of him for one night.

"What are you guys going to do?" he asked.

"I'm kind of tired," I lied. I felt as if I'd probably be awake for the next week. This was not a happy, fun drug we'd taken. This was a twist-your-head-up-in-knots drug. I just wanted it to be over.

"Mind if I hang? I don't like it when that guy goes off."

For the past week or so, right around midnight, someone on one of the upper floors had been letting loose with a series of bloodcurdling screams. We called him the Wildman. Legends had begun to appear scrawled in marker on the elevator wall: "Wildman Lives" and "Have you made your Peace?" While we all figured it was just some student with a twisted sense of humor and probably not the Angel of Death, the screams themselves were definitely unnerving.

I was a little surprised. "You're not scared, are you?"

"I just don't like it." Behind him, the dim hallway gaped like a mouth. He was vibrating slightly, possibly out of fear, but it could have been leftover nerves from the accident, or even just a trick of the hall light.

We let him in. Ed mashed up some saltines with water for Ella and put them in a dish. Calvin sat on the floor and took off his shoe. His ankle was swollen up like a grapefruit and had begun to turn a greenish purple.

"You walked on that?" Ed asked.

"I didn't know what it looked like."

"But you must have felt something," I said. "I mean, Jesus, that's ugly."

"I felt something, I guess. I don't know."

It was a bad moment. I thought he might cry. He kept staring at his ankle and shaking his head. "We should ice it," I said. Someone needed to take charge here.

"Where do we get ice at this time of night?" said Ed. He brought over our bottle of Jim Beam and some plastic cups.

I took the elevator back down to the Pepsi machine, pumped it with all our laundry quarters, got back on with an armful of cold cans.

Between the third and fourth floors, the elevator stalled. Then the lights flickered and went out. I stood there in total darkness holding five cans of soda, feeling their icy outlines against my ribs. From someplace high above, a person began to scream, making the kind of sounds that might come from someone being turned on a rack, or having their skin slowly peeled from them. I bent my knees and lowered myself to the floor. I decided to separate myself from this. Filtered through the elevator shaft, the sounds had a surreal quality, and I tried to imagine how one might notate them. After a while, I couldn't even tell if my eyes were open or not. I dropped the sodas and put my hands over my ears.

The howling stopped about a minute before the power kicked back in and the light returned. I collected the cans, stood and pushed the button for our floor again, taking comfort in the familiar graffiti, the fake wood-grain control panel, the ordinariness of it all.

———

Calvin sat with his foot up on Ed's bed. I arranged the Pepsis around his ankle.

"How's that feel?" I asked.

"Cold."

The pale blotchiness of Calvin's cheeks made me think of packaged supermarket tomatoes.

"Whoever that guy is," said Ed, "he's seriously whacked."

"Vietnam," said Calvin. "You know that guy with the blonde hair and beard who always eats by himself, wears an Army jacket?" He sipped at his drink, put it down hard on the edge of the desk. "He was over there. Went out on patrol with a buddy, and his buddy tripped a mine. Blew off part of his leg. That guy dragged a man two miles through the jungle, a guy who was already dead. When he found out, something in him just sort of snapped."

I knew for a fact this wasn't true. The guy with the beard who ate by himself was from Spokane, Washington, where he taught second grade and played piano at a Holiday Inn lounge, evenings. I'd talked to him once, when we'd both been waiting for the elevator. His name was Pat, and the main thing about him was his shyness. Of course, he might still have been the Wildman, but if so, it had nothing to do with Vietnam, or legs getting blown off.

"Where do you get your information?" I asked.

He shook his head. "Classified. I could tell you, but then I'd have to shoot you."

Ed coughed.

"You are so amazingly full of shit. I've talked to that guy. He's never been out of the country."

"Do you believe everything people tell you?"

"Do you believe everything that pops into your head?"

I looked over at Ella, who'd found herself a spot on Ed's bed, where she was busily licking one extended leg. The radio, which had been playing jazz, segued into crunching guitars. The water stain on our wall reminded me of something from biology class. I took one of the cans from next to Calvin's leg, tore off its pop-top.

He was silent, looking around the room. His eyes rested on my picture of Lili Arnot. "That your woman?"

I nodded. In truth, Lili Arnot would have probably been surprised to know I even *had* a picture of her, let alone that I was telling people she was my "woman." In the picture, she wore cutoffs and a white blouse and held a tennis racket under one arm.

"She gave me a blowjob once."

His face was a marionette's, grinning, wooden, vaguely evil. I hurled my open soda at it. The can glanced off the side of his head, continuing on to the wall, then to the floor where it spurted and frothed for a few seconds onto the stained carpet.

Considering his ankle, Calvin came at me with amazing speed. He threw me against the opposite wall. I'd cut him with the can, and blood dripped down over his ear. There was an oniony smell of perspiration about him, mixed with a sweeter scent of hair stuff. I put my hands around his neck and tried to choke him, while at the same time, he threw hard punches at my stomach and sides. There was a kind of purity to the moment, as when a thick August afternoon finally transforms itself into rain. This was where we'd been heading tonight, after all. If we couldn't beat up fags, we could at least beat up each other. I figured he might kill me, but I refused to worry. That was my role—the guy who worried—and I was tired of it. Ed shouted at us to stop, but we'd locked up like jammed gears. Calvin bit my shoulder and I jerked forward with all my weight, enough to push him off balance, causing him to step back. He cursed loudly and sat on the bed, where he pounded his fist up and down on the mattress.

"What?" I said. "What happened?"

"He twisted it worse," said Ed, going over to take a look. "Maybe it's broken."

"Fuck, fuck, fuck, fuck, fuck," said Calvin.

"You want to go to the hospital?"

"We can't take him to the hospital," said Ed. "They'll take one look at him and call the cops. Look at his pupils. They're the size of dimes."

"I'm all right," said Calvin, grimacing.

We decided on more aspirin and repacked the sodas around his foot.

No one said anything for a while. My sides hurt where I'd been punched, but basically I was OK, though I did feel a little stupid. Ed, who was wearing his "Bird Lives" T-shirt, started doing curls with a thirty-pound barbell. Calvin reached over and took my notebook along with a pair of number-two pencils off the desk, began playing drums atop my arranging homework. I didn't stop him, I just watched, painfully aware of my inadequate pencil marks on the stiff paper. They looked like a road construction project abandoned after only a few feet. Finally, I asked, "Did the lights go off here?"

"Lights?" said Calvin. "What lights?"

"When I was on the elevator, the lights died."

"Somebody should put that elevator out of its misery."

I sat down in a chair and had one of Ed's Kools. There were less than two weeks left to the summer. Soon, other people would have this room. It was wrong to think that our presence would linger on, though it was to this notion that I realized I'd been grasping all along, the idea that in some way we were etching ourselves onto the air, leaving shadows that would remain forever.

After a minute, Calvin put aside the pencils, took his knife out again and began flipping it. He seemed to have forgotten all about our fight, or the way we'd let him down earlier. He seemed to have forgotten about everything. I thought about the rockets we'd watched by the water, the way they rose in one big fiery line, then separated into smaller projectiles, burning out slowly in their own, solo descent.

"I know these two girls that share an apartment a few blocks from here," he said. "I met them at a record store. Very cool, very good-looking, and their parents are away. I'm serious—we could go over there."

"All three of us?" I said.

"Yes, all three of us." He was suddenly enthusiastic. "They wouldn't mind. We could say we were hungry, get them to make us eggs. That would get us in, then we could just see what happened from there."

"I am a little hungry," Ed admitted.

"You really want to go out again? " I asked. "You've been through a lot. Think about it. You got hit by a car."

He wasn't listening. "The hard part will be getting past the security guy at their building. We'll need a diversion. After that, we're home free." He dug a piece of paper from his wallet, and on it there was indeed a name, Nicole, written in loopy, high-school-girl handwriting. It was followed by an address. There was a distinct possibility that this was real.

"We'll get 'em to make us omelets," he said.

For a moment, I saw Calvin as a distillation of my own, ugly soul, and in his grinning, wicked eyes I thought I saw a reflection of all the bad things I'd done, as well as the ones I would do.

"It's really pretty late," I said, quietly.

But Calvin was already putting on his shoes.

VAQUITA

Edith Pearlman

"Some day," said the minister of health to her deputy assistant, "you must fly me to one of those resort towns on the edge of the lake. Set me up in a striped tent. Send in kids who need booster shots. The mayor and I will split a bottle of cold Spanish wine; then we will blow up the last storehouse of canned milk . . ."

The minister paused. Caroline, the deputy, was looking tired. "Lina, what godforsaken place am I visiting tomorrow?" the minister asked.

"Campo del Norte," came the answer. "Water adequate, sewage okay, no cholera, frequent dysentery . . ."

Señora Marta Perera de Lefkowitz, minister of health, listened and memorized. Her chin was slightly raised, her eyelids half-lowered over pale eyes. This was the pose that the newspapers caricatured most often. Pro-government papers did it more or less lovingly—in their cartoons the minister resembled an inquisitive cow. Opposition newspapers accentuated the lines under Señora Perera's eyes and adorned her mouth with a cigarette, and never omitted the famous spray of diamonds on her lapel.

"There has been some unrest," Caroline went on.

Señora Perera dragged on a cigarette—the fourth of her daily five. "What kind of unrest?"

"A family was exiled."

"For which foolishness?"

The deputy consulted her notes. "They gave information to an Australian writing an exposé of smuggling in Latin America."

"Horrifying. Soon someone will suggest that New York launders our money. Please continue."

"Otherwise, the usual. Undernourishment. Malnourishment. Crop failures. Overfecundity."

Señora Perera let her eyelids drop all the way. Lactation had controlled fertility for centuries, had kept population numbers steady. In a single generation the formula industry had changed everything; now there was a new baby in every wretched family every year. She opened her eyes. "Television?"

"No. A few radios. Seventy kilometers away there's a town with a movie house."

Golden dreams. "The infirmary—what does it need?"

Again a shuffling of papers. "Needles, gloves, dehydration kits, tetanus vaccine, cigarettes . . ."

A trumpet of gunfire interrupted the list.

The minister and her deputy exchanged a glance and stopped talking for a minute. The gunshots were not repeated.

"They will deport me soon," Señora Perera remarked.

"You could leave of your own accord," said Caroline softly.

"That idea stinks of cowshit," Señora Perera said, but she said it in Polish. Caroline waited. "I'm not finished meddling," added the Señora in an inaudible conflation of the languages. "They'll boot me to Miami," she continued in an ordinary tone, now using only Spanish. "The rest of the government is already there, except for Perez, who I think is dead. They'll want my flat, too. Will you rescue Gidalya?" Gidalya was the minister's parrot.

"And while you're at it, Lina, rescue this department. They'll ask you to run the health services, whichever putz they call minister. They'll appreciate that only you can do it—you with principles, but no politics. So do it."

"Take my bird, take my desk, take my job . . ." Caroline sighed.

"Then that's settled."

They went on to talk of departmental matters—the medical students' rebellion in the western city; the girl born with no hands who had been found in a squatters' camp, worshipped as a saint. Then they rose.

Caroline said, "Tomorrow morning Luis will call for you at five."

"Luis? Where is Diego?"

"Diego has defected."

"The scamp. But Luis, that garlic breath—spare me."

"An escort is customary," Caroline reminded her.

"This escort may bring handcuffs."

The two women kissed formally; all at once they embraced. Then they left the cool, almost empty ministry by different exits. Caroline ran down to the rear door; her little car was parked in back. Señora Perera took the grand staircase that curved into the tiled reception hall. Her footsteps echoed. The guard tugged at the massive oak door until it opened. He pushed back the iron gate. He bowed. "Good evening, Señora Ministra."

She waited at the bus stop—a small, elderly woman with dyed red hair. She wore one of the dark, straight-skirted suits that, whatever the year, passed for last season's fashion. The diamonds glinted on its lapel.

Her bus riding was considered an affectation. In fact it was an indulgence. In the back of an official limousine she felt like a corpse. But on the bus she became again a young medical student in Prague, her hair in a single red braid. Sixty years ago she had taken trams everywhere—to cafés; to the apartment of her lover; to her Czech tutor, who became a second lover. In her own room she kept a sweet songbird. At the opera she wept at Smetana. She wrote to her parents in Krakow whenever she needed money. All that was before the Nazis, before the war, before the partisans; before the year hiding out in a peasant's barn, her only company a cow; before liberation, DP camp, and the ship that sailed west to the New World.

Anyone who cared could learn her history. At least once a year somebody interviewed her on radio or television. But the citizens were interested mainly in her life with the cow. "Those months in the barn—what did you think about?" She was always asked that question. "Everything," she sometimes said. "Nothing," she said, sometimes. "Breast-feeding," she barked, unsmiling, during the failed campaign against the formula companies. They called her *La Vaca*—The Cow.

The bus today was late but not yet very late, considering that a revolution was again in progress. So many revolutions had erupted since she arrived in this plateau of a capital, her mother gasping at her side. The Coffee War first, then the Colonels' Revolt, then the . . . Here was the bus, half full. She grasped its doorpost and, grunting, hauled herself aboard. The driver, his eyes on the diamonds, waved her on; no need to show her pass.

The air swam with heat. All the windows were closed against stray bullets. Señora Perera pushed her own window open. The other passengers made no protest. And so, on the ride home, the minister, leaning on her hand, was free to smell the diesel odor of the center of the city, the eucalyptus of the park, the fetidity of the river, the thick citrus stink of the remains of that day's open market, and finally the hibiscus scent of the low hills. No gunshots disturbed the journey. She closed the window before getting off the bus and nodded at the five people who were left.

In the apartment, Gidalya was sulking. New visitors always wondered at a pet so uncolorful—Gidalya was mostly brown. "I was attracted by his clever rabbinical stare," she'd explain. Gidalya had not mastered even the usual dirty words; he merely squawked, expressing a feeble rage. "Hola," Señora Perera said to him now. He gave her a resentful look. She opened his cage, but he remained on his perch, picking at his breast feathers.

She toasted two pieces of bread and sliced some papaya and poured a glass of wine and put everything on a tray. She took the tray out onto the patio and, eating and smoking, watched the curfewed city below. She could see a bit of the river, with its Second Empire bridge and ornamental stanchions. Half a mile north was the plaza, where the cathedral of white volcanic stone was whitened further by floodlamps; this pale light fizzed through the leafy surround. Bells rang faintly. Ten o'clock.

Señora Perera carried her empty tray back into the kitchen. She turned out the lights in the living room and flung a scarf over Gidalya's cage. "Goodnight, possibly for the last time," she said, first in Spanish and then in Polish. In her bedroom, she removed the diamonds from her lapel and fastened them onto the jacket she would wear in the morning. She got ready for bed, got into bed, and fell instantly asleep.

———

Some bits of this notable widow's biography were not granted to interviewers. She might reminisce about her early days here—the resumption of medical studies and the work for the new small party on the left—but she never mentioned the expensive abortion paid for by her rich, married lover. She spoke of the young Federico Perera, of their courtship, of his growing prominence in the legal profession, of her party's increasing strength and its association with various coalitions. She did not refer to Federico's infidelities, though she knew their enemies made coarse jokes about the jewelry he gave her whenever he took a new mistress. Except for the diamonds, all the stuff was fake.

In her fifties she had served as minister of culture; under her warm attention both the National Orchestra and the National Theater thrived. She was proud of that, she told interviewers. She was proud, too, of her friendship with the soprano Olivia Valdez, star of light opera, now retired and living in Tel Aviv; but she never spoke of Olivia. She spoke instead of her husband's merry North American nieces, who had often flown down from Texas. She did not divulge that the young Jewish hidalgos she presented to these girls found them uncultivated. She did not mention her own childlessness. She made few pronouncements about her adopted country; the famous quip that revolution was its national pastime continued to embarrass her. *The year with the cow?* I thought about everything. I thought about nothing.

What kind of cow was it?

Dark brown, infested with ticks, which I got, too.

Your name for her?

My Little Cow, in two or three tongues.

The family who protected you?

Righteous Gentiles.

Your parents?

In the camps. My father died. My mother survived. I brought her to this country.

. . . Whose air she could never breathe. Whose slippery words she refused to learn. I myself did not need to study the language; I remembered it from a few centuries earlier, before the expulsion from Spain. Nothing lightened Mama's mood; she wept every night until she died.

Señora Perera kept these last gloomy facts from interviewers. "The people here—they are like family," she occasionally said. "Stubborn as pigs," she once added, in a cracked mutter that no one should have heard, but the woman with the microphone swooped on the phrase as if it were an escaping kitten.

"You love this sewer," shouted Olivia during her raging departure. "You have no children to love, and you have a husband not worth loving, and you don't love me anymore because my voice is cracking and my belly sags. So you love my land, which I at least have the sense to hate. You love the oily generals. The aristocrats scratching themselves. The intellectuals snoring through concerts. The revolutionaries in undershirts. The parrots, even! You are besotted!"

It was a farewell worthy of Olivia's talents. Their subsequent correspondence had been affectionate. Olivia's apartment in Israel would become Señora Perera's final home; she'd fly straight to Tel Aviv from Miami. The diamonds would support a few years of simple living. But for a little while longer she wanted to remain amid the odors, the rap blaring from pickup trucks, the dance halls, the pink evangelical churches, the blue school uniforms, the highway's dust, the river's tarnish. To remain in this wayward place that was everything a barn was not.

———

Luis was waiting for her at dawn, standing beside the limousine. He wore a mottled jumpsuit.

"Much trouble last night?" she asked, peering in vain into his sunglasses while trying to avoid his corrupt breath.

"No," he belched, omitting her title, omitting even the honorific. This disrespect allowed her to get into the front of the car like a pal.

At the airport they climbed the steps of a tipsy little plane. Luis stashed his Uzi in the rear next to the medical supplies. He took the copilot's seat. Señora Perera and the nurse—a Dutch volunteer with passable Spanish—settled themselves on the other two buckets. Señora Perera hoped to watch the land fall away, but from behind the pilot's shoulder she could see only sky, clouds, one reeling glimpse of highway, and then the mountainside. So she reconstructed the city from memory: its mosaic of dwellings enclosed in a ring of hills, its few tall structures rising in the center like an abscess. The river, the silly Parisian bridge. The plaza. People were gathering there now, she guessed, to hear today's orations.

The Dutch nurse was huge, a goddess. She had to hunch her shoulders and let her big hands dangle between her thighs. Some downy thatch sprouted on her jaw; what a person to spend eternity with if this light craft should go down, though there was no reason you should be stuck forever with the dullard you happened to die with. Señora Perera planned to loll on celestial pillows next to Olivia. Federico might join them every millennium or so, good old beast, and Gidalya, too, prince of rabbis released from his avian corpus, his squawks finally making sense . . . She offered her traveling flask to the nurse. "Dutch courage?" she said in English. The girl smiled without comprehension, but she did take a swig.

In less than an hour they had flown around the mountain and were landing on a cracked tar field. A helicopter stood waiting. Señora Perera and the nurse used the latrine. A roll of toilet paper hung on a nail, for their sakes.

And now they were rising in the chopper. They swung across the hide of the jungle. She looked down on trees flaming with orange flowers and trees foaming with mauve ones. A sudden clearing was immediately swallowed up again by squat, broad-leafed trees. Lime green parrots rose up together—Gidalya's rich cousins.

They landed in the middle of the town square beside a chewed bandstand. A muscular functionary shook their hands. This was Señor Rey, she recalled from Lina's instructions. Memory remained her friend; she could still recite the names of the cranial nerves. Decades ago, night after night, she had whispered them to the cow. She had explained the structures of various molecules. *Ma Petite Vache* . . . . She had taught the cow the Four Questions.

Señor Rey led them toward a barracks mounted on a slab of cement: the infirmary she had come to inspect. The staff—a nurse-director and two assistants—stood stiffly outside as if awaiting arrest. It was probable that no member of any government had ever before visited—always excepting smugglers.

The director, rouged like a temptress, took them around the scrubbed infirmary, talking nonstop. She knew every detail of every case history; she could relate every failure from undermedication, from wrong medication, from absence of medication. The Dutch girl seemed to understand the rapid-fire Spanish.

Surgical gloves, recently washed, were drying on a line. The storeroom shelves held bottles of injectable Ampicillin and jars of Valium—folk remedies now. A few people lay in the rehydration room. In a corner of the dispensary a dying old man curled upon himself. Behind a screen Señora Perera found a listless child with swollen glands and pale nail beds. She examined him. A year ago she would have asked the parents' permission to send him to a hospital in the city for tests and treatment if necessary. Now the hospital in the city was dealing with wounds and emergencies, not diseases. The parents would have refused anyway. What was a cancer unit for but to disappear people? She stood for a moment with her head bowed, her thumb on the child's groin. Then she told him to dress himself.

As she came out from behind the screen she could see the two nurses through a window. They were walking toward the community kitchen to inspect the miracle of *soya* cakes. Luis lounged just outside the window.

She leaned over the sill and addressed his waxy ear. "Escort those two, why don't you? I want to see Señor Rey's house alone."

Luis moved sullenly off. Señor Rey led her toward his dwelling in resentful silence. Did he think she really cared whether his cache was guns or cocaine? All she wanted was to ditch Luis for a while. But she would have to subject this village thug to a mild interrogation just to get an hour's freedom.

And then she saw a better ruse. She saw a motorbike, half concealed in Señor Rey's shed.

She had flown behind Federico on just such a bike, one summer by the sea. She remembered his thick torso within the circle of her arms. The next summer she had driven the thing herself, Olivia clasping her waist.

"May I try that?"

Señor Rey helplessly nodded. She handed him her kitbag. She hiked up her skirt and straddled the bike. The low heels of her shoes hooked over the footpieces.

But this was not flying. The machine strained uphill, held by one of the two ruts they called a road. On the hump between the ruts grass grew and even flowers—little red ones. She picked up speed slightly and left the village behind. She passed poor farms and thick growths of vegetation. The road rose and fell. From a rise she got a glimpse of a brown lake. Her buttocks smarted.

When she stopped at last and got off the bike, her skirt ripped with a snort. She leaned the disappointing machine against a scrub pine and she walked into the woods, headed toward the lake. Mist encircled some trees. Thick roots snagged her shoes. But ahead was a clearing, just past tendrils hanging from branches. A good place for a smoke. She parted the vines and entered, and saw a woman.

A girl, really. She was eighteen at most. She was sitting on a carpet of needles and leaning against a harsh tree. But her lowered face was as untroubled as if she had been resting on a silken pouf. The nursing infant was wrapped in coarse, striped cloth. Its little hand rested against her brown breast. Mother and child were outwardly motionless, yet Señora Perera felt a steady pulsing beneath her soles, as if the earth itself were a giant teat.

Señora Perera did not make much of a sound, only her old woman's wheeze. But the girl looked up as if in answer, presenting a bony, pock-marked face. If the blood of the conquistadors had run in her ancestors' veins, it had by now been conquered; she was utterly Indian. Her flat brown eyes were fearless.

"Don't get up, don't trouble yourself . . ." But the girl bent her right leg and raised herself to a standing position without disturbing the child.

She walked forward. When she was a few feet away from Señora Perera, her glance caught the diamonds. She looked at them with mild interest and returned her gaze to the stranger.

They faced each other across a low dry bush. With a clinician's calm Señora Perera saw herself through the Indian girl's eyes. Not a grandmother, for grandmothers did not have red hair. Not a soldier, for soldiers did not wear skirts. Not a smuggler, for smugglers had ingratiating manners. Not a priest, for priests wore combat fatigues and gave out cigarettes; and not a journalist, for journalists piously nodded. She could not be a deity; deities radiated light. She must then be a witch.

Witches have authority. "Good that you nurse the child," said Señora Perera.

"Yes. Until his teeth come."

"After his teeth come, *chica*. He can learn not to bite." She opened her mouth and stuck out her tongue and placed her forefinger on its tip. "See? Teach him to cover his teeth with his tongue."

The girl slowly nodded. Señora Perera mirrored her nod. Jew and Indian: Queen Isabella's favorite victims. Four centuries later, Jews were a great nation, getting richer. Indians were multiplying, getting poorer. It would be a moment's work to unfasten the pin and pass it across the bush. But how would the girl fence the diamonds? Señor Rey would insist on the lion's share; and what would a peasant do with money anyway—move to the raddled capital? Señora Perera extended an empty hand toward the infant and caressed its oblivious head. The mother revealed a white smile.

"He will be a great man," promised the Señora.

The girl's sparse lashes lifted. Witch had become prophetess. The incident needed only a bit of holy nonsense for prophetess to become lady. "He will be a great man," Señora Perera repeated, in Polish, stalling for time. And then, in Spanish again, with the hoarseness that inevitably accompanied her quotable pronouncements, "Suckle!" she commanded. She unhooked the pin. With a flourishing gesture right out of one of Olivia's operettas, conveying tenderness and impetuousness and authority too, she pressed the diamonds into the girl's free hand. "Keep them until he's grown," she hissed, and she turned on her heel and strode along the path, hoping to disappear abruptly into the floating mist as if she had been assumed. *Penniless exile crawls into Tel Aviv*, she thought, furious with herself.

When she reached the motorbike, she lit the postponed cigarette and grew calm again. After all, she could always give Spanish lessons.

————

Señor Rey was waiting in front of his shed. He clucked at her ripped skirt. And Luis was waiting near the helicopter, talking to the pilot. The Dutch nurse would stay until next Saturday, when the mail Jeep would arrive. So it was just the three of them, Luis said with emphasis, giving the unadorned lapel a hard stare. She wondered if he would arrest her in the chopper, or upon their arrival at the airstrip, or in the little plane, or when they landed at the capital, or not until they got to her apartment. It didn't matter; her busybody's career had been honorably completed with the imperative uttered in the clearing. Suckle. Let *that* word get around—it would sour all the milk in the country, every damned little jar of it.

And now—deportation? Call it retirement. She wondered if the goons had in mind some nastier punishment. That didn't matter, either; she'd been living on God's time since the cow.

FADO

Katherine Vaz

One morning I could not find Lúcia, my stuffed toy pig. I ran crying next door to Dona Xica Adelinha Costa. Xica buried her Saint Anthony and told him he would stay there until he helped us. Then she kissed me and sent me home. That night I saw Lúcia's cloven hoof jabbing out of my bed, and with a shriek I clutched her in a dance. Xica left Saint Anthony in his grave another day to teach him to be faster in finding what was lost.

When the Californian valley heat pressed down on us, Xica would lift my hair, so electric it leapt to greet her approaching palm, and she would blow on the back of my neck. Summers the fuchsia hung swollen like ripe fruit—the dancing-girls' skirts mauve, cherry, scarlet—and Xica taught me how to grasp the long stamen running up into the core and with a single sure yank pull it out with the drop of watery honey still glistening at its tip. My parents urged me to spend time with Dona Xica. We were lucky to be neighbors. I had never known my real grandmothers, and Xica would never have a real grandchild because a car wreck had made her married son an idiot.

———————

Bicho vai,
Bicho vem,
Come o pai,
Come a mãe,
E come a menina também!

The worm-monster goes,
The worm-monster comes,
It eats the father,
It eats the mother,
And it eats the baby too!

Mamãe walked her fingers up my leg singing this rhyme, and on the final line she attacked my stomach until I squealed with laughter. I would beg her to do it over and over. *O bicho* never got to my throat. I kept him down where it tickled.

I met worse night-things as I grew up. If I stared too long at those red and white pinpricks in my dark room, they rolled into constellations that burst alive, into pirates and dogs speaking guttural English. When they came for me I would sign crosses in an invisible picket fence around my bed. The beasts roared, but none of them could get me.

One night I finally kicked my sheets over the cross-fence and thought: Climb in with me. Xica is not afraid of you and neither am I. I am more afraid of being alone.

———————

The old stories said that our Azorean homeland was Atlantis, rising broken from the sea. We all have marks and patches surfacing on our skin. I have a fierce dark animal erupting from my side.

Xica had a wine-colored star in the cove at the base of her throat. When she drowsed in the sleeping net that swung between two trees dividing our yards, I liked to touch the star and the bones of her face. She had a long nose ridge, arcing like a dolphin's spine from between her eyes. Inside her hands and chest more bones floated, like those soft needles that poke unmoored in fish's meat.

My fingers could never drink up the rheum that always trickled from beneath her closed eyes. We are so sad, so chemically sad, that it leaks from us. The *fados* wailing from our record players remind us that without love we will die, that the oceans are salty because the Portuguese have shed so many tears on their beaches for those they will never hold again.

———

Xica Adelinha Costa could faint at will. She would quicken her breath toward that giddy unlatching when the spirit shoots from the body. Then all is cold and black, with a prickle of nausea. One day when I was thirteen I fell with her at the Lodi post office. We were in line to pickup the ribbon *do Nosso Senhor do Bonfim* sent from her cousin in Brazil, and suddenly Xica could not wait anymore. She shook so much I shook too, and then she collapsed into my arms and drove us both to the floor.

Most townspeople already knew that when Xica could not be without something another moment she hurled herself into the dark. Postmaster Riley did not rush over, but he tossed me Xica's package. I unwrapped the thin blue ribbon *do Nosso Senhor* and tied it around her wrist. She woke up because now she could make her pact with God. Xica whispered this prayer:

O Nosso Senhor: Heal my child. He has not spoken a single word since his accident.

O Nosso Senhor: You threw my husband off that whaling boat and did not return him when I was young and pretty in Angra—lift the fog from my son.

O Nosso Senhor: Make his wife love him again.

When the knot broke on its own, those wishes would come true. "Rosa," she said, "I can almost hear my boy saying my name." She smiled at the man offering her water and kissed the wrist tie that marked her as a woman of divine desires.

For sprawling in public with charms, my parents made me recite all the rosary Mysteries—the Joyful, the Sorrowful, and the Glorious—to scrub out my soul.

———

My father's lavender soap always drew me from sleep. The male-flowering scent came for me before dawn, as he padded around the house until his veins breathed open. He insisted I do his morning exercises with him. Out with the violet bristles protruding from the artichokes, there in the dark-claret light.

"Inhale with me, Rosa," said Papai.

In—let it fill you—*out.*

Sister Angela, my eighth-grade teacher, explained the heart:

Old tired blood of night and sleep starts out purple.

It goes through the heart to wash itself red.

The morning sky is red and purple to remind us that we walk in the air of burst hearts.

I would sit on the porch awhile holding my father's hand. It was the first time I already missed someone I still had, and my first lesson that true joy creates not memory but physical particles. My Lodi mornings hid embers in me that will float upward when I die, to burrow in someone else, because they have nothing to do with dust.

Mamãe would bring out mayonnaise-and-tomato sandwiches. We ate together before my father left for his milk route, and then she and I would go back to bed. Sometimes it is beyond endurance, the separateness of all our lives.

———

Manuel was soft and red-streaked as crabmeat now instead of big-framed and handsome. Xica led him by the hand and said aloud what everything was. He never spoke, but she refused to give up. When her ribbon broke she wanted him to awake with the world already learned. She told him about things that could be held:

Brier roses: Same genus as the strawberry. But you would never guess they were one family. Perfumed, pink. Careful how you touch it, love. Not a few big thorns but a hundred little stabs.

Cat: Venha cá, gatinha, gatinha! Here kitty kitty. It brushed your legs and then disappeared, Manuel. *Até breve, gatinha.* Don't cry, Manny.

Rocks: They stay in one place even if you turn away. Let me brush your fingers against them for you.

Brick: Watch me scrape my frayed ribbon against it to hurry your cure.

Before school I took Manuel's other hand. His wife Marina sat watching. An earthworm sometimes stitched its way around her bare toes in the mud, but she did not move. She liked belly crawlers: A recurring tapeworm let her stay thin and eat madly. We all ate pork—*vinho d'alhos, torrêsmos*—laden with invisible cooked trichinae, but only Marina would not flinch at finding alive in the ground what also churned dead in our stomachs.

In terrible heat she poured honey water or lemonade on herself, whatever was near in the pitcher, and her skin glistened with sugar. Marina was twenty-three, four years younger than Manuel, the most beautiful animal I will ever cross.

Because Manuel said nothing, Xica's morning lessons often veered off into history stories:

Lace: This at my throat, from my sister Teca. She lost her husband off the same boat that killed your father. She went blind hooking lace webs the old way, with an open safety pin. Flowers and faces white and matterless as the drone after the hive sucks him dry. The drone is left jelly. The drone is soft quiver.

Rosa Santos: Her blood grandparents are all buried home in the islands. Rosa came here as a baby and does not remember her birthplace. She has no brothers or sisters—her birth ruptured her mother's tubes.

Because Manuel still said nothing, Xica sometimes cried untranslatable words, things that could not be held or seen, anything that might unfasten the spirits in him:

Marulho: No single English word describes this roar-sound of waves as they crash on shore, Manuel. I think of the *mar* in *marido* filled with *barulho*, noise: an ocean inside a husband crashing. I watched you pace that night and drive off wildly because you could not stand being without her. She was only having coffee with a friend. She wasn't with another man. Marina can't tell time! She doesn't think!

Desacato: The purgatory where someone has not yet said good-bye, is playing along with another person's desires, but not out of love.

Saudade: More than longing. More than yearning. The aching person can declare: *Come to me. Although you are so much in me that I carry you around, I'll waste away if fate keeps us apart.*

Marina: You crashed into a tree and lost your mind over her. Stop fussing, Manuel. Rosa and I will lead you to her. The lazy goat Marina.

At the sound of her name his hand opened.

———

The Portuguese families in Lodi kept canaries. Some also raised parakeets or talking mynas and parrots. The birds gouged their cuttlefish and filled our houses with trilling and cracked seed. We needed their song to match our pulse and high nerves.

Mamãe wanted to murder the plumber. Mr. Fernandes fiddled with the leaking pipe under our sink until it lay quiet. Mamãe paid him. The next morning she needed him again. Mr. Fernandes returned three times. Finally the drips turned the under-sink cabinet into moss, and one night the pipe blew up. After shutting off the main, my silent mother drove our soaked towels to the plumber's house. She nailed them over some windows so that Fernandes would look right into mildew.

When she returned home she sang an aria with our birds.

———

Two lines from a *fado* my father often played:

> *Navegar é preciso,*
> *Viver não é preciso.*

This song of fate has two translations:

> To navigate is precise,
> To live is not precise.

or:

> To navigate is necessary,
> To live is not necessary.

A widow in our parish wrote a *fado:*

> As a child I thought love was for angels,
> But fate says that love is the unbroken horse
> Dragging us behind its sleek smooth haunches

From the moment we taste it
To the day we die.

———————

Manuel had once loved to comb the great matted snakes out of Marina's long hair. Every day in the sunlit yard he untangled her black knots, fixed a braid, and tucked flowers into her hair. She would lean her head back to kiss him with her upside-down face. They laughed when the kissing ruined the braid and Manuel had to do it over again.

Xica would bring out a pitcher of water flavored with cut peaches. She knew the most ageless secrets, my Xiquinha: The peach wedges looked like prawns with fibrous legs dangling, the scarlet legs that had clung to the peachstone's rutted face. She could take plain water and change it into an aquarium.

Xica left me when I still had so much to ask. When she set down the peach water for the lovers quietly, barely looking at them so that nothing would crack the spell, I should have asked the color and shape of the physical particle this love engendered. Maybe it is that blue anchor in the seat of all flames.

———————

During the Lodi heat we called knife-fight weather, Xica decided that Manuel wanted to relearn his wife's hair. We led him to her and used his clay fingers to tug her hair into rough skeins. Finally one morning the pulling made her wrench away and jump to her feet. "Stop it!" she screamed. "It's hurting me! It hurts!" She pushed us aside and ran off.

Manuel's half-closed eyes fluttered. "Marina," he said: his first full word since the accident.

Xica and I grabbed him. "Say it again," we pleaded. "Marina. Say 'Marina.' Say anything."

He could say nothing else and turned to watch her recede in the distance.

Marina's flight became the first entry in Xica's *Ofensa* ledger. Inscribing sins and proposed punishments in a great book was God's job, but once again He was asleep. Xica opened a large black diary and wrote:

#1. Marina Guimarães Costa, December 10. She abandoned us. Sawdust in her food will slow her. I'll turn her into a tree.

When boys started coming to visit me, I saw almost nothing of Xica and her wars. I set the table for my callers and bit my lips hard to make them red and swollen. Milk cartons then had lovely thick wax, and boys would scratch out my name with their fingernails. Tilting the cartons to the light I would read: *Rosa Santos loves Cliff. Rosa + Jimmy.*

My father told me to sweat my nerves back inside my skin. One day I had to plant scarecrows through our entire field using tin-can lids. The discs had sharp fluted edges, and I cut myself hammering nail-holes into them. I dragged a full trashbag of them through the tomatoes and fava beans and corn. I tied the lids with twine to stakes. The weakest breeze would lift them, teeth glinting, at the crows. No one in Lodi used straw men anymore. We got our scarecrows from cans.

I stopped planting my buzz saws because inside the thicket bordering our land I saw Marina, her clothes tossed onto brambles, colt legs splayed, with a man I did not recognize pressed to her back. She was in a sweat and did not see me. With a terrible moan the man dug into Marina so hard he lifted her into the air.

I ran home, and the cut metal I had seeded stirred after me.

Marina played with the saucers of glitter and straight pins. The crushed ice was to make the crackled lace candles, but she kept slipping pinches down her dress. She stuck holly into Manuel's hair and splashed the paraffin so that hard cysts cooled on our worktable. I was stenciling angels and wondering why I had come. Ever since Manny stopped working at the dairy, Xica and Marina had earned money doing needlework and raising chickens, and at Christmastime they sold candles. This was the first year I did not want to help. Manny was so peaceful cutting foil stars that I wanted to slap him. Xica was bossy, and Marina was all mouth. She stood at the refrigerator finishing a whole jar of olives, and then she drank the black-salt juice. She always needed to drain everything to its bedrock and bone.

Xica went into a rage when she saw Marina eating everything in sight. She hurled paraffin blocks, snowflakes, and sequined bells so hard toward the kitchen that I knew she had guessed the truth. When Marina escaped through a window, Manuel held out his arms and tried to go after her. We had to restrain him, and he fell down into the Christmas debris and twitched with shock. Xica and I rolled him onto a huge, padded tablecloth. We hoisted the ends and rocked him like a child in a hammock to stop his crying. Manuel spoke the last words he would ever say after his accident: *Marina. Marina.*

"Be quiet, sweetheart. She's here," Xica whispered, nodding toward me. "I'm here," I said.

I doubt we fooled him, but he quieted down. Our arms soon tired and he sagged to the ground, but we kept swaying, ignoring the tearing of our net, until the waves of lulling finally took him. When Manuel was asleep we got on our hands and knees, graying Xica and I, to pick up the trimmings and the stars.

———

Some entries I read in the *Ofensa* book of Dona Xica Adelinha Costa:

—#15. *Mr. Alfred Kearny, Lodi florist, January 20.* Fainting not enough anymore. Knocked over ten wreaths when I fell. Still he would not admit he is after my son's wife. Tomorrow I'll pour honey inside his store, and by nightfall black ants will be eating his flowers.

—#32. *Marina Guimarães Costa, March 2.* Twice, three times a day I wash her sheets! She comes home with that sin smell. It will travel down the hall to Manuel's room if I do not scrub and bleach it from her cloth. My hands are turning ghost white.

—#48. *O Nosso Senhor, April 17.* Why did You make her the one thing he has not forgotten? Untie this ribbon!

—#54. *Mrs. Lamont, May 1.* Spreading gossip. To teach her silence I'll phone her five times today and say nothing when she answers.

—#56. *The Sun, May 5.* Too hot. Bug and spider nests in house. Feel poisoned. Hate the Sun.

———

Xica finally packed Marina's bags and threw her out. Mr. Kearny hid her in his guesthouse and told his ragdoll wife it was the only charitable thing to do.

Father Ribeiro took Xica and Manuel sailing at Lake Tahoe. He meant well. Water calls to us if we avoid it too long, and he thought the Costas needed to answer the water's cry. Water would melt Xica's bile and teach her forgiveness, and it would soothe Manuel's heartbreak. I did not want to go, but Father Ribeiro insisted that I was one of the few friends Xica had left in the entire parish.

We were not far from shore. A young woman ran from the lapping water up the sand, tossing her hair as a man chased her. Even on our boat we could see the sparkling curves of their backs. She squealed while leading him farther from us. When he caught her, they collapsed together into a single tumbling dot on the horizon.

Manuel stared after them and suddenly threw off his life jacket. Father Ribeiro grabbed for him, but he was already over the edge.

Xica Adelinha Costa had tried to escape Portuguese fate by moving halfway across the world, to a dry inland patch, but there she was for the second time in her life on a shoreline wailing over the body of a dead man. Father Ribeiro, dripping and gasping, still giving the corpse the kiss of life, could not console Xica.

She grabbed a knife from a nearby picnic table and with one upward slice cut open the useless ribbon on her wrist. The ground was already claiming Manuel. Sand, leaves, and gravel coated his wet skin and filled his eyes and ears. Xica held him and tried to brush the debris away with the lament that convulses newborns, body blind and purple, the lament that told me she had already fallen into another world.

She wanted air to kill her instead of water. The day after she buried her son, she dressed in a long brocade gown and lay in the sleeping net. My parents fed her broth and told her to stop talking nonsense. "I'll be gone before dinnertime," she said simply. She closed her eyes and put her will to work.

Father Ribeiro came by to remind her that Manuel had not actually killed himself—he was a child, and when a child sees what he wants, a flash that speaks to memory, he flings himself toward it. His innocence meant he was in heaven. "So you shouldn't give up heart," Father said.

She did give up heart: She gave it to me. God still owed her a wish, and I was the only one who believed she could hold Him to it. My parents and Father Ribeiro were off discussing which doctors to call when Xica opened her eyes long enough to put my hand on her chest. "Rosa," she said. "My Rosa."

Her heart fluttered like a trapped hummingbird. Perhaps she was drawing all her blood toward it, because it beat harder and faster while her calves drained and her hands, face, and neck paled to chalk. Even the star in the cove of her throat dimmed. She was pulling up a winding sheet inside herself.

"Xiquinha," I said. I felt the bird fly up against her ribs, trying to break through and splatter on my palm. She was straining her heart upward as far as she could, loud and furious, directly into my hand. As I bent my face closer to hear the wing beat, the raging bird exploded, and then my Xica was gone.

————

After Marina had a miscarriage, Kearny's wife nursed her briefly and then ordered her out of their lives. Suddenly Marina had no more lover and no more baby. She took over Xica's empty house. Soon after Marina returned, I put a conch shell on her porch. No one can resist sealing the cold pink lip against an ear to hear the water echoing. I knew one widow who carried a conch in her purse to clap to her head like a transistor radio whenever she wanted to induce a good sobbing. Marina was such a glutton I knew she would fill herself with tides. She would probably take the shell to bed.

At the drugstore a week later I bought wax-candy skeletons. Children bite off the skulls, drink the cherry-water inside, and chew the wax until it disappears. I set the skeletons in toy plastic boats around Marina's windows and doors. Before leaving for school that day I heard her bellowing.

I punctured every inch of her garden hose. It spouted water everywhere like a gunned whale.

I hesitated after they found Marina aimlessly wandering the highway. Then I heard two women gossiping: *She killed her husband, and now she's queen of the house.* The next day I uprooted some plants from my father's aquarium, slapped them on an old doll, and left it strangling on Marina's porch.

One morning when Marina left to sell some chickens, I took the key from behind her mailbox, entered the house, and uncaged her birds. She would return to find them shrieking and pecking the apples on the table. She would never catch them. I hid hardboiled eggs and left a typewritten note: *Ten Easter eggs in here. Tear the place up before they rot.*

———

Certain delicacies in our cupboards were meant to last forever—the sulfured apricots, the grosgrain-tied bags of sugared almonds, the port with ashy mold around the cork. I stole them for Michael Paganelli, the boy who had come to work on the Bettencourt ranch. I had just started high school, and after classes he would be waiting for me in his pickup. We ate sweets and drank until I was gut-sick and brave enough to taste Michael's salt by licking his neck. I spanned parts of him: From his left nipple to his sternum was one strained hand stretch. My forefinger and thumb measured him nosetip to chin.

Alone at night I could put him back together. I spread my hand out on my chest and thought: Michael's breastbone is now crushed here. I have captured the size of him. The night breeze lifted my bedclothes as I touched Michael's lengths all over me.

It was worth lying to my parents. It was worth the stealing. My battle with Marina, and even the faces of my beloved dead neighbors, evaporated under the sheer height and weight of my new love.

———

Sex happens the way a pearl is formed. It begins with a grain or parasitic worm that itches in the soft lining until the entire animal buckles around it. With enough slathering it will relax into a gem.

The first time I made love was in water. Michael and I dove into the swimming hole outside town. The moon came down to be in the water with us, and in its round ghost center I measured Michael's erection so I would have it again when I was alone: more than my hand's widest stretch. Touch anemones at low tide and watch their tissue shudder and their color deepen. When Michael disappeared in me I cried his name, because this was how I had always thought of love—a jolt of swallowing someone alive. Sometimes we thrashed into deeper water. We submerged below the moon and kicked hard to come up choking on it.

Love had odd unforeseen glories. I came not from what he was doing but from arching against his rough belly. I would never have guessed that his tongue in my ear could cause rapture, or that not knowing how to ask him to speak my name could trigger such sadness. The sheer force of his coming thrust me from the water, and suspended in the chill, with stabbing pains and my blood on his thigh, I wondered why people are fated to have this torment forever.

They said the stench of rotting eggs drove her crazy. The house was a shambles, and here and there a myna chipped at the bright eggs putrefying on the floor. Mrs. Riley came by one day with an embroidery job and found the wild-haired Marina in a place smelling like a dead animal.

She took Marina to the hospital, where nurses closed her bulging eyes with cool witch hazel. They spoon-fed her purees and kept a night-light by her bed. Mrs. Riley called half of Lodi with daily reports. After a week doctors said that Marina was not sick enough to keep in the hospital, but she would never fully recover as long as she remained alone.

Michael acted as if he didn't know me. He stopped coming by after school, and when I went to the Bettencourt ranch he looked straight through me.

The next day I returned to the ranch and beat Michael's truck with a plank to chip off half the paint. Rust would set in before he could hammer out all the dents.

When love no longer recognizes us, we fall into the strangest outbursts and comas. I had restless sex with the first boy who came along at school, and then I collapsed into shock. I lay in my room until Mamãe tried to rub my shoulders and ask me what hurt. "Leave me alone," I snapped, wrenching away. That is the final curse of dryness: We forget about those closest to us and dwell suspended upon what has been snatched away. We who are robbed should be forgiven everything.

We recaged the birds, and I taught the mynas to speak so that the empty house would ring occasionally with throaty words. Marina liked the snapdragons and lilacs I planted for her. Marina: Do you recognize that plant there? It is what we call Our Lady's grass. Dozens of Azoreans smuggled it over here because they could not survive without its penetrating oil, only to discover that it grows wild in the hills.

I know what my punishment will be. Someday I will have to live a long time alone, long enough to imagine several times that I will never recover. Anytime I think *this cannot continue,* my sentence will double. This solitude will come after a great love has died, for then I will not be free so much as haunted with dead perfume.

One day, when mosquito bites covered Marina, I thought of Xica washing bruised Manuel outside in a large metal tub. She would keep the warm water and the soap out of his half-blind eyes, and as she worked, pouring long streams over him, she had such radiance that I knew she had the whole world there in her arms. There was not a trace of anguish as she smiled down at him. When she was done, she would lift the wounded man up into the light. Xica was so splendid before bitterness choked her, so glorious when she bore him aloft.

I found Marina writhing from bug attacks. They loved her sweet blood. I mixed some baking soda with water, and while cradling her I dabbed it over her itching red sores. I would have to keep the worms and spiders from chewing her. Marina could not stop scratching, and I remembered a touch my mother would give me when I was afraid at night. She would run her thumbs up under my eyebrows, along the bone and out to the temple. This sweeping over my eyelids always melted my nerves.

Marina rested back against my chest while I put her to sleep with my mother's eye-stroking. Here is the seal from which all grace comes: We must create Pietàs in order to live. Flesh that is torn, flesh that is dead or dying, even as it is rotting through your fingers—hold it next to your heart. Find ripe and tender flesh too, and hold it in your arms, because your life depends on it. Hold it for as long as you can, and ask for its blessing.

THE WOMAN IN
THE HEADLIGHTS

Barbara Croft

In dreams, the headlights make two narrow tunnels through the darkness. The woman appears on the right. The dun-colored grocery bag she carries shields her face, so that all that Chapin sees is a fringe of curly white hair and a white-gloved hand. He lifts his foot to apply the brakes, but something prevents him. He struggles and presses backward and feels the prickle of nylon upholstery on his neck. She starts to cross, and there is that moment that Chapin can't get past.

Then the bag flies upward in slow motion, cartwheels, and spills over the hood, dumping a shower of pickle jars and paper towels and Jell-O pudding boxes. There is no sound while this happens. There is no color, except the pearly pale green of a cabbage, tumbling slowly toward the windshield, casting its shadow over the dashboard, striking noiselessly.

Chapin awakes. The sheets are tangled around his ankles. Marilyn stirs but seems to know what has happened. It is the same dream, and not a dream. She reaches over and rubs his shoulder automatically.

Chapin gets up and walks down the hall to the kitchen. Sunlight is pouring in. He starts the coffee, feeds the cat, brings the paper in. The sea is brilliant. The light makes Chapin dizzy, and only opening the patio doors to the chilly, copper taste of the air clears his head. He goes out on the deck and down the wooden steps to the beach.

————

It happened two years ago, during a guest semester at Grinnell College. Someone had loaned him a battered white Toyota. He drove to Iowa City; he did that often. The woman must have been deaf, senile, something. The coroner said that she never knew what hit her. The verdict was that Chapin had not been at fault. The woman was eighty-one, had a history of erratic behavior, one of those reclusive types that lives in a crumbling house with a zillion cats. Chapin had, for once, not been drinking.

He stops at the little coffee shop on the beach. The girl behind the counter is wearing cut-off jeans that barely cover her ass and the sort of tight knit top they call a "sports bra." She is lean and tan. Her hair is, of course, blond. And when she hands Chapin the coffee cup, she lets her fingertips slide over his so lightly that he's not completely sure he feels anything. A faint disturbance of air, perhaps, that's all.

"Have a good one."

Chapin was not invited back to Grinnell. The department chair denied there was any connection. "Fresh faces," he said, "new points of view." And maybe, in fact, there wasn't any connection. Maybe they liked his work. Chapin remembers standing in the flat wash of late afternoon sunlight, he and the chair, on the walkway to Old Main. The chair's voice was like the hum of insects. Staring down, Chapin saw the bricks of the sidewalk begin to separate. They lifted and floated apart, but very slowly, the way dye spreads in water, the way clouds move.

————

Two children are playing on the beach. A golden retriever chases between them. They are six or seven, a boy and a girl. The sunlight striking the reds and blues of their clothing is almost painful against the pale sand.

His first impulse had been to just keep going. Independent of his will, his right foot pressed down hard. The pedal went clear to the floor, and the car surged forward. Then, again of its own will, his foot jumped off the gas and hit the brake. The car swung to the left. Chapin remembers revolving on the wet pavement, the car spinning slowly like a tired carnival ride. When it stopped he was facing the way he had come.

———

"It was two years ago," Chapin told his therapist. Seeing her was Marilyn's idea.

"And?"

Chapin bowed his head slightly toward her, raised his eyebrows. This was back in New York, three months ago.

"Have you been able to put it behind you?" she said.

Chapin surveyed the cluttered landscape of her desk: pictures of children—a boy and a girl—in various poses, in ornate frames, "Daddy" leaning into some of the shots; papers, folders, desktop toys, the kind of thing you give a professional person in order to show you are not intimidated. Underneath the gild of our educations, these things insisted, aren't we all just simply human beings?

"It's not really the kind of thing you 'put behind you,'" Chapin said dryly.

"Still having the dreams?"

"Dream. Yes."

She glanced at her watch, pulled a pad of paper from a desk drawer. "I'm going to give you something to help you sleep."

She scribbled quickly, folded the paper, and handed it over.

Chapin stood, extending his hand.

"The directions will be on the bottle."

He nodded.

"Take them," she said, looking into his eyes with professional concern. "Promise me?"

He nodded again.

He walked out, closing the door on the tasteful mauve carpet, the well-groomed plants. Smiling at the receptionist, Chapin crumpled the prescription in his pocket.

———

"Have a good walk?"

Chapin nods.

Marilyn is puttering with petunias in a cedar windowbox. Dirt streaks her long, freckled forearms. "Have Kit and Harry opened up their place?"

Chapin appraises her bones. Her lankiness delights him, the functionality of her frame. "I didn't notice," he says.

She smiles, for no reason. Why does she do that?

Chapin has decided to leave his wife, or, better yet, to make his wife leave him. It's too much trouble now, keeping it up. The daily exercise of marriage exhausts him, the effort of slogging through the little things: shopping and holidays, laundry, and brief and boring vacations to all the predictable places; her family and his family and their mutual friends. And, he thinks, any kind of change . . .

"I'm driving into town later," she says. "Want to come along?"

He shakes his head.

"You could drive."

He says nothing.

"You know, you should get back to it," she says. "Start driving again, let go of the past."

"Why?"

"Oh, David." She tilts her head to the left. "Come with me."

"I just don't want to," he says.

────────

The moment she goes, he feels a sense of relief. Not happiness, but the freedom to be depressed. He feels almost lighthearted. He changes into swim trunks, selects a paperback book he's been meaning to read, finds a beach chair on the deck, and goes down to the sand.

The sea is a flat gray-blue. No breakers today. The waves uncurl in creamy ruffles and pull back with a sigh. Other than the scuff marks left by the children, there is not a footprint anywhere, not yet.

How to do it. Quickly. How to make it easy and all right. She has this loyalty thing, and so domestic. A good soldier, Marilyn. He doesn't want to hurt her.

When they met, she was seventeen. He was two years older. It seems impossible to ever have been that young. His parents and her parents belonged to the same club. They met at the pool. He remembers showing off, pulling funny stunts on the low board; he almost feels it physically: the cannonball, the fake fall, his arms and legs cocked at odd angles, dropping through sunlight, falling, falling; then the cold explosion of the water. In the silence he almost hears her laughter.

The girl from the coffee shop walks by, smiles at him. He gets the feeling she does this to every man. It amuses her to turn them on, gives her a sense of power. Chapin on the beach, the grizzled hair on his sagging chest, the blue-veined legs, the twisted toes with their horny, yellow nails, is no longer the man young women yearn for. He knows this. He feels satirized.

She sets up near him, makes a show of spreading her yellow towel, bending at the waist to give him ideas. Then the meditation: standing, left knee bent. She must have seen this on a postcard somewhere. Her left hand fanned on her left hipbone, she puts the right demurely to her brow, shades her eyes, and looks out on the sea, pensive. Ah, my dear, Chapin thinks. Such an amateur.

Chapin opens his book and tries the first paragraph. Individual words make sense, but not the whole thing. He tries it again. He reads the first two pages. Nothing grabs him. He flips to the middle and reads a passage or two, goes back and starts at the beginning. Three pages in, he is still not connecting. He turns to the back cover and finds out what the book is about.

"Good?"

Chapin looks up.

The girl nods toward the book.

"Not very."

"Those bestsellers are always a disappointment."

Like she would know, Chapin thinks. On the other hand, . . .

An airplane goes over, a prop plane, pulling a gaudy banner. The drone of the engine sounds like a giant insect. They ought to ban those things, Chapin thinks. An Airedale trots by, yards ahead of his owner. No leash, Chapin notes. And the rule is, always has been, all dogs must be leashed.

"Would you like to get a drink?" This comes out so predictably Chapin would have felt negligent not to have said it. Of course, it was inevitable. So much is.

She smiles. "Love to."

She has that kind of downturned smile that Marilyn always makes fun of, the kind that says, Ain't I cute? Well, why not? She is.

They walk to The Cove, an ersatz pirates' lair, and order daiquiris, which, Chapin thinks, is just about perfect.

———————

"You had an affair."

"I had a fling." He told Marilyn right away.

"With a woman who drinks daiquiris." Marilyn is a scotch drinker. Glenfiddich, no ice. "Were these banana daiquiris?" she says.

Chapin says nothing.

"I'm more hurt than angry. You know that." She lights a cigarette. "Now you've got me smoking again," she says.

The hard part is that it would be so easy. Just the one word—"Sorry"— would probably do it. Marilyn loves him. As though he were worth it. Amazing.

———————

Chapin sees the girl again, more daiquiris, and, yes, as a matter of fact, they are banana. She is a comfort, someone that he can't hurt. Ironically, the tacky nautical setting of The Cove, all fishing nets and lobster traps, the overripe appearance of the girl, make the thing look a little like cartoon lust: an aging intellectual with a faithful, classy wife making a fool of himself with a nubile gum-popper half his age. He can imagine his therapist shaking her head.

But with such insight.

———————

Hurricane lamps on the glass-top table, white linen, a small crystal bowl full of unassuming, pastel flowers. The table is set by the patio doors, which are closed against the wind. Dusk. The glass reflects them at their dinner—ghost marrieds, keeping it under control.

"'Through a glass darkly,'" Chapin says, nodding toward the glass doors in which an echoing Chapin is nodding back. "I feel watched."

"I'll open them," Marilyn says

"No, don't."

Chapin's wife is an excellent cook. She does simple things, but in such a way that the essence of the dish—in this case, chicken simmered in a light wine and tarragon sauce—presents itself. Chapin eats quietly, slowly, savoring a glass of chilled Chablis.

"Why don't you say something?" she says.

"Me?"

She looks around the room pointedly. "Do you see anyone else?"

Chapin nods discreetly toward the patio doors. "Mon frère." Marilyn smiles.

"It wouldn't take much," she says, "to save it."

"I know."

Sand drifts across the patio floor. The darkness deepens. Chapin puts down his fork and stares out to sea.

———————

Once you have killed, it is easy to kill again. Crossed the line, something like that.

But how?

He and the bimbo discovered in bed? Tacky. Chapin rejects it. Suicide attempt? Too predictable. The silent treatment takes too long, and uncontrollable lapses into happiness intrude, set you back for months. Something quicker.

Marilyn is sleeping in a canvas deck chair, an old *New Yorker* open in her lap. The sun bleaches her out. She seems transparent, no more substantial than her magazine. She has pushed her glasses up on her forehead, and Chapin watches her eyes. REM beneath the eyelids. Does she dream? Her hair is down. Chapin lifts a lock and tickles her ear. She tosses her head like a colt but doesn't wake. He slicks it into a thin red strand and holds it under her nose—a Fu Manchu, drooping, comic, Yosemite Sam.

Which came first, the chicken or the egg? Chapin makes a low, cluck-clucking sound. The fact is, he is not a very good writer. Or, maybe he is, and his style is just not in fashion. In an age of memoirs, Chapin avoids first person, strives for a clean narrative line, shaped by character. Character is the heart of fiction, Chapin tells—used to tell—his students. Plot is just revelation. But which came first?

Her hair is a paintbrush. He trails it down her neck, dusts the hollow at the base of her throat. She stretches as though responding to a caress, and

Chapin notes how fine her hair is, how the color reminds him of strawberry jam. The midday sunlight ignites it, and just as he is about to kiss her, Marilyn awakes and smiles at him.

————————

Chapin's wife believes he is suicidal. No, he just wants his life to fit. The mismatch of their spirits causes her pain. So, this is a love story after all.

"I called for reservations," she says.

She is dressed for dinner in beige silk and stands before the hallway mirror, primping. Chapin watches. Thinking, thinking, he cannot find a way out. Guilt would be easy, but Chapin, in fact, is not guilty. So much for a ritualized release.

"Want to drive?"

Chapin shakes his head.

"Do you good."

How can he tell her he doesn't want good done?

She tilts her head, fastening an earring. Light falls on the delicate curve of her neck, a simple thing that almost breaks his heart.

"There won't be any traffic," she says.

"I don't know."

She puts her arms around his waist. "Do it for me," she says.

They take the dark blue Crown Victoria, purchased with money from Marilyn's father's estate. It's four years old, but looks brand new, and Chapin delights in the feel of the wheel in his hand, the way the engine responds to the slightest pressure on the gas. They take the narrow two-lane road to the restaurant, the one that winds southwest through the forest preserve. The night is damp, the road like satin; the smell of the pine trees hits them like a jolt of pure oxygen.

"I'm glad to see you doing this," she says.

Chapin doesn't take his eyes from the road. "Like riding a bicycle," he says. "I thought I'd forgotten."

"Feels all right?"

Chapin nods.

Marilyn settles back and closes her eyes. "Things are getting better," she says. "I know it."

Chapin's eyes are riveted on the road. He senses the depth of darkness to his left but dares not look into it.

"Were you working this morning?" Marilyn says.

"Sort of. Looking over some old starts."

"That's great."

"What's so great about it?"

She smiles. It's an indulgent smile. Chapin hates the triumph he sees in her face. Doesn't she know that the question is still open? The ancient, cosmic question of chicken and egg. Was Chapin's character the causal egg, the "accident" a revelation of sorts? In that case, the sour downward spiral that brought him here was, in classical terms, inevitable.

"What about the novel?"

"I've got pieces," Chapin says. "Some of them pretty good, but . . ."

On the other hand: wasn't he just like everyone else until then? Promising, compromised, flawed. In that case, killing an old woman, lugging pudding boxes back to her flat, was impersonal, circumstantial, truly an accident, and in that case, . . .

"So?"

"I can't sort it out, I guess."

Unjust.

"Not true," Marilyn says. "You 'sorted out' that magazine piece in—what was it?—three days?"

"How I spent my summer vacation."

"You made some very clever observations."

"Dreck," he says.

"Why do you insist . . ."

"What?"

Marilyn says nothing.

"You think everything can be fixed," he says.

"If you want it fixed, yes, I do."

The road has modulated into a series of tricky curves, poorly banked so that Chapin has to fight the wheel for control. They seem to come up faster than he expects.

"Slow down," she says.

The woods close in. Only six o'clock, and yet a smoky blue-green darkness hovers around them.

"I'm thinking omelet," Chapin says.

The curves get tighter. They're like a puzzle with no clues. You have to guess the way the road wants to go.

Marilyn shifts in her seat. "Want me to drive?"

Chapin feels he is getting the hang of it. The trick is to accelerate through the curves.

"There's a great one-liner," Chapin says. "Groucho Marx, I think."

"Watch the road."

"'She criticized my apartment, so I knocked her flat.'"

"Let me drive." Marilyn says. "Really."

"Get it? 'Knocked her flat.'"

"Oh, for God's sake, David, let it go."

Chapin rounds a corner, and the landscape opens out. The pine trees fall away on either side, and the road runs straight, perhaps forever, toward the sun. Chapin is lost in the brilliance. It is finally too much. Chapin throws his hands up, lets go of the wheel.

Suddenly the windshield is spattered with shadows. Someone screams as the car jolts down an embankment, through a tangle of weeds. The engine quits. The wheels sink in mud, and the car stops.

Chapin is out and, oddly gleeful, circles the car, dancing. The crash has started a scatter of birds that whispers up from the grass. They lift and fan out across the sky, released.

Marilyn is still facing forward, but when Chapin arrives at the passenger window, she turns. And, finally, the look on her face is one he has never seen before.

"Are you all right?" she says.

Chapin leans in close and whispers: "You said, 'Let go.'"

———————

Marilyn's car is a practical white Ford Escort. It stands at the gate with the doors open. A small blue train case and a matching Pullman lay on the back seat.

"Well, that's everything," she says.

He says nothing.

"Unless . . ."

Chapin can't meet her eyes, won't meet her eyes. He has to hold out just a little bit longer.

"I hadn't realized," she says. "I'm sorry."

Seconds pass. Chapin, half-turned away from her, his hands in his pockets, feels her holding her breath. There is a perfectly round bruise over her right eyebrow, like a shadow, oddly beautiful. Chapin feels her shift her weight and pretends to notice something on the horizon. Of course, there is nothing there, but it kills any impulse she might have had to make some sort of gesture, to reach out and touch him.

"We don't have to do this," she says.

He turns. He faces her. He looks her in the eye and says, as though in casual conversation, "Do what?"

———————

"So. Things are improving."

The therapist has cut her hair. She looks younger, happier somehow. Chapin wants to support her in the illusion that he has been "helped."

"Definitely."

"I'm so glad."

They stare at one another. Does she like daiquiris?

"I know you haven't been taking your medication." There is no accusation in her voice. "Any particular reason?" she says.

Chapin shrugs. There are a thousand reasons. And, there is, finally, no reason at all.

"I killed someone."

He thinks she may want to argue about the verb. Usually she corrects him: "I was responsible for someone's death." But this time she merely nods her head. "An old woman, you told me."

"Her, too."

———————

The beach house is empty, filled with Marilyn's things. Chapin can barely endure it. Daiquiri is still available. She telephones now, now that Chapin's alone, and one day he invites her over, a first. She arrives with all the eagerness of a college girl out on a blind date and carries a grocery bag with a loaf of French bread and a stalk of celery sticking out of the top.

"I thought we'd cook."

"Fine."

She stands there. "So? Where's the kitchen?"

Chapin shakes his head like a man awaking from a long, convoluted dream. "Sorry. It's this way."

He leads her back through the narrow hallway, takes the bag from her hands, and puts it on the countertop.

"Drink?" he says.

"Sure."

He opens the freezer for ice, fills two glasses.

"Scotch?" she says, already resisting.

"Just try it."

"I don't know."

She takes a sip and wrinkles her nose. "Ugh," she says. "It's bitter."

"Yes, a little. You get used to it."

AFTER

Lucy Honig

She had been out of class for three or four days and he had missed her: the dry wisecracks, those bright green eyes letting him know with the slightest narrowing or shift if he had stopped making sense. When he saw her in the hallway, finally, before first-period bell, he folded his big arms across his chest. All the ninth graders called him Mr. Clean behind his back, and he knew he looked like the character who advertised the cleanser, with his massive shoulders, the exaggerated athletic build, even the smooth-topped head. He was not altogether bald yet, but getting there, too soon. He folded his arms across his chest and made his voice even gruffer than usual. "Hey, you, kid! Where've you been? You owe me a book report!"

Her eyes flashed in panic and her face began to crumble, tears brimming.

"Hey," he said softly, putting a hand on her shoulder.

"Didn't they tell you?" she asked.

"What?"

She sighed, then whispered: "My father died. Last Wednesday."

"Oh, Jesus." He hugged her, but she accepted the hug as if she were standing there alone. Nobody had told him. He became furious. *His* star, and no one told him. Goddamn principal, goddamn jerks.

"El, I am so so sorry."

"Not *here*," she groaned, reacting not to his words but to the feeling in them, an intensity that she more than matched with the sudden, deep adult intimacy of her voice. "I feel like I've been gone a hundred years," she said. She swung her head back so that her dark, stringy hair swept over her shoulders. "Here, I have it here, the book report."

"Oh, Ellen, no! I didn't mean—"

She fumbled in her bookbag and retrieved the papers, folded and slightly soiled. "Here." She handed them to him.

He touched her shoulder again. "You idiot," he said. He opened up the folded pages. "Oh, no." She had picked Faulkner, read *As I Lay Dying*. The irony had already registered fully in her eyes when he glanced back at her: a momentary flicker of her humor.

"I'd read it just before. I didn't want to fall behind. Yesterday I wrote it up. It's not very good."

"Who cares," he said. "How's your mother?"

She shook her head no. "It was rough." The irony was gone now, leaving just the tiredness and distress in that thin little fifteen-year-old, smarter-than-anybody face. It was creased and lined, as if she had been sleeping on a damp, wrinkled pillow. She looked down at her feet.

"Come talk," he said.

───────────

When she ran it was like flying, and the driveway was not long enough, she ran along the highway to the dirt road that went up toward the Kozaks and the Sayer farm. Fields of young alfalfa spread out on either side. When she came to the steep hill downward, she took it with arms stretched out, banking like wings, and hurtled down faster and faster, her feet barely touching the ground. She created a whoosh! of a breeze around her, and she became the breeze around her: she and the air merged in the sheer speed of flight. And if there was a wind, a strong wind just before an evening rain—

oh, how she could fly through it, running with all her might, and then she *was* the wind, she dissolved into millions of molecules of motion, pure motion. How wonderful she felt when she flew!

But when she stopped, the things around her collected, drew together into a wall: the trees and the house, the grass and the sky arranged themselves into an impenetrable layer at one grasp beyond her. Everything was flat, as if the world hung before her on one straight, solid curtain. And weaving in and out of it as they went through the motions of a day, were her sister, the sleepwalker, and her mother in a new, awful silence, flat as glass.

At five-thirty in the morning the light was fine and gentle and cool, slanting though the pines in pale strands. He took the trail at a medium jog, pacing himself steadily as he went along the ravine, down to the stream, which was swollen brown with springtime torrents, across the bridge, and, after the sixth mile, back up to the main road. Charlie Marshall passed in the pickup at the usual spot, exactly halfway between the Shell station, shut tight, and the Matthews' barking mongrel. He waved at Charlie, then picked up speed and felt the expansion in all the muscles of his thighs. He was in the full power of his youth, not yet thirty, and yet he was—had always been, it seemed—haunted by the specter of decay and immobility. Something he'd picked up in books, his wife insisted: his family all lived robustly until their quick and late and quiet deaths. He ran and lifted weights, built himself stronger, a human fortress, immense and invulnerable.

In the faculty lunchroom, Ginny Firth, the girls' gym teacher, sat beside him, a big, bony, smart lady. His wife said Ginny Firth liked women. He didn't know; he didn't care; he liked Ginny. She leaned over to him and said, "Are you training her?"

"Who? What?"

She laughed, her smile reaching up to immense cheekbones. "Ellen Frisch. She's my best runner. For all these years, completely unexceptional in phys ed. And suddenly she's winning every race, I mean it, *every* race."

"I hear you're running," he said. She sat on top of a desk in the front row of the empty classroom, swinging her feet, her face still marred by those strange wrinkles. He wondered if all the thinking was doing it, the intensity of her thoughts somehow engraving her flesh.

"Just in the driveway. Down a back road," she said.

"How far?"

She shrugged. "I don't know. Not very. But I go fast."

"Better not take it too—" He stopped, watching her face, and saw that she did not simply run. Her running was something else. Whatever it was, the rules of fitness would not apply.

"I run like the wind," she said, and then she giggled. "Sometimes . . . it's like I'm not even there. The *me* part of me, that voice."

"Is that what you want?"

She blushed. "Yes." She spent a minute thinking, the colors of her thoughts rising and falling in her cheeks as she swung her feet, her wrinkled face wrinkling more.

"It's a release," she said finally.

He almost said, "Like sex," but stopped, remembering she was a child.

"If I could believe in God," she said, "it would all be easier."

"Well hell, El, don't expect *me* to tell you to." He scowled, to match the gruffness of his tone. "You know I'm a son-of-a-bitch atheist."

"It *would* be easier," she said again.

"Yeah, and then you'd be like *them*," he said.

"Them!" she cried. "*God* forbid!"

————

When she waited for the school bus, standing in the shelter of her father's vegetable stand, Mr. Spinner went by in the little gray Volkswagen and waved. She had learned the sound of his car, the putter of the Bug's engine. Even from inside the house, upstairs, doors closed, she could tell when he was going by and picture his massive frame filling the tiny cab.

Putt-putt-putt. In the afternoon when she had no reason to be there, she hid in the shadow of the stand and watched the small gray car toodle past, a wind-up toy, filled with *him*. She wished he would see her and stop, but she stayed hidden, listening to the sound of him trail off, grow fainter as he rounded the hill, and fade away completely in the wind. Then she turned and ran as fast as she could, back down the driveway to the house.

————

He gave a groan and slowly, very slowly, lowered the last barbell. Sweat oozed down his limbs, glistening on the bulge of muscles. His big arms trembled. "Shit!" he said gruffly to himself. From the doorway of the cellar room, his wife laughed. He spun around and aimed a frown at her. "Watchit!" he said fiercely. She stuck her tongue out, laughed, and disappeared up the stairs.

Her father walked down the driveway from the stand. He stopped beside the row of bushel baskets, knelt down, and examined the tomatoes. She walked toward him from the house, calling out. He looked in her direction but did not seem to see. She called out again. He turned and walked away and she followed, breaking into a run. But she never got near him. She awoke.

She sat on top of the desk, dangling her legs. She wore white socks, sneakers, a heavy, rough-textured pleated skirt—not a summer skirt, though it was the first week of June. "And I feel like it's so completely *real*," she said, looking down into her lap. "Each time I have the dream, I know he's alive. There's no question. And it's so un*fair*!" Her voice rose angrily.

He sat and listened. She turned her face toward him, the anger in it now directed at him. Livid red. "He wasn't even nice to us most of the time, you know."

"I didn't know, no."

"He yelled and hollered. No matter what we did, it was wrong. Once a friend of mine came over and I was so embarrassed—he threw a fit at my sister for getting eighties instead of nineties on her report card. It was awful. I didn't know why he was like that. But my friend was there, I had to explain it, so she wouldn't think I had a monster for a father. So I said, 'He's a sick man. He's had a bad heart ever since he was a kid. He's so angry about always being sick, sometimes he blows up at the rest of us for no reason.'" She paused, biting her lip. "And as soon as I said it, I knew I was right, or near enough. And after that it was different. I could talk to him."

She stared down at her lap again. He waited.

"The last few months," she said slowly, "we talked. A lot. I came home from school and told him about my day. He listened." She stopped and swung her legs in that ungainly way, her stringy hair hanging about her eyes.

"After the funeral," she said, "I just wanted to tell him about the funeral."

———————

The uncles decided the girls should run the stand that summer—his stand, his business, an enterprise only *his* heart and soul had ever entered; they had always detested helping there. They fought their uncles, but with such listlessness they had no chance of winning. And Muriel still barely spoke; her fight was gone. She worked all week in town. On the weekends she went to market, bought the produce. Ellen and Jackie dragged themselves out in the mornings, sometimes close to noon, and like zombies they arranged the baskets of tomatoes, beans, and squash, the mounds of sweet corn and heaps of melons, and the boxes of maple-sugar candy left from the previous year, now aged to a granular pallor. The shelves were barely covered: a match to the girls' half-heartedness.

She hated customers. She hated having to be polite or answer questions or make change. Jackie went to summer school each afternoon, and Ellen sat in the little Shaker rocking chair with a book in her lap. The traffic whizzed by, cars and trucks all of one flat piece with the gray asphalt. "Don't stop, don't stop." She repeated the incantation if cars slowed down. Across the road, at the motel but as near to her as the single dimension of the road, Nelson the hired man whistled as he slowly pushed the laundry cart from one room to the next. Sometimes he waved; she waved back.

And then one day that woman stopped, the silver-haired woman with the jangling bracelets who came every year on her way from New York City to Saratoga. Years ago she had given Ellen a wooden doll that Ellen had cherished. And now, with her make-up heavy, perfume strong and foreign, she grabbed at baskets of cherries and peaches, she made a pile on the counter with zucchini, peppers, onions, and corn. "Every year! What would I do without it! You have no idea what a relief it is . . . yes, yes, to leave all that behind. And the humidity! You lucky child, here in the fresh air!" She made a big fuss, chattering without stop, until finally she bit her lip so that the dark lipstick cracked suddenly to a pale white patch, and peered sharply at Ellen. "Now. Where's that father of yours?"

Ellen tried to speak, but it was as if a hard plug of metal blocked her throat. To get the words out, the metal plug had to be pushed. The city woman frowned at her, fading into the flat, pale wall of road, motel, sky. Everything dimmed. She tried to remember the wooden doll, tried to unblock her throat. But the metal stayed. Everything dimmed more. Finally she spoke. "He died." The words crashed into the air, and she felt a rapid spinning. The woman from New York cried out, "Oh, my *dear!*" and caught her.

———

Sometimes when he drove by he saw her at the stand, that tumbledown shack with the peeling gray paint. She waited on a customer, her shoulders drooping, or sat in the back where it was shady. And sometimes he saw the flash of movement in the driveway, the dash of her quick sprints. She seemed utterly alone. But because it was summertime and school was off and nothing seemed amiss, he did not think to stop, but waved and putt-putt-putted his way up the road, around the hill, and home.

———

She dove into the pool and swam underwater in strong, steady frog strokes just inches from the bottom and all the way down the length of the pool. Then she did a quick turn, kicking off from the rough concrete side, and swam back, still deep underwater, still pushing out with strong frog strokes, lost in the water's caress. She forgot air, she forgot the limits of her lungs, she forgot the limits of her skin, which now interjoined with water. And she felt the ecstasy of being nothing but water and motion, the pure push through blue space, the stretch and reach of her arms now an energy that seemed to come as much from outside of herself as within, and the power in her legs, kicking out, the very same as the power of the water's resistance. She reached the other end and turned, propelling herself off the concrete with the strong agreement between her knees and the soles of her feet. But then: she had pushed upward and her head surfaced, and she breathed in the hot air, gasping like a fish that did not want air, and this air in her lungs and on her shoulders and around her face seemed to pull her body and mind into separate parts again. She grabbed onto the side of the pool and looked around. The road shimmered with heat, and across it was the gray stand, dwarfed by ancient pines. And everything composed a flat canvas, one pale surface, color and depth gone. She put her hand out to touch it, but it was not there to touch. She filled her lungs, plunged under the cool water again, and swam down, down to the safety of her own dispersion.

––––––––

It was as if the Volkswagen had driven off the road and into the driveway on its own volition. There is *nothing* you can do for her, he told himself, cutting the engine. She sprung out of the rocking chair and stood, very nervous and brittle, regarding him with an angry panic as he got out, straightened to his full height, and approached. Her hair was shorter, cut bluntly and shiny clean.

"Hello, El," he said.

"Hi."

He juggled two peaches in his large hands. They were fuzzy and pale and not ripe. The basket was not even full. The shelf tipped at an angle. She looked down at her feet, then around at the display that was not up to snuff, and her face showed signs of another panic. He put the peaches back in the basket.

"Hell," he said, "I don't want to buy anything."

"Good," she said. "I don't want to sell anything." Suddenly she grinned.

"Are you running?" he asked.

She sighed. "A little. I swim more now." She squinted again, pointing past him, across to the motel where he could see the turquoise glimmer.

"Not much of a pool," he said.

"It's enough," she answered. The energy seemed to be collecting in her chest, about to come charging out in a torrent of words, he knew, if he waited. She squinted at the road as a car slowed down. The car drove on. Her eyes brightened. "I've started swimming underwater. I do laps underwater and it's as if I don't even need to breathe, I get into this rhythm, and the water takes over and there's no difference between the water and me."

"It must feel good," he said.

"Yeah." She paused. "It's really the only time I ever do feel good."

His heart seemed to contract.

"And all the chatter in my head is quiet. What a relief!" She gave a little laugh. "It's like I don't have to be there any more. It's enough that there's energy and water and—and feeling. When I'm underwater, I don't have to keep talking to myself."

He smiled.

"I don't have to keep listening to myself, either," she said, smirking.

He smiled again. She needed to lose herself in those sensations, and yet the sensations rendered themselves into words, almost despite her. Then the words sought *him.* And he wondered if she would stay with her body, in the energy and sensation, or if someday she would abandon it, to wander off entirely in the chatter of her head, locked irrevocably into articulation.

He said, "Keep swimming, El."

"I know," she said.

He turned back to the Volkswagen, opened the door, and folded himself up to fit in. "But for Chrissakes," he yelled sternly. "Don't forget to breathe!"

―――――――――

She watched the gray car get back on the road, she heard one gear shift, then another as it passed the mailbox and the pines—and it was off, dissolving into the world of one dimension. But here it had stood out, as he had, in its entire form, all dimensions. Everything had, while he was here. Even the bushel baskets of fruit had suddenly jumped out at her, alive with their own color and shape. Peaches round. Baskets square. He had stopped to talk to her! And by stopping, he had made the world fill out and occupy itself again, so that there was within her vision a distinct near and far, a brighter and duller, a center and an edge. There were spaces between things, there was *here*, and there was *there*. He had stopped, for *her*, in the middle of a summer afternoon!

―――――――――

Like the year before, he sat at his desk, facing her, as she sat atop a front-row desk, a tenth-grader now, no longer in his English class but *there*, after school, alone. She wore nylons now instead of socks, but still swung her feet in the old ungainly way. Her shoes had fallen on the floor. She sat there, reciting by heart the T. S. Eliot poem he had once mentioned that *he* knew by heart, and she did it with fine intonation, tender feeling, not a word wrong.

"Hey, pretty damn good," he said when she finished. She beamed at him with good color in her face, the wrinkles gone, her dark hair showing blond sun-streaks, her eyes full of light.

"It's good to have the old kid back," he said softly.

Suddenly the light and feeling in her face vanished. "I am *not* the old kid!" she shouted. "And I will *never* be the same!"

He saw at once that she was right. She would blossom—had already begun to blossom—into all the facets of adulthood from that single stem, her father's death.

"El," he said.

She looked down at her stockinged feet. "It's no use. I'm sorry. I didn't mean to yell. It's just that everything seems ruined."

"Hey, El. You were never what I'd call a happy-go-lucky, carefree sort of kid to begin with. You *think*, remember? It's what distinguishes you from the apes." He coughed. "And a few other people we know."

She smirked, almost as if she would laugh. But she did not laugh. "I know." Her face darkened. "But this is worse."

"You miss him," he said softly.

She shot that angry look at him again. "It's *not* that easy!" she shouted hoarsely. Then her voice lowered. "Don't you see? If you, if someone had mixed feelings about a person to begin with. . . ." She stopped, shook her head. "Okay, yes, I loved him, he was my father, but he was difficult. Don't you see?"

He nodded.

"And everybody comes up to you and says, you must be *heartbroken*. Well, that's not it! I'm not such a good little girl! But it's death. It's so final. I was in the *middle* of something with him!"

They were silent for a minute. Then he spoke. "You can't say, 'Poor, wonderful Daddy, he was a saint, only the good die young.'"

"Right," she said, almost triumphantly.

Again they sat in silence. Again he broke it. "And you can't hack through the rest of your understanding of each other."

She sighed. "Yes," she said.

Another silence occupied another minute. Finally he said, "Well, hell, El," deliberately elongating the rhyme. "If I were you, I'd be pissed as hell at him."

She nodded. "There," she said.

"Don't," he began, and then he paused, wondering if he should say it, because he didn't *really* know, did he?—except from some mute instinct. "Don't let anyone stop you."

————

She lay absolutely still in bed, but her mind began to rush out, further and further, hurtling into a black space that had no end, it went—she went—at a dizzying speed, racing outward through the blackness, which was suddenly infused with faint sprays of light, then utterly black again. The force and speed of her mind's propulsion into blackness erupted into a buzz, a hum, that grew into a grinding racket that got faster and louder and faster again until the sound itself exploded into white light, a terrible flash! And still she hurtled into space, all directions at once, until—what was it? Everything began to contract in upon her, the vast oceans of space dipped inward, faster and faster, it all came hurtling back at her, whirling up a storm in the spaces of her head. The blackness streamed inward now. She lay there. In the box. With blackness. The voices around her were distraught. Her mother, her sister, her aunts were all weeping. No! I am *not* dead! She tried to cry out. But the furious streams of movement, in a sudden whoosh! swept her core into their current so that in this fraction of a second she felt herself ebb away, the all of her gone, except for the thinnest thread; and there was nothing but the vast quiet that she would not even know, but for this thread. . . .

She awoke with her head pounding violently; she realized that even awake she was still on the thread's end overlooking the negation of her self. And she could not bear it, this complete encircling with all her senses of the core that was her death, the knowledge itself as total as the emptiness it knew—and for a brief second the two were in balance, the thread stretched taut. If it broke, she would not be there to know it or to know the rest of the world going on. "No!" she cried aloud, and the thread brought her back into herself, so that in another second she could not even imagine where she had just been.

"And I was dead," she said matter-of-factly. She had summoned him for a talk during lunch instead of waiting until the usual time after school.

"Except for this thread—no, not even a thread, like a fragile spider-web hair, that's all. That's all there is between life and death. Now I know exactly what it is." She spoke with intense animation, her face flushed. "It snaps—and then you're gone. All I had was this thread; I felt the rest of me flow out and leave. I heard them talking around me, at the funeral. And then I was gone, and all that was left, beside the thread, was the nothing."

She shuddered. And it was about time, he thought, because he had felt his own hair—what was left of it—stand straight on his head at the start.

She went on. "But then the thread pulled me back enough into being alive that I was *aware* of the death, I had a complete grasp of it, just for a fraction of a second. Not the dying, exactly, but the *not being there*. And *that*," she paused, eyes bright with fierce assurance, "was horrible. I can't de-scribe it."

"You just did," he said.

"Oh, no. You can't imagine."

"Give me a chance."

She laughed nervously. "But even *I* can't imagine. Not now. Even right after it happened I couldn't. Because as horrible as it was, I did try to bring it back. But I couldn't. I tried very hard to summon it back."

They sat in silence for several minutes. Finally he said, cautiously, "Do you think if you can get back there again—into death—you'll find him there?"

Her response was not at all what he expected or what he feared. She burst out laughing. "How mystical!" she cried. "Oh, God, no, that's not it at all," she said, laughing harder. And then, her laughter subsiding, she said, "No, I just want to *know* what it is, that's all."

And although he thought he was relieved, the hair stood up straight once again.

———

Thwop! The piece of maple went splitting out into two big chunks. Thwop! All the muscles of his back rippled in the motion. He stacked half a cord of wood from an hour's work, which was still not enough. He needed more: not more wood, he had mounded up enough, during the summer and fall, for another three winters, but more motion.

He put on the worn running shoes and took the trail at an even pace down the hill and along the rushing stream, but instead of climbing up to the main road, he turned and took the stream trail back again, lost in the music of his own footfalls. At the flattest stretch he thought he'd try it *her* way, just for once, and he took off in a sprint. But after fifty yards a deep ache started in his lungs, and not long after came a knot that seized the muscle in his right calf. Then both knees buckled.

Later, as his wife massaged the leg, she said, "A cramp in your leg usually comes right before your foot goes in the grave."

"Hey!" he barked. "That's not funny." And tears of pain moistened the corners of both eyes.

———————

Putt-putt-putt. She heard the under-rhythm of the Volkswagen in the distance and waited in the shadow of the stand, boarded up now, grass growing high around it. Across the street, Nelson pushed the laundry cart along in his slow, quiet routine. At last she heard the sound more clearly, putt-putt-putt. It set off a pounding in her chest as it grew closer. She stood motionless, knowing she was hidden, and watched the small gray car putter past with him gigantic in the front seat. She felt the first surge of a yearning so new, so vague, so light a flutter in her throat, that she hardly knew she was feeling anything at all. And then the putt-putt-putt faded and was gone.

She took off down the driveway and forced herself into *his* rhythm, so that she could feel the lifting from the ball of one foot and the firm landing of the other. What was the point? Plod—plod—plod—she jogged along this way, *his* way, the length of the driveway, down the highway the short distance to the dirt road, and halfway up to the Sayer farm. Then she broke into a sprint, filling her lungs on the first leap, and tore out of the jog in a burst of her own breeze. The air brushed her cheeks, her hair flew out, her feet barely touched the ground, and she flew! Along the road and down the hill the wind was her very soul, and as she dissolved into the wind she felt herself become life, pure life, her surge through the air matching the push of blood through her veins. She was the same as that force and no more than it, she was the thread of life, flying down a country road.

———————

In his quiet classroom after school, she sat at a desk by the long row of windows, her geometry book open next to a sheet of lined paper and two sharpened pencils. She had already worked out the answer to the first problem in her neat print and careful triangular drawings. But now she dropped the third pencil beside the book and looked out the window. The afternoon sunlight filtered across the deep green soccer field and through the row of stately maples at the far border, where it wove a gold pattern on red leaves. As the breeze blew, the gold tones shimmered. The air around them seemed to shimmer, too. She watched the breeze waft through the grasses below, which leaned gently. And then the team of boys in shorts and sweatshirts came running down one side of the soccer field, the whole group at the same brisk jog along the field, then toward the trees. They were all caught by the slant of sunlight and lit momentarily by the golden hue, and from the gold they jogged into the trees and disappeared. Ellen stood up to watch the last boy fade away, the gold light closing back in around the space where he had been, and a peacefulness, which had not been disturbed by the runners but made somehow more luxuriant, now redistributed itself along the grass and trees and sky.

He came and stood next to her, looming so close that if she looked sideways but an inch or two she saw the thick brown and black wool weave of his jacket, halfway down the arm. Her heart began beating wildly; a hot flush spread from her forehead down her face and throat to her neck. Why was he standing so close? She stole a rapid look up at his face, which stared out the window where her own look had just been fixed. She saw the coarse bristle of a new day's growth on the underside of his chin. His huge, square shoulder jutted out beside her head. She stopped breathing. Then she could hear *him* breathe. Just as she turned her head to face out the window again, she felt his look begin a downward, sideways glance at her. Too close, much too close! The heat rose back from her neck into her face. She would explode.

The heave of his chest and a puff of air yielded a sigh. She did not look back up toward his face, but fixed her glance out the window, seeing nothing, taking no breath, paralyzed. If he said one single word her pounding body would burst into a million pieces. But *why* was he still there? It could not have been even a full minute that he stood where she could hear each of his breaths and know the fibers of his sleeve, but it was forever.

At last he turned, and she sensed the movement of his shoulder hoisting up, heard the soft rustle of his clothing. And then, with one hand cupped, he touched her head just below the crown, he lay his hand upon the spot with an exquisite, tender firmness and drew it down another inch, without lifting it or even loosening the pressure, and there, above the nape of her neck, pressed his fingers a bit more firmly with the same awesome tenderness. Then the touch lightened, lingered a second more. . . and was gone. This unimaginable caress had lasted three seconds, at most four, and was gone.

He left her side, slowly turned and walked up the row of desks back to his own. He sat down. She reached up and felt the spot, as if to make sure it was still there. She cupped her own hand and laid it firmly on her head, capturing the touch. Then she let her hand drop limply to her side. She kept her look fixed out the window and let herself take a breath. She breathed again, she began to pace out each breath as if she were sprinting down the road, taking air deeply into her lungs, slowly releasing it, breathing in again. Each new beat of her heart pounded a bit less wildly in her chest. The light in the maples now shone with a glint of silver laid over gold. The wind had shifted, the time had changed. A stronger breeze skimmed through the grass. She sat down at the desk and looked ahead, at him. He corrected papers, reading intently, his forehead furrowing.

She picked up a pencil and looked at her book. Then she glanced one last time out the window to see the stream of boys running another lap down the field and through the trees.

WAITING FOR GIOTTO

Adria Bernardi

At dusk, he crosses the threshing floor. The soles of his wooden shoes hit against the stones. The stones fit closely, embedded into the ground, squared blocks pressed tightly, one against the other such that no weed can grow between them. The threshing floor is Apennine sandstone, slate-grey, and not easily splintered.

––––––––

When he exhales, his breath is visible in the faltering light. Below, to his left, in the valley, a bell pounds five times, a hollow knocking toll. He pauses and looks. In Ardonlà, minute lights begin to flicker; the river has already disappeared in the dark. The mountain peak and ridges are looming hunchbacked beasts.

He whistles, a sharp, cranium-piercing whistle, and Diana the goat trots up beside him and follows. He is a tall, gangly man, all limbs and neck. He approaches the stable, leans a shoulder into the door, loosening it, lowering his head as he passes underneath the lintel.

Inside, he lights one candle and sets it up high on a shelf, out of the way, so that it will not be accidentally toppled. A tunic falls to just above his knees; it is a plush material, a purple so deep it is almost black.

Diana the goat settles into the corner and is sleeping like a patient dog.

He takes a panel from the corner, unwinds the piece of sackcloth that covers it. He hangs the cloth on a wooden peg. The panel of chestnut has been planed and smoothed, then coated with lime, which dried, and then was rubbed and smoothed some more. He lays the wooden panel on freshly scattered straw and drops to his haunches, his long legs bent and splayed, the heavy cloth of the tunic draping over his knees.

With jagged fingernails, he scratches his scalp and his arm. Patches of skin have turned white, then red, and he must try not to touch them. The skin throbs and pulls apart from itself, and when he can no longer tolerate it, his nails nick hatch marks into the skin, and the sting relieves his incessant discomfort.

Bartolomeo de Bartolai stares down at what he has drawn: three faces, one floating above the other. Three bodiless beings. Each face is round, with wide, almond-shaped eyes that stare out, impassive and severe, orbs that nearly fill the socket. Each pupil is obsidian, a perfectly round stone. Above the eyes, the thick brows merge together and form a painted gash. He gives each face a tiny, set mouth. In the place of a body, there is an arc, a boat whose prow and stern fan upward into wings. He has copied these figures from angels chiseled in stone above the door of his farmhouse, the work of his grandfather's father. The men of the mountains all know how to work with stone, they can chisel celestial beings from it. His nails are dirty. His fingers are scraped and cut, stiff from the cold. He comes into this stable at night, while the others quietly drink their aqua vita in front of the hearth, dulling their hunger, numbing their sores.

By day he tends the sheep, in the evening he comes to the stable. It is the second night of November in 1560.

———————

The winter is long. Bartolomeo de Bartolai sits drawing on a flat piece of rock, over and over. He draws with clay dug from a ravine and ash taken from the hearth. He draws with charred twigs of chestnut and hawthorn, with charred walnut shells. He makes drawings on flat stones and rough wood. Drawings of what? The usual things. The things that he knows. Sheep. Goats. Everyday things.

———————

Bartolomeo de Bartolai lives in a remote narrow valley, far away from a city, but knows the story of Giotto, the greatest artist in the history of the world, word of Giotto has made its way even this far. He knows how Giotto's father was a simple fellow who gave his son sheep to tend. How the boy was forever drawing on stones, on the ground, in sand, on anything, and how, one day, he was discovered, by the great painter Cimabue, who saw the boy drawing a sheep on a flat, polished stone. How Cimabue asked the father for permission to take the boy Giotto to Florence, and the father lovingly granted permission. Bartolomeo de Bartolai knows this story, the holy men themselves disseminated it, and he has heard how Giotto, single-handedly, restored good design and drawing to Christendom after it was corrupted by the infidels.

———————

So many others have left to find a way in the world. Others younger than he, who were babies when he was already tending sheep.

He watched them leave with canvas sacks upon their backs, depart and not look behind. From his spot near the river, he was stunned and astonished: They were not waiting. How did they conceive such a thing?

He wanted to say, Stop! You are not ready to go yet! You are too young to set off in the world. This is not how you are supposed to do it. You are supposed to do it like this: sit here by a river, drawing, like me, drawing, drawing, shapes and lines and figures, making them look like they are moving in three dimensions. It is very difficult. You will not necessarily understand the shapes you are making, but you must keep making them and a picture will emerge. Slowly, slowly, until one day, they will dance upon the rock. This is how it must be done. You must serve an apprenticeship, here.

But they did not. They were bold. They told the priest, You have nothing more to teach me. They said to their parents, I break with you.

He watched them leaving, climbing the hill, through the gate of the walled town, up the side of the mountain toward Faidello, up higher toward the house of Abramo, toward the Long Forest and over the hill toward Cutigliano, on to Pistoia. Pistoia, where they have invented a tool, a hand-held weapon that exhales explosion. A pistol. These people who were younger than him headed past Pistoia, past Prato, where abandoned babies are left at the hospice of the Misericordia. They went down the slopes of the foothills, where grapes and acacia grow, onto the plain, into the river bed of the Arno, into the city, Fiorenza.

He envied them, but crossed himself and prayed, because *invidia* is a sin. The envious sinners in purgatory, between the Wrathful and Proud. He saw the others leaving, bounding away, and thought, Do they not risk worse sins?

No, he wanted to shout. Wait. Wait right here with me. Wait your turn. Do not risk abandonment. Come sit beside me; I have been practicing, practicing for years. Come wait with me.

He opened his mouth to shout, he could see them up the hill, but his throat was dry and no sound came out.

Before he can make his way down from the mountains, he must learn the principles; this is his understanding. And so he has prepared and prepared and prepared. Before you even begin to contemplate the journey, you must understand certain things. The principle of perspective. Vanishing point.

Bartolomeo de Bartolai sits making figures on a panel of wood, over and over, waiting for Giotto.

He scavenges and hoards, and whenever he finds a broken plate, a cracked vase, a shattered bottle from the midwife, he gathers the pieces in a canvas sack that hangs from his waist. This sack is called a *scarsella*, an alms purse. Since no one in these mountains possesses coins to fling to beggars, a *scarsella* is any type of gathering sack, whether for mushrooms or for chestnuts.

Whenever he goes to town, to Ardonlà, on market days, he wears the *scarsella* and walks behind the shops on either side of the street to see what has been discarded. Once he found an apothecary jar, broken and without its lid, decorated with blue and yellow scrolls. He gathered the pieces of this ointment jar, wrapped the fragments in a rag, then put the bundle under his cloak. He looked to see what was behind the shop of the blacksmith. Nothing. And behind the tinker. Nothing. Beside the church, he found a broken chalice, made of wine-red glass, which the priest had unblessed and thrown into a heap. Behind the tavern, he found a broken string of beads, pieces of flat blue glass, and he took these as well.

For this scrounging, his mother cuffs the back of his head. At least leave intact our dignity, so that we are not seen picking up broken things from people who have as little as we do. They will call us mendicants and hoarders. But Bartolomeo de Bartolai cannot stop himself from squatting down to pick up a shard if it glints.

He saves the collected fragments in a chest inside the stable.

––––––––––

Halfway down the valley, the windows of the villa are filled with panes of glass. When the Signore married a lady from Ferrara, he put in glass that came all the way from Venezia. In Venezia, he has heard, there are hordes of men and women and children, arrived from the mountains, who work in shops making glass. How dazzling it would be to live there. Bartolomeo de Bartolai imagines a city of glass, color reflecting everywhere. He imagines heaps of glass everywhere, glistening like the mounds of jewels inside a sultan's tomb. Whenever a glassmaker makes an error, or inadvertently drops a bottle, he tosses the broken pieces into a heap. He has heard of a young person who travelled to Venezia and is etching spectacular mountains on the insides of vases. In Venezia, the brilliance would only blind him and cause him to wince. Here, instead, he can keep his eyes open, scanning the ground for the rare discarded colored piece.

––––––––––

How were those others able to leave so soon? Not sit up here and wait? He saw their proud chins jutted forward. He saw how they waved to him as they passed by. He believes they saw him as a simple person, sitting there with his sheep. He wanted to remind them that Giotto was a shepherd, but they would not have cared. They would have said, You are left behind by time. They do not even recall Cimabue, he is irrelevant to them, and their gazes are fixed beyond the mountain pass.

He sits and waits for a master, someone to tap his shoulder, to lift him up, usher him by the elbow. Invite him into apprenticeship. Perhaps Giotto himself, stern in profile, will see the drawings, his fine collection of shards, and will say, Yes. Then lead him away, down out of the mountains.

Once, he went to see a great man as the entourage passed on the road above, he had heard he was a great painter. Everyone clapped and sang as the man approached, reached out their hands to him. Young men carried the great man on their backs, on a chair fastened to poles. They sank down in the mud to their knees. From the side of the road, Bartolomeo de Bartolai stretched out his arm, and the great man mimicked the way his hand trembled.

He looks up into the face of each stranger passing through, wondering if he is the Master. Each season, the Giotto he envisions has a different face.

He sits and he waits for Giotto; he knows better than to wait for Cimabue. Too much time has passed. He lives below a narrow dirt road, a mule path no more than three men wide, the only road that passes through the mountains and links one city to another. He lives in a cluster of ten houses that is too small to be called a hamlet. One house touches the other, and they are all made of the same grey stone as the cliff. The houses sit on a ledge supported by a single granite column. It is called *La Gruccia, the crutch*, because from a distance it looks as if it were perched on a walking stick.

Giotto might travel some day along the mule path above. He might stop because he needed to sleep. Or because he needed to eat. Because his horse was tired. Giotto would somehow know that Bartolomeo de Bartolai was sitting by the edge of the river drawing figures of sheep on stone, just as Giotto himself had done, and surely, he would appreciate this diligence.

Did the ones who have gone down receive a call? Because no one goes down without an invitation. How did it enter their minds that they were worthy enough to knock on the door of the privileged? A shepherd does not go through the gates of a rich man's house, not even to a door around back, unless he knows that there is someone who will answer. He knows he would be apprehended, arrested, beaten, put outside the gate to starve. He would be mistaken for a vagrant. Who are they, the ones who went down?

These privileged ones who have taken it upon themselves to go down to a master's shop?

—————

He knows that the ones who have left would mock him: That old man, what do you want with that old man? He has nothing to teach you. No one has anything to teach you that you cannot learn by yourself. You are wasting time; your life is passing. Count the days already gone. In winter you could die suddenly of pneumonia; in summer, contagion travels up from the plain. What do you wait for? An invitation on parchment? With gilt edges, rolled tightly into a scroll? Bah, they would say, these young people with sacks hoisted over their shoulders, their chins in the air. Bah. There is no messenger that brings correspondence intended for these parts; the only messages are those that travel through, being carried from one city on the plains to another. This Giotto you wait for is archaic. His students have moved beyond him. They have already stood on his shoulders and seen things he could not dream of. You are too solicitous, too timid. You defer, when you should demand.

But I am only a simple shepherd.

—————

The bell down in the village bongs seven times, a slow weighted rumble. Outside the shed, the sky is black.

He sits on straw in the stable at night and remembers a fresco at a church, the pilgrims' destination, the monastery of San Pellegrino, built on a pinnacle where three valleys come together. The monks say this fresco was done by Giotto.

He carried away the fresco, holds the picture inside his head: San Gioacchino is asleep on the ground in the mountain, chased from the temple into the mountains because he has fathered no children. He wears a rose-colored robe. He is sitting, head on arm, which is resting on his knee. While he is asleep, an angel announces that his barren wife is with child, and that the child will become the mother of God. A shepherd leans on a crutch. One sheep stands on a granite scarp. Another one sleeps. A black goat looks away, while a ram sits wide awake. They are all fat, healthy creatures. The halo of the sleeping saint is golden. A gorse plant nearby is flecked with yellow.

On a piece of stone, Bartolomeo de Bartolai imitates the way the rib cage of the shepherd's dog is visible through its skin, the way the goat's hoof splays as it steps down the side of a cliff.

––––––––––

When Bartolomeo de Bartolai looks around, he sees that all the young people have gone down out of the mountains. One, whom he called friend, Martín de Martinelli, patted him on the head, and then was gone like the rest. He last heard that Martín was in Fiorenza preparing walls for frescoes.

When he left, Martín de Martinelli did not look back or sideways; he had always been preparing to leave. Those who move away carry off what they wish and remake in their minds those who have stayed, while the ones who remain behind are left to wonder what has become of those who depart. Some who stay in the mountains close their hearts tight to forget the ones who have left; some turn the departed into heroes, making them more than they are. And if those who have ventured out should return, the ones who have remained lose voice in their presence because the returning emigrants claim the expertise of the world.

As a child, Bartolomeo de Bartolai followed after this friend, imitating him. He was intrigued, intimidated. It was excessive adoration. His heart is hardened, and yet he still hopes for a single message. Like a puppy dog. Then he wishes to kick himself for this suppliance, but does not. He turns back into himself and makes marks on stones.

––––––––––

Why was he so dazzled by Martín de Martinelli, a person who treated others like servants? Finally he understands what he had refused to see for so long: Martín de Martinelli is the earth and everyone else is a planet circling.

Martín de Martinelli would occasionally glance over his shoulder as he sat bent over a panel of wood, commenting upon his progress. Bartolomeo de Bartolai wants to know if noteworthiness is like this? Others watching to see if you might be recognized, if you are the one who will go to work in the shop of a master. They watch, afraid of approaching too close lest you remain forever hunched over, eccentric and obscure. It was an infatuation, he decides, a kind of being in love with Martín de Martinelli, with a person incapable of listening. How do you comprehend the world if you see only yourself, over and over and over? Do you see yourself finally as a spectre? As spectre, you then consume the air around you like a flame. And while some pull up cushions to sit at your feet, you fail to notice that others have wandered off, neglected and stung. One person in town called Martín de Martinelli a trinket maker of worthless things, spoiled, and Bartolomeo de Bartolai said, No, there is genius, wait. I was young, he thinks now. Spellbound. But the truth is, I wanted his way of being for myself, his ease and his boldness. Now I see that these thoughts were a form of Envy, and that this elaborate infatuation was Covetousness, and that I coveted his signature.

———

He blames others for his timidity:

His great-grandmother who was once a lioness and now does not know her own daughter.

His grandmother who must tend to her and grips his wrist when he passes by.

His mother who drinks a bitter liquid made from distilled walnuts, each time the great-grandmother wails.

His father who leaves the house and wanders into the woods to escape. Bartolomeo de Bartolai stays in the corner waiting to see if his mother will call out for him; when he leaves, his father pats him on the head, and calls him his favorite child, though he knows his favorite child is the one who has stayed, the one who is huddled in the kitchen with a wrist being gripped.

He stays. He waits. He holds his great-grandmother's hand in the dim light while she moans. His grandmother begs him to tell her what is beyond the threshold and he describes the garb of the pilgrims. The painted cart of the book merchant and the books laden onto the back of a mule. Bartolomeo de Bartolai puts a cool cloth on his mother's forehead after she has fallen asleep. He unbolts the door for his father when he comes back home. They all grow old.

It is a new era, the ones who left have said. The old order is gone. Be bold, be deferential no more.

———

There is calm as his hand moves across a flat, polished stone. He draws, draws, draws, and on his way back from the fields into the house he tosses the stone into a pile in a corner of the threshing floor. The literate call the threshing floor an *aia*. Aye-a. Like a scream. From all the being beaten down. The peasants like him call it an *ara*, which also means *altar*.

––––––––––

Before they go off, when the journey is still before them, do they feel the twinge of misgiving? In the months before they leave, the impending journey has already changed them. Every encounter becomes a question: Will this be the final encounter? So that in the future you will say, The last time I saw Martín, he was at the fountain in town. But if you should see him once more, this is how he is remembered: The last time I saw Martín, he was in the tavern, playing *tresette* and winning. Once he announced his desire to leave, he could never be Martín in the same way again; he became Martín-who-will-leave-in-September. Once he revealed his intention to leave, he ceased to be part of the daily flow of mundane activity, bodies leaning into plows, planting, training vines against a trellis, harvesting, threshing, butchering a hog, coming into a stone house silently from the snow. He could not be part of the winter's circle around the hearth, or, when the sun emerged in the spring, he was no longer one who replaced slate tiles upon a roof or gathered early berries. At the moment he said he was leaving, Martín de Martinelli placed himself outside all this. It was irreversible. Even if he had changed his mind at the last instant, others would have thought, This year he stayed, but next year? He was no longer part of day-to-day movement, taking tools to the blacksmith or standing against the side of the mountain at the mill as grain was being ground, talking loudly above the roar of the cascade. When the wax of candles dripped onto the stone floor of the church at midnight on Christmas, he was not part of the chanting.

––––––––––

But wasn't it always so, the leaving? Is not the Holy Book that is read on Sunday the story of departure, one after another after another? Were not these mountains populated by nomads with tents and sheep? The Etrurian people coming up from the plains, some of whom buried the bones of their dead, some of whom buried their ashes in urns. They were followed by Christians who prayed in caves and, then, by Roman soldiers deserting, who were followed by the red-haired, blue-eyed ones with their bagpipes made of sheep gut who built stone huts here, warriors from the north with massive beards and long, consonant-filled words. Then the descendants of Esther fleeing the walled cities on the plains, accused of killing infants. They all fled into the mountains, staggering up here, burying their dead along the way. Trying to outrun war and pestilence. For centuries and centuries, they came up into the mountains. Bartolomeo de Bartolai is all of them. Who can say where he began, and who was the one who begat the person who begat him, who begat that person, all the way back to the beginning? Back to the gods of the northmen. Back to Job.

A man who came back from the Orient with Marco Polo was beaten in Venezia; they beat him on the stone floor under an alcove in the calle dell'Arco. And this man made his way southward to Ravenna, from which he was driven to other cities, Forlì, Ímola, Bologna, skirting the edge of the mountains, persecuted the entire way, until he was driven into a blind alley in Modena by thugs, nearly set afire, and he fled upward, up, up, up, into the mountains. He ran to the highest point, until he could go no farther without descending. He begged for mercy at the feet of the oldest woman of the village who stared down at this man with pitch-black hair. He did not want to go back down onto the plains; he begged her in his native tongue, and because he had a wide smile like her last-born son who had fallen off the mountain, she said to him, You may stay and be safe. As she spoke, the others dropped their clubs; one man gave him a massive shepherd's coat, a coat made of skins. He showed the others how to weave reeds into mats of intricate patterns. He built a strange, stringed instrument. He married, and his wife bore twelve children, six of whom survived. Scattered stone houses hold altars dedicated to a forgotten god whose name means immeasurable light.

The ancestors, yes, were nomads and people in flight, but, once here, they stayed put and lived their lives according to the rhythm of the bell, resounding morning, noon and night; and the seasons, summer, autumn, winter, spring; and all the rituals and holy days that are repeated in order, in an endless variation. His ancestors of long, long ago were people in motion, but they were followed by people, he believes, who should remain in this same place, immovable and bound to this soil.

He crosses the *ara* in the fading light of autumn. He sits on straw in a corner of the stable. He picks up a stone and draws. When he is exhausted, he returns to the house and lays his head on a mattress filled with wood shavings and scented with thyme to keep away insects. He dreams of a tap on the shoulder. He dreams about forms, a dog's paw, the curve of an angel's chin. A scaffold. He sees his hand move across a piece of stone, leaving identifiable marks, a sparrow, a lamb that looks as if it could bleat for its mother. He dreams of drawing pictures whole.

At the church of San Pellegrino, he once saw ten angels in a storm-blue sky, and they were all lamenting what occurred below. One threw its head backward, open arms and palms outstretched downward as if pushing away the air. One scratched and tore the skin of its cheeks with its fingernails; another pulled golden strands of hair outward from its scalp. One held a pale yellow cloth up close to its open eyes, as if wanting to conceal the view. The bodies of these angels tapered, then disappeared like flames.

The fresco in the pilgrims' church was a copy, painted by someone who had imitated a fresco down lower in the mountains, which was in turn an imitation of one in the foothills, which was a copy of one from down lower still, an imitation of a fresco in a town on the river, which was a modified version of a fresco farther downriver, a fresco which was an imitation of one in the city. The first one to copy it was called a follower of Giotto, and even after all these copies, the fresco in the mountains at the pilgrims' church site bears the great man's name.

He dreams of drawing pictures whole, but whenever he begins, he falters.

Martín de Martinelli said, Once silenced, we have been unsilenced.

But Bartolomeo de Bartolai sits there knowing that he still stutters, tentative, trepid, trembling.

Tiresome, he knows, and reminds himself he possesses worldly goods: he has a pallet with blankets. He has spiritual wealth. He has all of his fingers and teeth.

When he opens his mouth to say he is timid and weak, to say he cannot speak, a voice behind him says, What, then, is the sound coming from your mouth?

———

Do you remember how in our youth we rebelled? Martín de Martinelli had said before he left. Do you not recall?

Bartolomeo de Bartolai had replied, *Yes*. But all he remembered were words half-formed in his mouth.

Do you remember how we added our names to the list of demands signed by Iacomo de Petro, Lorenzo de Contro, Rolandino de Berton?

Yes, he said. But in truth he could not write his name.

Boldly, they took down the banner of the duke, and hoisted up another at night in the dark. They fled deep into the woods and sang songs around a fire, and when the sun rose in the morning, the people in the village of Ardonlà woke to find the sky-blue herald of the dissidents suspended from an arch.

Certain reproaches still clang in his ears: The hierarchy has crumbled; we are no longer serfs.

———

When, on the mule path above, a handbell is rung six times but not at the sixth hour, it means travellers are passing through and are looking for food to purchase. Itinerant merchants, soldiers. Or pilgrims en route to holy places:

> *San Pellegrino dell'Alpe*, they chant,
> *scendete un po' più giù*
> *abbiam rotto le scarpe*
> *non ne possiamo più.*

The penitent traveller says this aloud walking toward the relics of San Pellegrino, the hermit who lived in a hollowed-out beech tree.

> San Pellegrino, they mumble aloud,
> come down a bit lower,
> we have broken our shoes
> and cannot go any farther.

Once, eleven years ago, when he heard the bell ringing, Bartolomeo de Bartolai carried up a wooden pail filled with milk; he had no cheese to sell. He climbed the footpath up the side of the mountain, the branches of the hedges brushing his arm, the saw-toothed canes of blackberries pricking through his leggings, the sun beating down on his back.

He arrived at the road out of breath. It was July and pilgrims were travelling south and west toward the mountain pass on their way to the monastery of San Pellegrino. A pilgrim gestured to him. Bartolomeo de Bartolai saw that despite her simple garb of hazel-colored wool, despite her display of poverty, she was privileged; she wore a thick gold ring on a golden chain around her neck. Her alms purse was bulging. Bartolomeo de Bartolai stood in front of her, holding his pail, looking at the ground, waiting to be spoken to.

Mid-conversation, she spoke to another pilgrim. She was not going to the pilgrimage site of San Pellegrino, like the rest, she said, but rather to the south and east, toward the city of Fiorenza. Then she began speaking of the master Giotto:

Giotto apprenticed with Cimabue for ten years.

Bartolomeo de Bartolai stared at the ground, listening.

The Pope called him to Rome for the Jubilee in 1300, and Giotto worked on the basilica of San Giovanni in Laterno.

Bartolomeo de Bartolai offered her the pail of milk. She batted him away and called her lady-in-waiting.

In that city, he made a mosaic called La Navicella in the portico of St. Peter's, a mosaic of Christ walking on water.

He listened, open-mouthed. The lady-in-waiting approached and grabbed the pail from him.

In Padova, he painted the Scrovegni chapel, where I myself have prayed, and there is an imitation of it at the pilgrims' church in these savage mountains.

The lady-in-waiting handed the pail to a manservant.

In Assisi, he painted San Francesco's life.

The manservant poured the milk into a large metal flask. The servants watched their lady speak.

He painted the great poet Dante from life.

The manservant thrust the pail back to him.

As she turned to go, Bartolomeo de Bartolai bowed his head and asked the lady, *And, please tell me, on these journeys, what kind of materials does the artist Giotto pack into sacks and transport?*

The pilgrim backed away from him, wrapping her cloak around her, covering her mouth and her nose, and said, *What do you think I am, a book?*

He had seen what a book looked like, he had seen people with their noses looking down into books. So when she said to him, What do you think I am, a book? he was stung, humiliated. He did not know how to understand her insult. He knew that she was not a book; a book is an inanimate object. A book is made of paper, which is made from trees, and the trees come from forests in the mountains because all of the great forests of the plains have been leveled. No, she was not a book, she was a woman with raven hair visible at the edge of her hood.

But he remembers to this day what the humbly clad pilgrim said, what he overheard: Giotto painted Dante from life. Bartolomeo de Bartolai does not understand this expression. How else would he have painted him? From death? No, because a painting or mosaic comes from an idea, and an idea is alive. Something you hear or see or smell or touch or taste puts a picture into your head, and this causes you to put down a mark. She was trying to impress them with her knowledge of the world down there, of how far she had travelled, then became offended because she was asked a question she could not answer: What materials does Giotto use? Of course Giotto painted Dante from life; he painted everything from life, a goat with splayed hooves, a shepherd with a tattered hem.

Of course, Bartolomeo de Bartolai knows what a book is. He has seen them at the villa of the Signore. He was shown a page once, during the month of August, when he and his father were summoned to the villa. They were asked to move a wardrobe from one room to another. They hoisted it with great difficulty and carried it on their backs across the hall into another room. The Signore was not sure where he wanted it placed, so he went upstairs to ask his wife, the lady from Ferrara for whom he had put in glass windows. They set down the wardrobe, and while the Signore was gone, Bartolomeo de Bartolai gazed around the room at the polished marble floor with its swirling of onyx and pavonazzo purple and umber.

In the corner, Bartolomeo de Bartolai saw a strange piece of furniture. As tall as his waist, it stood on a single leg, like a crane, a *gru*. There was a tray at the top made of two pieces of wood that fit together and lay like a bird's open wings. A book rested on top. The Signore's voice and footsteps were still upstairs, and Bartolomeo de Bartolai peered down into the open book, careful not to breathe on it.

One page was a wall of marks. One page was a drawing. The drawing was this: two circles side by side. Inside the circle on the right was a form with a rounded back, the profile of a monster with a single eye of ultramarine. Inside the other circle was a pair of curved claws that reached up toward the monster.

The Signore swept in and saw him looking. His father raised a hand to cuff him, but the Signore stopped him and said to Bartolomeo de Bartolai, Do you like my book? I bought it in Venezia for three *scudi*. You can buy any book you want in Venezia; it is where most of them are published. In that city, a man is free to think his own thoughts and ideas circulate freely. The thoughts of the reformers are openly discussed. Some doubt the existence of hell, some deny the Trinity.

He pointed to the book and placed an index finger on certain marks, pronouncing the words *Orbis Descriptio*.

This is a map of the world. He pointed to the circle on the right. This is the Old World, and this blue oval is the Mediterranean. We are the Old World.

Then, he pointed to the circle on the left. This is the New World. The Arctic, the territory of Florida, the Terra Incognita of the interior, which all belongs to Spain. Below, America of the South.

Bartolomeo de Bartolai would like him to point out other places, for example, where is Fiorenza? He would like to see where Giotto has travelled. But instead, the Signore says: I have decided after all to put the piece of furniture back into the room where it was originally. On the way out, the Signore tells them that behind the stables there is an old pine board from a table top which they are welcome to take.

At twilight, that evening, he went back down to the villa. He walked through the villa's forest-garden, where the Signore planted pine trees so they formed the letters V and L, the initials of the Signora. In a corner of this walled forest-garden was a heap of discarded objects, and there Bartolomeo de Bartolai found the pine board.

For months the board has lain untouched in the corner of the stable; he is afraid to make a mark on it, does not want to spoil it.

Each night, he walks out to the stable, seeking a respite from the house where his great-grandmother sits on a mat in the corner and moans and rocks, her eyes wide and staring at nothing. His grandmother feeds her chestnut gruel with a wooden spoon. The great-grandmother spits the food back out. The grandmother clears her mother's lips with the edge of the spoon. His grandmother grabs the wrist of whoever is nearest, whoever is passing by, whoever is most alive. In springtime, his mother sings of the harvest, *The day laid on the threshing floor is flayed.* She sings love songs all day long. His father bends his head under the granite lintel as he passes through the doorway; his shoulders brush the frame, though he is not a large man, and he slams the door shut. His grandmother grabs him by the wrist and his mother sings. In the day, he takes his cloth hat from the bench and follows his father out the door. He goes off into the field, and watches after the five thin sheep and the three emaciated goats.

In order to pay for grazing rights for a season, when he was a boy, his mother cut his hair. She pulled it tight, away from his head, cut it close to the scalp. Then she sold it to a pillow merchant passing through. After she cut his hair, he would run down the path into the field, where everything was blurred from tears, and he pointed out the grass to the beasts, showing them which blades to eat.

As he stands up to go out to the stable, he carries a lantern because darkness comes early. They begrudge him oil for the lamp. His mother says, Where do you think more oil will come from? You think it will seep out of a crack in a stone? His father says, When a spark turns into a ball of fire what will we do then? This is the discussion every night, every night at dusk, when his uncle and great-uncle, his grandfather's brother, get ready to tell the stories they have told again and again, the same ones, how a grave robber dug up the bones of San Sisto in Rome and tried to sell them to priests all the way up into the mountains, but no one believed him, and, desperate because he was high up in the mountains in winter and without any money, he sold them to a wealthy old woman, who bought the bones with one gold *genovino* and a sword and a bundle of candles, and as soon as he handed the relics to the old woman, he was turned into a pillar of stone, and she had a chapel built right there. He does not want to hear any more of these stories, he has heard them every night of his life: how the poor young man found a key that let him into the princess's heart, how the charcoalmaker's son solved three riddles. He begs them for oil for the lamp. His mother accuses him: *spende fina i capei;* he would spend even the hair on his head. At the villa of the Signore, the lanterns burn all night long, yet they accuse him of being profligate for trying to extend the day.

His father hollers, And if you start an inferno? His mother hollers, If we run out of light? Then his grandmother grabs his wrist and holds it up to them and says, You cut his hair, you sold it, now give the child some light.

If he could, he would write the master Giotto a letter. Tell him that he is ready to come down and work in his shop, to mix plaster, to clean paintbrushes. If only to rake, with a wooden pitchfork, the stall where his horse sleeps at night.

————

In the stable, he cleans a spot on the dirt and lays the panel on the ground.

We are isolated, but we hear things. We are remote, but we see things.

He hears rumblings of what goes on below; the sounds echo up three valleys, the Valley of the Scoltenna, the Valley of the Dragon, the Valley of Light, and by the time the sound makes its way up into the mountains, after having bounced off mountain walls, it is only a faint echo. The sounds arrive belatedly, sometimes centuries later. He has heard the priest speak the word, FRACTUM. This is the way the sound comes up, in pieces. After something has already happened to fracture the whole into pieces.

He spills out the pieces of terra-cotta and broken glass and sifts through what he possesses.

————

What do you think I am, a book? He hears the words again and again. I have never left these mountains, but I know something of other places because people travelling through bring word, the itinerant monk, the copper seller, the merchant who buys flock and hair. They carry up messages from down below, and this is how it is possible to know something of other places. I have seen certain things with my own eyes, like the frescoes at the pilgrims' church, the saint sleeping in the mountains, ten angels wailing in the sky.

In his head, he continues to fight with Martín de Martinelli, ten years gone, thinks of how Martín de Martinelli said to him: Wake up! Raise up your eyes!

And how he replied, I have been taught to keep my head bowed and not to swagger, to not be a braggart and spendthrift like the prosperous shepherd who sees a little of the world, sells his fat sheep down on the plains, and comes back with coins in his pockets, blaspheming and knocking over tables in the tavern. I have been taught to be simple, honest, laborious. Labor is honor. All I have ever seen are heads bent over and down; look at the way everyone's shoulders are curved.

Look up, said Martín de Martinelli.

And Bartolomeo de Bartolai answered, You look up and you see misery. You see how the lords overrun one another's territory, spreading disaster, spreading strife. You see how brigands steal anything that glistens. How soldiers bring contagion and take away flour. You see starving mothers who leave infants to die on the mountainside so that the ones at home survive.

And Martín de Martinelli replied, The days of a peasant's false humility are over. Do you not see that a new day is coming which will do away with antiquated ways? Do you not see that there will be new systems to classify, new instruments to understand the world?

Bartolomeo de Bartolai asked him, Does it bring comfort to think that there will be instruments to measure cold and heat, that will measure the strength of wind and the weight of air? Will they not take away the hours of the day, the days in their merciful order? The seasons that make this life, with its empty stomach and lesions, bearable? Will it not take away the calendar that begins with the feast day of the Blessed Virgin and ends with the feast day of San Silvestro? Would you have me break this whole?

Martín de Martinelli said, I would not have you break anything. I am not here to cause you to do anything. I can only say what I am going to do: I am leaving. I am not going to remain up here, my stifled voice vibrating against the vocal cords. Do you know how it is when you have a great sadness, a great anger, and try to make no sound? Do you know how it is when you hold it inside your throat? Of course you know, because you are a mountain dweller, made of stone, and you think you can outlast the pain without opening your mouth.

Bartolomeo de Bartolai answered, I notice no such pain.

Martín de Martinelli said, If a dog catches his paw in a trap, and the paw is cut, it yelps and howls, and then, if the dog survives, and the wound heals, he becomes accustomed to the pain and merely winces each time he puts his weight upon the paw.

_____

He must turn away from the admonishments; he must turn away and try to recall something else. Something beautiful. A mosaic. On the other side of the river above Ardonlà are the ruins of a fortress that sits on a steep bluff. Below it is a cave. The entryway is hidden among bushes and rocks along the riverbed. The passageway opens into caverns where Christians hid when they fled into the mountains. They were followers of Sant'Apollinaris of Ravenna. They built an altar in a cave, and, on the vault, they made a mosaic like the ones they had left behind. When it became safe, they built their altars above ground, and the ones below were forgotten. The forest above was cleared and a landslide buried the cave's entrance.

_____

He saw the mosaics only once. He was a child. He was taken there by his great-grandmother who is now being fed like a baby. She was not afraid of wolves or bears, and she took his hand and led him there. He was not afraid because she was not afraid. She was bent over as she walked beside him, leaning on her wooden walking stick, which was shaped like the letter T. She told him she was going to show him where a saint was buried, told him that no one else remembered, that they were too afraid to look. As she walked, she became transformed and stood up straight; she threw away her walking stick. She moved like a goat from one rock to another and she was not afraid of slipping on a wet stone. All the lines were erased from her face; her blue eyes were lights; she balanced on one rock, and then another, along the bank of the river.

He is trying to see the mosaic again. There was a strange source of light. There were foreign plants and creatures. A palm tree with leaves that grew out from the center like the legs of a spider. A turtle climbing out of the water onto a bank. There were two cranes drinking from a pedestal fountain.

At night, he crosses the *ara,* and sits on the straw with a sackcloth blanket covering his legs. The lantern hangs on a wooden peg. On the floor, there is a jar containing mastic, which he has made from the resin of pine. Before him on a rag, he has spread out the fragments of broken glass and painted terra-cotta. Each night, he lays out a row, edging one piece against another.

He thinks, We hear things up in the mountains. We are isolated, but we hear things, just as we heard of Giotto. Just as we have heard that in France on the other side of the river called the Var, men slaughter each other. One man slashes the gullet of the other, like a pig is killed before dressing, from ear to ear, without remorse. Except they are doing this in every season and pigs are only killed once a year, in the autumn, when the weather is cold, just before water freezes. They hang the bodies upside down, bound by the feet, suspended from a tree, and the blood is left to drain out onto the ground. An itinerant bookseller said this.

One man massacres the other over the right to name God. One man slays one man, then, there is retaliation, and five more are slain. Each sect buries its dead in trenches, all together, one body piled on top of another, because there are too many bodies to give each soul its own grave. The foot soldiers of the holy war do not allow firewood to pass through their territory into the towns; there are no trees left to be cut. The wealthy possess furniture to burn, but the poor man, who has already burned his one table and one bench, freezes to death. The warriors are violating women, and the women who survive are left with the hated seed. They are slaying children who are not yet steady on their feet.

They say that Peace, herself, is revolted, and that she holds her stomach and retches; she has hidden her face under a hood and has started to walk away from the battlefields, following along in the ruts made by the wheels of carts, dragging herself along a muddy road that is lined with corpses, not even bothering to lift the hem of her cloak.

This is what the merchant passing through said. We hear things. We hear it in fragments, we hear it in imperfect remnants.

———

Remnants like the tunic he wears, a *saltimindosso* it is called. Giotto's shepherd wears a *saltimindosso* like this, with a hem torn in three places. The tear must have been recent, otherwise the shepherd would have repaired it, because it is the only garment he possesses. Bartolomeo de Bartolai's shirt is made from clothing discarded from the Signore's villa, a deep black-purple of a fine heavy material. But who is to say this *saltimindosso* is made from a discarded article of clothing? Perhaps it was a blanket that covered his horse.

———

Each night, he looks at all the irregular pieces and stares at them. A dot, a line, a wave. At times, he has to look away; the pieces seem to be moving, clattering against each other like hundreds of rows of broken teeth.

———

He scratches his scalp, the discomfort is great.

Even as a child, he got scabs on the top of his head. He would stand with his back to his mother, who sat on the bench and looked through his hair at his scalp. She applied an ointment which she made from beeswax and mint and rosemary and lard. She put this on his scalp in the morning and at night before he went to sleep. She told him the skin of his scalp was drying out, and that his scalp was drying out because his head was too hot from thinking. She asked him again and again about the thoughts inside his head. You have to let your thoughts escape with breath. Otherwise your mind will get too warm, and strange things will begin to happen. As a way of encouraging him to speak, she asked him questions constantly: Do you think it will rain tomorrow? Do you think the frost will come early this year? She would ask him, What are the thoughts bouncing around inside your head? He would try his best to answer her, to describe the thoughts in his head. Why, if the bell tower in Ardonlà blessed by San Bernardino is supposed to keep away storms, why then did the roof of the house called Le Borre collapse? And his mother said, It was from the weight of the snow and it was the will of God. He asked her, If an angel dropped a string from the sky, could you climb to heaven, and, if you could, would your weight pull the angel down? She answered, Angels do not need rope, that is why there is prayer. He asked, Why did the side of the mountain fall into the river and smother the cave with the mosaics? She said, Because the earth has grown heavy and swollen with pride.

In the kitchen, in front of the low stone sink, she grabbed him by the shoulders and shook him, told him not to tell anyone about the sores and not to scratch his scalp in public. Otherwise, they will tell the priest and he will call you before him to ask you what you are thinking. They are burning even humble people at the stake for what they are thinking. When I was a girl, they wanted to execute a miller in Savignano because he was going around saying that the world created itself, that God Himself did not make it. His mind was working too hard; he was burning up with thoughts.

His mother put more salve on his scalp and stopped asking what he was thinking. She asked which plants the sheep had eaten and how many weeds he had pulled from the soil.

Talk, talk, she said to her son, putting ointment on his scalp. Let the heat escape. She urged him to speak, but to not say anything.

He must not speak, and so he listens. He listens when the priest speaks in church about books, saying how books are like people. How each one is made differently, how some contain holy thoughts, how some contain impure thoughts, how some contain heresy.

The priest says a book is like a human being; it has a spine, and if the book is opened roughly, too quickly, the spine can be snapped, and that a book can scream in pain, yell out, hurl out words, shriek.

A book, he also says, is like fire, and if there are unholy things inside, when the book is closed, the marks on the pages rub against each other, embering twigs, one on top of another, smoldering, burning low as long as the book is closed, and then, the moment the covers are opened, the pages ignite and the book explodes into a ball of fire, singeing the skin and blinding the eyes.

An evil book, he says, can be the Devil himself, taking an elegant, refined form, with the hems of his garments embroidered with gold thread. He can take the form of a book, its covers decorated with fine-tooled leather, its pages fluttering like silk. And at night, the priest says, the book changes shape and goes to each of the people sleeping under the roof and puts impure pictures inside their heads so that they dream of sinning in unimagined ways.

He speaks about books in the small round church, even though there is no one present who can read.

Bartolomeo de Bartolai cannot read, but he knows this much, that inside a book there are pages. And on those pages are marks. And those who understand the marks get pictures inside their heads. The marks look like vines in spring, brittle and dark, clinging to a wall washed white with lime. He does not understand how to adjust his eyes, the way one does when moving from a field into a forest. In a field, you look for the hare's round shape against the tall straight blades; in the forest you look for a glint of white, the spot on the animal's hind. It is a question of teaching your eyes how to look. This is the secret of understanding a book, he believes, but he does not know how to instruct his eyes.

At night, in the stable, the fragments he has assembled assault his eyes and mock him: This makes no sense, a band of gorse yellow here? Why, Fool?

All the fragments laid out together, separately inarticulate, broken, chipped. It makes him dizzy. It is an untrained swirl, and he becomes so confused he must look away.

He fans the pieces out carefully.

In one pile, the fragments of blue.

Giotto's angels tore their hair, clawed the skin of their faces. And he has made three faces like theirs.

He has sketched them out on the panel, and is now forming them with tiles. But on his panel, in his shed, there are not mere angels. The top one is a god, who, like the Signore, is the most powerful. The one in the middle is a god who is the next most powerful and is his heir. Below him is another god who is the least powerful, but has other powers the other two do not, because he is also light. Bartolomeo de Bartolai has made three gods; he believes they are three and distinct and separate, each having his place in the hierarchy.

He believes he has made a picture that is holy and sacred, but if the ambitious priest were to hear of it, a priest who wants to escape from the mountains and be allowed to return to the plains, Bartolomeo de Bartolai would be interrogated. Why have you drawn this, my son? You do not really mean to say that God is three different beings? The priest would turn to Bartolomeo de Bartolai, ask him to renounce the work, to redefine it, reminding him that God is one and indivisible. That God created light. That God is not light.

He shows the panel to no one, not because he considers this dissent, but because it is a peasant's habit to conceal. For the cheeks, he has saved his most precious glass, pieces of Asian porcelain tinted pink.

———

It is nearly winter. No one passes through on the narrow road above. Snow has already fallen. Bartolomeo de Bartolai tells himself he must admit what is obvious, that Giotto is ancient and it is unlikely he will travel up into these mountains.

———

He returns to the stable each night, crossing the *ara*. He hangs the lantern on a wooden peg, burns the precious oil. He throws the goat Diana a piece of crust he has saved. He stares at the dried-out board of pine, dreams of pictures he has seen before. He is no longer waiting for the great man. Great men do not arrive. He will never go down out of the mountains. He will soothe the foreheads of his elders, and the past will be his future.

Bartolomeo de Bartolai sits on the ground on clean straw under a dim yellow light, his fingers aching with cold. He fans out the pieces before him. He examines his few shards of cobalt and azurite blue. He begins to set them in mastic, though he has not collected sufficient fragments to complete the sky.

Authors' Biographies

GEOFFREY BECKER is assistant professor of English at Towson University in Towson, Maryland. His stories have appeared in *Ploughshares, Colorado Review, Poet and Critic, The Iowa Journal of Literary Studies, The Chicago Tribune,* and *Crazyhorse* and have been included in *Best American Short Stories* (2000), *It's Only Rock and Roll,* and *Short Takes: Fifteen Contemporary Stories.* His novel *Bluestown* was published in 1996.

ADRIA BERNARDI received the 1999 Katharine Bakeless Nason Prize for Fiction for her novel *The Day Laid on the Altar.* She is also the author of *Houses with Names: The Italian Immigrants of Highwood, Illinois,* and has translated literary works from Italian to English, including Gianni Celati's *Adventures in Africa,* Rafaello Baldini's *Page Proof,* and Gregorio Scalise's poetry.

DAVID BOSWORTH is a professor in the University of Washington's Creative Writing Program, where he was Director for five years. He has been a National Endowment for the Arts fellow and recipient of an Ingram Merrill Foundation Fellowship. His novel *From My Father, Singing* was selected for the Editors' Book Award.

JENNIFER CORNELL is associate professor of English at Oregon State University. Her short stories and essays on popular culture have been published in numerous literary reviews and anthologies, including *Irish Cinema Reader, The Brandon Book of Irish Short Stories, Cabbage and Bones: An Anthology of Irish-American Women Writers,* and *Writing Ulster.*

BARBARA CROFT has taught at Loyola University, DePaul University, and Columbia College, Chicago. Her collection *Primary Colors and Other Stories* won the 1989 New Rivers Minnesota Voice Project competition. Her short fiction has appeared in such literary reviews as *The Kenyon Review, Colorado Quarterly, Plainswoman,* and *Poet & Critic.* Her awards include the Pirate's

Alley William Faulkner Society Prize for Novella, the Katherine Anne Porter Prize for Fiction (honorable mention), the Daniel Curley Award for Recent Illinois Short Fiction, and the Pushcart Prize. She has also published a work of scholarship: *"Stylistic Arrangements": A Study of William Butler Yeats's "A Vision."*

RICK DEMARINIS is emeritus professor of English at the University of Texas at El Paso. His novels include *A Clod of Wayward Marl*, *The Mortician's Apprentice*, *The Year of the Zinc Penny*, *The Burning Women of Far Cry*, *Cinder*, *Scimitar*, and *A Lovely Monster*. He has also published five collections of short fiction and one nonfiction book, *The Art and Craft of the Short Story*. He received the Independent Publishers' Award for Best Book of Short Fiction for *Borrowed Hearts: New and Selected Stories*. He has also won The Jesse H. Jones Award for Fiction and The American Academy and Institute of Arts and Letters Award in Literature.

ELIZABETH GRAVER is associate professor of English at Boston College. She has published two novels, *The Honey Thief* and *Unravelling*. She has received the O. Henry Award three times, and her short stories and essays have been included in *Best American Essays* (1998), *Chick-Lit 2: New Women's Fiction Anthology*, and *Sacred Ground: Writings About Home*. Her third novel, *Night Light*, is forthcoming.

RICK HILLIS has been a Jones Lecturer in Fiction Writing at Stanford University, a Chesterfield Screenwriting Fellow, and a Writer-in-Residence at Reed College. He has written numerous screenplays and published short stories in journals and anthologies, including *Voices 1: Contemporary Short Fiction*, *An Ounce of Cure*, and *Voices 2: Canadian Short Fiction*.

LUCY HONIG is associate professor of International Health at the Boston University School of Public Health. Her novel, *Picking Up*, was the winner of the 1986 Maine Novel Award. Her short fiction has been published in a number of literary journals, including *Ploughshares*, *The Gettysburg Review*, *Oxalis*, *Indiana Review*, and *Antaeus*. She has been the recipient of an O. Henry Award, and her work has been included in *Best American Short Stories* (1988), and *Inside Vacationland: New Fiction from the Real Maine*.

ELLEN HUNNICUTT has won numerous awards for fiction including the Herbert L. Hughes fiction award, the fiction prize from *Indiana Review*, the Council for Wisconsin Writers prize for book-length fiction, the Banta Award, and the Writer of Distinction Award from the International Reading Association. Her stories have been published in *Story*, *North American Review*, *Prairie Schooner*, *Mississippi Review*, *Cimarron Review*, *Michigan Quarterly Review*, and *Crab Orchard Review*. She has published one novel, *Suite for Calliope*.

JANE MCCAFFERTY is assistant professor of creative writing at Carnegie Mellon University. She has won the Great Lakes New Writers Award and two Pushcart Prizes, and six of her stories have been included in *Best American Short Stories*. Her first novel, *One Heart*, was published in 2000; her second, *With Lily by the Sea*, is forthcoming in 2002.

REGINALD MCKNIGHT is professor of English at the University of Michigan. He is the author of the nonfiction books *African American Wisdom* and *African American Wisdom, Revised and Expanded*. He has published three novels, *I Get on the Bus*, *White Boys*, and *He Sleeps*. His stories have appeared in numerous literary reviews and anthologies. He has received many awards, including the Addison M. Metcalf Award from the American Academy of Arts and Letters, the Whiting Writer's Award, a Special Citation from the Ernest Hemingway Foundation, the Bernice M. Slote Award for Fiction, and the Pushcart Prize.

STEWART O'NAN has published stories in journals including *Colorado Review*, *Glimmer Train*, and *Ploughshares*. Named by *Granta* magazine as one of the twenty best young American novelists, his fiction titles include *Everyday People*, *A Prayer for the Dying*, *The Names of the Dead*, *Snow Angels*, and *The Speed Queen*. He has also published a work of nonfiction, *The Circus Fire: A True Story*, and edited *The Vietnam Reader: The Definitive Collection of American Fiction and Nonfiction on the War*.

EDITH PEARLMAN has published more than one hundred short stories in literary reviews, magazines, and anthologies, and an equal number of nonfiction pieces in newspapers and magazines. She has been the recipient of the Pushcart Prize and two O. Henry Awards, and her stories have been included in *New Stories from the South* (2001) and two editions of *Best American Short Stories* (2000 and 1998).

JONATHAN PENNER is a professor of creative writing at the University of Arizona, and the author of the novel *Natural Order*. His previous novel, *Going Blind*, received several awards as an outstanding first novel; *The Intelligent Traveler's Guide to Chiribosco* won the Galileo Press Short Novel Prize. His short stories have appeared in *Harper's, TriQuarterly Review, Antaeus*, and other magazines, and in *The Norton Anthology of Contemporary Short Fiction*.

RANDALL SILVIS writes poetry, fiction, and drama. He is the author of eight novels, including *Excelsior, Dead Man Falling, On Night's Shore*, and (forthcoming in 2002) *Disquiet Heart*. His screen and stage plays have won first place in the National Playwrights Showcase Award (three times) and the Ruby Lloyd Apsey Playwriting Award; in 1983 he won both the drama and the short story awards at the Deep South Writers Drama Conference.

MAYA SONENBERG is associate professor of English at the University of Washington in Seattle, Washington. Her short fiction has been published in numerous literary journals, including *Alaska Quarterly Review, Gulf Stream, Santa Monica Review, Columbia: A Magazine of Poetry and Prose*, and *Grand Street*.

KATHERINE VAZ is the author of the critically acclaimed novel *Saudade*. Her second novel, *Mariana*, has been published in six languages and is a bestseller, in its fourth printing, in Portugal. Her short fiction has been published in *Glimmer Train, Tin House, The Gettysburg Review, The Antioch Review, The Iowa Review*, and *TriQuarterly Review*.

W. D. WETHERELL is the author of thirteen books, including the novels *Chekhov's Sister* and *Morning*, the short story collection *Wherever That Great Heart May Be*, and the memoir *North of Now*. His work has received three O. Henry Awards, a National Magazine Award, and The Strauss Living Award from the American Academy of Arts and Letters. His stories have appeared in major journals, magazines, and anthologies; one story, "The Bass, the River, and Sheila Mant," has been reprinted more than thirty times, and appears in textbooks for high school and college students throughout the country.

ROBLEY WILSON is emeritus professor of English at University of Northern Iowa, and former editor of *The North American Review*. He has authored several fiction titles including *The Book of Lost Fathers, The Victim's Daughter*, and *Terrible Kisses*, as well as poetry titles including *Everything Paid For, A Walk Through the Human Heart, A Pleasure Tree*, and *Kingdoms of the Ordinary*.